THE BOY WHO LOVED SCIENCE TOO MUCH

SIERAN LANE

Cover design by Muhammad Kaleem
Book formatting by Brady Moller

CONTENTS

Xakroff
Kanithee
Upido

Lumion Sea

Peakuyu

① Coas-Glow

Hopha

Darra

Fartha

Norlithien Sea

Zachilael Anera Oftonoss
Reenosco

Gena

Uwian

Cantor

Quillin

Sarrare

Raiyad

Princalen

Drifeas Buviorim

Achamae Minispee
Chacleur Hosgown

②

③

Wilophera
Sea

Lochta
Merra
Temecore

PLUTORIA
OCEAN

Itheris
Ishiri

④

Orunkey
Mixa

Ytruss

Uncisu Wotia
Agrille

Citchera

⑤

Emerau

⑥

CADRA OCEAN

MAP OF DRELL

Bosdreen

Lakra   Otustry   Eirloe   *Findaire*
                                      Sea
Naian   Dasturn-Mink
                              ⑦
Marelor
Shophinia

Trenquillis
Craie   *Geranian Sea*

Achelée
Sea

Linthae   ⑧
Eena

Preshal Jerroci   Plascent   Winera   Ovi

                         Tuvuti   Chros
PLUTORIA   Givinia
OCEAN   Riktai
                    Cinery
                              Healeva   Jaivela
                    ⑨   Ambiyu
                    Nualyss Mulbaster
                                   Oestus

                         Vénus   Flinid
                                             Biennae
DAPONO OCEAN   Keephae   *Sea*
                 Brininor

THE SUPER SECTORS:

1 — AQUILINE   4 — BAYTA   7 — NOLA
2 — OVAL   5 — SWIRNIS   8 — JADICE
3 — FOREST   6 — TUN-SNOW   9 — PERA

To everyone who supported me in completing this story, and to my fellow writer friends, Haidan and Annette, for their constant encouragement and inspiration!

The hero of this story, Lark Arias, lives on Drell, a planet in a galaxy far from the Milky Way; humans discovered and lived on Drell countless millennia after the publication date of this book.

ONE
THE JOURNEY THAT STARTED IT ALL

The five-year-old little boy stood at the counter with a defiant look on his face.

"No, I do not have any money, but I need the chemicals."

Haus, the middle-aged man who ran the shop, grinned in an attempt to calm the boy. "I'm sorry, Lark, but I can't give you chemicals for free."

Those chemicals in question sat demurely in rows of see-through flasks on a dark shelf behind Haus; these liquids, gases, and solids that Lark desired touched him in their enigma and crystalline beauty.

Lark frowned. "Can we not figure out another way? I must have them for my experiments."

He eyed a few elegant bottles of amber gas, as well as a tall flask of river-blue powder—there was so much that he wanted!

"I know you love your experiments, but you can't get something for nothing," said Haus. Lark was about to reply again when Haus continued, "But I do have one solution. You can do something for me and you can have all the chemicals you'll ever want for free."

Lark's eyes dilated in disbelief. Could Haus be tricking him? What did the man have up his sleeve? But regardless of what was up, Lark's heart and mind still raced with excitement, as though they were illuminated by a bright, seeking light. He asked, "What do you want me to do?"

Haus grinned. "Hold on a moment," Haus said, and reached for something from his pocket. Lark narrowed his eyes and his body tensed, afraid that it might be a weapon. But instead, it was something long, narrow, and flat, gleaming with the shade of bronze. "Here," Haus said. "Take this shrim strip and spread it over your forehead."

"Why?" Lark asked.

"Just do it, or else there will be no chemicals for you," came the reply.

With great reluctance, Lark rubbed that strip on his forehead. Immediately there was a tingling sensation, but that only lasted for a second and thankfully didn't hurt. (For the sake of simplicity, I will use our terms of seconds and minutes instead of their Drellian units. But I will use their term "cores," of which one core means two hours in our language.)

Haus smiled. "All right, thank you. Now step over here if you please. Your forehead has been marked as 'friend, not intruder,' so you will be allowed entrance." Haus opened a wide, grey door behind him and invited the boy to go in. Lark was only bent on getting his chemicals so he followed the man without question. They came into a great, spacious room immersed in blue light. The blue was in fact an electric blue, so that you had to squint if you accidentally glanced at the glaring parts of the room. Lark squinted painfully.

Haus said, "Now, little boy," Lark winced at the call of that diminutive. Haus continued, "Will you look at this?"

A few steps before them, in a large transparent case, something resembling a chrysalis swam in a pool of purple. The chrysalis was silky, glue-like, and gelatinous, if you could call something like that gelatinous.

"What is this?" asked Lark, his natural curiosity of any unusual looking chemical coming over him.

Haus stroked his beard. "This is a brachiorsor (pronounced "brack-kee-oar-soar"). Pretty, isn't it?" Lark didn't care whether anything was pretty or not. If they achieved their purposes, he supposed that they would automatically be "pretty." But Haus went on and said, "The brachiorsor is what my clan and I use to...perform our annual ritual."

"What ritual?"

"You are so impatient," Haus said with a desultory, demeaning gesture. Lark frowned. Haus said, "The brachiorsor is what seals our loyalty to each other, by—"

"How?"

"You shall see. Anyway, the thing is, this brachiorsor is causing us a little trouble. You see," at the sight of Lark's grumpy face that signaled, "Hurry up or I'm leaving," though Haus believed that this boy would be too eager to get those free chemicals to really leave, Haus continued, more quickly now. "There's a light attached to the purple pool here. Would you like to see it? All I need to do is press this button."

Lark wished that he didn't have to talk to him like he was a little kid, though he was a kid. But Lark just wished that people would stop babying him because he could understand a lot of things that many adults couldn't. Or at least, that was what Lark believed.

Haus pushed an oval button that was floating in the air, and a flaring yellow light flooded the purple pool and pierced its transparent container; the yellow light also flooded out and mixed with the blue lightning lights all over the room, forming some kind of strange green color, and Haus said, "Impressive?"

Lark shook his head resolutely. He didn't care. He just wanted this adult to hurry up.

Haus was disappointed at this lack of appreciation. Usually little boys were easily impressed by great visual displays like this. Haus cleared his throat. "Anyway, as I was saying, the brachiorsor needs to be ignited by—a certain chemical reaction."

"What reaction?" came the instant reply.

"You really are so impatient," teased Haus, and he cleared his throat again when he faced another glare from the blue-eyed boy. "Well, this is something like aerobic respiration, you know what that is—you learned it in school already, right?"

"Of course," Lark said, tapping his foot.

"Okay. Well, the brachiorsor uses something similar to that. But instead of transforming oxygen and glucose into carbon dioxide, water, and energy, this transforms nitrogen and other strange chemicals into— well, very complicated chemicals that I wouldn't want to tell you about."

"Tell me about them anyway," Lark commanded.

Haus knew he was going to say that, and he grinned. "Okay, as you wish, my boy."

Don't call me my boy, Lark thought.

"These chemicals," Haus said, "are called octamethyst (pronounced "oct-tah-mee-theest") and trichloroes ("try-clor-roes"). Remember that?"

Lark nodded. "Octamethyst and trichloroes." Lark bet that he could even spell them and look them up in a database immediately to find out all he could about them. He might have even heard of them before. But Lark was one of those people who might have heard of any chemical, considering the innumerable hours he poured daily into investigating, researching, and learning as much as he could about science and chemistry. He already had a thorough knowledge of countless chemicals—the number of which could put any average elementary school science teacher to shame.

"Octamethyst and trichloroes," Haus said. "A purple and green pigment respectively. Well, okay, they are more than just pigments. They have functions as well—"

"What functions?" Lark asked, with an expectant look at Haus. Unfortunately, something else grabbed the adult's attention; the yellow light that had gone on and flooded the room had suddenly disappeared. Haus cursed and feverishly pushed a number of buttons.

Lark wanted to help him—not out of the desire to help, but out of a desire to speed the process so that Haus could tell him what exactly he had to do to get this endless access to free chemicals.

But only a short while later, Haus got the light to come on again; he heaved a sigh of relief, and smiled. "Anyway, the octamethyst is a fixing agent. I suppose you already know what that means?"

Lark nodded impatiently. Of course he did. "But what are you aiming to fix?"

"Never mind about that. Anyway, the trichloroes is to generate energy."

Lark perked up at the sound of the word energy. "What do you want that energy for? Do you not already have a source to charge up your whole store and home?" Drellians had invisible power sources installed in their indoor spaces, which cost nothing at all. The energy was all from nature, including the sun and wind. So why would anyone need any additional energy?

"We, I mean I, need this trichloroes energy to uh," Haus tapped his head, "charge me up."

"What do you mean?"

"I need this to activate my brain circuits to enhance my intellectual abilities when I come to play the Great Annual Game."

"What is that?"

"Well," Haus said slowly, "My friends and I—"

"How many friends?"

"My five friends and I—six people in total," Haus said. "My five friends and I would gather once a year, in fact, in just a few days, to hold a competition between us. Whoever can write out the highest quality of poetry, or draw the best picture, wins."

"So what is the prize?" Lark asked, his head building up a picture of this whole story.

Haus stared down at him with a big grin. "Something like this," he said, and fished out something that looked like a pink ticket from another one of his clothes pockets.

Lark didn't bother asking what this pink object was this time because he fully expected Haus to explain it. But Haus didn't. Lark scowled; yet he couldn't ask now as that would be mortifying.

But Lark still managed to say, "So?"

Haus ignored him and put the pink ticket-like object back into his pocket. "No more about that now. Just know that I want to use this brachiorsor to do something amazing with my brain. However, the brachiorsor needs more fuel and—" Haus paused a second as if expecting Lark to jump in with a question. But the boy didn't this time. So Haus continued, "And I need you to help me find that fuel."

"But why do you want me to find it? Can you not find it yourself?"

"There's a little thing, you see. I—have this illness right now so I can't travel far—"

"You want me to travel far?"

"Not that far," assured Haus, but Lark doubted his words.

Haus continued, "Come on, I can show you a map."

"Yet what kind of fuel does this brachiorsor use? If you cannot use the ordinary energy sources that everybody uses?" Lark said, astonished that Haus would not even have the presence of mind to tell him that first.

Haus was not bothered by the terseness of Lark's question, however, and hastily mumbled something.

Lark couldn't catch a word of that—it sounded like "parter" but he wasn't sure. Regardless, he didn't want to make himself look stupid so he didn't ask.

Haus flashed up a liquid crystal map into the air before Lark's eyes. He pointed somewhere. "See? That's where I have to go to get the par-the-air. A pink liquid with a very high boiling point."

Par-the-air. Lark wondered if it really had something to do with the air. But now was not the time. Lark said, "That is too far. My parents would never allow me to travel such a distance."

"Ho ho. Can't you go somewhere without your parents' permission?" Haus teased.

Lark shot the man a dirty look. He wasn't a goody-two-shoes, but going so far away without letting his parents know seemed a little much even for him. Plus, he wasn't sure if the place was even safe. Though the Order—the intersector organization to prevent crime—was amazing and had monitors just about everywhere on the planet, there were some very deserted or unpopulated places that the Order could not survey.

They also could not survey indoor places, as people inside the buildings had their right to privacy. What's more, due to a debate in the past where people feared that the Order would have too much power over the world, the law also dictated that though the Order could monitor most outdoor places, they were not allowed to record any of these surveillances.

There was expectedly much controversy over this latter law, as some stated that this would render the Order less capable of searching for kidnapped persons trapped indoors, for instance. Nevertheless, the compromise remained that the Order could monitor most outdoor areas but could not record them on film.

Thus, Lark naturally wondered if this would be a dangerous mission and his mind kept generating the possibilities of things that could happen to him. He wasn't a coward, but he was not above fear for himself either.

(The term "intersector" is like our term "international," because their "sectors" were like our nations and countries; each sector was also grouped with several other sectors to form a "super-sector"; please see the map at the beginning of the book.)

Nevertheless, Lark said, "Tell me how I can get there."

Haus raised an eyebrow at him. "Have you never used public transport before?"

"I have," Lark said, thinking "obviously," "but only with my parents or teachers." Then he added, "But I suppose these transportation systems would be very easy to learn. I have been on them countless times before, so I can very easily work this out."

Haus loved how this kid was so full of himself and so protective of his ego. It was amusing to watch him. Haus grinned, and said, "Just take the Coaster there, and then—take the Hyure."

The Hyure were flying machines, local transportation driven by human drivers. They were long, slender, and swift vehicles of any color, including bright pink and lilac. There was also yellow, blue, green, orange, and more. However, not that many Hyure were black, grey, or even white. It just so happened that the designer of these vehicles did not like dull colors because they thought that black, grey, and even brown were way too depressing. They didn't mind silver, though. These Hyures were sleek and swift.

Coasters, on the other hand, were large white transporters that traveled over longer distances, even across different sectors of the planet. However, to be precise, there were different types of Coasters of different speeds. The slowest were the intra-sector ones, those that only travel within one sector. Faster ones were the intra-super-sector Coasters, which travel within the same super-sector. And the fastest were the inter-super-sector Coasters, and these travel across the seas and oceans between super-sectors.

"So where am I supposed to find the money to travel, then? Since my parents would not know?" Lark asked.

"I'll pay you."

ON THE COASTER, LARK WONDERED WHY HE HAD NOT ASKED Haus what kind of illness he had.

This question consumed the five-year-old boy for a while. Mysteries bugged him easily and he fell readily into deep trances thinking about certain things that puzzled him.

Intensely white walls inside this Coaster ran to form a huge chamber-like compartment. Blue seats decked almost the entire perimeter of this interior; and windows perched above most of the seats like circular beams of light.

At this moment, while he was sitting quietly by himself, he saw a lady seated opposite him; a little girl, probably aged three, sat beside her. Both wore Creemas, a kind of one-piece attire that was silky and soft. Lark himself was wearing a thick black Iminis (pronounced "imm-min-nis")—his happened to be furred but rough in texture; most other people preferred to wear smoother and gentler Iminises.

It was a rather cold autumn day, so Lark had no idea how the lady and little girl withstood the low temperature in their relatively thin garments.

The lady looked like she was in her early thirties, or late twenties, barely older than his own mother. Lark, despite himself, felt a twinge of guilt at the thought of deceiving his parents that he was off to buy something for the family—he had promised to buy more food supplies. His parents were surprised that he actually wanted to do something for the family, for once. But they were happy that perhaps, just perhaps, their boy was finally turning "normal," good, and sweet like any other child that they would desire to have, and they let him set off early in the morning.

Yet, Lark was not one to be so easily overwhelmed by guilt. He was a person who could brush things aside and focus on what he was doing.

The lady opposite seemed to be gazing at him. He stiffened. Then to his relief, she glanced up again. But now the little girl beside her was staring at him. He glared at her, hoping she would be scared and thus look away. But she didn't. She just kept on staring at him with such a dismayed expression on her face that he frowned terribly and looked somewhere else. When the Coaster reached his stop, Lark breathed a sigh of relief and got up to leave. Then suddenly he heard the girl cry out, "Hey mommy, that boy doesn't have a grown-up with him!"

Lark knew what was about to happen. So he made a run for it. Unfortunately, he was not a fast runner. Too much time shut up in his room designing, investigating, and thinking about things instead of running around in the playground like every other kid really taxed his physical abilities. And thus, the little girl easily caught up to him right after he stepped onto the platform that the Coaster had landed on for this stop. She blocked his way. "Stop," she said.

"Please go away," he said. Hopefully the "please" would make her go away. But she didn't. And her mother approached too.

The mother said, "Little boy, where's your mom? Where are your parents?"

Lark was tempted to say 'I have no parents' out of annoyance, but instead he said something incoherent; he mumbled, shrugged, and moved away. But the woman and her child stopped him again.

"I can help you find your parents, child," the woman cried—or at least that high pitched voice of hers sounded like crying to him. This was just extremely irritating and Lark had to find a way to escape her as quickly as possible. "Let me take you to the Coaster Order." She made a gesture for Lark to come but he refused to budge. In fact, when she made the gesture again, Lark immediately sprinted away. The little girl ran to catch him and she did. Lark was fuming with frustration and he wanted to kick her. But he was not a violent person. Superior as he was, he did not kick or injure mortals. They were not worth his time.

But since he could not run as fast as they did, Lark decided that he would let the little girl and her mother lead him away for now, and see if he could deceive the Coaster Order and break free. Or somehow get them to let him go.

So he grudgingly walked back to the woman with the little girl by his side. As they went towards the small building where the Coaster staff worked, the little girl started to chat, "So, what's your name? Mine's Alyssha."

Lark couldn't care less what her name was. So he kept quiet.

"What's your name?" the annoying girl demanded.

"Lark Arias," he said resignedly and hoped that she would not bother him anymore for the rest of the way.

Unfortunately, of course, she did. "So, um, what's your favorite color?"

Was this all girls thought about? Evidently, Lark Arias did not have much experience with girls. To be more precise, he did not have much experience with human beings. Was he obliged to answer? No. And thus Lark did not answer.

But the girl was really determined. She yanked at his sleeve. "I said, what's your favorite color?"

He gave a really deep frown. He wanted to say blue, because that was probably his favorite color. Yet, he wasn't quite sure. He did like solid greys—or anything that reminded him of metal too, or ice. But he also seemed to like dark greens. Nevertheless, Lark just thought this girl was unbelievably annoying so he decided not to answer her and hoped that she would just shut her mouth.

As she was getting absolutely no response, Alyssha tried something else. She asked her mother to interrogate Lark.

Her mother rolled her eyes. If the kid didn't want to talk, then let him stay that way. The kid probably had reasons of his own for being so reserved, and perhaps this reason had something to do with how his parents were not with him. She wondered vehemently where his parents had gone, but the three of them were almost at the Coaster Order's. Still, for the sake of her dear Alyssha, the mother asked, in a gentle voice, "What is your favorite color, Lark?"

Lark still did not want to reply, but since it was the adult who spoke to him this time, he thought he had better respond, lest she do anything to deter him even more from his path. So, without any emotion, he replied, "Blue." There was no need to elaborate on his answer to mere mortals.

WHEN THEY GOT TO THE COASTER ORDER'S OFFICE, THEY entered a small, cramped room painted predominantly in shades of cool green. They were told that the lead Order member was out, but a junior member was there. He was in his early twenties. "Hello, how may I help you?"

"Hi," said the mother, "this little boy here is lost and without his parents."

"I am not lost," Lark said; he didn't know what he could say about his parents, though.

Nevertheless, the Order member started plying Lark with questions. The poor misanthropic boy frowned with feeling as he was forced into a sustained human interaction.

"Where do you live?"

"I do not want to tell you."

"Come on, kid, let's make it easier for ourselves, eh?"

"I do not want to tell you," he repeated in a monotone.

The Order member put his hands on his hips, and his lips were pursed. The three-year-old Alyssha jabbed Lark in the ribs and he shot a warning glare at her. She was utterly undaunted and shot a tongue out at him in response. Lark was obviously unamused at this atrocious immaturity.

"I do not want to tell you," Lark said. "If I may be truthful, I have an errand to run for a friend," he winced at the word "friend," as no such thing existed for him except for science, if you counted a subject as a friend. "And I would greatly appreciate it if you would terminate this interrogation and set me free."

The Order member, the mother, and the annoying three-year-old stared at him. "What errand?" the latter asked.

"It is none of your concern," Lark said, still in a monotone. He internally began tapping his foot.

"Oh please, tell us!" Alyssha said.

But the more they pleaded him, the less willing he was to explain in further detail. "Please," he said, "I am but five years old. I do not need to be questioned like this."

The Order member grinned. "Exactly. You are but five years old. That's why we need to help you find your parents. So I hope you will be a good little boy and cooperate."

Alyssha gave him a wide grin as well. He really wanted to kick her; but he had never kicked a person in his entire life of five years; and he was too full of pride to need to kick anyone anyway. Instead, he closed his eyes in annoyance and hoped that some scheme would come to him. However, though Lark was hyper-trained in scientific and mathematical thinking, his sharpened skills and intellect in these areas did not transfer to real life. His escaping tactics were no better than anyone else's.

Thankfully, he did understand how to go on the Coaster and Hyures after just a few trips with adults. About Hyures, he hoped that they would not be too hard to accost, because he suddenly realized that a lone five-year-old like him may not be treated seriously enough to be allowed on the vehicle. In fact, the Hyure driver would likely be just as exasperating as these two adults and Alyssha were: the driver would either refuse to give him a ride, or ship him back to his parents and therefore sabotage his mission. But he needed those chemicals!

So he formed a hasty plan. "Actually," he started. Everybody stared at him in eager expectation; an eagerness that scared him. He continued nevertheless, "this errand of mine is very simple. I need to buy some items for my friend—who is an adult, because he has an injury and thus cannot travel far."

"You have to travel far?" blurted out the Order member.

"Yes, unfortunately my poor friend cannot do it himself. And—"

"But then," interrupted Alyssha, "you can still go with your parents to buy whatever you want to buy, right?"

The high pitch of her voice was irritating. He replied, "My parents are busy. Plus, my friend wants to keep what he is buying a secret. Because— he would not want anybody to see how juvenile he is to buy kiddy potions." Lark smiled inwardly at the ingenuity of what he had come up with.

Kiddy, or "toy" chemicals, were 'inoculated' by a special industrial process to make them safe for children to use. Inoculated chemicals would not explode, corrode, poison, irritate, or burn anything or anyone. But some chemicals were too potent to be made safe by the inoculation process, so those chemicals were unfortunately inaccessible to children. Nonetheless, Lark thought toy chemicals were for mere amateurs; he deserved real chemicals.

Alyssha seemed amused by Lark's explanation of this errand for his "friend," as were Alyssha's mother and the Order member. The little girl said, "Ooh, I've always wanted one of those toys." No, you didn't, Lark muttered to himself. Alyssha continued, "But why would your adult friend want a kiddy potion set? Does he have kids to buy these for, but then he wants to surprise them because it's a birthday present?"

Stupid girl. If he did, then why would there be any problem telling his parents about it? He told her about the flaw in her argument.

Alyssha simply replied, "Your friend is weird."

Lark hoped that this would be it and he could proceed to stage two of his plan, but then Alyssha began again, "You still haven't explained to me why this grown-up friend of yours would want this ridiculous potion set."

Why must he explain to her? Yet, since the eyes of the two grown-ups —grown-ups had power—were on him, he was obliged to answer, "Because—my friend has the heart of a child." This was obviously something that Lark memorized from his literature classes, though he had no idea what the expression meant. "He also trusts me," Lark said.

The trio stared at him. Lark wished that they would keep their eyes to themselves.

"Uh," said the Order member, "so your friend didn't think that he could lie and tell your parents that you're buying him...food or something?" He sounded surprisingly timid for a member of the Order.

Lark was astonished at this man's obtuseness. "If he were to lie, then my parents would come with me, see what exactly I am buying, and discover his desire for a child's toy! Does that not sound humiliating to you?" He endeavored to act like a faithful friend and they did seem convinced. "So," he said, getting extremely uncomfortable because he had never begged people to do him a favor before, or at least that he could remember, and asked, "since you all now know about this affair and are all strangers who would not be able to embarrass my friend, would you be so kind as to help me get to this place to buy him his kiddy potions?"

It was an instant yes. Lark smiled to himself at his fabulous, but expected, success. Wasn't he an amazing boy genius? he thought.

Lark now pondered what he would do once he got to Phuore—the place Haus had pointed out on his map—as they would soon figure out that Lark was not getting kiddy potions. Perhaps he could try to lose them once they got him to his destination. But how?

As the Order member couldn't leave his post, Alyssha and her mother accompanied Lark by themselves on the next Coaster after changing from the previous one. When they sat down, he tried to still himself and stare straight ahead. He avoided thinking about how the little girl and her mother were sitting on either side of him, as their nearness was unsettling. Lark especially resented the little girl's proximity, as she was bound to deliberately annoy him. Why couldn't they both sit on either his left or right side so that he at least had one side free?

But the little girl had insisted on the need to "guard" and flank the boy so he didn't run away without an adult again. Her mother thought this unlikely as it would be easy to catch such a slow runner of a boy, but she humored her spoiled daughter anyway and sat on the other side of him.

Sadly, Lark was unable to complain. Well, he could, but it would be beneath him to reveal his feelings, especially to strangers, under such circumstances.

Alyssha took a big yawn—how imprudent!—and said, "So, uh, Lark, what was the name of this place where we're going?"

Lark wished that she wouldn't say "we." It disgusted him that he had to travel with anyone already, let alone be associated with them by this pronoun. So he said nothing.

"Mama," Alyssha said, "Lark isn't answering me again."

That's because I hate you and wish you were gone, thought Lark bitterly.

Alyssha continued, "Mama, can you make him say something to me? I'm bored."

"Oh," her mother, Mrs Juess, said gently, "I could talk to you and then you wouldn't be so bored anymore. There's no need to disturb your new friend."

"I am not her new friend," Lark couldn't resist blurting out.

The little girl looked like she was about to cry. Lark couldn't see this, though, as he was still glancing ahead. She was probably faking this look anyway to make her mother do something about it. Mrs Juess sighed inside and wished that her daughter would be a bit more understanding. It was very clear that this little boy wanted nothing to do with her daughter or with anyone at all, but her Alyssha was an innocent soul who was too naïve to see anything. Her mother also loved her way too much, and was too used to spoiling her that she yielded to her daughter's whims and spoke to Lark.

"Hi, Lark," Mrs Juess said, not expecting him to answer and indeed he didn't. "Would you tell us the name of the place where we're going again?" This, she thought, was a stupid and pointless question. If she did not know the name of the place they were going, then she wouldn't be able to escort—chaperone him in the first place. And little Lark told her just that.

Alyssha made a very upset face and stuck her tongue out at Lark, which he also did not see because he could not deign to look at either of them. "Why are you so mean, Lark?" Alyssha said.

Lark glanced around to see if there were any seats freed near him that he could retreat to and escape from this aggravating child. Unfortunately, the Coaster was full.

"There are five more stations left," he said absentmindedly in the hope of diverting them to something else so he wouldn't be obliged to answer them. Lark didn't dislike talking per se, as it was just a fact of life like breathing, eating, and sleeping. But he disliked purposeless chatter and small talk. He simply despised useless things. This could be a contradictory claim, however, because Lark liked things that were potentially useless, at least to the wider public: who on Drell cared whether this substance called amosti could glow in the dark when it was dipped into ice or not? How would that change anybody's life? Yet, it would radically change Lark's life, because each new scientific discovery made him happier; to know more about chemistry was to open a new world.

Lark's attempt to divert their attention failed with Alyssha though, as she just started prattling about the diverter instead. Were all girls so tremendously and relentlessly chatty?

Mrs Juess shook her head at the insensitivity of her child. She tried to get her daughter to talk to her instead, but Alyssha had no interest in her mother's attention and continued to bother the poor boy, probably because little children preferred to talk to other children about their age. But why was Alyssha so inexorably chatty? It couldn't have been in her genes, right? Mrs Juess herself was never this sociable, at least not in her memory. And her spouse was normal too. Maybe it was her daughter's friends who influenced her.

Mrs Juess also thought that Alyssha's greater desire to talk to Lark was precisely because he was so unapproachable and rejecting. Some people derived a certain pleasure out of annoying those who most wanted to be left alone.

Here, Alyssha yawned again and said, "Okay, you don't want to talk about that, huh?"

Lark didn't even know what she was talking about, because he wasn't paying attention. He thought that what came out of this little girl's mouth was rubbish, and a person of his stature should not pay any heed to such filth in case they contaminated his mind.

Being a boy of science, however, he should know better than to think that mere small talk would "contaminate" one's mind. Listening to others may influence you, but you always have the choice to reject the influence. Lark loved the sciences in general, but he was not as taken by psychology, for the simple reason that he didn't like human beings. Finding out how human minds worked was useless information to him. He didn't mind biochemistry or biology, however, even though these subjects were related to humans. Perhaps it was because the biological sciences could be reduced to chemistry, and the latter never failed to pique his interest.

About science enthusiasts, some people preferred simpler things, so they liked physics best. Some liked the complex, especially the organic, so they most loved biology. Yet, there were also some like Lark, who loved a particular science best (chemistry, in his case), but could appreciate both complexity and simplicity. To him, complexity was something that promised richness and deep abundance—a more complex system was more satisfying to study because it was so intricate, full of convolutions, and took longer to understand; and, as you know, the longer one took to understand something, the more rewarding it was to finally get it.

As for simplicity, Lark liked it because it was neat. He liked precision. And maybe it wasn't just precision. It was orderly. Exact. Clean. Pure. Like seeing a tiny spider's web in the center of a vast space of purple sky— where there was no ground to obstruct your vision, nor clouds. Only pure sky and transparent gas. You know that magical feeling when something is so simple, yet its implications are so various? Lark often felt that way, though not consciously.

(See "The Names of Academic Disciplines[1]" under "Drellian Society" in the glossary.)

For a moment, Lark was hopeful that this obnoxious girl was going to shut up once and for all, because she was silent for a while; but then she started talking again, and he pitied himself.

"So," she said, "do you like to dance?"

What a joke that was. Did he, a master scientist, like to dance? Lark didn't bother answering her. He just hoped against hope that his perpetual nonresponses would eventually make her clam up.

He was disappointed, however, because Alyssha was not a girl to be easily deterred. After failing to elicit a response from Lark about dancing, she proceeded to ask what his favorite lamina was (laminae were like our animals on earth); and his favorite sport? For the first question, he liked laminae, but he felt no inclination to answer her. As for sports, he detested them, so that was double the reason why he completely ignored her question. Well then, what was his favorite school subject? This he was tempted to answer because this was the only question that lingered close to the one thing in the world he did care about. He was going to say, "Science. Chemistry in particular."

Yet, he resisted giving this aggravating girl the satisfaction of his response, so again, he kept quiet and stonewalled. Soon, he even shut his ears with his palms and concentrated hard on thinking about the latest chemical formulae, mechanisms, and reactions that he had looked up. Hopefully science would save him, as it had very often done in the past.

But Alyssha, unexpectedly, yanked at his hand. This was ridiculous. Mrs Juess exclaimed, "Alyssha! Stop that!" But her daughter didn't stop, and Lark kept yanking back his hand, which he was finding a bit hard to do as he was not a particularly strong boy: he had been spending too much time in his lab performing delicate matters that required no strength, as his robots and machines took care of all the heavy duties for him.

Alyssha, on the other hand, was perhaps a particularly strong girl, even for a three-year-old. Lark felt like his hand would soon be successfully yanked from his ear, and his poor ear would be filled to bursting with an onslaught of nonsensical chatter. In fact, she might even shout the nonsense into his exposed ear and deafen him forever. Not that this would be much cause for alarm, because Drellian technology would be able to cure that very quickly and easily.

Mrs Juess eventually managed to pull her daughter's hands away from Lark's. He breathed a sigh of relief inside when suddenly Alyssha began to cry. And she didn't just cry, she bawled. Oh my, what had he gotten himself into?

Mrs Juess was terribly embarrassed by the scene her daughter was making, and this wasn't the first time this sort of thing had happened either. In fact, this happened very often, to Mrs Juess's constant aggravation. Yet, she often could not quite override her tendency to be soft and friendly towards her daughter. She simply did not have it in her to be unkind or harsh towards Alyssha because she loved her child so much. However, she did, in this case, pluck little Alyssha from Lark's left side and place her daughter onto her lap.

Alyssha was still bawling and Lark thought he would go deaf anyway just from hearing her cry. Lark thought he was going to die if they didn't get to that station soon.

But luckily, Alyssha had predictably just cried for show, to get attention. More importantly, to try to get Lark's attention because he had been so obstinately and successfully ignoring her, which she resented very much because she thought she was the most adorable, attractive, and irresistible little angel that any sane person would automatically love and serve.

Her pompous and supremely self-confident attitude was obviously a result of her upbringing by her mother. As misfortune had it, her father pampered her as much as her mother did. Perhaps even more so, depending on how you looked at it. Her father especially loved to buy his daughter presents, countless presents of whatever she wanted and whatever he anticipated she wanted. To his credit, he often anticipated correctly and consequently his daughter loved him very much—for his presents.

So, Alyssha was crying her head off and Lark pitied himself to the extreme for having gotten into such a scrape. He almost regretted asking for her mother's help—he would have come up with a clever solution to induce the Hyure driver to get him to the place anyway, but now was not the time to dwell on such regrets. He longed to punch the girl on the mouth to silence her, but with some hope her mother would do that for him so that he would not have to resort to violence—he was not a violent person.

Unfortunately, Alyssha's mother didn't help him do so. She just made a lot of useless shushing sounds.

At this moment, Mrs Juess received a call. More trouble, Lark thought. It was her beloved. "Honey!" she cried. "Your daughter's crying, please comfort her!"

(See "Computers in General[2]" and "Communication via Computer[3]" under "Technology" in the glossary.)

Computers were silvery-white networks that were transparent and nonphysical like projections of light; these networks were the size of an adult human. People could ask computers to follow them around, much like a loyal digital companion. But most of the time, people chose to keep their computers invisible.

One second later, a face hologram of a man in his early thirties appeared, and he widened his eyes at his wailing daughter. "Oh, Alysshie, don't cry, Daddy will buy you more presents next time. What present do you want?"

"I don't want any presents!" Alyssha managed to say between her sobs.

Just then, the Coaster touched down at the next stop and a number of people left to get off at their station. Lark thanked his lucky stars and rushed to a now vacant seat away from the Juess's.

(For an explanation of how Drellian parents pass down last names to their children, and what surname the parents choose to title themselves, see "Middle and Last Names[4]" under "Drellian Society" and "Social Conventions".)

"No, Lark, come back!" Undoubtedly that was Alyssha.

"Who's this?" asked her father. "Your new friend?"

"Yeah, but he's not very nice. That's why I'm crying."

"Oh no, did he hurt you?" The father glared at Lark, who paid no heed to the little hologram.

"Yeah!"

"Where?"

"In here!" She poked her chest where her heart should be.

Mrs Juess sighed. "Honey, she's just having one of her tantrums. She wants to talk to a little boy that we met but I don't think he likes talking to people," At least she understood that much, thought Lark, "but we need to go with him to Phuore to buy uh—a chemistry potion set for his friend." And she explained the whole situation to her elemen.

"Elemen" meant spouse. This translation "elemen" reflected the meaning of the original Drellian word: "element," as in "in one's element." The term implied that one was in their element when they were with their spouse; or, they felt so bonded to their spouse that they felt they were made of the same element, and that they lived in this same element together. Mrs Juess's elemen Mr Juess wasn't amused at this moment, however.

"Are you sure the kid's not lying? He could be a runaway, you know?" he whispered this very quietly.

But Mrs Juess said, "Darling, you suspect too much. The kid doesn't look at all like the crafty type. I mean, he's extraordinarily antisocial, but some kids are like that. And he looks like an innocent little boy, so I think we should trust him."

"You are a little gullible sometimes, Evervessa."

"Dron, you are a little too untrusting sometimes. Remember when you first met me?"

"Oh come on, dear, why bring that up now?"

"Because!"

And the couple went on like this for a while, and nobody cared about Alyssha.

Lark gazed out the window that was opposite him as if he were in a dream. He thought of something. What if he poured lava into a vorte cup? Would it melt it? Presumably not, as these cups were made of some of the sturdiest materials alive—materials were alive for Lark—however, if it did melt it, then what would happen? Would the liquid then evaporate? Because the lava was so hot? And so Lark entertained himself with those thoughts for a while, as Alyssha wailed and her parents, well, love-chatted.

When they got off the Coaster, Alyssha said that she needed to go. Good riddance, thought Lark, and he crossed his arms as he waited for the two outside the washroom. (There is a Drellian equivalent for this word, but for now, let's simplify it and say "washroom.")

Now Lark sighed and asked himself again why on Drell he was doing all this. Yes, it was for all those free chemicals, but could there have been an easier way to acquire them? Why didn't he try to bargain with Haus? Maybe because Lark wasn't a bargaining person.

The five-year-old boy sat down on a short, flat rock in exhaustion, and he rested his feet on the damp soil below. He put his chin on his hands and his elbows on his knees. He watched a little green stalk on the ground that seemed to be growing. It wasn't really growing, but Lark imagined that it was.

While he was observing that specimen out of sheer boredom, he could have been reading on his computer instead as he carried his books everywhere. Yet, this was one of those strange times where he didn't feel like reading; sometimes he preferred to look at real objects rather than at the holograms that were conjured up by the books.

(See "Books and Electrospaces[5]" under "Technology" in the glossary.)

After peering a little while at that plant, Lark closed his eyes.

He imagined a scene playing in his head: a bunch of people wild in their joy, dancing in the sun, around who knew what. Lark was obviously not in the midst of them. He didn't even want to join in. But this scene was so disjointed from his normal train of thoughts that Lark dismissed this as one of those alien thoughts that people always had.

His parents and teachers had schooled him well on this strange and unsettling phenomenon: certain thoughts in a person's head do not correspond to a person's true nature, and even try to lure the person away from their real self. Lark was not absolutely sure what this meant, at least, in a deep way, but he didn't care much. It was just that whenever he did receive any of these bizarre thoughts, he would know perfectly well that they were foreign from him, and thus he would not be disturbed by them.

Lark then had another thought. Of a distressed looking person, eyes begging, staring at Lark, as if entreating him to lend help, to save their life. Lark shuddered. His parents had also warned him that some thoughts were more arbitrary than others. But to Lark, this was not just arbitrary; it was dark. It was not as if he were an incredibly cold-hearted person who would never lend a helping hand to someone in great need; but the fact was, he had never encountered a situation where somebody was truly in need of aid. And the prospect of having to save or help someone in the future daunted him even more than the person's distress.

He kept his eyes closed, and his head spun around some equations he had mentally retained using a memoria.

(See "Memoria[6]" under "Technology.")

Lark was in the middle of pondering about what variables he could use to substitute 2 from the equation—. His mind was whirling with calculations when he heard someone call his name and break his concentration.

---

1. The Names of Academic Disciplines

You might have been wondering why Drellians would still use some of our academic categories on Earth, like psychology, chemistry, biology, and physics. Firstly, these terms simply indicate the "level" of complexity for the subject under study. Physics involves the study of fundamental matter, energy, and their interactions; chemistry focuses on the structure, properties, and transformations of substances; biology is about living organisms and their processes; and psychology studies mind and behavior, to name a few examples on this continuum from the most basic to the most complex subjects.

Thus, these names of academic disciplines just mark a certain "level" of study on this continuum; this type of categorization is simply a social convention that most on Drell follow, though others like to use different categories. For example, some like to put what we call "physics" and "chemistry" in the same group, since they both talk about the physical, material world that is not necessarily living.

Next, one reason why Drellians still had professions like "psychologist" and "chemist," was because most people favored certain categories on that continuum of complexity over others: Lark liked the complexity level of chemistry best, for example. Many people were happy to hold more than one title, e.g. both a chemist and a physicist, if they had wider interests. But most professionals would only pick one academic discipline to specialize in, as there was obviously a great deal to learn within any one discipline already.

At the same time, Drellians did not have the danger of overspecialization or developing tunnel vision from these academic divisions, because scientists and other experts regularly talked to those outside their fields, to gain interdisciplinary insights. Even experts as antisocial as Lark was would eventually recognize the value of such inter-field discussions.

2. **Computers in General**

A computer is an invisible or transparent air network. It is normally invisible, but when you want it to become visible, it becomes a white, silvery, and transparent network in front of you. These computers can follow you everywhere if you choose to bring them.

They can often be voice commanded, even if you speak softly; just articulate clearly. Computers are quite intelligent at interpreting ambiguous vocal signals, and are usually even better than humans are at interpreting speech. Of course, you can also press buttons, use joysticks, draw or touch things on the computer air panels (airborne keypads) if you wish—or just control everything by voice. But sometimes it's easier to communicate using your hands or visuals instead of by words, so you might want to use these tactile or visual techniques instead.

You can also command the computer using your thoughts and mental images. However, this method can be difficult as thoughts tend to be interrupted very frequently by distractions, which may confuse instructions to the computer, or even lead to the wrong commands.

Computers have such a massive memory that it feels infinite. Apart from their amazing memory, computers are also almost indestructible. Very few viruses and bugs can affect them, but even these are easy to exterminate.

3. **Communication via Computer**

The contacting function is built into the computer. You can use holograms, two-dimensional faces, just voices, just words, or just images. More than one person can participate in the conversation, of course, in any of the above forms of communication.

4. **Middle and Last Names**

Couples typically use one of these two options in passing down last names to their children. The first is to have the child receive their last name from one parent, and their middle name from the other parent. For instance, if the parents were Kate Snow and Joachim Fraser, the child might be called Lezlie Fraser Snow, or Lezlie Snow Fraser.

Alternatively, the child could themselves decide which parents' last names to use when introducing themselves to new people. Since Drellians usually only mention their first and last names for convenience to new acquaintances (or, more commonly, just their first name), Lezlie would either call herself "Lezlie Fraser" or "Lezlie Snow."

Couples with more than one child may choose to name the siblings differently, for instance, "Lezlie Snow Fraser" and "Bonzo Fraser Snow," though couples usually opt to keep the siblings' middle and last names the same. E.g. Lezlie Fraser Snow and Bonzo Fraser Snow. Or, of course, parents can let the children choose which names to use when introducing themselves to new people.

As for the couples' way of addressing themselves, spouses tend to decide on whose surname to stick to, such as Mrs and Mr Snow, or Mrs and Mr Fraser, as well as what titles to use. Mr, Ms, Miss, Mrs, Mx, Misc, and Ind. are common titles. These are approximate English translations of the Drellian titles. However, some other couples do change whose surname to follow from time to time, or some may even wish to switch their titles throughout their life.

The naming conventions for non-monogamous couples are more complex, which I will not go into detail here, but basically it involved a great deal of negotiation for which children get whose surnames, the possibility of multiple middle names, and many other considerations.

In this story, as an example, "Juess" is Evervessa's maiden surname. Her spouse Dron adopts Juess as his surname as well; his original surname was Phelia (pronounced "fee-lee-ah"). They call themselves Mrs and Mr Juess, or Evervessa and Dron Juess. Their daughter's full name was Alyssha Phelia Juess, or just Alyssha Juess for short.

5. **Books and Electrospaces**

Drellians still read their books in words (whether by looking or listening to the words), not in direct mental images or any other fancy nonverbal modes of communication—though fancy nonverbal books are available to those who want them. Drellians also think, like some of our Earthly friends, that written words are too beautiful to eradicate, no matter how ambiguous and flawed in expression they are. And often it's because they're so opaque and able to be interpreted in so many ways, that written language is so endlessly attractive and interesting. So Drellians (and the many generations of human beings before them) decided to continue the writing of words in their culture.

Books are electronically stored, so they're like our e-books. There is basically infinite storage space—not literally infinite, but the memory is so massive that it feels infinite for all practical purposes.

Such electronic books can be read directly from the computer, where the computer projects a page of words in front of you like a phantom book; there is also no backlight, so your eyes can read comfortably. Alternatively, you can put the book into an electrospace. Electrospaces are like e-readers, except the shape and size of the screen and device, as well as their thickness, can be changed any time to your liking. You can ask the computer to hold the electrospace for you too, if it ever becomes too tiring to hold up yourself. There is also no backlight on electrospaces, for the same reason as detailed above.

Plus, the books' pages are automatically adjusted to the person's comfort. The word sizes, fonts, and spacing can be controlled either via words or touch panels. If you want to turn the page, you just need to signal to the computer in some way: press a button, touch a screen, make a gesture, nod, tap your hand on your knee, say something, etc. You program the signal you want to use.

6. **Memoria**

This helps in generating a kind of permanent memory. The memoria is a feature in the computer. It's a code that sends electrical signals to your neurons and other brain cells to make your memory permanent. You choose the exact thing (target) you want to remember, which prevents you from remembering any extraneous and unwanted things, like the smell of food wafting into your nostrils at the moment you were learning something new.

However, your brain hurts if you use the memoria too much for an extended period of time. But different people have different levels of stamina. Some people can do one core (two hours) of nonstop memorizing. Some can do only half a core (one hour). Thus, you must rest for a while until your brain stops hurting, before using the memoria again.

You can also delete unwanted memories that were acquired using the memoria. You probably can't delete naturally formed memories, though.

The memoria is how even five-year-olds can know so much already about science and other things. Therefore, people like Lark who spend a disproportionate amount of time studying would be able to become an expert even at the age of five, albeit just a mini-expert who knows more than the average adult does.

TWO

KARRIN TREEK

T o his surprise, instead of seeing Alyssha or her mother, he looked up at a boy clothed in a blue and white Dracana (pronounced "druh-cah-nah"), a loose-fitting garment with long sleeves commonly worn in the fall. The boy had brown hair and sea-green eyes, and was currently juggling a light blue bubble ball the size of his palm. Bubble balls were rubbery, bouncy, and ranged from opaque, translucent, to fully transparent and could be any color.

"Fancy meeting you here!" the boy said.

This brown-haired boy was Karrin Treek, one of Lark's classmates. Karrin was one of those people who tried to reach out to Lark by introducing themselves to him. He was also among the few who didn't see Lark as a freak, believing instead that he was just an extra unique person.

Karrin's father, Hlen Treek, was a psychologist, and he had told his son to never judge others because everybody's brains processed the world in different ways. In fact, Hlen recognized Lark as the type that was passionately obsessed with one thing, which consequently made Lark uninterested in other human beings.

On Drell, by the way, everyone knew that there was no such thing as innate talent. There was only innate interest in specific things. But most people did not have an extreme desire to do just one thing, so most people did not reach the greatest possible levels of human achievement. But if a person had such an intense, focused passion as Lark did, it was certain that they would soar to that pinnacle of excellence.

In contrast with people like Lark, Karrin Treek was a relatively balanced and sociable child, who preferred to be with his friends than to be alone.

Moreover, science did not move Karrin in the least. He was much more into acting and dancing, the performance arts. Perhaps Karrin had more similar interests with his mother, a mostly silent woman who was good at and loved dancing, as well as silent acting. She was not actually shy or inhibited, however; she was just one of those people who did not feel the need to talk and didn't like talking.

At this moment, Karrin slipped the blue bubble ball back into one of his Dracana's pockets, and asked, "So, Lark, what are you doing here?"

Lark was in no mood to answer; he gave Karrin a nonchalant look.

This would have offended any five-year-old kid, but Karrin was not just any five-year-old. Since his dad had told him to be more tolerant towards Lark, Karrin was patient, and said, "Ooh, what an interesting plant you were looking at. What's it called?"

To Karrin's relief, Lark did reply this time, in a low tone, "A quimemoris."

"So what does it do?" Karrin tried to make Lark say more. Unfortunately, Lark did not respond, probably because he had lost all motivation to say any more. It was already a miracle that Lark had told him the name of the plant.

"By the way, Lark, do you have a favorite lamina?" Karrin asked.

Lark displayed a frustrated expression, frowned, and turned away.

But Karrin moved to face Lark again, to the latter's infinite annoyance, and said, "Um, by the way, my dad and I bought some trooflées, would you like some?" Trooflées were bright green and shiny, rubbery, firm, but squishy soap-bar-shaped snacks; they had the perfect degree of sweetness that made you feel happy.

But Lark was not a kid who was particularly interested in food in the first place.

This sad scene of Karrin trying to get Lark to open up happened all the time in the classroom as well, but Karrin still thought he could someday turn Lark into a friend.

Karrin believed that anybody could be befriended given time. There was just, as his father had always told him, a complex that prevented certain people from socializing or receiving warmth from others around them, something that blocked them from interacting with and liking the world outside. Karrin was determined to break this "complex," even though he was discouraged every time he tried. Not so discouraged that he ever despaired, though.

Regarding this difficulty, Karrin had a female friend called Eeera who told him what she thought about this. This Eeera had long hair in a chestnut-brown ponytail, and she gazed through pale green eyes. Her physical similarity to Karrin in hair and eye color was likely one reason why they had become friends. And Eeera, like Karrin, was a rather sociable person. She wasn't hyper or bubbly, but she was relaxed, confident, and approachable.

Once, Eeera had pulled Karrin aside, and said, "Kari, don't you think we should try to approach Lark in a different way? He really doesn't like us talking to him."

"You mean we should give up? And leave him with no friends forever?" Karrin was shocked at her suggestion.

Of course this was not what she meant. She, like an older sister, shook her head at him. "No, no, no. I mean we should be gentler. Ignore him for a few days and then try again, don't try to um...storm at him every chance you get."

"Oh, but then he won't have anybody to talk to for the whole day for several days!" exclaimed the good-natured Karrin. "You know that apart from us, only a few people occasionally try to talk to him, but you can tell that their hearts aren't really in it because Lark always rejects them."

Eeera laughed inside at the purity of this child Karrin. "He always rejects us too. Maybe we should give up."

"Eeera!" he cried though he knew that his friend couldn't have meant that.

"Let's just be patient and leave him alone for a while and see what happens."

So they indeed left Lark alone for some days; three days. But to Karrin's disbelief and hurt feelings, Lark not only did not seem sadder, he looked visibly happier that nobody was bothering him anymore! Karrin just could not understand it. Sometimes he wondered if he would be able to keep to his father's advice of accepting everybody and not judging. He couldn't resist admitting that he thought Lark very weird and incomprehensible in not needing any friends or company. But again, Karrin told himself not to think this. It wasn't right to call someone eccentric just because he was different from you. From Lark's perspective, Karrin would be the weird one. So Karrin urged himself to wait and be patient.

But after these three days, Karrin couldn't resist again and ignored the advice of his kind friend Eeera. In the classroom, and before the teacher came, Karrin said, "Lark! How are you doing today? What's up?" A frown immediately darkened Lark's face, and Karrin felt he was being repulsed once again.

Karrin didn't give up, however. He said two sentences about how he himself was doing, and then asked, "What are you reading?"

"Nothing that would interest you."

Lark spoke! At least that was a start. But then Karrin thought he should ask Lark to show him the name of the book. Lark ignored him. Karrin begged him repeatedly, and Lark stood up and started walking away. Karrin was about to follow when Eeera held him back. "Just let him go. If he doesn't want to talk to you, then don't force him to. You know, people develop at different rates. He just—likes his books, learning, and science more than people, that's all. That's what your dad told you, right?"

He nodded grimly, his pity rising for his poor, friendless classmate.

Karrin simply didn't get how some people could be perfectly fine with no social contact at all. According to his father the psychologist, people felt happy when they got to have a social interaction, when they could spend time with others and talk, laugh, or play together. However, there did seem to be a minority of people who...didn't seem to feel particularly uplifted by social contact.

Some of these folks even felt sad, angry, or perplexed when they were with others. And some, like Lark, couldn't comprehend social relationships at all, such that when he had to read literature and stories for class, he didn't really understand the interactions and relationships between the characters. He understood the literal meaning of the words, but not the emotional overtones.

Now, Karrin was about to give up on getting Lark to say more than just the plant's name, when he suddenly heard someone else call for Lark.

Unhappily for the latter, this someone was Alyssha. The little girl arrived, looked at Lark and then at Karrin.

"Hi," Karrin said, thinking that the little girl was quite adorable.

"Mmm," said Alyssha with curiosity at this new kid. "Where do you live?" she said randomly.

"Oh," Karrin was surprised at this question, but he answered, "In Dillas. You know, just a few stations away from here?"

"Oh Dillas. I've been there so many times I can't count," Alyssha boasted, and Karrin well knew she was, but little three-year-old girls had to be indulged in this way, he thought, so he let her go on. She said, "As for me, we live in Vermint. You know where that is?" Little Alyssha felt very happy that she found a playmate who was more appreciative of her attentions and chatter than Lark was. Whilst Lark was happy that he had gotten rid of both children in one blow—without even doing anything.

Just then, Mrs Juess announced that it was time for them to go.

"Aw, Mom, just a while longer. I need to tell Karrin about that new chrisjaras you bought me—"

"No, Alyssha, we promised Lark to help him go to Phuore, remember?"

"Phuore?" Karrin said, surprised. "Lark, you've got to take me with you."

For once, Lark spoke, "But do you not need to go somewhere with your parents?"

"Uh...I'll tell my dad when he comes out of the washroom. Oh, there he is." Karrin sprinted towards a brown-haired, dark-eyed man who looked a bit like him; Karrin announced to the man the presence of his classmate Lark, and asked if they could go with Lark to Phuore, because Karrin "had always wanted to go there." This dark-eyed man, Mr Treek, walked with his son to where the Juess's and Lark were, clarified the details of their mission, and then agreed to go with them. Karrin jumped into the air with joy.

But Alyssha was even more elated by this. "Yay! Now I can take all my time to tell you about my chrisjaras!"

"Sure, take your time," said Karrin. Mr Treek patted his son on the head and said his greetings to everyone. When he saw Lark, he gave the latter a nod. Lark didn't nod back, but for Mr Treek, who was a psychologist and by definition an expert on all sorts of people, especially the most deviant ones, he wasn't surprised in the least. He would be astonished if the boy gave any verbal response at all.

As for Lark's opinion, Lark thought that adding two more people should not make a difference to his mission, as he figured it would be equally challenging to get rid of four versus two people once he got the par-the-air. So he shrugged to himself and let these people eagerly chat themselves up.

"Where's your mom, Karrin?" asked Alyssha.

"Not sure. Probably busy dancing."

"Oh my, she dances?"

"Yeah," Karrin said enthusiastically. "My mom's really good at it and I'm training myself to be better at it too."

"Woah, you practice every day?"

Karrin looked embarrassed. "Not yet, but I'm planning to do that."

"Well, you better start early, or else you won't get good at all," Alyssha warned.

When they all got into a Hyure, Lark noticed the bright blue sheen of its wing. He thought there was something peculiar about this wing and mentally noted that he would think about this back at home. Perhaps he could simulate whatever the thing was that just struck him and study it intensely. Lark studied everything intensely, or at least as much as he could. And he often saw peculiar things in objects, whether in color, form, volume, shape, texture, or any other property. He noticed and paid much more attention to inanimate objects than to human beings.

When the Hyure took off, the sky rushed down to meet them and Lark could feel the wind. He liked the wind. Just because he spent most of his time indoors didn't mean he didn't like outdoor things. He liked plants too, for example. These were just different phenomena to investigate in addition to the usual chemicals he bought. And since the wind was made of air, it intrigued him because air was a composite of many compounds, elements, and mixtures of things. You could say the air was an alloy of some sort. He daydreamed about that new concoction he would make with this certain brownish-yellow liquid with that blue smoky chemical. He wondered if such a mixture would explode. He hoped it would.

His reveries were cut short when he heard Alyssha's loud laughter. Apparently Karrin had told her something very funny. But whatever it was, Lark was sure that it wasn't. Lark never found anything funny; humor was something completely alien to him.

THREE
KREESHA AND GRAHAM

Now let's leave Lark Arias and his cohorts for a moment and talk about Mr and Mrs Arias.

Mrs Arias, Kreesha, leaned back on a light orange seat and stretched her arms. "Darling! Graham!"

"Yes, honey, I'm coming." The speaker, Graham Arias, floated into the airy living room with a platter of food. "Dessert's ready, my sweet." With a sweeping grace, he placed the platter on a circular glass panel and flew flamboyantly to his elemen, where they shared a deep, consuming, and infinitely delicious kiss.

"Oh Graham, your kisses are always so sexy."

"And what about my person?"

"Your person is even sexier than your kisses."

Graham Arias gave his elemen yet another unbearably sexy kiss and his elemen swooned. She was still conscious, however. But then something overcame her and she swooped out of her seat onto her feet, her long, red hair flowing and her green eyes bright with life. Graham stared with enraptured awe at his mate's beauty. "Kreesha!"

"Graham!"

"Kreesha!"

"Graham!"

And she flew into his arms and they shared a million kisses again. "Graham dear, let's go..." She blushed, but she pulled him towards their room anyway, and her elemen only followed dumbly, as intoxicated with her as she was with him.

So you see, Lark's parents were one of those rare couples who were still deeply and insanely in love with each other after so many years of marriage. Well actually, a lot of couples were still deeply in love, but most did not show their love so openly. And though they were passionate about each other, most couples' passion was suppressed so that they could interact as mature adults, for practical purposes.

But Lark's parents' mutual passion was unsurpassable and unassailable. They desired each other immensely hour by hour. They simply could not keep their hands off each other, which obviously nauseated their son. He did not care in the least what his parents were doing with each other, but it still disturbed him to be living in the same place as two people who were so opposite from him. His parents would never understand him but he didn't care.

Here, you might think that there was a hidden sadness in how nobody would ever understand Lark because he was so weird and different. But no. No sadness. Lark was just Lark and he was perfectly happy to stay the way he was.

Back to the story.

So, as you may expect, Graham and Kreesha Arias were embracing each other on their velvety blue bed and kissing endlessly.

They did wonder why their son was taking so long at his errand to buy those food supplies but at the moment, they didn't really care. They just wanted to enjoy each other and make tons and tons of affection, to show the other how much they still loved them, how passionately they wanted and needed them. They so deeply longed to be in such a union with each other and really were in such a deep union that they were just short of becoming the same person.

After a great length of time, with Kreesha's hands tangled in her mate's reddish-brown hair and Graham hugging her shoulders, they finally came back up to the surface to breathe. She was blushing but flushed with deep pleasure, and he was too. And then more rosy romantic scenes happened. It took some time before Mrs Arias zoned back out of her trance and asked her elemen, "Dear, where do you think Lark went off to?"

Unfortunately, her elemen was still locked in his fanatical adoration of her, and he replied, "I don't know." He still looked so dreamy and he couldn't tear his attention away from her. Well, it was the same situation for his mate and they stared into each other's eyes for a thousand cores more.

At last, when Mrs Arias moved, Mr Arias stopped her, pressed her down to the bed again and smothered her with kisses. She giggled and kissed him back. So there was more love and nothing was really being done. The two should be worried that their son had not come back after such a long time but they seemed to be drugged by one another. They were so lost in another world. They could persist in that same lostness till the end of time—till their son died.

But eventually they did snap out of it. "Darling," cried Mrs Arias. "We've got to do something. Call the Order or something. Our son— where did he go? Larky, where are you?"

"Oh poor Larky!" his father exclaimed as well. "Who knows where our little lad has gone off to. But I don't think we need to call the Order. I'm sure he hasn't really gotten lost. It's more likely that something has fixed his attention again and he's spending tremendous amounts of time investigating it." They knew how astonishingly attached their son was to science. They couldn't see what there was to be crazy about in such a subject, but they respected their son and encouraged him to do what he liked.

This vast difference in both temperament and interests between Lark and his parents might make one wonder if they were actually related. Even their eye and hair colors didn't quite match, as Kreesha had red hair, green eyes; Graham reddish-brown hair and blue eyes; and Lark blond hair and sky-blue eyes. But Lark really was their biological son. The quirky couple was just curious and playful when they chose to give him those colors via genetic engineering before he was born.

Nonetheless, most couples had no wish to play around with their offspring's hair or eye colors, even with the reassurance that there would not be any side-effects; so the Arias's were just an exception.

Kreesha now stretched her legs, and hopped off the bed, to her elemen's disappointment. But he understood. He was not very worried about his son, but he was getting worried now since his elemen was worried. You see, this couple were so supremely connected to each other that if one got sad, the other would too in a matter of moments. If one got frightened, likewise, the other would as well in a matter of seconds. They were like two pieces of metal that conducted heat (or electricity) with a startling rapidity.

Lark's mother paced the room. "Graham, are you sure we shouldn't be worried?"

"I'm not sure anymore!" her elemen admitted, and started pacing the room with her too. Well, not side by side. He was pacing somewhere else and occasionally met her and separated, then met, then separated, and so on. But eventually he joined her side and they wandered round and round together. Really, they were such a sight. It was their habit to sometimes pace rooms together. This kind of strange behavior drove Lark crazy; but since he didn't care, he simply retreated to his room to hide from his bizarre parents.

After several cores of pacing, Kreesha stopped. She mopped a hand over her eyes. "I can't do this anymore, Grae Grae. What will have become of our son?"

"Oh, don't you think he's on one of his uh, intellectual expeditions again?" her elemen suggested.

"What do you think?" said Kreesha. Normal people would have interpreted this as resentment or annoyance, but not Graham. Kreesha would never be resentful of him, just as Graham would never dream of being mad at her. What she just expressed was a simple desire to know her soulmate's opinion.

"I think that we should stay here a little longer and then go out and find him."

"Oh, can we go out and find him now? I'm so worried!"

Graham didn't want to distress his elemen anymore, so he took her hand, and the couple flew out of their house.

Without even thinking, Kreesha called out, "Lark? Lark!"

Graham was about to join her but then he said, "Should we call the Order after all?"

"Maybe we should. If we search by ourselves, it'll take forever."

"Oh, but if we do call the Order, should we stay back home just in case Larky does come back by himself? We wouldn't want him to come back to a barren hearth, would we?" Graham cried.

"No, we wouldn't! You're right. Let's go back in." But then she paused. "Grae Grae, I just thought of something."

"What's that?" By the way, it never seemed to trouble the couple that they were always wandering around in romantic, sentimental, and melodramatic wonderland, and that they were so wishy-washy and not at all time-efficient, and so perpetually relaxed, and so comically taking their time even during emergencies.

The couple was so used to this style of life and so satisfied with it, that they could not for their life understand why their Lark was so agitated about their lack of speed—and why he would just hurry on his way to do whatever he was doing and dump his parents.

Kreesha and Graham weren't—too hurt by such dumping because they were used to it; plus, they understood that their son was a special kind of human being, who required special treatment, and had special needs. Their son worked in a different way from how they did. He wasn't exactly another species, but they accepted that he deviated from most people. They were obviously very disconsolate about this, but not as disconsolate as most parents would be, as they were very optimistic people.

Lark was actually a fairly optimistic person himself, at least when it came to science, but he clearly wasn't ebullient like his parents. As a matter of fact, he held a great amount of contempt towards bubbly people, as he thought they were shallow to the extreme; he, in contrast, was somber, serious, severe, and therefore a profound being.

Now Kreesha was crying out, "Oh, wait a minute. I thought of something. Would our Larky want to eat Kraeks?" Kraeks were a Drellian delicacy, a kind of snack that was crunchy, brownish-yellow, and kind of golden. It seemed to be something that Lark responded relatively more favorably to.

But here, even Graham was dismayed. "Oh Kreesha, why would we want to wonder about that now?" Even though he kind of knew what his elemen was getting at. But he just said that so he could hear her voice again.

"Grae Grae, don't be silly." She wrapped an arm tenderly around his neck. "I was just anticipating Larky's return home and that he would be hungry. Yes, of course he's very into his science, but even young genius scientists need to eat, don't they?"

"Ah, you are so intelligent and thoughtful, my dear!"

Yes, Graham and Kreesha regularly acted out these overly romantic and childish little plays, where they would say things as if they didn't know them; both would understand what the other meant, and what the other wanted them to say, and they would say it all accordingly. It was as though they were always singing a duet, a kind of call and response that went on forever.

"Okay, shall I help you make those Kraeks?"

"That would be much appreciated, my jewel," Mrs Arias said. But then she said, "Oh but let us call the Order first."

You would wonder why the couple was so unhurried and scatter-brained at this moment, but that beats me. They were genuinely quite worried, but they seemed to be unable to get out of their trance and dance. But at long last, the Order was called, and the Order leader assured them that they would find their son as soon as possible.

"Now, let's get back to the Kraeks," Mrs Arias said cheerfully, as if her dear son was already back.

LARK THOUGHT ABOUT WHAT HE SHOULD DO NOW. THEY WERE all on the Hyure, and almost at Phuore. Karrin was so excited. Lark didn't care about his classmate's enthusiasm except that it might make him harder to get rid of.

They soon alighted from the Hyure onto a sandy path flanked by thick grass and sun-yellow flowers, where the air was relaxed and fresh. Karrin, as expected, waved a very friendly and polite goodbye to the Hyure driver, and cried out, "Take care!" You could see why Karrin tended to be quite popular with adults as well as with other children. Now Karrin said, "Hey Lark, so you can go find those toy chemicals you want now, huh?"

Lark didn't bother nodding. He didn't think it was necessary to respond to Karrin because it was ultra obvious that searching for those "toy chemicals" was what Lark was going to do. He took out an electronic map from his computer pouch, adjusted this map so that he was the only one who could see it, and started walking.

(See "Computer pouches[1]" under "Technology.")

"Where are we going, Lark?" Karrin asked.

"Yeah, where are we going, Larky?" copied Alyssha.

Lark frowned. Only his parents were allowed to call him "Larky." If he were any ordinary five-year-old boy, he would have fumed openly and turned on that ignorant, silly three-year-old. But he was no ordinary boy, so he ignored her and kept walking in a certain direction.

Mrs Juess soon said, "But you're wandering away from the main shopping places. Are you sure you're not lost, dear?"

Why did adults always have to call him by names like dear, darling, honey, or sweetie? He didn't want to reply, but not answering an adult could lead to consequences, so he said, "I am not lost." Maybe he should have said more, but this was Lark, who just did not know the social norm of elaborating on something that did not need elaborating on, and so he didn't.

He continued to walk until Mr Treek also asked him where he was going and why he was wandering away from the main shopping locations. Lark reassured him that he knew what he was doing. The others did not seem convinced, but Lark was not bothered about that. He would think of a way to get rid of them.

He was quite lost, however. His map told him exactly where to go, but this was taking forever. Should he consider taking another Hyure? But would that arouse more suspicions?

Meanwhile, Karrin was chatting with Alyssha. "So, what do you like to do best when you're not at school?"

"Oh, lots of things," Alyssha said. "Like the other day, I was playing in the water world in Bricalo and—"

Lark tuned out the rest of her words here. She was irritating and he didn't want to hear her voice anymore. But then something caught his ear.

She was whispering, but not so inaudibly, "You know Lark?"

"Uh huh," said Karrin, encouraging her to go on.

"I think, I think—"

"What?"

"I think Lark needs a friend."

So that was all she wanted to say? Lark was not impressed. Everybody thought that he needed a friend. Absolutely everybody. His parents with great worry thought it was abnormal for a child to not have any friends, especially if he was perfectly okay with it.

"You know what I think Lark really needs to do?" she asked.

Karrin said that he would be honored if little Miss Alyssha could tell him.

She delightedly did. "He needs to talk to more people of his age, and to find someone he actually likes."

"But he doesn't like anyone," Karrin said, not unaware that Lark was listening. Karrin was hoping that by voicing his thoughts aloud like this, he would be able to somehow convert Lark to their side, make him normal and able to make friends like everybody else. Karrin had no intention of making Lark lose his specialness of being the science expert and fanatic, but Karrin just thought that this was for Lark's own good, because sooner or later, Lark would have to make friends.

"Yeah, he doesn't like anyone," Alyssha said, shrugging.

"So," Karrin said, with a deliberate slowness. "Do you think there's anything we can do to help him?" Lark was obviously not paying attention to them, Karrin thought. But who knew? Maybe he was only feigning inattention. Karrin continued, "Do you think there really is any way we could help him, Alyssha?" He took care not to call her little baby names, like "little Alyssha," because he knew that that would infuriate kids like her, notwithstanding that he himself was also a kid. He personally did not mind it much when adults babied him with these affectionate names, however.

Alyssha said with a shrug, "I'm not sure if there even is a way. You know, he just—ignores you, if you know what I mean."

"I know exactly what you mean." Karrin did not mean to taunt Lark or anything, but he just wished that Lark would say something in response. An average boy would definitely have said something by now because of how disrespectfully they were speaking; but Lark was, again, not an average boy. He had an abnormally high self-control. So, Lark was a contradictory character in that his pride was easily hurt, and his ego easily offended; yet at the same time, he was so good at ignoring people and pretending that they didn't exist.

It seemed that nothing Karrin and Alyssha said would induce him to even turn around to look at them. There were times when Karrin observed that Lark's head shifted just the slightest bit. It was during those times that he felt inordinately hopeful; but right after that, Lark's head would prove to have never shifted, and that Karrin had been hallucinating yet again; Lark was as immovable as ever.

Finally, Karrin said, "Alyssha, would you like to go someplace?"

"What do you mean? Aren't we going to find whatever Lark wants to buy? Those toy chemicals or whatever?"

"No, I mean, you know, Lark isn't ever talking to us. He never even looks at us. This shows that he doesn't like us and wants us to leave. So maybe we should all really leave and not bother him anymore and leave him to his own quest." Karrin really hoped this would do the trick. He called to his father, "Daddy, since we're in Phuore already, maybe we should leave Lark now and not bother him anymore."

Mr Treek was dismayed, but little boys nowadays were strange, he thought. "Okay," he said, just like that.

Karrin hoped his father could see what he was trying to do, and that his "okay" was not serious. Alyssha also asked her mother whether they should just leave Lark. Expecting an okay from her, she was surprised when her mother did not conform to the group's new mandate and she said instead, "Alyssha darling, we promised Lark that we would go with him. He's just a little kid like you. He needs a grownup around."

"But—"

"After Karrin and his Daddy leave, Lark would still need us, right?"

"Oh, but—" Alyssha wanted to say: but Lark is so boring....but she didn't say it. Perhaps this was one of those rare times when she actually felt like being decent and sensitive. Her head drooped. She did not know that Karrin was using this ploy in an attempt to provoke Lark. Unfortunately Karrin's plan did not work.

Next, Karrin thought of something else. He said, "Hey Lark, look what I've found here? Wow, have you ever seen anything of this color?"

Lark did not turn around or even react to this because Karrin had tried this trick on him before, and Lark was not one to be tricked a second time.

Karrin was very disappointed, and his dad gave him a glance, meaning that he understood what his son was trying to do, that he did not really mean it when he said he wanted to leave Lark alone. Mrs Juess, however, did not get this dynamic. She glanced at Karrin and his father—the Treeks—with puzzlement that they were still walking with them. But of course, since she was a humongously polite person, she did not say anything. She just glanced at her daughter, at Lark, at Karrin, and at Mr Treek.

So Lark, Karrin, Alyssha, Hlen, and Evervessa walked awkwardly together, and Alyssha and Karrin desperately said things to fill up the silence.

But Lark was at the moment trying to figure something out. Was there something wrong with his map? A part of him wanted to seek help. Maybe the adults would know something about this. Lark was experienced with his map to some extent as he did need to make short trips here and there to buy stuff—but he had never been out so far before—his parents would never let him go anywhere that required the Coaster or the Hyure, let alone both, by himself. Yet here he was. A part of him yearned to get help, because there really seemed to be something dreadfully wrong with the map. But he had too much of an ego to ask for help.

Lark clicked at that section of the map marking the distance left to go. It seemed that it would be "just around the corner"; yet it was "just around the corner" many minutes ago too! Right now, they were in a vast grey plain. It wasn't completely vast because there were a lot of gray, brown, and black buildings around them. Some buildings were silvery. A few were mud yellow.

In stark contrast, the place where the Hyure first dropped them off was colored in much brighter and more vibrant shades. It was luxuriant. In that far more vivacious place, there were also some snowy looking buildings that sparkled like real snow. There was snow, rain, hail, and sleet in Drell too.

Now Lark was just puzzled at the inaccuracy of his map. Maybe it was the technology's problem, or maybe there was something wrong with the place itself. That last suggestion gave Lark an involuntary shiver; but he immediately chastised himself for shivering, because getting scared was not something that Lark did. It was cowardly to be scared. Yet, no matter how much he wanted to deny it, it still gave him the creeps.

He fixed his eyes on the map, trying to figure it out all by himself; and despite how much the situation chilled him, he was unwilling to turn around and dispel his fears by looking at his companions. Not that looking at his companions would do anything to help him anyway, since he didn't like people and that people in general had no positive effect on him.

Lark was thus staring with intense concentration at the map, when Karrin bounced in front of him and waved a hand in front of his eyes. Lark snapped away in annoyance, his face expressing disgust. He wanted to say, "Can you not see that I am busy?" but then he decided that silence was the best punishment for the likes of people like Karrin, and how right he was.

Karrin was filled with the utmost disappointment at this devastatingly incessant rejection. He sighed inwardly and wondered if he would ever "conquer" Lark and make him his friend. Things seemed to be going nowhere—but Karrin was not one to let anything pull him down. He would never give up! Karrin was getting all giddy and pumped up again.

Karrin tried again, "Can I help?"

Lark wanted to say yes, but then he turned away.

Karrin was let down once again, but he brightened up when his dad asked Lark the same question.

Now, you know already that Lark did not respond to adults the same way as he did to other children. For him, adults were more useful creatures —more likely to be truly helpful to him. So he made a sign with his head that he would indeed welcome help. Karrin was going up in frizzy yellow balloons that Lark had finally reacted to someone.

Lark said to Hlen Treek, "Mr Treek," he remembered my last name! Karrin thought bubbily, like an elated and surprised fan boy. "There appears to be a problem with this map. As you can see here, the distance between our current location and the target location is only four qworts. However, the map has been showing 'four qworts' for many minutes already."

Now a "qwort" was approximately four meters. How could they be sixteen meters away from something, and after some minutes, still be sixteen meters away? At this time, Lark realized his mistake, because by showing an adult his map, he was revealing the true location that he wanted to go to; and if the adult knew anything that Haus did, he would figure out what Lark was up to.

Mr Treek, however, was very kind, and took a good look at the map without betraying any signs of noticing anything odd about Lark's desired destination. There were times when Lark disparaged a human being a little less than usual, and this was one of them.

"The thing is, my son," Mr Treek fell again in Lark's esteem because he just used a diminutive like all the other adults did; and Lark couldn't help feeling disappointed. "Your map ran out of electricity."

That struck Lark like a lightning rod. It ran out of electricity? Really? The Great Lark's instrument ran out of electricity and he didn't know? He didn't figure that out?

Mr Treek must have seen the very unhappy and bewildered look on Lark's face (just because Lark didn't like talking didn't mean he had an expressionless face. On the contrary, Lark's face was often very expressive, probably to make up for his distaste for talking to people who had nothing interesting or useful to offer him), because Mr Treek said, "Don't worry, old chap, I used to always wonder what happened when my pop would tell me that it had simply run out of electricity!" He laughed good-heartedly.

Lark did not hear that goodheartedness, however. He just thought he had undergone a supreme humiliation. This was one of those times when the illusion of his grand superiority broke down, and he saw the real him, that he was flawed and weak like everyone else. Lark Arias was struck dumb with mortification.

And unfortunately, despite his supposedly fantastic social skills, Karrin was not sensitive enough this time to restrain his laughter, though it was as good-natured as his father's. "Oh that's funny. Yeah, don't worry, Lark. That happens to me a lot and I would get so puzzled every time, but every time someone would just point that out to me and—" and he collapsed into more laughter. Lark did not find this very funny at all and he frowned at the Treeks.

Surprisingly, here Alyssha begged to differ and she actually put a comforting hand on Lark's shoulder. Yet Lark saw her hand not as a comfort but as a threat, a challenge. He glared her down with a look so hard and sharp that the little girl withdrew her hand and was very scared all of a sudden.

Her fear was irrational, of course, because in spite of Lark's eccentricity, he was as harmless as a lily. He couldn't even run as fast as a three-year-old girl anyway, as we have already seen. And there wasn't much to say about his other physical abilities either.

"Okay, so do you have any electricity sources?" Lark asked. If they were indoors, devices would be automatically fueled with electricity in Drell. However, once outdoors, things would be disconnected from that magical supply of electricity, and one would have to rely on portable electricity source packs. Lark was here talking to Mr Hlen Treek.

But Karrin piped up helpfully and said, "Yes, use mine!" He dug out a soft black object. Without even waiting for Lark's permission, Karrin gently squeezed the black blob, and a haze of gas issued from the opening. The gas gathered, streamlined, and thickened into a liquid; it plunged into Lark's map, spread itself everywhere, and seeped into the device. The map immediately updated itself and showed that they were past their location by about twenty qworts. Lark was infuriated.

Karrin tried to calm him down. "Hey, it's okay..." Lark refused to look at him. But Lark was a rational person after all, so he ignored his classmate and stomped back toward the place they had passed. Karrin and the rest, but especially the obsequious Karrin, stomped to keep up with Lark.

Now that Lark was at the head of the group, you may wonder whether he was a person who liked to lead. But the answer was that he had no desire to either lead or follow, because he wanted nothing to do with people.

Lark kept staring at his map. Yes, they were getting closer, and closer, and closer. And then they were here. He looked up.

Everybody else looked up too.

At a grey, metallic sky.

Nope, they were not inside a building. They were literally looking up at a sky.

Lark's first irrational thought was: really? It was in a mysterious outdoor place? Am I supposed to expect the par-the-air to fall through the air, out of the sky, and into my hands? But then he suddenly saw this dungeon-like hatch in front of him.

"Oh my gosh, where have you led us, Lark?" Karrin asked, in a sort of pretend grownup way that was very annoying to the other boy. Poor Karrin kept trying to entertain and engage, but the tricks that worked on most people failed completely on Lark.

"Oh no, will there be anything dangerous lurking inside there?" asked Alyssha timidly. She sounded genuinely frightened. Karrin was genuinely frightened too, and so was Lark. But the former boy tried to hide it with grins, and the latter, well—never admitted fear even to himself, as you already know.

Mr Treek said, "Hey, Lark, are you sure we came to the right place? This doesn't look like a place where they sell toy chemicals, right?" he said, smiling, trying not to convey any sense of intimidation, threat, or disbelief to Lark. He tried to come across as friendly and helpful. Yet to Lark, he came off not as friendly but as perfectly neutral.

Mrs Juess was dismayed like everyone else. But she kept silent and waited to see what the other people would say.

Lark glanced at Mr Treek briefly. "This is the place my friend asked me to go to." He wondered if he should tell them the real story. It was so tiring to keep making things up. He now nervously looked around to see how he could get inside that building. Scared to death as he was—he really was—he had to get in if he wanted his limitless supply of chemicals.

"Um, son, I hope you don't mind me saying this, but is there something you need to tell us?" Mr Treek asked him.

Lark, again, did not like how Mr Treek disappointingly called him "son" like everyone else did. Really, it was quite thoughtless of Mr Treek, who was a psychologist, to not realize that some kids resented being diminished by these names. But he was only a research psychologist, not a clinical or a counseling one. And he was far less interested in interacting successfully with people than in understanding human psychology on the theoretical level.

---

1. **Computer pouches**
   Computer pouches use space tunnels, space pockets, space wells and the like to carry around physical objects within virtual, electronic space; and computers can easily retrieve these physical objects whole when the user needs them. However, once again, these carried objects must be portable-sized, so you can't carry a house or a large vehicle

with you—excessively large objects can damage the computer. Similarly, carrying way too many albeit portable-sized objects can also damage the computer.

Nonetheless, even with these size and number limitations, Drellians rarely have to hand-carry anything they bring anymore, unless they want to, or if they didn't bring their computer. Some people still like to carry bags with them, though.

FOUR
LARK'S "CHILDHOOD PROBLEMS"

et's skip back over to Lark's parents again. We shall rejoin the boy shortly.

Kreesha was sitting and crying on a stretch seat at home.

(See "Stretch seats[1]" and "Floating panels[2]" under "Objects" and "Household objects and places.")

Her elemen lay beside her on another stretch seat, patting her back. "Darling, don't cry. He'll be all right."

"But I'm so worried! What if something really did happen to him this time? Oh I should never have been so indulgent to him!"

As thoughtless and silly as Lark's parents were, they genuinely did care about their son's welfare; and it was all their fault for being so careless as to let this happen. So Kreesha broke down. Graham sort of broke down too, but less visibly. He wanted to be strong for her. But he was as weak and sentimental as his elemen deep down.

And Graham was indeed an extremely expressive person; he went on frequent bouts of emotional adventuring with his mate, and they always had prime times together in their mutual hyperness and excitement—these were some great reasons why they were always so close, so bonded, so attached, and so deeply in love all the time. They electrified each other with a never-ending stream of pleasure and energy.

The two were such wildly enthusiastic people that they were good at sparking up energy in a room too. Others often admired their liveliness, and many wanted to be infected by their jubilance. Others envied or resented them. Some were simply annoyed by hyper animated people in general, because they stood out from the crowd too much. Or, as in Lark's case, they simply thought that hyper enthusiastic people were too loud, too noisy, and too raucous; and they wished that these people would quiet down or even better, shut up, so they could dwell quietly and calmly on their own nebulous thoughts.

Now Kreesha was still crying, and Graham desperately wanted to join her.

"Don't cry, darling!" he cried uselessly. She held his hand tightly, as he did hers, and then she started bawling. Only, to Graham, it was not bawling. It was music of the very sublime sort. The only thing that was more beautiful than her crying was her talking, or her singing. In fact, any sound related to Kreesha, even the swish of her clothes, was divine music to Graham.

You might think that his perceptions were ridiculous. How on Drell could somebody be so miraculously celestial and perfect looking? But, well, Graham was deeply in love with her, and when you're in love, especially if you are still so deeply in love after more than five years of marriage, then you would be completely blind to your partner's faults.

In fact, Graham felt that he was such a lucky fellow to be able to marry her and be blessed by her love and esteem. He sincerely thought he was the luckiest man alive...except for Lark, her son, who also got a fair share of her love.

You might wonder whether dear Graham felt any sense of competition with Lark for his elemen's love, but no. Graham was above jealousy—because he felt so secure in his mate's affection. As lucky as he felt he was, he never thought he would ever lose her, because she was always there right beside him; and though he kept reflecting on his supreme good fortune, he was constantly reminded that this dream was his reality.

Moreover, Graham sincerely loved his son too. The boy was a dear treasure to him, though Lark may not be aware of this, seeing how severely insensitive to warmth this boy was. We don't even know whether Graham loved Kreesha more or Lark more. He didn't quite know himself and sometimes worried that Kreesha would be jealous that he gave so much of his love to his son.

But Kreesha was not jealous either. Because she too really loved and cherished her son, no matter how antisocial he was, no matter how much he seemed to resent and repulse his parents. It hurt both of them that their son had never been close to them. Well, perhaps when he was a baby, he was close enough; the little baby boy seemed quite happy receiving so much love, hugs, kisses, and caresses from his mama and papa, and he did seem to genuinely enjoy their affection, and he did look as though he felt himself to be a very blessed boy—to have such adoring parents who spoiled him like no tomorrow. But...it was somewhere around when he was two—or maybe it was one? That he started changing.

Lark Arias just...didn't seem to like their caresses anymore. He stopped smiling. And wriggled out of his parents' arms and cried to be let down so he could crawl. He crawled very early and walked very early. Yet it took him longer than usual to learn how to speak. He did not develop any speech, writing, or reading difficulties, however. They were okay. Well maybe even better than okay, because his grades were well above average.

(See "The Drellian School System" under "Drellian Society" to see how educators abolished grades and marks, and replaced these with a wholly different method of evaluation.)

So this baby boy of one and a half years began to repulse his parents. At first, it wasn't that bad yet. Kreesha and Graham thought that the baby just wanted a bit of independence, so they happily let him crawl around by himself, though they made sure that the enclosure in which he crawled did not contain anything potentially dangerous. Kreesha and Graham, though they were very permissive parents who gave their son so much freedom, were very protective of him too.

Yet, not long after, Lark began to cry more often when he was in their arms. He refused to stay in their arms for long, and they didn't know when the nightmare happened—when Lark seemed to cry every time they picked him up. And when they touched him, he would move hastily away.

Kreesha cried her heart out at the tragedy and Graham did too, though he tried to restrain his emotions just a little bit so he could comfort his elemen.

They took their baby boy to see the psychiatrist.

To their dismay, the psychiatrist said that there was absolutely nothing wrong with their baby boy, biologically, physiologically, or neurologically.

And psychologically, he was normal too. The psychiatrist said that he was simply a boy who had one of these very strange personalities. Strange not as in bad, but as in he was one of the minority.

Those with this personality were completely captivated by one thing, unmoved by anything else, and tended to hate humanity, or at least be astonishingly indifferent to humanity. Some psychologists called these individuals the "natural obsessors." (For more details on this personality and how it relates to Lark and his love for science, see "Natural Obsessors[3]" under "Drellian Society.")

Presently, Graham said, "Kreesha, baby, don't cry, don't cry. I'm sure the Order will find our son soon." He tried his best to soothe her, but she was inconsolable. Now, most elemens at this point would have thought Kreesha extremely annoying and get frustrated or resentful or even disparage her. However, Graham was not like most elemens, and he genuinely felt so sorry for her. Plus, he himself was distraught at what his son might be doing, and where he might be. Had he finally gotten into danger? Had the dreaded day come at last?

Poor Kreesha and Graham Arias worried constantly about him— when they were not creating and expressing their love for each other or bursting with joy at their lives in general. They feared that their little boy would run into trouble one day, because other people might not like him; he was so incurably antisocial.

The Arias's really did try to educate him on a bit of social skills. But the boy would just stare at them impassively and disdainfully. His parents were immeasurably distressed and pained to see that disdainful look that was permanently in his eyes—when he did deign to look at them. After a little while, he would get up and leave before they finished speaking or demonstrating some basic social skill. Kreesha was especially distraught, because she felt that the situation was so hopeless. Would their son really just pack up and leave them one day? How would she live?

Graham fearfully told her not to think like that, because she would always have him. And they had another one of their many million moments of tenderness, where they embraced, caressed, kissed, and did much more. Really, the pair had such a tremendous desire to express their love to one another, and constantly too. It also didn't help that they were both in the same job, so they almost literally saw each other constantly.

They were simply very worried that their sonny boy would turn out very poorly and really hate them—if he did not already do so now. They wondered whether Lark would completely rebel against them and throw things at them, shout at them, or do something even more frightening and heartbreaking than that. At the moment, though Lark seemed to clearly despise his parents, he was quiet and did not explode into outrageous behavior—except the few times his parents were too intrusive like when they accidentally broke his favorite device.

The Arias couple, being such naturally optimistic people, were thankful that at the very least their son was relatively calm and stable, no matter how he felt—unless the situation was simply too terrible for him to keep his feelings under control.

So Lark was like a rebellious teenage son who distanced himself completely from his parents, except he wasn't a teenager. Such a total distancing from his parents since he was two or one was what made this whole situation especially poignant. Lark would always shut himself inside his room, working on his science, his chemistry.

Since they loved their son so, they wanted to please him and buy him all the chemical toys he could desire—fortunately these were relatively cheap. But recently he had been very frustrated (he showed this on his face, though he felt much too superior to throw tantrums) that he could not get anything beyond kiddy chemicals. He wanted real ones. But as much as they wanted to indulge him, they could not possibly buy him real chemicals because he could hurt himself. In fact, they were one hundred percent certain that he would hurt himself, so they refused point blank to buy him any. And so, they watched with pained hearts their son retreating quietly and sullenly back to his room.

They honestly did not understand what the hype was about science. They did not understand it. As they were never interested in it, they chose not to pursue any further education in it, so their son was already way advanced compared to them because he had already learned so much about both contemporary and historical science and chemistry.

Very often, the couple, especially Kreesha, wished they knew more about this subject and perhaps they would be able to...connect with their son more, and maybe their son wouldn't reject them so completely—maybe they would even have a chance to befriend their son, or at least be slightly accepted by him. But there seemed to be no chance of that happening, from what was going on now. Multitudes of times before, Kreesha, Graham, or both of them wanted to really learn some science so they could talk a little with Lark.

Like there was that time when Kreesha forced herself to figure out this new scientific discovery. She couldn't quite understand it but she just took out the little that she got out of those articles, and went to her son while he was eating. At the very least he was willing to eat outside, with his parents; though he completely ignored them, and seemed visibly happy when his parents had to leave him to eat by himself because of something they had to go to.

So Kreesha started talking to Lark about orbitals and how interesting these mu and gamma rays worked to...she said a bunch of things she read from the article that she didn't really get, and she humbly asked Lark if he could explain it to his poor mama.

With a spark of hope, she heard that he indeed started to explain, though with extreme condescension, about what orbitals were like—Kreesha and Graham had unfortunately even forgotten about most of the basic chemistry from their school years—but then the boy started mumbling and lost interest in finishing his explanation, probably because he thought his mother, and by association his father, were too daft to understand anything about science, so he stopped explaining and went back to his dinner.

When he ate, he always had that distant expression on his face, evidently thinking about some new topic in science that had caught his fancy. There was a time before when he would look at his food with curiosity. His parents at first were delighted that their son showed some sign of normalcy at last as all kids should be interested in their food.

But their delight soon died when they saw their son use his computer to input notes and analyses, and referenced several information sources about the food he was eating. He was studying it from a scientific perspective again. Their son seemed incapable of looking at anything the way normal people did, like how tasty or attractive the food was, rather than what chemicals it was composed of. He just had to be so analytical.

Sometimes Kreesha would feel a little resentful of science, because it was taking their boy away from them—she would feel jealous of it, though it was only a realm of knowledge and not another human being. Graham didn't feel resentful of science, though. He just felt extremely sad that their son didn't like anything that they liked.

What Graham and Kreesha liked was a plethora of many things, including the humanities, like politics, sociology, history, psychology, cultural studies, and economics; management, marketing, and promotion, especially in making aesthetically pleasing things to attract customers; sports, travelling, and languages; and the arts, particularly in designing graphics and advertisement films.

(See "Graphic Design Software[4]," "Virtuals,[5]" and "Films and Movies[6]" under "Technology.")

So as Kreesha and Graham had a pretty vast range of interests, though they aspired to be and were connoisseurs of some things, they did not understand why their son was so completely obsessed with one subject. Life was so varied, wonderful, colorful, and beautiful; how could only one part of it stimulate you and the other parts induce nothing but indifference?

They also did not understand how one could be so indelibly attracted to one thing that it became an obsession. To Kreesha and Graham, the idea of an obsession was alien to them, as they were fond of so many things but were not "madly in love with" any of these subjects or activities. The only thing that they were really obsessed with was each other, and their love.

At this moment, Mr Arias was stroking his elemen's hair, begging her to stop crying, even though he himself was crying too.

After a while, Kreesha got up, and wiped her tears. She stared numbly at the sheet-white wall opposite her. "Why didn't the Order give us an answer yet? It's been some minutes now."

"Patience, my dear," he said, though he himself was not very patient either.

They held hands and both stared at the pale wall opposite them for a very long while, meditating.

Later, they did get a call back from the Order, but it was bad news. They still had not found their son, which meant that he was indoors; because if he were outdoors, they would have easily tracked him with their intersector monitors. Indoor surveillance was illegal, as explained earlier.

However, they did receive notice from one of their Coaster Order members that a little boy of their description (the Order sent out an image of Lark to all their members) came to see him with a woman and a little girl. And that this boy had wanted to go to Phuore.

"Phuore!" Kreesha and Graham immediately gaped. There was finally something they could snatch upon.

The Order checked all their monitors in Phuore, but they found nothing; so Lark was definitely indoors. Next, they asked all the shopkeepers in the Phuore area to keep a look out for a boy of this description—they sent out a hologram of Lark's image. But still, nothing came up.

"So if Larky isn't in any of the shops, where could he be?" Kreesha said desperately.

The Order also sent out messages to people in the public buildings through screens of moving pictures. However, the bad thing was that Lark was far from the only kid, or person, or living creature, who was missing. Things like this happened every day, and it was hard to ask people to look out for so many different people at once. But the Order was well organized and had well-trained Order members who could look for many missing people at once, so the Order leader reassured Kreesha and Graham that all would be well. Their Lark would come back home to them in no time.

Kreesha wanted to believe them, but she couldn't. She clutched on tighter to Graham's hand and knew he thought the same thing. "Grae Grae, what should we do?"

He wished he knew. "Let's wait, and have faith in the Order," he said, hugging his elemen close to him to give her comfort.

---

1. **Stretch Seats**
   Can be stretched out onto any surface, to a long length (1, 1/2, or 1/4 qworts, i.e. 4, 2, or 1 meters). They are held up securely in the air by strong magnetic forces.
   You can adjust its texture, level of softness or hardness, the location of the armrests and backs, and the lengths and shapes of these armrests and backs. You can also compress the stretch seat into a small enough size for carrying. So furniture is easily transported when you have to move into a new house.
2. **Floating Panels**
   Floating panels, like stretch seats, are held securely up in the air by strong magnetic forces. These panels can be used as tables, seats, supports, or simply useful surfaces. You can't adjust their texture or softness, and there are no appendages, and thus they are

cheaper than stretch seats. But you can compress the floating panels into a portable size just like with the stretch seats.

3. **Natural Obsessors**

Natural obsessors are people like Lark who are supremely obsessed with one thing, uninterested in everything else, and tended to hate humanity, or at least be astonishingly indifferent to humanity. Some psychologists call these individuals the "natural obsessors," though some experts prefer to use a more pleasant sounding term.

However, some other psychologists think that it's very prejudiced to call a particular personality by a special name; because by doing so, it's like saying they have a mental disorder, that there is something "wrong" with them—but there is clearly nothing wrong with them! They can live very happily and healthily just the way they are, with their one life obsession and their shunning of fellow human beings, and being perfectly content with that.

There are, of course, lots of psychologists who argue that natural obsessors are suffering from a mental disorder, because their condition ("their personality!" the other psychologists correct them) necessitates their having no friends. Absolutely no friends, though some people may still grow to love them and hope that they will one day love them back. And having no friends is obviously impacting their psychological and social sphere.

A lot of debate then raged up about how "having a social life" had become an essential thing in life. Why do you need it? Of course, it's very good for preventing depression, protecting against stress and early death, and it boosts your immune system. Yet for these natural obsessors, their immune system is perfectly fine, and their likelihood of developing trauma, depression, stress-related diseases, etc. is exactly the same as the rest of the normal population's—no different from the average normal person with an average number of friends and social contacts.

So these "natural obsessors" are just a very strange phenomenon. They do seem to be naturally self-sufficient. Their only problem is that they don't fit in with society. The only problem is that other people are bothered by their extreme obsession with one thing, and their perpetual unfriendliness, coldness, and unresponsiveness.

But it is true that some natural obsessors, like Lark, whose realm of obsession does not require a lot of physical activity or much outdoor work, may be physically a bit weaker, and have a weaker immune system than the average person. This is not because they are in this "unhealthy" category of "natural obsessors," though, but because they simply don't spend much time outside, or much time exercising.

Of course, there are some natural obsessors who handle themselves very well by exercising. (Just because they're obsessive doesn't mean they're stupid. They too can acquire knowledge about basic health, and understand that they have to eat well and exercise enough, sleep well, etc.) But then there are some natural obsessors, like Lark, who don't bother exercising. Not because he's lazy, but because he's too drawn to his one great love.

The natural obsessor expectedly finds it extraordinarily hard to disengage from their favorite activity. They have to be literally torn away from their work. Perhaps they would kick and scream, but no matter. And since they have a harder time than most people do in disengaging from tasks, they just have to work extra hard to disengage themselves anyway, because they later learn that to succeed or survive in life, one has to balance oneself a little bit.

People explain to them that if they want to carry on doing the thing they love best, they had better learn to take care of their health, so they do so. But kids like Lark don't quite understand yet, so they don't trouble themselves with exercise. Also, some natural obsessors, just like a lot of "normal" people, understand that they need to exercise, etc., but they still don't anyway! That is why they tend to be physically less fit. However, these natural obsessors are the same in fitness as an average inactive "normal" person.

And when I say Lark was ultra passionate about science, I meant both a) He could not live without science, could not survive without science, could not imagine a world without science; and b) He loved science with an astounding fervour. So what I mean is, he was not just driven by a survival necessity; it was not just a psychological need. He was also driven by a genuine, fanatical pleasure to do and learn about science. It was a sublime, high, and pure pleasure. It was a joy and passion from the head, from the heart, and from the soul. It was a sense of deep, inexplicable connection to that larger realm of that something called science.

4. **Graphic Design software**

You can press keys, draw or scribble on pads, etc. to create your design electronically. But you can also use your voice to speak to and ask the computer to do things for you. You can even connect to and deliver your mind's images to the computer.

Unfortunately, the mind image communication is not so successful because images from the imagination tend to be very blurry. But the few people with very clear and detailed imaginations tend to do better with this approach to the graphic design software.

5. **Virtuals**

Similar to virtual reality, but are for shows, movies, and the like. You can go inside these virtuals and feel the physical environment (but be protected from e.g. excessive heat or cold) of the show or movie, but the characters and creatures in that show or movie will never be able to touch or see you.

6. **Films and Movies**

Drellians have moving pictures as well as virtuals, because people don't always want to immerse themselves bodily into that movie. Sometimes they just want to see it quickly.

FIVE
OH, PARENTS!

Meanwhile, Lark and his crew had indeed entered that creepy-looking building. Inside, it did not look that creepy. After they had gone to the end of a very short, dark corridor, they immediately emerged into a lit room. Mr Treek had wanted an explanation from Lark, but Lark did not give any. All Lark said was that he pleaded Mr Treek to have patience, and that all would become clear in time, and please would he bear with him for now. Mr Treek was a kind person after all, so he bore with him. Karrin and Alyssha gave Lark a baffled look.

Now Karrin said, "Hey, look at those stars." There were indeed starry decorations all along the walls on either side of them. Those stars were yellow, light green, and light blue. They were skillfully arranged to create some aesthetic effect. Out of this party, Karrin was the most artistically and aesthetically inclined and he said, "Ooh!" Alyssha also said "Ooh!" Lark, however, took no notice of the stars, as he had never been into the aesthetics. The only beauty he ever saw was the beauty of systems, chemicals, math, and all such matter to do with science.

Alyssha pointed at some of the fancy decorations on the walls and ceiling to Karrin. "What are those?" After listening to Karrin's answers, she pointed to a painting of a huge lamina above them. "And that?" The lamina seemed to be watching them, and its mouth was open, teeth bared.

It was a quadruped with whitish-yellow fur, strong muscular legs, long pointy ears, a muzzle, and sharp claws erupting from its four paws.

"That's a velocip. It's usually friendlier than this, but I guess this is a guardian velocip."

"I'm scared," said Alyssha unnecessarily. She didn't look at all scared, though. She glanced at Lark to see what he thought of the creature above them. But as expected, the boy paid no attention whatsoever to what the other children were saying, and he was walking straight ahead with quick strides. "Wait up, Lark!" she said, and everyone hurried after him.

This room with the starry walls was lined with very neatly arranged rows of furniture: stretch seats, floating panels, and the like. All this may have been fun to examine, but as they had no time to spare, they left this room and entered another. This room was not as bright as the one before, but it was still as bright as a typical room. Yet the walls and machine-looking structures around them were a very dark blue, which made the room look dimmer than it actually was.

Lark peered curiously at those machines. Karrin wished he knew about those fancy devices so that he would have a chance to get Lark to talk. Alyssha started counting the number of machines they passed for fun. Ten, eleven, twelve,...,twenty one, twenty two, twenty three...but eventually she lost count and started chatting with friendly Karrin again out of boredom. This room was a lot longer than the previous starry one.

All of a sudden, they heard a thump. Everyone, including Lark, froze.

"Who comes here?"

Everybody was still frozen.

"Oh come on, who comes here? I won't bite. I'm just a human being." The voice was gruff and male.

Lark was the one who de-froze and spoke. Now was the moment when his crew would know the truth at last. Too bad he couldn't think of a plan in time to shoo them all away, but that did not seem to matter now. And secretly, he was glad that he hadn't gotten rid of them, because he was quite afraid when he was walking through this shady and mysterious place, and could not imagine how it would be like walking alone; though of course, he would not admit that he was scared.

Hence, Lark was a puzzling creature. Sometimes other people gave him no comfort for his fears. But sometimes, despite how antisocial he was, the presence of other people did reassure him. Thus these "natural obsessors" were much more complicated than you may think. Lark said, "I came from Haus, and I have come to get a vial of par-the-air for him."

Par-the-air? Hlen Treek and Evervessa Juess thought. But though they, non-chemists as they were, had no idea what this was, it was nevertheless evident to them that Lark was not buying toy chemicals. From the moment they looked at the door of this building, they knew that Lark had been lying about those kiddy potions all along. But they still went through with him as it would be stupid and a waste of time to make such a long journey and suddenly to tell the whole party to turn back without doing anything.

"Ah, Haus," the person inside said. Then he came out. He was an old-looking guy, probably in his sixties. Haus was either in his late forties or early fifties. "Is this what you were looking for?" He held out a vial of pink liquid and handed it to Lark. The two adults behind the boy wanted to warn him from taking it but he already did, and it seemed that it was not doing him any harm. He was just holding a vial with a mysterious chemical inside.

Now Mr Treek asked Lark what this par-the-air was, and why his friend Haus wanted it. But before Lark could make up a story about that, the man in his sixties explained to him what it was, that Haus needed this chemical to help him enter a competition with his friends every year.

"That's it?" Mr Treek said in dismay. "Just a competition with his friends? Are you sure there aren't other people involved?"

"Well, he has a lot of friends," the man said, grinning. "And his friends are all very competitive, so if he doesn't use any chemicals to do some tweaking, then he would be doomed to die of humiliation; because he knows that by his ability, he has no chance of doing even averagely in the competition."

Mr Treek thought that this Haus must be a loser to need to do averagely. It was probably just some crummy competition that should not be taken seriously anyway. Notwithstanding Hlen's general open-mindedness towards others, he sometimes judged them like most of us did. "Is this competition very important to him? To his friends?"

"Oh, very. If he doesn't participate every year, he will lose all his friends." Then he said to Lark, "Now run back and give this vial to Haus, okay, little buddy? That's a good boy." And with that, the man walked back into wherever he came out of and disappeared.

Even when Mr Treek called out for more explanations, he still wouldn't come out. But as Mr Treek, Mrs Juess, and Karrin were decent people, and Alyssha felt like copying what everyone else was doing, and Lark just wanted to go back to Haus as soon as possible, nobody moved to pursue that strange man.

"Let us go now," Lark said, for once speaking to the group. Karrin was glad that he said something, and Karrin led the way for the group. But Lark seemed to want to lead the way instead and moved ahead of Karrin. Karrin shrugged and let him lead. Lark didn't actually want to lead; he just wanted to be at the front so no one would be obstructing his view. Lark was one of those people who were indifferent to leadership, after all.

"Phew, that was fast," Alyssha said again unnecessarily.

Mrs Juess had been holding onto Alyssha's hand ever since they entered this building, anxious that her daughter might get lost, though that was an impossibility because Alyssha had grown quite scared and wanted to stay as close to the party and Karrin as possible. But parents were often over-frightened about things.

Soon they were back in the starry room and Karrin relaxed a bit. Then they were in the dark corridor. But blessedly, the corridor was only about two to three qworts long. And then they were out in the open air again.

Just as they wanted to go home, a Hyure swooped down from the sky right in front of them.

"Mr Lark Arias?"

———

KREESHA AND GRAHAM WERE DANCING WITH JOY. THE ORDER members had indeed found their son at last, in a rather remote place in the Phuore. There were apparently two adults and two children with him; one man, one woman, a little boy, and a little girl. The Arias's were wondering if the two adults were abducting all these children, but then they learned that the girl was the woman's daughter and the boy the man's son, and they soon also learned from the Order's quick reports about Lark's story from Mr Treek's account.

Mrs Juess didn't say much during this journey. She was only concerned for Alyssha's safety; she didn't care very much about anything else. She was one of those people who hilariously did not care for much except for the people she cared about.

As for Lark, he was only slightly irked that the Order had captured them right after they came out of the building. The adults convinced the Order members to let Lark bring his little vial of pink liquid with them, after insisting that it was important to him. Mr Treek even made up a story for him, saying that it was important medicine for a certain friend of Lark's who was too sick to go get it himself.

Lark was frankly quite surprised that his classmate's father was willing to lie for him. Yet, that did not induce Lark to feel grateful towards him. He never felt any gratitude for anyone, ever.

Though Lark knew that they would deliver him straight to his parents, he was very calm about this, calmer than any ordinary kid would be. Karrin just thought this all a very delightful adventure, but was pleased that they were going back home—and on an Order's Hyure too!

Alyssha, on the other hand, was sad that she would have to leave her new friends soon. Well, she probably wouldn't miss Lark, but she definitely would Karrin. She asked Karrin to exchange contact codes with her and made him promise that he would contact her sometime. After exchanging those codes, the two children were mutually pleased at making a new friend.

And then came the time to depart.

Karrin was quite touched that Alyssha was actually crying. He didn't know he had so much in him to make her miss him so. "Come on, Alyssha, we can always see each other or talk to each other again, right? We've got each other's contact codes!"

She still sniffed anyway.

Of course, during all this time, Lark looked not their way at all; and though he heard what they were saying, he was not listening. He was just planning what he would say to his parents when he got home. How could he keep the pink liquid without his parents becoming hysterical and throwing away his par-the-air?

But Lark was being quite unfair to his parents. As dramatic and sentimental as they were, they were not that irrational to throw things away without a thought. Lark severely underestimated his parents' intelligence, just as he did everybody's.

As Alyssha waved goodbye to them, Lark just stared without feeling, then turned away again to ponder over his own matters. Karrin glanced at Lark and sighed inwardly. His classmate would just never be more tender-hearted towards anyone. Poor Alyssha! he thought. When it was time for Karrin and his father to go, the latter said, "Lark, my boy, tell me after how your friend does, eh?"

Lark gave him a desultory nod just to shut him up. Karrin and his father waved to him. The son waved with particular enthusiasm.

WHEN LARK HIMSELF GOT HOME, HIS PARENTS BURST OUT THE door and seized him into their arms—well, Kreesha seized their son. Graham only did the bursting out.

"My Lark, Lark, Larky, Lark!" She squeezed her son tight and showered his airy blond head with kisses. It was quite embarrassing, and Lark hoped that she would be careful not to crush his par-the-air whilst she was hugging him.

"Welcome home, my poppet," Graham said, patting Lark's head.

Would his parents just leave his head alone? And when was his mother going to put him down? One reason why Lark didn't try to thrash out of Kreesha's arms was that he was holding the par-the-air and who knew how fragile the vial was. He wouldn't want it to break because who knew what would happen if he got any of that chemical on his skin?

He notably didn't consider what would happen if it got onto his mother's skin. Please don't take this as a sign of cruelty or selfishness, though. Just see it as Lark not thinking about other human beings as usual, because other human beings did not really exist for him; at the very least, they were never important enough in his life for him to care at all.

Poor Kreesha mistook her son's absence of struggle as a sudden relenting of his coldness towards her, that maybe after the long journey, her son was actually glad that he was safe in her arms again? That perhaps he had finally enkindled a little bit of affection for her and her Graham?

Those happy thoughts spun through her mind as she clutched her son more tightly. Her son was also clutching his par-the-air more tightly.

Now Graham held out his arms and Kreesha handed Lark to her mate to hug. Oh gosh, Lark thought, as it was his father's turn to hug and crush him, and even kiss him. When would his parents finish? Needless to say, Lark was not particularly fond of affectionate people, and his parents were two of the most effusively affectionate people in the world. That was just his bad luck.

When this embracing spree was really taking too long, Lark mumbled, hoping he would be heard, "Please, let me down."

"Oh, sorry, darling," said Graham, and finally placed his son back onto the ground, and his son heaved a huge sigh of relief. He then darted into the house and made a beeline for his room.

"Just a second, young man!" Kreesha barred his way to his room.

"What is it, mother?" Lark had never been affectionate enough to call his mother by the more familiar "mom" or "mommy"; the Drellian language had terms roughly corresponding to mom, mommy, and mother too. Of course Kreesha and Graham were aware of Lark's stiff formality, and this added to their pain that their son was so cold to them.

"Please, explain to us what happened. All we know is that you somehow have a friend who was very sick, who asked you to go to Phuore to get that medicine. So who was that friend? How did you know this friend? And who were those other people with you and how did they come to be with you?"

Lark figured that she would ask that. He calmly said, "My friend is my friend, and it is none of your business who he is. As for the other people, the woman and her daughter were from the Coaster and I asked them to accompany me to get the medicine. The other boy and the man were my classmate and his father. My classmate happened to see me on my journey and demanded that he come with me."

Graham and Kreesha were stressed that Lark would not tell them who this mysterious friend was. But Graham asked, just out of curiosity, "Which one of your classmates was this?"

"Karrin Treek," Lark said.

Graham noted to himself to contact Karrin's dad later to gather a bit more information about all this. Kreesha meanwhile was trying to convince her son to spill out more to them.

"Please, dear, tell mommy what happened? How did you meet this friend of yours?" she asked sweetly.

It was not sweet for Lark, though. He could not see sweetness. "I told you already. It is none of your business."

"Now, Lark, don't be cruel to your mother," Graham said, trying to put on a stern expression but failing. Lark always noted this failure of his parents to try to be harder on him. The best his parents could do was physically force or drag him somewhere. In speech, they were always soft and weak. Meek. He furrowed his brows with scorn, the usual scorn. He looked down at the hard, glazed floor and wished that his father would stop bothering him. "Look up, son." He didn't, and hoped again that his father would stop pestering him.

Kreesha presently began to cry. She couldn't really control her feelings, as you can see. Her elemen was doing much better at this. He too wanted to cry as their son was always like this. Even after this dangerous excursion, Lark was still as cold, indifferent, and rejecting as before. What did he have against them?

But Graham did not dare ask this question out loud. He wanted to ask it every time, but he never had the courage. He never even had the courage to tell Kreesha that he wanted to ask that. And he kept trying to hide that question from himself. He so much dreaded getting Lark's answer.

Little did Graham know that if he really did ask Lark, Lark would simply stare at him with dismay, because Lark himself never had a reason for treating his parents this way. His parents were simply like the rest of the world. He did not like human beings except for himself, and his parents were simply part of this humanity that he despised. He had nothing personal against them.

Perhaps he was particularly annoyed at how opposite his parents were compared to him, how ridiculously sentimental and in love his parents always were, and how excessively, ravishingly affectionate they were too. But then, all human beings were exceedingly annoying and exasperating in some way anyway. Lark felt no extra hatred towards his parents.

Still, you had to feel sorry for Graham and Kreesha because little Lark Arias didn't trust his parents either, or even tell them anything about his life. Kreesha would love it if her son would tell her just one thing, just one little tidbit about the science that he was always so interested in studying, even if she didn't understand a word he said.

Graham, on the other hand, wished that maybe one day Lark would be less extreme. Perhaps he would learn to like a few things that his parents liked, and not be so separated from them. Graham understood from what the psychiatrists said that this obsessiveness was the hallmark trait of his son's condition, or personality; but Graham still held that secret hope that someday his son would become "normal," or at least approach that ideal.

By "normal," he didn't mean ordinary or boring. He meant a happy, healthy, balanced kid. I've already told you that the Arias's were always worried sick that Lark was not getting enough—well, any—exercise, though he seemed to be pretty healthy; and worried that Lark had absolutely no friends, hated everyone, and that he didn't seem at all bothered by his current state. All that Lark was doing (or not doing) was making them so uncomfortable. They wished they could do something about it, but the psychiatrists weren't helping.

Perhaps if they went to another psychiatrist, they would have gotten a more satisfying answer; but this psychiatrist that they went to happened to be one of those who embraced diversity, and said that if they thought "natural obsessors" was a disorder that needed to be fixed, then the "more neurotic" people, those who were more negative, unhappy, and anxious than the average person, would definitely need to be "cured" as well.

So the psychiatrist refused to do anything to "fix" Lark, and said to his parents that the boy had a right to be what he wanted to be, and that they did not have the right to change him. The psychiatrist meant this very kindly, but his parents, especially Kreesha, thought this very harsh of him to say so; but they thanked him, and lived in despair with Lark.

But they were not in utter despair. Kreesha still dreamed about the day when Lark would start softening and warming towards them again, and return to the happy baby that she had once fed and nursed in her arms. And Graham simply hoped, and believed, that something would change.

Yet, right now, Lark turned away from his parents and crossed his arms. He wanted to scoot into his room, or someplace, but his mother was blocking him and his father was on the other side, so he was stuck. He could escape through the sides, one of which he was currently facing, but escape was highly unlikely as his parents could both run faster than him.

So all he could do for now was to stand his ground and hope for the best. He hoped that his parents would hurry up with this ritual and go away, so he could calm down in his room, and that next time he went to school and made his way back home, he could hand the par-the-air to Haus and he would gain free access to chemicals forever, without his parents ever knowing.

"If you don't want to speak to us," Graham said, "at least give papa your pink liquid." He extended a hand towards Lark, and Lark shrunk away. "Come on. Don't make me take it from you."

Lark still clutched at it. "Please, father. I know what I am doing, and I do not need to hand this over to you."

So the Arias's were stuck in this stalemate. Who would win? Who knew?

Suddenly, Kreesha said, "Graham! I've got an idea." She pulled her elemen aside and whispered some words in his ear.

Her elemen's face immediately brightened with delight whilst his son's immediately blanched with fear. "Larky," he said, "Come and see what we've done to your room."

Lark knew that this must be a trick. A pretty blatantly fake ruse, in fact. Even his parents should not have been this stupid. Nevertheless, he was still worried. "What have you done?" he asked accusingly.

Graham smiled, and went to open Lark's door. Lark's eyes widened. His room was completely...pink.

"What have you done to my room?" Lark's face was completely blanched with both horror and anger. He didn't think very highly of his parents, but he hadn't thought that they would stoop this low!

He shot into his room and was about to slam the door shut when his parents slipped inside with him and then closed the door. The three of them were trapped together. Lark backed away like a prisoner of war, until he reached his bed, where he felt relatively safer. He stared at his parents with eyes of pure fright.

Some parents might gloat over this moment because they had finally cowed their rebellious son. But not the Arias's. Both were sad that it had to come to this. That their son could become so afraid of them. What had they done? What had they done wrong to deserve this constant punishment from their son?

In this really sad moment, Kreesha cried, and Graham was comforting her. He really wanted to shoot a reproachful glance at Lark, but he just didn't have the heart to do so. Graham restrained himself on the outside from breaking down emotionally; but on the inside, he was crying with just as much feeling as his elemen was.

Lark, at this time, was utterly indifferent and oblivious to all that was going on inside Kreesha and Graham. He just sat there hoping that his parents would make it fast and go away. In fact, Graham was considering going away, when Kreesha said, "Larky, do you know why we did this?"

"How did you do this?" Lark asked.

"It was easy. All we had to do was ask the computer," she said calmly, or not so calmly.

Lark wondered why he was so upset when he could easily reverse all the coloring effects by asking the computer himself. Perhaps because his room was now forever tainted in his memory, because his parents had meddled with it and made it look hideous.

Kreesha continued, "We're just, quite unhappy, Lark."

Oh no, here it came again. Lark rolled his eyes inside and really hoped that she would get it all over and done with. He looked down at the ground yet again.

Most people would feel the tension in the atmosphere and feel very nervous and perhaps even start sweating. But Lark felt none of these things. He was very calm, but also very irritated that this was taking so long as he could have been learning more about science instead. All his parents ever did was waste his time. He leaned back in fatigue.

"Lark, Lark!"

"Yes, mother?" he said without looking up.

Kreesha said, "Lark, your father and I are very upset that—"

"Yes, I know, I know. You are displeased that I always behave so 'coldly' towards you and father. May I be left alone now?"

"No, not yet," his mom replied softly.

Graham sighed.

Kreesha said, "Couldn't you just...change a little bit? Come out of your room more often? Come with us to activities more?"

"That is what you have always been saying. And my reply is the same. I am sorry but I need to devote all my time to studying science, because as you know, there is nothing in the world I love more."

Graham and Kreesha exchanged a glance. They really didn't know what to do with this or what to do next.

Lark interrupted their thoughts impatiently, "May I ask the computer to revert the colors of my room now?"

"Yes, you may," Kreesha said, and she started to retreat out of the room. Her elemen clutched her hand to stay, however.

And Graham said, "Lark, really, son, I don't want to be mean, but you have got to change that attitude of yours. It makes us very sad, do you understand?"

"I understand that perfectly, father. You have been explaining this to me scores of times. Such repetition cannot fail to elicit a thorough under-standing."

"But I'm afraid you don't really understand, darling."

"Oh, but I do," protested Lark.

"Then explain to me what you do understand."

"Grae Grae!" Kreesha said. "He's five. We can't expect him to be able to verbalize something like this yet." Her words were still very soft.

"Well?" Graham said. He sighed, as Lark obviously did not reply. "If you don't understand, at the very least, please, I beg you, come out of your room more often—and actually—talk to us, son."

"I am talking to you," Lark said.

"Of course you are, but that's not what I meant."

"What do you mean?" Lark said irritably.

"Talk, as in, talk to us about what you're interested in. Tell us about what you like, tell us about your life, your experiences. Tell us about your feelings."

Lark narrowed his eyes. "I do not intend to tell you anything more about my 'friend,' if that is what you are implying."

"No, I didn't mean that. We don't have the right to pry into your affairs, and I trust that you are a sensible enough boy not to make friends with bad people, right?" Without waiting for Lark's reply, Graham contin-ued, "All I'm saying is that your mother and I would be extremely happy if you could just—talk to us a little bit about what you care about."

"I care about science," Lark said flatly, because this was the most obvious thing in the world.

"I didn't mean that either."

"Then what do you mean?" How frustratingly slow and indirect his father was, just like his mother. Why were both his parents so annoyingly relaxed and indirect and everything? This was taking so long.

"I mean...what you've just done was simply tell us what you care about."

"Is that not what you requested?"

"That is very good, that you've told us what you care about, but—tell us a little bit more. Tell us why you like science. Why do you like chemistry?"

"Why must I tell you?"

"Because we don't understand why, and would really like to know why." For fear of this sounding resentful when no resentment was intended, Graham added, "Because we want to understand you."

Lark shrugged. "Why do you want to understand me? Whether or not you understand me is none of my concern, and neither should this concern you."

"Oh but it does concern us," his father said, and his elemen nodded. "It would mean the world to us if only we could see what you can see! We would be so happy if we could understand what you like."

"You are not making sense," said Lark. "You know perfectly that I like science and chemistry. You understand that fact already."

"It's not just the fact, Lark." Oh my gosh his father was taking forever to express himself. How long was this going to take? Lark edged away, but his back was soon pressed against the bed. His father went on, "We would really like to know more about your life. About your feelings."

"I do not have feelings," Lark said.

"Oh, yes you do." Graham did not say this in an irritated way, though. He really meant this statement to be a matter of fact. "We all do. We're human beings."

"Well, apparently, I do not have feelings."

"Why do you have to keep denying that you have emotions, Lark? There's nothing to be ashamed of in having emotions."

"Of course there is nothing to be ashamed of. I simply do not have feelings, and I am very sorry if this simple fact displeases you."

Graham was about to give up. "Just—why don't we take this one small step at a time?"

"Father, how much longer are you going to lecture me?"

"It won't take much longer, I promise." It was kind of sad that Lark, as usual, had the upper hand and was controlling his parents, while all Graham and Kreesha wanted was a talk between equals. "Just, please. Tell me why you like science."

"I like science because I like science. Because it interests me." Was that a good enough response for his father?

"Very good. Then what are the latest things that you've learned in science?"

"You would not even be interested."

"We would—"

"Even if you were, you would not be able to understand a single thing I say, so it is useless for me to try to explain."

"True, but—"

"Father, you promised that you were about to end this tedious and fruitless talk."

It was fruitless indeed, Graham had to agree. So he did give up, and began to withdraw from the room, with Kreesha trailing behind him, casting a very wistful look at Lark. It was extremely hard to be the parents of a "natural obsessor."

SIX
THE GREEN SUBSTANCE

When his parents were finally gone, Lark Arias was finally at peace. He closed his eyes for a moment and smiled. The sweetness of solitude. And as everyone was gone at last, he could now rest and relax, and reengage himself in the safety of his room.

It was funny how despite his annoyance with his parents, Lark really liked his room. He was quite attached to it. With equanimity, he commanded the computer to transform all the pink in his room back to the original thunder-blue, sharp white, and pitch black tones.

And then he dove back into his books.

He was reading about this sea lamina with golden fins—twelve fins all around its translucent body. He wondered how this creature could generate that sustaining light inside it...and then it struck him.

Since he had the par-the-air with him, why didn't he try some experiments with it first, before he took it away to Haus? Surely getting a mere droplet would not hurt.

Excited now, little Lark Arias whispered his commands to the computer to pinch a minuscule amount of liquid from the little vial into a very small container that Lark had.

It was done. The pink liquid sat discreetly in that tiny container. Lark gazed at it eagerly. What would happen if he mixed this with—oh but what about—what about—his mind was jumping all over the place. He was alive with too many ideas. The possibilities were endless! Oh why was science so intoxicating? His eyes shifted across the computer's catalogues of the current chemicals that he had. They were all kiddy chemicals, of course, so they were very safe. But once he used a bit of par-the-air, it would not be so safe, right?

Now, Lark was not one of those hopelessly impulsive thrill seekers, so he wouldn't do anything silly like risking his life; but...in this situation, he couldn't help being exhilarated. The possibilities were still flashing and storming in his head. He couldn't decide what he should do.

Of course, he could obtain even more of the par-the-air; but if he took more, Haus might notice that he had pinched away some of his chemical. And who knew what Haus would do if he noticed? Lark would probably lose his right to all Haus's chemicals in the store, and that would be tragic.

Lark racked his brains for the best idea, but he just couldn't decide. And like all the times he was stuck on a mystery or a science or math problem, Lark stared at the wall. Hopefully a solution would magically unravel itself into his head.

He soon came up with a tiny tint of an idea. Remember that amosti I told you about? That chemical that glowed in the dark if dipped into ice? Lark thought that he could try depositing a bit of amosti into the par-the-air, and see if the amosti glowed. Par-the-air was not ice, but—it was an energy source, wasn't it? And glowing was a sign of light energy, was it not?

You could see how amosti was a pretty benign and innocuous substance—it was just a fancy chemical that could easily be made into a glowing lantern in the dark. A nice visual trick to amuse kids—it even amused Lark, showing that deep down, this boy was really just a kid, like everyone else.

So, without further hesitation, he commanded the computer to take out a tiny drop of amosti, and release it into the tiny container of par-the-air.

Lark was expecting an explosion.

He was disappointed.

But then something did happen. A color change. Amosti was transparent whilst par-the-air was pink. The pink...for some reason turned green. A light, yellowy green that reminded one of fresh spring. A very pleasant, green apple kind of green—not that Drellians had apples, but they had some similar looking fruits.

Lark stared at it for a moment without blinking. Then, realizing that nothing else was going to happen, he sighed. Now, when Lark commanded the computer to do anything with chemicals, the computer automatically protected his eyes and body with a shield, in case of any chemical spills or eruption.

He rubbed a hand over his face. Not because something got into his eyes, but because he was still disappointed that nothing happened. He really wanted to see something thrilling, something entertaining. A mere color change didn't impress him. He wanted to see smoke or fire, as the kiddy chemicals would never permit inflammatory reactions.

Yet, he did not despair. He got up and stared at the wall again. Then he thought of something. It was so simple that he wanted to punch himself for not thinking of this before.

He didn't try heating up the concoction.

After berating himself for such unbelievable foolishness, he swiftly commanded the computer to heat up the concoction to 100 °C. (Actually, Drellians use a different temperature measure, but for the sake of simplifying things, I'll just use Celsius.) Bubbles appeared in the concoction as it started to boil.

Amosti had a similar boiling point to water, which was why Lark ordered 100°C specifically—he was a wise boy, and did not want to risk killing himself, so perhaps just making the amosti boil was enough to cause an effect but not a fatal effect? Okay this was obviously not as wise as Lark thought, but well, he was not an experienced scientist, after all; he was only five, so we might as well forgive this little boy for this blunder which might end his life.

The bubbles fizzed with increasing speed and grew larger and larger. Lark watched with mounting eagerness as steam, spring-green steam, started to rise from the mixture. Was the steam going to corrode something in his room?

"Corroding something in his room" was no doubt a bad thing; but Lark, in his scientific fervor and madness, took leave of his senses, as all he wanted to see were clear, powerful, and poundingly exciting results.

Unfortunately, nothing seemed to be corroding. The green steam just rose higher and higher until it touched the ceiling, and spread. All the while, the computer protected Lark from its vapors, so he was safe. The only thing that was notable in this experiment was that much of the green vapour, when it reached the wall and ceiling, left green marks on them. Doubtless his parents would notice it next time they came into his room; but at this moment, Lark was too absorbed in all that was happening to care. He often became quite heedless when he was deep in an experiment.

Soon enough, those green vapours started to subside, until they were no more. This was strange, because normally things did not just stop steaming before its chemicals ran out. In fact, the concoction even stopped bubbling. He checked the temperature and it was still a mere 120°C.

Now Lark was fascinated. A mixture of amosti and par-the-air could make the concoction bounce back to its original insipid and calm state after only a few minutes. He quickly noted down these facts on the computer's note-taking device, by voice command.

Lark regained his composure after a while, but he pondered on what happened. He was still leaning forward to gaze at that silent green mixture. Was it going to do something? Something unexpected? Or perhaps even wild? He waited for a quarter of a core, but still nothing happened, even though the temperature was now 200°C. With a sigh, Lark turned off the heating system. Was something going to happen now? Was Lark's sudden thought.

Then his eyes widened.

Indeed! That green liquid was congealing into what clearly looked like a solid. In fact, cracks were forming on the walls of its container. It was freezing! Now, Lark knew that if one put ice into amosti, the amosti would glow, but he had no idea that when one mixed amosti with par-the-air, the mixture would turn to ice after heating and cooling. Or was it ice?

Lark Arias was extremely curious and was itching to touch the concoction to make sure. But he was not a silly boy, after all, despite his age, so he ordered the computer to feel the concoction for him.

This was a singular device where the user of the computer would extend a computer's—robot's—hand into the concoction, and the computer would send corresponding electrical signals to stimulate the nervous sensors on the user's hand and fingers, so that the user would feel the exact sensations felt by the robo-hand. The user could also control how exactly the robo-hand moved whilst touching and handling the chemical too, just by moving their hand. Thus, scientists in the Drellian age could now happily manipulate and "feel" chemicals without endangering their lives—or hands.

Lark was amused to find that the solid felt quite gelatinous and tacky. It was definitely wet, not dry, so it wasn't completely solid. And the strange thing was that when he touched it, there was something "glowy" about it. Imagine a faint light glowing inside a lantern in the night, and imagine that feeling on Lark's fingers.

Thus, this chemical mixture had gelatinous parts, hard solid parts, and some liquid remains. Lark wondered if he could extract this chemical from its flask. So he commanded the computer to lift a bit of this out of the container.

A tiny stream of stuff stuck to the robo-hand (this robo-hand was made out of an inert and extremely durable substance that could resist almost any corrosion, heat, or even rust.) And then the stream thickened, as some of the substance miraculously climbed up the string.

Lark was amazed. Why was it going against gravity? Or maybe it wasn't going against gravity. Maybe these sticky strands were just so extraordinarily attracted to each other that when one left the container, the rest of it just had to come up as well. Lark winced. That reminded him of his parents.

Speaking of his parents, Lark was suddenly vigilant, hoping that his parents wouldn't come barging in. Of course, his door was locked, as usual. But what if his parents felt especially upset after that outburst, that scene, and decided to get the master key to open his door and check what he was doing?

Lark told himself that that wouldn't matter a jot anyway, though, because his parents were nutheads when it came to science, and that any chemical manipulation he was doing at the moment would look the same to them. They would not be able to tell that he was using that mysterious, non-kiddy par-the-air. His parents didn't appear to notice his pink chemical much anyway. They were so focused on making him "talk" to them, whatever that meant. And so Lark comforted himself as he concentrated on this chemical manipulation.

The chemical traveled up this pulled up string, but not all of the chemical moved up. You might have been wondering how such a tiny amount of chemical could generate so much steam, and why Lark would even be able to pull strings out of it. I have no idea, except that strange things happened in Lark's lab. Strange things happened in Drell.

Before long, the chemical stopped traveling up. It was a longish string of stuff that was one eighth of a qwort long. So, what does it do? Lark thought.

He meddled with this chemical for a very long while, until it was time for his dinner. You might have noticed that Lark left for the Phuore place in the morning. He had his lunch in the Coaster while he was traveling to Phuore. As usual, Lark was reluctant to leave his room, but he heard a knock on his door.

"Lark?" It was the sound of his father's voice, and he sounded tired. Lark, expectedly, did not hear the fatigue in that voice, nor would he be able to empathize anyway.

The boy was sullen when he came out, and he plopped down into a transparent orange seat that was cool, almost cold, to the touch. His parents sat in similar orange seats and all three Arias's faced a large, oblong glass panel where several platters of food lay.

Kreesha made a shy smile at her son. Graham was probably doing the same, but Lark wasn't looking that way and he didn't care. He saw the food in front of him, and though Kreesha and Graham (they liked to cook together) tried to cook something that their son seemed slightly more partial to, Lark thought that the food today was exactly the same as the food he got any day, so he chewed without speaking until he was done.

Whilst he was eating, his parents chatted to one another, nervously, watching their son. They both wanted to say something to Lark, and at the same time they both wished the other would say something to him; but in the end, nothing was said. Lark finished his food so quickly anyway that they had no time to reflect. When the boy leapt off his seat to go back into his room, Kreesha called for him to come back, that there was something else she wanted him to eat.

"What is it, mother?" he said, not amused.

Kreesha tried on her greatest smile ever, and she brought out something green, and her elemen also brought out something green.

At the sight of this new food, Lark froze. Green. His heart stopped. Could his parents know…could they know…He glanced to the floor very quickly, then reassured himself with his rational side that of course they didn't. His parents were total science outsiders. They would never know. And they didn't survey him in his room. His parents may be goons, but they couldn't be so bad as to install surveillances on him, would they? That would be a serious breach of his privacy. He resolutely told himself to set this aside as a coincidence.

To satisfy his mother, he plopped himself back to their dining facility and stared at the new food. The green was spring green, and it was gelatinous. There was a little bit of liquid remaining, and something like cracks and icy frost caked the sides of the see-through container. Lark continued to stare at this green "dessert." And he felt very sick.

"Lark?" Kreesha asked worriedly. "Lark?"

Graham likewise looked his son over. "Larky? Son?"

Lark did not respond, rapt as he still was in his own thoughts and sensations. He didn't feel so good. At long last, just when Graham and Kreesha were about to get up and touch him—which he definitely did not want them to do—he took a deep breath, and spooned up some of that green substance and stuffed it into his mouth. Instantly, he felt disgusted, nauseous, and had to leave.

"Lark!" Kreesha cried.

Please, mother, release me, he thought, as he made his way to the washroom.

Lark threw up. Every part of his insides wanted the green matter out of his system immediately. Thank goodness he hadn't swallowed any of it yet, so he quickly got rid of any greenness left on his tongue and mouth by rinsing them with water. He sighed, suddenly exhausted, and sat down.

"Lark? Son? Are you all right?"

His parents again, outside. If only they would just leave him alone. Most children his age would welcome their parents' comfort and aid when they were sick, but Lark didn't.

They knocked really hard. But Lark didn't care and he was too tired to move anyway. He wished, almost implored, for the two to leave. Why couldn't they just go away? While Lark thus stewed in his thoughts of frustration, something unexpected happened. He cried. He was crying!

Now by crying, it wasn't outright bawling. That would be disgraceful and mortifying to Lark. What happened was simply the heating up and wetting of Lark's eyes, and then the moisture subsequently slipping out of his eyes, and streaming down his cheeks. He sniffed and commanded the computer, in a soft voice, to wipe his tears away.

But the tears kept coming. He didn't actually feel sad, that was the strange thing. Yet, he did feel an unrestrained urge, or even desire, to cry. This felt disturbing and abnormal to Lark, because he did not cry often, if he ever did anymore. Lark was definitely not a crying person! So why on Drell did he suddenly want to cry? This was outrageous, irrational!

In this perilous moment, Lark dared not quit the washroom. He knew his parents were outside, and by how raucously sentimental they always were, he could imagine how explosively they would react if they saw him crying. Perhaps they had even heard him sniffing earlier. Hopefully not.

"Darling, do tell us what's happening. Are you feeling all right?" said his mother.

Evidently he was not, but he didn't want anybody to come in and help him. He would find the cure himself. Spontaneous crying, he thought, and instant nausea after tasting green stuff...he believed that these symptoms had nothing, absolutely nothing to do with the spring-green substance still whirling around in his room. Yet, why did his parents coincidentally bring him that strange new green food that looked and felt so similar to what he was experimenting on just a moment ago in his room?

While Lark Arias speculated on the possible explanations, he heard his parents hammering on the door. They were not really hammering, though. It was just that Lark's distressed and confused state of mind was magnifying his perceptions.

His parents were now screaming for him to open the door. Again, his parents were actually asking in soft voices, but his agitation was making him exaggerate the stimuli that he perceived. The five-year-old covered his ears and breathed, and breathed, and breathed; and wished that his nausea would disappear.

Lark peered around, and looked at the place where he could take a bath. Maybe he would feel better if he did. But since he couldn't get his clothes—he could ask the computer to get them, but his parents would see

—then all of a sudden, Lark just didn't care anymore and nudged the door open with his foot.

"Lark," said his mother happily and with relief. She, as Lark expected, attempted to grasp him into a hug. His father was looking down at him with a curious expression.

"Are you okay, son?" he asked.

"Of course I am," Lark frowned. He hobbled towards his room without much awareness of what he was doing. He just wanted to be safe, alone and comforted in that warm enclosure.

"Lark! Please, honey, stay here. You don't look so good. You look so pale."

Lark ignored her and slowly reached the door of his room; Kreesha wanted to yank him away because she was so tormented with worry about him, and Graham was about to prevent her from such a desperate measure, but Lark had already opened his room door.

Kreesha screamed when she saw what was inside. Graham screamed too, but his yell was softer—he made it softer, and his elemen's scream covered his anyway. The walls and ceiling of Lark's room were speckled all over with an amorphous, insidious looking green. "What. On. Drell. Is. That. Dear?" she said, quite frightened.

Lark didn't care to respond. It was simply the green steam that had hiked up his walls and ceilings and plastered themselves there. Plus, the green wasn't literally "everywhere." They were just hanging around on the side that he was experimenting on—which was the wall that one saw first when one opened the door, exactly the side that his parents were now seeing, and therefore this was why they had the misperception that the green stuff was really "all" over the place.

"Son, come back out this instant." Graham, in a jiffy, scooped up a protesting Lark into his arms. Unluckily for Lark, his father was far stronger and more athletic than he was. Both Graham and Kreesha were more athletic than the average person.

Lark was still protesting when his father took him out and sat him down on a stretch seat. "What was going on in there? In your room and in the bathroom?" Graham asked with concern and tenderness. But Lark, as you may have expected, heard none of this tenderness.

"Father, please," Lark said, still struggling. He still did not understand why his parents bothered to meddle with his affairs at all. It wasn't that he thought himself an unworthy person to be loved, or that he somehow secretly wanted to be loved. He just thought that it was stupid of people to meddle in others' affairs.

Graham was frowning and so was Kreesha. Kreesha said, "Lark, tell us what's wrong. Did you really hate the Ruminence we made for you? I'm sorry for making you eat it—I thought you would like it," she said.

"Ruminence...," Lark muttered.

"Yes, Ruminence. It glow—" But Kreesha stopped herself when she saw that Lark had a very agonized expression on his face as if he were about to throw up. "Grae Grae, take him back to the washroom."

Lark threw up again. His parents looked at him worriedly and placed him on the stretch seat in the washroom. They sat with him for a long time without speaking.

As melodramatic and noisy as this couple was, they were not wholly insensitive to the emotions of those around them. They understood that too much talking would simply upset their poor son even more and perhaps make him feel even more ill. It was too bad that they weren't always sensitive—they tried so hard to get their son to talk to them, to tell them about the things he learned and cared about, when it was more than exceedingly obvious that Lark had no intention to ever reveal to anyone what was going on in his mind.

Lark was just hanging there in Graham's clutch when he threw up. After throwing up, Lark didn't seem to have the strength to do anything else. Normally, when his parents tried to pick him up or touch him, he would fight back and attempt to escape, but this time he felt so drained that he didn't even want to move.

Kreesha put a hand on Lark's shoulder, in an attempt to calm and soothe him. But you know Lark. Things that would be soothing to normal human beings were aggravating and bothersome to him. He longed to wrestle out of Graham's grip right now, but he just didn't seem to have the energy. In fact, he feared that he might want to cry again and embarrass himself. Embarrassing himself in front of his parents would be especially damning and disagreeable.

At this time, there was a signal from outside. Kreesha and Graham exchanged a glance. It was a signal from one of the household computers that something was wrong in the house. Both parents immediately thought of the noxious green substances in Lark's room, and both shivered. But at the moment, both of them wanted to stay with Lark, because they were worried that he would really collapse or lose it if they were even a moment away from him.

They did not realize that this would not be the case, however. Lark would be perfectly fine without their comfort and support. Yet at the same time, independent as Lark was, it wasn't absolutely certain that he could take care of himself that well—when he was sick. Perhaps his parents' support helped more than he realized. But it was certain that their presence was doing nothing to help Lark emotionally. Regardless, he wished his parents would go away. He mumbled something of that sort, but they seemed not to hear. Instead, they casted sympathetic gazes upon him, which irked him even more.

At long last, though, Kreesha said, "I'll go and check what's wrong. Grae Grae, take care of Lark." And she left.

A moment later, Kreesha hesitated in the doorway to her son's room. The green...slime, or whatever it was, was slowly creeping down the wall. She still did not see that the green substance was only streaking down one wall, not around the whole room.

Panicked, she tiptoed into the room and peered around. She finally saw that the other walls were clean. She also saw that the protective chemical shield was still up from the computer, and that the robot arm was still there.

But unhappily, Kreesha was not familiar with Lark's equipment. The couple sometimes would use robots to help them measure exact amounts of ingredients for cooking, but they were people who preferred to do things hands-on, by themselves without the computer's help, because it was simply much more fun to cook by hand.

She whispered, "Computer, check for viruses and other microbes in this green chemical and its vicinity."

"Negative. No microbes in the green chemical or its vicinity."

Kreesha ought to breathe a sigh of relief after this announcement, but she was now even more worried because the source of Lark's illness was not microbes, but some unknown force she was less familiar with. Could it be something to do with radiation? Toxic effects? But wasn't the computer shielding Lark when he did his experiments, as it was now shielding her? She gave a shudder at the thought that she was being protected from some unknown entity or force that had ailed Lark. What should I do? she thought.

All of a sudden she had an idea. Could Lark's illness be due to some mysterious chemical reaction between the green substance and the yellow Sheavus she was making yesterday?

Kreesha and Graham had been trying out some new experiments with food. In fact, all three Arias's were people who enjoyed experimenting. They were all dissatisfied with the status quo, of how their food or chemicals were like. They felt that trying new things, and combining substances to hopefully get remarkable new results, was tremendously fascinating.

Kreesha as a child was very intrigued by the swirling of food together in their containers, platters, and whatnot. She liked to mix and mash things together to see what she would get. Her parents were worried that what she made would get her sick, so they tried to take away her new concoctions as soon as she made them, if they caught her; but to be kind to Kreesha, they always recorded the 3D simulations of her food. (See "3D Recorders[1]" under "Technology.")

As she was a mild child, however, she didn't seem to get too upset when her parents took her newly invented food away. Yet, this was more because she was naturally easy-going and amiable that she didn't like to throw tantrums—she simply didn't like expressing her anger towards others. She preferred to be happy and vivacious towards everybody so she could influence them with her jubilance. She also felt it her responsibility to cheer people up and energize them. She had this belief that people who were born with a particularly happy disposition should use their gift to affect others who were less fortunately disposed.

Now, this adorable little girl would do all sorts of things to mix different colors, textures, and temperatures; she stirred up solids with liquids, gases with solids, or gases with liquids. Once, she even tried mixing blood with her drink. Kreesha had accidentally cut her finger, but instead of screaming as she would naturally do, she suddenly thought that she should take advantage of this opportunity to try something radical. It was fascinating how those droplets of red swirled and swirled, and danced in that clear, sky-blue liquid that was her drink.

At that time, it did not occur to seven-year-old Kreesha that this mixture was horrific. As a matter of fact, she thought it was very beautiful. It was a piece of art with something bright red lingering and moving inside that clear, beautiful liquid. And it was extra captivating because that red liquid was from her.

But when her parents realized what Kreesha was doing—they found their daughter gazing intently at her cup, and then they saw her finger—they, with panic, yanked their little daughter away from the cup, and she protested in a mild but vivacious voice, "Mommy, Daddy, it's so fun! Look! Don't you think it's so pretty?"

"There's nothing pretty about what's happening to—whatever that thing is." Kreesha was quite let down that her parents didn't appreciate what she was creating. They never seemed to comprehend her love of experimenting with food and drinks. But then she was used to this lack of understanding.

Kreesha also had a little sister, who was six at the time, called Lilla. She was an odd girl. She was shy, inhibited, and easily embarrassed; yet, she could become very aggressive and kick and punch if she felt threatened; and she would bite, slap, pinch, or even trip her enemy. She would also be very verbally aggressive, by cursing the other person as strongly and hurtfully as she could. Of course, she never meant any of it. She was just acting in self-defense.

On the other hand, Kreesha was a child normally quite outgoing, affable, cheery, carefree, and confident. And even when she felt threatened, she would not physically fight or verbally abuse the threatener. She would instead try to reason with them, or say sorry for what she did wrong—if she thought it might have been her fault, whatever she just did—or she would try to calm the other person down, by speaking extra sweetly and delicately to them. There you have the two contrasting sisters.

The two sisters loved each other, and Kreesha liked to hug poor little Lilla and kiss her cheeks. She was really the model older sister in how she took care of and always stood up for her younger sibling.

Her future elemen Graham too, had a sibling, a brother who was two years younger than him. Graham sincerely loved his younger brother, but he sometimes teased and made fun of the younger boy in a friendly way that made the latter cry.

Graham always felt sorry after his younger brother, Rai (rhymes with eye) cried, and he would apologize like crazy. Yet, despite his teasing Rai, it might contradict your expectations in that Graham was the more sentimental and soft, nurturing, and feminine sibling; and Rai was the more boyish one. Not the very masculine type, but more like a stereotypical boy according to our Earthly stereotypes.

Coming back to Kreesha, what often occurred was that her parents, Mr and Mrs Blé (pronounced "blay"), would scold Lilla sternly about how she had just behaved—because she had thrown one of her very violent tantrums again. But Kreesha, when she was around to hear this, would come out and gently tell her parents that it was not Lilla's fault, that it was the perpetrator who started it for being so mean to her, that you couldn't blame Lilla.

So, that was a brief story of Kreesha. Now let's come back to the present, or rather, the recent past: As I was saying, the day before, Graham and Kreesha were experimenting with some new food and Kreesha made some yellow Sheavus (the name she gave to her creation). Graham made some blue and white Angielle (the name he gave to his creation) that was swirly and creamy.

Kreesha was uncertain about her Sheavus, because it was made from relatively volatile, strong-smelling ingredients. It wasn't exactly perfume; it smelt strange, but she wanted to try it anyway just for the sake of it. To her delight, despite its odd—but not repulsive—smell, she loved the taste of it.

She let Graham try and he loved it too and praised her lavishly as the couple were wont to do for each other all the time. She also enjoyed his Angielle but she liked her own creation slightly better. Maybe it was because it had a more unusual, though very pleasant, taste and feel in the mouth. She not only liked strange concoctions. She liked strange smells and tastes as well.

"Many smells become aromatic once you get used to them"—was her philosophy, and this statement seemed to hold well for her most of the time. She was a kind of Stravinsky, you could say. Like that brave musician, she liked to stun her audience—her tasters—with her daring and electrifyingly new experiments, which may be jarring and even unpleasant to those who were not very open-minded; but she understood that after a while, any radical food, as long as it was made well, would be accepted and loved in time.

Graham, on the other hand, did not aim for the radical as much as she did; he aimed more for beauty, though he cared about audacity and courage too. Kreesha likewise also cared about beauty, but she was more intrigued by the wild and shocking—she wasn't completely out of control, however. She aimed for the striking, provocative, yet elegant and very tasty kind.

As Lark had parents who were so in love with each other, who loved him so much, and who regularly created new, exciting, and delicious food, Lark was actually living in Heaven. So it was such a shame that he was the one person in the world who could not appreciate any of these three things. He disliked effusive love, whether it was passionate or tender; he could not care less how much or little affection others had for him, as long as they left him alone; and he didn't give a jot about the beauty or deliciousness of food, because to him, food was simply energy—a charger that had to be used as quickly as possible in order for him to return to more worthwhile matters.

Now, I just want to tell you a little more about Graham and how he loved to make beautiful food. At home when he was young, such as when he was seven and his little brother Rai was only five, Lark's current age, Graham would carefully pour in sweet things, colored things, and things that had interesting but delicate patterns—like the lovely edible plants one could find in stores, and many other pleasing ingredients; then he would stir, mix, and style everything with such extreme care as if he were creating a meticulously fashioned masterpiece.

One of the desserts he had made back then was a light-green curling structure, its sides beaded tastefully with little fruits all around it. It glowed like a jewel yet looked like it was something from nature at the same time. Rai immediately asked to eat it and Graham fed him the first scoop.

It was fortunate for Graham that his parents did let him eat what he made—unlike with poor Kreesha—as long as he let his parents check what ingredients he used first, and then they would usually give him permission to taste it.

In contrast with his older brother, Rai was quite uninterested in making food. If you told him to make something for you, he would make you the simplest, easiest, most overdone dish ever, and he would make you that same dish every single day. It was lucky for Rai that his brother enjoyed making so many different and aesthetically appealing dishes, because as unenthusiastic as Rai was about cooking, he really loved to eat and had a great fondness for attractive food.

The huge elation Rai expressed when viewing Graham's especially beautiful experiments, was probably one reason why Graham was so keen on making strikingly handsome food, if one could describe food in that way. You could see that Graham was quite susceptible to the feelings of others around him. It gave him pleasure to make his brother happy. And this made up for all the many times Graham made him cry.

At the present moment, Kreesha was panicking that her strong-smelling Sheavus had very likely reacted with the unknown chemicals in Lark's room. Such a reaction between their food and his chemicals had never happened before—but it wasn't inconceivable.

"Computer, check the source of this problem."

She thought that this was a rather vague instruction, but hopefully the computer would understand, as it often did, because computers were generally extremely intelligent and astute creatures. Yes, some Drellians liked to see their computers and electronics as having lives of their own, and that they were people just like flesh-and-bone human beings.

The computer made a noise that sounded like an acknowledgement that it had heard Kreesha, and started searching around the room. She was impatient that after some minutes, nothing had turned up. But then without warning, the computer answered her and its voice took her aback.

"Source uncertain. There is a strange aura in Master Lark's room."

She knew it.

"The strange aura," continued the computer, "is—"

But the voice was covered by a loud shout from the washroom. "Mother, please do not do anything with the chemicals in my room. I was in the middle of a very important procedure, and I promise to restore the wall and ceiling to their original condition."

Kreesha knew that what her son wanted her to do was not right. There was evidently something wrong with that enigmatic green substance and she would remove it. Amid the background noise of her elemen trying to soothe Lark, and her son continuing to discourage her from any action, Kreesha looked around the main room and found what she was looking for.

It was the "grey beam." Now, this item was not as depressing as its name suggested. It was called grey because the rays it emitted were used to neutralize whatever excessive acidic or alkaline levels there were in the places the rays touched. Kreesha hoped that this would do the trick. But she had a problem now, because the grey beam could not penetrate the protective shield that the computer had erected around the green chemicals. Should she remove the shield and then shoot with the neutralizer? Or was it too dangerous to attempt such a thing?

"Please, mother, let me deal with what is happening in my room."

Kreesha paid no attention to him, however, as she knew Lark would more likely investigate and experiment with his chemical instead of fixing the problem. She was also puzzled as to how the kiddy chemicals that she and Graham had bought for him could create such green masses around the room. She had a faint suspicion about how, but it was useless to go into that now.

She wished she could call Graham to discuss with her what to do, as the couple were very dependent on each other. But again, she didn't want Graham to leave Lark alone and didn't want her elemen to move Lark either, for fear of making her frail son feel even more uncomfortable—though he wasn't really that frail.

At this point, she paced outside his room. She tried to aim the neutralizer at the protective shield again, hoping that it would miraculously penetrate it and reach the green substance, but of course that was to no avail.

It was some time during her pacing that she began to feel a bit sick herself. She felt like she couldn't breathe properly, and she closed Lark's door, fearing what was happening, and sat down on a stretch seat outside his room.

Seeing his elemen thus, Graham called out, "Kreesha darling, are you all right?"

She mumbled that she was, and would have asked him to come over and help her, but she didn't want him to move their son. She also felt a mounting migraine. She could fortunately still breathe, but her breaths were less full than they usually were. In great discomfort, she clutched her head.

"Kreesha?"

"It's okay, dear. Take care of Lark."

Torn, Graham decided to move slowly to his elemen with Lark in his arms. Lark was too tired, drained by whatever was affecting him to try to slip out of his father's clutch; his eyelids were also drooping. Was he being affected by some kind of narcolepsy in addition to his bouts of nausea and uncharacteristic crying? What was happening to him? But the urge to sleep was so strong, and he was just about to succumb when he heard a shriek.

---

1. **3D Recorders**
    Will record a hologram of whatever object or living thing you want. You can also turn on its smell or touch (or even taste, if applicable); touching this hologram will let you feel the original texture of the thing. 3D recorders can even capture the objects' sounds.

SEVEN
RECOVERING FROM THE ILLNESS

I
t was not from his mother.

It was from someone outside the house. Graham hurriedly left his sick son and elemen for a while and rushed out to see what was going on outside. It turned out that the cry had come from their neighbor's daughter, who was seven years old. She pointed with alarmed eyes at something on the Arias's wall. "Look, Mr Arias."

He turned around. On this vast wall was a long streak of green, and inside this streak, were swarms of tiny winged and straggly laminae with millions of legs. These laminae were quite common around Drell, but they existed only in the rural areas; Drellians had invented technology to keep pests like these away from their towns and cities without killing these creatures—it was unethical to annihilate another species without a very good reason.

Graham felt like he was about to faint. But he wasn't suffering from an illness like his son and elemen were. He just didn't like those chresins (pronounced Kree-sins). They gave him the creeps and absolutely disgusted him—thankfully they were almost never in the urban areas—but they populated the rural areas.

So, aside from his fear of these disgusting laminae, he wondered how these chresins could get into this area and how they ended up on the wall.

Whatever the reason, it evidently had something to do with the green slime that had accumulated and was creeping down their wall, and it was most certain that the green slime was from his son's room; yet, he still wondered if there was an additional reason. He was no expert in chemistry, but was there some magical ingredient in that green substance that attracted these small laminae to fly all the way from the rural areas to here?

But this guess would also be ridiculous, because the gases that the urban communities had sprayed all around must have repulsed all of these troublesome and gross chresins. So could it be that these tiny obnoxious laminae had not been forced out of the urban areas, but that they had simply gone into hiding, perhaps even underground?

These chresins were whisking their wings and twitching their legs about in the ugliest manner imaginable; and Graham averted his head, not bearing to watch anymore.

What should he do right now? He saw that Kreesha had the grey beam with her, but should he try to neutralize the green slime that was so atrociously and conspicuously on their wall? But would the neutralizer just exacerbate the already frightful-looking green thing? Perhaps he should call the Order? But calling the Order twice in a single day...There must be experts on things like these.

He decided to get the neutralizer anyway and see what would happen. When he returned to his elemen and son, he was amazed to see Lark fast asleep in his mother's arms. The child's face was contorted into a painful expression; the mother was not looking very well herself.

At that moment, Graham denounced himself for being so thoughtless, and so selfishly concerned about getting rid of something that he was personally repulsed with first, without thinking about how his family was suffering—how could he? He didn't realize that the nasty green thing and little critters outside could very well be linked to what his elemen and Lark were going through, and that to eliminate the problem outside may help the people inside.

He crouched down by his mate and son's side, touched their foreheads, and was relieved that their temperatures seemed to be normal. "Lark?" he whispered. His son seemed to be really asleep. Kreesha looked at him weakly, supplicating him to help them. He gripped her hands in his, and called the medics.

MEANWHILE, AT THE TREEKS' HOUSE, KARRIN WAS HAPPILY telling his mother about his adventure in Phuore, and she listened with interest, though she didn't speak much. Some kids might be discouraged by such an unresponsive and reserved mother, but not Karrin: he was used to it and was way too cheerful a child to be set off by such insignificant things. Besides, he understood that his mother did actually care about what he was saying.

"That sounds great," his mother said with an emotionless expression. But no matter how emotionally flat she both sounded and looked, Karrin still saw an animacy of great feeling in those green-gray eyes. Her eyes were the kind that seemed grey if you looked at them in one way, but green if you looked at them in another.

"And then the Order found us and gave us all a free ride home," concluded Karrin proudly.

"That's fantastic," his mother replied with the same implacable monotone. But Karrin again sensed a lot of dynamic emotion in that seemingly deadpan voice.

He said, "Ma, tell me about your day. What did you do while I was gone?"

She made a little inner grimace, because she was forced to speak, but this grimace was contradicted by the simultaneous rise of pleasure she felt that her son cared enough to ask her about her life. So she calmly told him about the dance routines she went through, and which combinations of moves and music scores she had chosen.

This would have been an extremely dry and boring conversation to the average person who didn't know anything about dancing, or even to the average dancer; but Karrin wasn't at all bored. This kid so idealized his mother and was convinced that everything she said held a lot of deep significance and poetry. His mother was so artistic and beautiful, he often thought.

By the way, everybody in Drell was equally physically beautiful, thanks to technology; but what was most important, was that different people still had different standards of beauty. It was just great that Karrin's standards met how his mother looked like, and there was of course that effect where the more we like or love someone, the more beautiful they will appear to us. That was exactly little Karrin's situation.

Hlen Treek was smiling at how his son and elemen got along. Not many people understood his mate, because she was always so quiet and morose. But thankfully his son did. Hlen was also very thankful that Karrin was such an understanding boy, and thought that their parenting must have been quite successful.

Karrin chatted with his mother for a little while longer, though he did most of the talking, and then his mother asked him to go do his homework. He looked a little disappointed that the conversation was already over, but he nodded, uttered a "See you later, Ma!", and padded towards the corridor lit with yellow light that led to his room. But his father called to him right when the boy reached his room door. "Karrin?"

"Hmm?" Karrin turned around.

"I just want to say—keep a look out for your Lark classmate, okay? I'm quite worried about that chemical he got. I was wondering if I should have asked the Order to take it away, but at the same time, I felt like I would be betraying the kid if I did, you know what I mean?"

"I think so, Daddy."

After Mr Treek spoke a few more words to him, Karrin pulled open the light blue door to his room, and went in to do his homework.

The fact was, Hlen Treek was a strange person. Maybe it was because he was a psychologist that he had a different perspective on how he saw other people. Although he was well aware that this pink chemical could be dangerous to the little boy, or maybe even his family, some strange intuition made him trust Lark.

He thought that to immediately wrest the vial from the boy's grip would be something akin to treachery, especially from their camaraderie during the excursion. (He forgot that there was no such thing as camaraderie for Lark; that no such "bond" had developed or ever would develop between them.) He also felt that they were both boys, brothers from a certain standpoint, so he should trust that what Lark was doing was sensible and right. The boy was helping his friend, right?

Actually, the more Hlen thought about his decision to lie for Lark and let him keep his vial, the more troubled Hlen felt, and the more he regretted his decision. Had he endangered the little boy now? And who knew who this "friend" of Lark's was? This "friend" was moreover associated with someone who lived in a secluded place barred by a dungeon-like door.

Yet, once again, Hlen felt that if he forcefully took the boy's chemical away, he would be making the boy unhappy and ruin Lark's purposes. Hlen had no idea what real purposes the boy had, but he felt that a person who was a "natural obsessor" would have intentions different from everyone else's, and that "normal" people like him had no right to discredit them.

So you see, Hlen Treek had wound himself into one of those intellectual confusions. From his psychology background, Hlen got into the habit of sympathizing with absolutely every kind of person in the world, respecting all, and trying to understand all even if they may still seem bizarre to him. This respecting of all kinds of people included respecting their decisions and feelings.

However, Hlen over-applied this general principle of accepting psychological diversity here and forgot about the objective principles that were important to every person. He forgot about personal safety.

Well, he did have personal safety in mind, but his psychological training made him so focused on the "respect" he should pay Lark and how he should give Lark his "autonomy," and "trust" him. It did not occur to him that in this particular situation, he should treat Lark like any ordinary little boy and protect him from danger. He had, in a way, seen Lark as a unique and idiosyncratic individual who needed to be given freedom to express himself, rather than a child who needed physical protection. Such was the danger of intellectualization.

But what could Hlen Treek do now except to ask his son to keep an eye on his poor classmate? It did occur to Hlen though that his poor son could not establish any form of communication with Lark, because the latter really was an oddly antisocial fellow, after all. He could also ask the teachers and Lark's parents to keep watch, but doing so would necessarily mean showing them that he had the audacity to lie for Lark while being very much aware that he may be endangering this child.

Thus, he could only trust Karrin for now, and of course, his elemen. He and Ella trusted each other much like many of the other couples in Drell did each other. Although there were still dissatisfying marriages in

Drell, such misfortunes were quite rare. Most couples enjoyed very happy and long-lasting marriages.

Those were the last thoughts in Hlen's head that night as well—about both Lark and his blessed marriage—as Hlen drifted off to sleep in his elemen's arms.

"DAD?" KARRIN SAID THE NEXT DAY AFTER BREAKFAST. "YOU don't look so good today, you all right?"

"Sure I am," Hlen said, making a smile. "And you look quite sprightly yourself, dear. Are you expecting yet another new and exciting day?"

"You bet!" The little boy sprung into the air and twirled around. But then he said, "Daddy, you still haven't answered my question. Are you feeling well?"

"Of course," Hlen said again, unconvincingly. He waved his son a goodbye anyway, and heaved a sigh of relief when Karrin was gone.

"Honey?" That was his elemen, Ella Treek. She was currently sitting on a stretch seat that was soft, firm, and tinted with peach and purple. "Karrin's right. You don't look too good. What happened?"

And as Hlen trusted her more than his life, he told her everything, from the beginning till the end. As he expected and to his relief, she did not interrupt, nor did she seem too disturbed. She looked calm as usual. But Hlen knew that his elemen was not in the habit of showing her emotions. He could only hope that he didn't frighten her too much. She glanced at the ground a moment, then turned her bright eyes up at him. "Darling, I don't think you need to worry."

"No?" He knew that his elemen tended to see things differently from how most people did. But still he was surprised at her response.

"I don't mean we shouldn't care about this Lark's safety. I'm just saying we should tell his parents what happened, and then think about what to do later. What if Lark really has a friend that needed this...par-the-air? If we take the chemical away from him, wouldn't we be hurting someone else?"

"But the man said that the par-the-air was only for enhancing this

Haus's performance in this...strange game he plays with his friends every year."

She shook her head. "You are so naïve as usual, Hlen. Did you really believe that? That is a ridiculous story. I'm pretty sure that they were using that tale to mask a real reason. But what that reason is, though, I am not sure. I don't know if it's for some strange sickness, but that is a possibility."

The two elemens were quiet for a while. Then Hlen said, "Ella, what if this Haus guy really was suffering from some illness? Would Lark catch it too? And who knows where Lark met this 'friend'? Anyway, I still feel suspicious whether it is indeed a friend of his. Karrin says Lark doesn't like making friends."

Ella didn't care if Lark liked to make friends or not and she told her elemen so. "What does Lark like most?"

That question caught Hlen off guard. "According to Karrin, he likes anything to do with science, especially chemistry. Science and chemistry are in fact the only things that Lark likes in this world."

His elemen nodded. "Then this Haus man must have something related to science or chemistry that Lark really wants, and offered this as a prize in exchange for Lark's help."

Hlen gaped. "Simple psychology!"

"Simple psychology," Ella said too.

Shortly before school started in the morning, Karrin swung about in the playground around a contraption with ropes. There were long, thick, and strong rubbery ropes called elastoropes that were tied to some poles. Karrin was attached to one of these elastoropes and he was running around the playground with it, along with three of his friends who were also attached to elastoropes.

"You can't catch me, you can't catch me!" Karrin shrieked.

When it was time to enter the classroom with everybody else, Karrin glanced around the crowd and noticed that Lark was absent. Could this have something to do with the pink chemical Lark found yesterday?

But Karrin knew that Lark, though obsessed with science, was not one who would miss school just to stay at home with his science. He caught Eeera's eye and they both wondered the same thing.

———

GRAHAM STARED AT THE TWO MEDICS, A MIDDLE-AGED MAN and woman, both with orange-brown hair and staring eyes. They faced him with a stern expression as they stood against the glaring white walls of the medical building. "Your son is suffering from a relatively rare disease called charmia. Your elemen is too, but it's a lot milder for her. The disease charmia manifests in different ways in different people. For your son, you've already seen that it's in nausea, narcolepsy, and even uncontrollable urges to cry."

"To cry?" Graham said, bewildered. He glanced at his still sleeping son's face but there were no tears. Evidently Lark had commanded the robots to wipe his tears before he came out of the washroom, Graham thought.

"Yes. And as for your mate, she suffered from labored breathing and a migraine. There might be occasional itches in various parts of her body too, but thankfully for her, that didn't happen."

"It won't happen," Graham said, more to himself than to the medics. He felt the warm weight of his elemen leaning on his shoulder; she shifted with clear discomfort on the long brown stretch seat they were sitting on together. His son, on the other hand, had awakened briefly earlier and had demanded that his parents let go of him, so he now lay in slumber by himself on the next stretch seat, a good distance away from his mama and papa.

"But both of them suffer from an onslaught of exhaustion. That's why your elemen can barely talk now," the medic said.

Kreesha made a faint smile at them all, since she was indeed too tired to speak. Graham patted her cheek to reassure her that she did not need to. "So what is the cause of their illness?"

"A group of chemicals called troptomyces. These are not microbes or viruses, but troptomyces are abnormally strong. They can definitely penetrate through any ordinary lab shield, especially if it was a kiddy chemical set shield."

Graham wanted to ask them about the strange collection of chresins, but he asked instead, "How long will the medicine take to help them fully recover?" The medics had previously fed Kreesha, and force-fed the sleeping Lark, some bluish-purple liquid.

"It depends. But most patients only take one decaweek. However, if you're talking about the general fatigue syndrome, that should only take a hexaweek." On Drell, instead of a seven-day week, they counted in terms of a ten-day week, called a "decaweek," or a six-day one, called a "hexaweek."

"Will the recovery time be different for adults and children?"

"It may be faster for children, but as your elemen is still quite young, she will recover very quickly as well, don't worry." The middle-aged woman then shot him an even more serious look. "But may we ask that you bring us to your house to remove the green unknown substances?"

"Of course." Graham was wondering when they would do that, and help him get rid of the chresins while they were at it.

When the medics left, he rested Kreesha on his arm instead of his shoulder, as she was slipping off. He spoke soothingly to her, repeating what the medics said about her getting better. It'll all be over soon, I promise, he said. And he glanced anxiously at his sleeping son. The previously anguished expression on Lark's face seemed to have relaxed. He did not look happy, but at least he seemed at peace. The medicine was probably taking effect. Soon, Kreesha would be able to walk, talk, and be herself again too.

Four days later, in the morning, Kreesha had her arms round Graham and they were still drowsing in their bed. They gradually awoke and Kreesha kissed him softly on the lips. "Get up, baby. And don't worry, I've got almost all my strength back, I can breathe better than I could four days ago, and the migraines don't come so often anymore either. And even if they do, they're not as strong as before."

He stroked her hair. Thank goodness his darling was indeed getting better. He was watching her complexion recover more and more of its bloom over these four days. Of course, Graham, being his elemen's devoted mate, was probably imagining things when he saw the "increasing bloom" in her face, because really, how many gradations were there of facial bloom? So the two lay there together for some time more; and they stroked, patted, and kissed to comfort one another. They didn't need to hug because they were already in an embrace.

In the other room, before school time, Lark Arias was already up and reading. He stood his silver-rimmed electrospace on a floating panel, and sat in a dark green orb chair.

(See "Orb Chairs[1]" under "Objects" and "Household objects and places.")

Graham had finally permitted him to go to school on this fourth day. This time Lark wasn't reading about science, surprisingly. He was reading for his other subjects in school, as he wanted to catch up for the lost time when he was sick.

What he was reading at this moment was a story about a little boy who was climbing a building, by grasping vines. Lark wondered how he could do that. Even an athlete would find such clinging hard without technology, and he remarked on the silliness of literary stories in general. When the little boy in the story went over the wall, triumphed, but then fell and hit his head, Lark rolled his eyes and thought: you deserved it.

Lark seemed to be a very callous fellow. Yet, it was possible that he wasn't really callous, that he was just unconsciously hiding his real feelings even from himself. He was possibly completely human and capable of empathizing with others deep down. Still, it would be hard to explain away the yawns that frequently came to him while he read these stories.

⸻

ABOUT THE GREEN SUBSTANCE, THE MEDICS HAD BEEN astonished at what happened, and said that they couldn't believe the Arias's would let their five-year-old son play with such dangerous chemicals as that. Graham hastily explained to them that all he and his mate bought him were toy chemicals, which were guaranteed to be safe.

"Guaranteed?" said the middle-aged woman medic. "There are risks with any chemicals, no matter how protected they may seem on the surface. You have seen the consequences of this playing." The medic had such a severe facial expression that she could easily have been Graham's mother, and Graham indeed felt like an awkward and cowed son in front of her. As a matter of fact, Graham and Kreesha were both still very young, in their late twenties. He was twenty-nine and she was twenty-eight.

Graham then explained to the medic that apart from his toy chemicals, Lark also had a pink chemical that he got for his "friend." It did not occur to Graham that Lark might have used par-the-air in his creation of the green substance. Graham only mentioned this pink chemical since the medics were here and Lark was asleep, so that these experts could test what it was once and for all.

The medics were expectedly very curious to see what he meant by this "pink chemical." In fact, they demanded to see it, but Mr Arias said they would have to find it themselves in his son's room as he had no idea where Lark had hid it.

Upon hearing that, the middle-aged man and woman medics, as well as their team of helpers, grunted and went into Lark's room; they were protected by special screens that their computers had generated. The medics had already screened Graham, his mate, and his son before they came to the Arias's house.

Now Graham got to survey Lark's room himself. That green substance was even more frightful up close, and to his disgust, but not to his surprise, several clusters of chresins now festered in his son's room, even in some places where there was no green substance.

He couldn't resist asking the medics about them this time, and they replied, "Chresins are very attracted to troptomyces chemicals." They didn't explain why there would be such pests in the urban area when they should all have been banished in the first place, but Graham thought that they would be very annoyed if he asked such an irrelevant question, so he didn't.

The medics gestured to each other to take certain medical weapons. But first of all, they turned off Lark's lab shields. They blasted the walls and ceilings with their weapons and gradually the green substance peeled away; the chresins scuttled away too. Whilst some of the medics were cleaning the Arias's house, some others were looking around Lark's room for his pink chemical.

Graham was, in truth, not very happy that these strangers were snooping about in his son's room, but at this moment, Lark's and his elemen's safety were more important than the preservation of privacy, he told himself; but still he could not help feeling quite unsettled by this thorough searching and scouring of his son's room.

To everyone's surprise, no one could find Lark's chemical.

"Your son must be very smart," said the middle-aged female medic, with a sardonic smile.

"Couldn't you scan for the chemical?" Graham asked.

"You think scanning for them is so easy? We first of all have to know what exactly the chemical is, not just that it's pink. Plus, chemicals that are put in secure containers, which I have no doubt this chemical is, are extremely difficult to detect."

Graham frowned. "But couldn't you just detect the container then?"

The medic laughed at him again, and in a very maternal tone, replied, "You think detecting anything is so easy? Let's see you try it! We have to know what exactly this kind of container is, and what its materials are."

"But aren't there only a few common materials that make up these containers?"

The medic looked at him. "Young man, you don't know much about science and chemistry, do you?" Graham shook his head sadly. "Nowadays, containers can be made out of anything! Provided that they're layered by inertizers, and that the materials are relatively sturdy and hard to break. Understand?" Graham nodded, whilst hoping that she would stop mothering him.

So, after a few more moments of fruitless searching, the medics gave up and left. They only bid Graham look after his son and elemen, ensure that they took their medicine at the set times, and that they both got enough rest, water, fruits, and vegetables. Graham was half expecting them to say "get enough exercise" too, but he then brushed that thought off as silly, and anyway, the medics didn't mention it.

IN THE PRESENT MOMENT, LARK WAS MOPING BECAUSE HE thought it was absolutely stupid to keep studying this story he was reading, but he had to do it.

As he read, he constantly criticized the protagonist for being abnormally dim, but perhaps that was realistic because human beings in this world were so stupid anyway, he thought. Lark did sometimes imagine a world where everyone was exceptionally bright like him. How would he feel in such a society? Accepted? Happy? Or would his sense of superiority be threatened? But did he really need to feel superior?

Lark imagined that an alternative reality where no one was stupid could be quite interesting, but he didn't evaluate whether it would be a good thing for him or not. Perhaps one advantage of that different universe was that his privacy would be more respected; nobody would ever intrude upon him again, and he would live in eternal bliss as a consequence.

But would it really make him that happy to have complete independence and solitude? Lark was a very withdrawn person, who desired nothing but the continual study and discoveries in science, and he honestly did not need people, except to satisfy his physical needs like shelter and food—like from his parents. However, I'm not quite convinced that Lark would be completely independent of human beings emotionally. Wouldn't he, to some extent, feel deprived if people around him, his parents, everybody, were gone from him?

Lark did sometimes fantasize about a world where he was the only human being existing. He imagined that with a naïve happiness. At least, I think it was naïve. He probably didn't understand himself. There was no evidence to suggest that "natural obsessors" like him would be able to feel emotionally healthy in a world with absolutely no human beings, because such an experiment would require every human being to die, which was obviously unethical.

So what I propose is that the apparent antisocial-ness of these "natural obsessors" was not as extreme as some may think. Perhaps Lark thought that he wanted absolute silence and solitude because there was so much stimulation and bustle around him. But if his surroundings had no social stimulation at all, would he still welcome that supreme silence?

I often still speculate on whether poor Larky would ever make a friend. Perhaps he would one day even befriend Karrin and others who desired his friendship. Maybe he would develop more modesty towards his parents. I would not expect him to become an effusively affectionate child towards Kreesha and Graham, but he, maybe, could become someone who was more understanding and accepting? He likely wouldn't become very warm and friendly towards his parents, but perhaps he would become less cold?

Lark now glanced at the time keeper that was in the computer network, and leapt up to go to school. He could very well walk to school, but he preferred to take a transport. However, his parents, though very permissive in general, demanded that he walk. They even threatened (very contradictory to their expected reactions, but you know, people contradict themselves all the time) that they go with him to school if he took a transport.

Lark could take a transport without his parents knowing, but he needed to save enough money to buy the books and chemicals that he needed. The money that his parents gave him wasn't generous, though it wasn't too modest either. He decided that doing a bit of physical exercise for a short while was a worthy sacrifice to make in exchange for a lot more intellectual nourishment.

Meanwhile, at the Treeks' place, Hlen and his elemen had gotten hold of the Arias's contact code by asking the school. Normally, the school would not reveal such personal information to other parents, but when Hlen and Ella explained that it was for a very urgent matter, though they could not reveal the details, the school relented and gave them the code.

Hlen gripped his fists in anxiety whilst his mate tried to calm him down with a hand on his shoulder. "Relax, Hlen. If you can't, let me deal with it."

Hlen said that it was all right and he could do it himself. Ella shrugged and let him proceed.

Very soon, a 2D image of Graham appeared. Kreesha was away preparing herself for work. Graham was astonished that he was looking at Hlen Treek—after the latter introduced himself—and Graham gave him a friendly smile.

Hlen Treek went straight to the point and told the other father about the dubious circumstances that led to the acquisition of the "pink chemical." Graham shivered inside. "Mr Treek, please tell me more."

THE BOY WHO LOVED SCIENCE TOO MUCH

But Hlen did not have any more to tell, except the story that the man gave about Haus needing this par-the-air chemical in order to "do averagely" or "decently" in this "annual poetry competition" with his friends.

"Poetry competition?" exclaimed Graham.

Hlen nodded. "It's completely nonsensical, isn't it?" Graham nodded too, though he liked poetry; but it was just pathetic for someone to rely on chemical means to enhance their intellectual capacities for poetry instead of on their own abilities, even if they lacked them.

Graham also wondered whether there were chemicals that enhanced emotions and sensibility, because these sensitivities and perceptivities were clearly more important for writing great poetry than "intellectual" ability. Graham, moreover, did not appreciate how some people demeaned poetry by thinking that it was a competition. Poetry was not about competition; it was about a free expression of oneself. How could some people not understand that?

The parents now discussed that they should find out where Lark was going and stop him before he did anything silly. That was obvious, but people sometimes had to say the most obvious things to get their thoughts organized before they felt confident enough to do anything.

KARRIN TREEK AT THIS MOMENT WAS WONDERING WHAT Lark was thinking while the latter was reading yet another book. Karrin was relieved that his classmate was back at school and he asked Lark how he was and what happened. Karrin got only brief replies that Lark had been "sick," but Lark refused to elaborate. This mystery intrigued Karrin, and he chatted with his other friends about this, including Eeera. Eeera was the chief person he liked to speak to on matters concerning Lark.

BACK TO HLEN AND GRAHAM. THEY DID NOT THINK THAT they should do anything as drastic as to call the Order, because that may prove to be making a mountain out of a tiny sand hill. What if there wasn't anything the matter after all? Perhaps Lark had really found himself a friend at last.

Kreesha later came into their conversation, and slapped a hand on Graham's shoulder, at which the latter did not flinch, because he was used to her habit of slapping his shoulder without warning; and he really did not mind because this only proved her affection towards him. Kreesha initially widened her eyes when she found out that they were talking to the father of Lark's classmate; the couple had never talked to the parents of their son's classmates before, as their son had never befriended anyone.

"Graham," she was careful not to say "Grae Grae" in front of someone who did not know them well, in fear of embarrassing him. In truth, Graham would probably not have minded much. "Why don't we monitor Larky? He could really have some trouble coping with whatever he's in right now. It's possible that he really made a new friend at last but then is so desperate to maintain this friendship that he's willing to do anything this new friend wants and so he—" She paused to catch her breath.

Hlen then remembered, and added what Ella had said about how the "friend" was probably giving Lark something concerning science and chemistry, since Lark loved these subjects so much.

In the end, the parents concluded that they indeed must do something to help poor Lark cope with whatever he got into, and so they launched a plan that did not involve the Order.

---

1. **Orb chairs**
   These chairs mold themselves perfectly around the sitter's back to ensure maximum comfort, and have armrests as well; but they can't change shape or size like stretch seats can. Nevertheless, orb chairs are beautiful, smooth, and full of grace, just like a tough but supple jelly.

EIGHT
RARERUS

After school, Lark immediately went with his par-the-air to Haus. To his great dismay and disappointment, the man was not there.

Lark paced in front of the shop counter with both fury and agitation.

Graham and the other parents had wanted to monitor Lark, by secretly contacting Karrin and asking if he could follow Lark. Karrin was going to—from a distance, but then Eeera pulled him aside to help a little boy who was crying.

"But I need to—" started Karrin.

"You need to what?"

"Um..." But Karrin couldn't tell her because he promised his dad not to reveal what they were doing to anyone, especially as they did not even know what was going on, and that this matter seemed very important to Lark. So Karrin hurried over to that crying boy and talked to him soothingly. He was a small boy, in both height and skinniness. Karrin was of average size, and Lark of average height but very skinny.

Karrin's friends often went to him to be comforted when they were down. He was pleased that so many people trusted and depended on him, but sometimes it really became too much: too long, too frequent, or too intense. But maybe he was still a very young boy, that he didn't know how to reject these requests for assistance. He asked his dad what to do when this happened and Hlen told him to just refuse politely. "Tell them honestly that you're busy or can't take it anymore. Since they're your friends, they'll understand."

Hlen seemed to imply that since Karrin's friends probably didn't understand, they were not really friends. Karrin felt a tiny bit of this insinuation, but he was not consciously aware of this hidden message. Yet, the next time someone asked for his help, he never had the heart to refuse them. He sympathized with them too much.

And so, after helping that little boy, Karrin was not surprised to find that Lark had already long gone, and when Karrin returned home, he gloomily reported to his father what happened and that he had failed in following Lark. Hlen sighed, but muttered that he hoped Lark didn't try to do anything. When he saw the guilt-ridden look on his son's face, he patted his shoulder and said, "Don't worry about it. You're just a very good friend, that's all." The boy was slightly cheered by this, but not much cheered.

Karrin brooded on this more at home, still burdened with self-blame, and he worried about what would happen to his classmate. And worry he should indeed, if he knew what Lark was about to get into.

The latter, meanwhile, was still stalking impatiently in front of Haus's serving panel, expecting someone to appear. As was Lark's habit during nervous moments, he thought about recent scientific discoveries in chemistry, biology, physics, and even mathematics.

But today, he couldn't seem to focus on anything except for that strange par-the-air, and his amosti, and how mixing the two combined to form a green chemical to make him sick. And why was it related to his parents' Ruminence? If at all? And the medics saying that it was all because of troptomyces?

He mused, analyzed, reasoned, and hypothesized, trying his best to unravel, or at least make some sense out of this whole labyrinth of a mystery; but to no avail. After a very long while—or at least, it seemed long to him—Haus was still not there.

Lark wanted to wait a bit longer, because he really wanted those chemicals and as quickly as possible. Who knew when his parents would find out what he was really doing, or when this man would withdraw his offer? But it was really taking too long, and Lark was conscious that he was wasting precious time that could be spent on studying, learning, and pondering; so with great reluctance and much frustration, he turned around for home.

But just at that moment, a familiar voice called his name. The man he had been waiting for had finally come out of the backroom.

"Little boy! You came!" Haus said. He looked jollier and more affable than usual today, for some reason.

Without smiling, Lark handed over the par-the-air, thinking that it was finally over, that he could get all those free chemicals to take home at last, and maybe even get the most dangerous, and rarest chemicals in the world to do a gazillion tests and investigations on; imagine what he could be capable of in the future. He would be unstoppable from now on!

As these thoughts and fantasies whirled through his mind, Lark was staring fixedly, with his characteristic lack of social sensitivity, at Haus, expecting feverishly that dramatic moment when he would finally get what he wanted, when he heard Haus laugh and say, "Oh no, no, no, my boy. You can keep the par-the-air! You'll find it more useful than I would myself."

Lark was aghast and confused. "What do you mean?" He wondered if this was some trick or if Haus was just teasing him.

The man beamed—with a noisome smile, thought Lark—and explained, "I'm sorry for fooling you all along, but I had to make up a story—"

"You made up a story?" Lark should have guessed. He was mad at himself for not realizing it earlier. He was even more enraged at himself for his naivety than at Haus for deceiving him. What was going to happen to his limitless supply of chemicals now?

"Let me finish, please. You see, me and Marius, that man you met in Phuore, needed to recruit. We put you on this mini mission of getting par-the-air to test both your wits and courage. You know, we wouldn't be able to tell how brave, resourceful, or determined you are just by interviewing you! We had to see if you had the personality traits and smarts to help us," Haus finally blurted out with a large grin.

Lark was open-mouthed. "What sort of recruitment are you talking about?"

"Well, Lark, my friends and I are involved in a secret mission against— I will tell you later. We need someone who's brilliant in chemistry. But not an adult, because he would just dismiss us as silly. You, on the other hand, are perfect. Still a child, and only five years old, but already an accelerated prodigy in chemistry. Just envision what you will be able to do by the time you're an adult!"

Lark was flattered by the truth of that statement, but he nevertheless said, "How do you know that I would not dismiss whatever it is you want me to do as silly as well?"

Haus smiled. "As un-childlike and unsmiling as you always seem to be, I know that you wouldn't turn down our invitation. So what do you say to joining my friends, Marius, and I in our underground secret force?"

"You have not even explained what your 'secret force' does, nor even what it is called, nor of what kinds of members it is composed." And Lark added, "Nor if there are any other children in your secret force."

The man smiled apologetically. "There are children, I promise. But none are as young or as ingenious as you are. We are the Rarerus team, and we unite as one to combat what are called the Arach."

Notwithstanding that "Rarerus" sounded like the comical and pompous "rare-are-us" (this pun worked in the Drellian language as well), Lark bid him define an "Arach."

"Gladly. You see, the Arach are alien parasites from an unknown planet which we believe may or may not be from our universe. And these Arach, among us now, are aiming to turn—more and more humans into antimatter."

"Antimatter?" Lark had very often wondered what turning a living being, himself, or one of those other human beings, into particles of the same mass but opposite electrical charge—antiparticles—would be like. "What happens when the Arach succeed with this—"

"We call it antimattering."

"—antimattering?"

"Yes, I know it sounds fantastical, but—"

"What happens to human beings and other life forms when they are antimattered?" Lark demanded.

Haus now looked uncomfortable. "Uh...you don't want to know, kid."

"But I insist that you tell me, or else I will refuse to join your—Rarerus."

Now it seemed like it had come to a stalemate. But eventually, Haus groaned. "I don't really want to tell you, because you're only five and—well, antimattering a person has something to do with disintegration. Please. I don't want to say any more about that."

Lark let the information sink in, then he asked, "What do you do to prevent the Arach, then?"

"Oh no, not so fast. I haven't explained everything to you yet." Lark listened. "You see," It was very annoying how Haus had a constant need to say "you see," and Lark obviously did see without Haus asking him to do so, "since the Arach are viruses, your naked eye will never detect them. They get onto your body and lay a web egg on you, and this egg erupts and spreads its web until it covers your whole body. And during this whole time, you won't be able to see or feel anything.

"Then they hypnotize you so that you will walk to an unknown place —to their chambers underground where they use special gases to solidify that web on you. After twenty-four hours, when it fully solidifies, you're anti-mattered," he said. "What we can do is use some of the octamethyst to digest and annihilate their webs. But this only works before the web fully solidifies in those twenty-four hours."

"So this is where the octamethyst comes into play," Lark mumbled. "Then what about all those other chemicals you mentioned? The brachiorsor, the trichloroes?"

Haus grinned. "You'll learn about those soon enough."

"Then what about this par-the-air that I got for you? Were my efforts all for naught? Was this chemical merely to 'test' my wits and courage and to keep me intrigued before you 'invited' me to your shady group?"

"Woah, woah, woah," Haus put out his hands. "Cool it, kid."

"Please do not call me by diminutives."

"Oh. Sorry. I'm used to calling kids as kids." He shrugged.

"Then just refrain from doing so for me, if you please," Lark said with exemplary politeness.

Haus shrugged again. "Sure. As for the par-the-air, it's for you to keep and study at your pleasure." He grinned. "So, would you like to join our group now?"

He still didn't strike Lark as a man on a serious mission, but Lark was genuinely curious. He didn't nod, but he said, "Show me your hideout, and then I will decide whether or not I will join."

"Suit yourself. Come with me." Lark was surprised that his request was so readily granted, and the boy padded after him into the electric-blue room housing the brachiorsor. Haus whispered a command to a computer and a door opened on the opposite side of the room from where they were standing. "Come in."

The new room they entered, which was both long and wide, had shifting lights of lilac and periwinkle blue, which was rather discomforting. There was a man sitting in the center of the room on a stretch seat next to a floating panel. It was expectedly the old man from Phuore, Marius. The old man waved lightheartedly to them. "Hi, Lark! I'm so glad you decided to join us—"

Lark clarified that he had actually not decided to join yet until he was allowed a full scrutiny of their compound.

"Okay," said Marius, his cheerfulness unflustered. "Actually, this is only one branch of our organization—the Dillois (pronounced "Dill-lwah") branch. Our Center is in Vénus."

Dillois was the city where Lark, Karrin, and Eeera lived, and Dillois was in the Fartha Sector. Vénus was the capital sector of Drell, as well as the most affluent sector. Many important intersector events and organizations took place in, and were established, there. So the Rarerus also being in the capital did not at all surprise let alone impress Lark. And while this old man was happily prattling on about some irrelevant details of their organization that did not interest Lark in the least, the boy glanced around the room for any other doors or openings. There appeared to be none.

Eventually, Marius stopped delineating the types of metal and materials used to design the walls and furniture of their establishments, as well as the perfection of their aesthetic use of colors on every surface of their buildings. You may have expected Lark to care about the building materials, because it should be related to chemistry, but he didn't this time. All Marius told him was about the standard, mundane, completely expected way of constructing buildings that Lark already knew all about. He had waited very patiently for the man to finish off his ebullient detailing of these insipid matters.

"Okay, Lark. Time for you to get to know us. Haus and I are two members on the Scythe level. Ahem. Our Rarerus society is organized into five levels of authority. On the first and topmost level, is our wonderful leader, Liara Grae." Her last name reminded Lark disturbingly of his father's first name Graham and his mother's last name Blé; and "Liara" (pronounced "Lee-air-rah") reminded him of his own name, Lark Arias. This leader already gave him the creeps.

Marius's eyes had filled with glittering stars after uttering their Rarerus leader's name; when the stars finally cleared, he continued, "The second level right below her are the Beams. Two people are on this level. Next, the third level are the Spikes. Three people on this level. Level four, us the Scythes, four people. And finally, level five, the Drills, of five people. All other members have no commanding power but they are nevertheless loved, accepted, and respected as part of our family."

I see, thought Lark. "Where are the children in this—organization, then?" he asked.

Marius and Haus faced him with wide grins. The former turned to the latter. "Did you tell him yet?" Haus shook his head. Marius said to Lark, "Did you know that there are only two children in the Rarerus so far? And that they are the two Beams?" He beamed. "Liara likes children better than adults, we sometimes think. But we don't mind, because we too like children better than adults, even though we love the other adults too."

"How old is your leader?" Lark asked.

An ordinary person would have thought this question exceedingly rude, but Marius didn't seem to mind, and he said, "Seventeen."

Lark was dismayed. "Then she is also a child. There exists an organization where a child can lead?"

"Eh, it depends on what age you define one to be an adult. Even if we say twenty, why, she's only three years shy of becoming an 'adult,' and she's doing a fine job in organizing our missions so one must not be ageist." It was very obvious that they were ageist anyway by their all favoring children over adults. And about ages, one had to be twenty to be considered an "adult," and Drellian years were also longer than Earthly ones.

(See "Calendar Days, Months, and Years[1]" under "Time" and "Quantitative Measures.")

"Anyway," Marius continued, "if you want to know, our previous leader, Jax, was also seventeen when he first ruled. He is now thirty, and no longer wanted to rule because, uh—uh—"

"Maybe because he was too tired of all the responsibility?" suggested Haus.

"Yeah, probably. He didn't say. I know what you're thinking, Lark. No, we do not always elect seventeen-year-olds as our new leaders. They can be of any age, as long as the current leader thinks they are fit for the job to take over after they retire."

"And Jax is now out of the five levels. He is without a level," Lark said.

"Not exactly. He's now one of the seniors. The seniors are those who used to be leaders, or they are respected wise people who have decided to help the Rarerus. The seniors, of course, do not have to be at least the age of thirty. Some are in their twenties."

There was still something Lark didn't understand. "How old are the two child Beams?"

"Oh, one's a girl, aged twelve, Amber. The other's her little brother, aged eight, Eventii (pronounced even-TIE)."

"Nobody else in the society are seventeen or younger?"

"None."

"Then none of the adults in this society ever had children who became part of this society?" Lark asked. "All the children who happen to be here were invited from outside Rarerus?" You might not have expected Lark to ever think about such social logistics, but well, this was all just a system to him, no matter social or chemical, and he just had an instinctive urge to understand systems to the full.

"Oh." It was evident that Marius had never thought that Lark would ask this. Marius looked to Haus for help, but the latter just shrugged and returned the look.

So, Marius helplessly added, "Actually, most of us in the Rarerus are single and many choose to stay single, because none of us want to—come to love someone more than our own life, only to see them, um, anti-mattered, you know?"

He muttered something about romantic love making one blind to all the beloved's flaws and problems too; but Lark didn't see this muttering as important, so he ignored it.

"And," Marius went on, "we also rarely recruit those who are already married or romantically involved with someone, for the same reason. But of course there are exceptions. You will see a few married couples there."

"So the children of these married couples are automatically in the Rarerus," Lark said, thinking that if it were so, then how could the three children be the only children there?

"Uh—not really. A couple who is in the Rarerus keeps it a secret from their children as well because—the fewer the people who know about the Arach, the better. Those who know are constantly in danger for their lives, if they aren't antimattered instead."

Something occurred to Lark. "Do the Arach have specific targets? And what are they trying to achieve? Do they attack everyone who comes within reach? How would—"

"Hold on," Marius said. He chuckled—Lark did not like chuckling people. "The Arach are a sentient species. (Yup, five-year-olds in Drell already knew what 'sentient' meant, among a thousand other things.) They never attack randomly. If they did, everybody on Drell would be gone by now." Here, Lark wondered what he meant by "gone." "Instead, the Arach have certain...plans. There are patterns to the people they choose to attack, but we are not sure what. We just sense a pattern. What makes it hard is that we only discover a small percentage of their targets. Liara estimates that we only find ten percent of their targets—"

"How did she come up with that number?"

"Ugh, go ask her yourself. I'm not a math whiz." This disappointed Lark, but he let the old man go on. "Despite our lack of knowledge on how they target victims, we know for certain that they have some important motive behind all this."

Lark couldn't resist saying, "How do you know that every Arach does not actually have different individual motives in approaching their victims, and that is why you find it so exceedingly difficult to identify a single, collective pattern to their targeting? The Arach, I assume, are individuals after all, not just pieces of a coordinated system."

Marius looked like he didn't want to deal with any more of these kinds of questions. He looked troubled. Lark sighed inside at this man's uselessness. Marius just mumbled, "Maybe you're right. But why don't you just ask Liara?" He cleared his throat and tried to regain some of his former dignity—which, to Lark, had never even existed from the start.

Marius continued, "We're not really sure what their big motive—or motives—to antimatter certain people are. We don't even know what exactly happens to people when they are antimattered. Some brave scouts who have broken into Arach chambers and survived told us that they couldn't see any signs of the human victim. The victim was just all gone. Except they sometimes left some hair, or some skin particles that we detected. But this basically means the victims left nothing behind because everybody sheds dead skin particles and hair all the time."

"And you have been investigating this matter for how many years?" Lark asked.

"More than thirty years," Marius said with shame. "Yet, scientists often investigate a phenomenon for way longer than thirty years and still don't find any answer, right?"

"I suppose so," said Lark. This analogy did make him despise their Rarerus society less. There was really something magical about Lark and the word "scientists."

Marius continued, "Now when a person is antimattered and disappears, the Arach must cover up their tracks and get a replacement for the vanished victim, so their friends, family, and colleagues won't find out."

"Replacements...as in clones?" Lark asked.

"Clever boy," Haus said.

Marius went on, "Yes, and you know how the Arach do that?"

Lark sniffed. "This is an elementary question. Any ordinary child of my age knows this, let alone myself. The Arach obviously simply collect a bit of the victim's DNA—from a strand of hair, some skin—and create the clones. But how do the Arach imitate their victim's habits? An individual's actions and speech are not entirely determined by their genes."

"Well, you might not believe me, but the Arach seem to have discovered a way to suck out the essences of the victim's minds and souls so that the clone can imitate them to perfection."

Lark gaped. "That is not possible! Even the most advanced scientists cannot replicate a person's mind, let alone their soul. A person's 'essence' is precisely called so because it is essential to them and cannot be pulled out of their body."

But Marius just shook his head. "We have to admit, our Drellian scientists are not very advanced, after all, because these alien viruses have found a way to do it."

This actually left Lark quite agitated. "Perhaps the Arach have not really extracted the person's essence. Perhaps they have simply discovered a way to imitate the victim's habits and idiosyncrasies by—working out the person's neuronal and glial firing rates, among other things."

"Whatever." Marius shrugged. It was evident that Marius and Haus were people who did not really care about the exact science and mechanisms behind things; they were more into practical applications and what they actually did. Lark no doubt looked down on people who only cared about what they did and didn't use much brain power. It was unthinkable how one could not bother to figure out all the exact logical intricacies of how all involved systems worked in a given situation. "Anyway," Marius said, "would you like to know how we can detect whether or not a person is an Arach clone?"

"Yes, of course. That was what I was about to ask," Lark said.

"This is a very straightforward process. You may remember, the four DNA bases in a human being are—"

"Guanine, cytosine, adenosine, and thymine," Lark said impatiently. "And?"

"And Arach DNA, fortunately, contains, in addition to these four bases, two other bases—bluamine and zanyliline. So, ATCG and now BZ."

"So all you have to do is take a bit of the person's DNA and check if there are any Bs and Zs," Lark said. He guessed from what Marius had just said that the Arach viruses must be retroviruses of some sort. In other words, viruses who had the ability to turn their RNA back into DNA and to insert their DNA into the host, where the latter would be the human clone.

Marius and Haus also assumed that he guessed this already, and Marius was just glad that he did not have to explain all those scientific details himself. But he added, "Yes, so the Arach use the DNA they have inserted into the clone to control the clone."

Lark nodded curtly because that was the most obvious conclusion in the world.

Now Haus said, "And since I've already told you about the octamethyst, I say we give your brain a break for now. Phew, that was a real information overload, huh?"

Lark frankly did not mind the "information overload," because he filled his brain with info nonstop during all of his free time anyway. He was like a super-efficient machine that would never stop taking in and processing information, a very info-greedy machine. Lark wanted these two men to continue so he conjured up half a million questions in his head, but one question in particular stood out to him.

Lark asked, "Yet, have any Rarerus members ever asked the Arach what their motives are, or what happens to the antimattered victims?"

Marius squeezed his eyes shut with both pain and aggravation. "Yeah, some of us have asked. But none of the Arach clones we've talked to could give us a straight answer, because the Arach apparently are very careful with their information. None but the central control Arach know what the true motives, purposes, are, let alone what antimattering exactly does to victims. None of the Arach clones know who these central control Arach are either, except for the central controls themselves. But the central control Arach's commands are still distributed to their subordinates." Marius paused. "Their motives must be some deep, dark thing if they have to be kept that secret!"

Lark thought of another matter. "You cannot speak directly to the Arach? You must speak through Arach clones?"

Marius nodded. "Unfortunately, that's right. Well, it's possible that, with some years—or centuries—of investigation, we will be able to work out Arach language to communicate with the viruses directly. But as the Arach viruses never speak to us directly via their own language anyway, I don't see that ever happening."

Lark frankly thought Marius was being rather pessimistic; yet, being able to talk to the viruses directly probably would not provide them with any more enlightening information, unless the Rarerus could decode Arach virus language such that the Rarerus could "eavesdrop" on the viruses' conversations, and garner secret intelligence from the Arach world.

In fact, Lark was uncertain whether or not this "ignorance of the Arach's true motives" was just a cover story the Arach clones were all commanded to tell. Who knew if they were lying or not? And perhaps the Arach all did have individual motives, but they had simply learned to work together as a species to keep all of their individual motives and intentions a secret.

Yet, before Lark could voice these thoughts, Haus heaved a sigh and said, "So would you like to go to Vénus to meet Liara?"

The boy glanced around in shock. "Does this mean that your branch here only consists of this small room?" The long and wide room that they were now in did not contain much, aside from some seemingly out-of-place emotographs on the walls, and strange curled gel or plastic-looking objects at their feet.

Emotographs were like our photographs, two-dimensional but displaying the emotion of the person in strongly expressive colors and shades. So something like a perfect mix of expressionist and realistic paint-ing. There was one picture of either Haus, Marius, or another man (the picture was too blurry) that was cyber blue—or rather, the blue of midnight. The expression on the man's face was either of despair or fear. Lark quickly looked away from this blue picture because it was unsettling him in a way he did not want to admit, and he did not enjoy intro-spection.

As for those gel or plastic-looking objects, they coiled around the humans' legs quite unpleasantly. Lark had not the remotest idea why the men would pave their floor with these. Maybe they thought these objects cushioned their legs comfortably?

Haus answered, "There is indeed more to our branch than what you see here, but—"

"You are not prepared to show me more," Lark said.

"Not exactly. It's more like you are not yet prepared to be shown more. We do not want to overwhelm your young mind with too much new stimuli at once."

"Just show me."

"You don't understand, we—"

"Just show me," Lark repeated.

Haus exchanged a glance with Marius. Then the former replied, "All right. But not today. Come back and visit another time." He paused and smiled. "So have you made your decision whether or not to join us yet?"

"I will make my decision, but not today," Lark mimicked.

So Haus resignedly led him out of this room, as well as the brachiorsor room, and back out into the shop. "Will you have time for another visit tomorrow?"

"I am not sure," said Lark, about to leave.

"Remember not to tell anyone about Rarerus, okay?"

"You have my word," the boy said casually, and left for home.

When Lark arrived back at the Arias's house, his parents interrogated him about why he came home later than usual. It was his misfortune that it was one of those days where his parents got to leave work early and were thus instantly aware of his absence. Lark mumbled something incoherent and attempted to retreat to his room.

A sad-eyed Kreesha stopped him, and Graham tailed him. "Sweetie," his mother said, "We're very worried about you, so we want to make sure you haven't been—meeting up with anybody we don't know."

Lark jolted inwardly at this, but thankfully his changed expression was well hidden as he was glancing down. "Mother, apart from this Karrin Treek and a few other of my classmates that you have managed to make me name in the past, you do not know any of the people I meet every day anyway," he said matter-of-factly.

"You know we don't mean that," said Kreesha, still sad-eyed. His father also annoyingly placed a hand on his shoulder, further restraining him. Lark would have roughly tossed his hand aside, but he knew that doing so would only make it even less likely for his parents to release him any time soon, so he bore with it. Kreesha said, "Larky, we'll be honest with you." She exchanged a glance with Graham. "We know about your par-the-air chemical and how you got it from Mr Treek."

Lark knew that his classmate's father was not to be trusted, after all. He felt no disappointment from this, however, because he never expected anything better from another pesky adult who was the father of a pesky classmate. She said, "So we are all very concerned that you might be trying to meet with this 'friend' of yours to give him your chemical. We don't know who this 'friend' may be, who would make you travel so far to get something that might be dangerous. And we also know that—you don't like to make friends."

Lark snatched on that instantly and said, "How do you know that I do not like making friends? I tell you I have finally made a friend, two friends, in fact, and they are both much kinder to me than the two of you put together!" With a burst of fury, he pushed past his astonished mother into his room and bolted the door.

He heard the voices of his parents outside. "He says he's really made a friend, and two as well! But these friends of his sound so dubious...and the par-the-air...the green...so strange..." The voices gradually drifted away as Kreesha and Graham walked off to talk somewhere else.

Lark was proud that he managed to lie once again by saying that he had indeed made friends. There was now hope that his parents wouldn't pry into his matters anymore. As irritating as they were, they were probably not as obnoxious as to stop him from "spending time with his friends," right?

But he did not realize the damage that was done by uttering that his "friends" were "much kinder" to him than both of his parents put together.

At this moment, Kreesha was crying and saying what a worthless and horrible mother she was; and Graham was crying and saying what a worthless and horrible father he was, and trying to comfort Kreesha at the same time. After a few more moments, the couple finally got tired of crying and stared with sorrow at each other instead. "Oh Grae Grae, what should we do? Our son is associating with shady friends that we haven't even seen before, and now he openly admits that he doesn't like us!"

Graham was clasping Kreesha's hands in his, and squeezing them to make her feel better. He didn't say anything for a while, and then he said, "We will just have to keep watch on him somehow. Relying on his classmate...didn't seem to help, so we may have to—" here he lowered his voice to a whisper, "survey him using our monitoring robots."

His elemen widened her eyes in shock. "But we would be intruding on his privacy. We can't do that no matter what!"

"But what other choice do we have?" asked Graham sadly. "If we don't intrude on his privacy, then we have no way of keeping him safe."

"Yes, but—how would you like to be secretly surveyed every moment of your life, Grae Grae?" Then realizing that she might have sounded too harsh, she softened her voice and said, "Sorry, I didn't mean to say it like that. It's just that we can't do this kind of constant surveillance on our son. Everybody deserves to have their privacy respected."

Graham sighed resignedly. "Then what do you suggest we do?"

She took her hands out of her elemen's grasp and closed her hands around his instead. "Why don't we—try to trust our son? We can ask him to always come home safe no matter what."

"Do you really think that will stop him from coming to harm, though?"

She bit her lip. "Not really." She looked down in concentration.

"What about—" the two elemens said at the same time. They glanced at each other.

"You can go first," Kreesha said.

"No, you go," Graham insisted, and even made a gracious gesture with his arm.

So Kreesha began slowly, "Um, this might sound—awful to you, but I thought maybe we could...give him an incentive not to go looking for those 'friends' by buying him real chemicals?"

"Real chemicals?" Graham cried out in shock.

"Yeah. That was what Lark wanted from the very beginning, right? Maybe we can ask how scientists could help us protect our son by...inoculating the real chemicals?"

"But not all chemicals can be inoculated. Some are just inherently more likely to burn or explode!"

"Then I don't know...," Kreesha said. "What about you? What was your suggestion?"

"I—" Graham blushed. "I simply thought we could give him more pocket money as an incentive." Drellian parents indeed also gave pocket money to their children.

"Oh," Kreesha laughed. "That's a better idea than mine. It's less dangerous. So let's do that."

Graham frowned. "But wouldn't you say that giving him more pocket money might make him greedier? At the moment our Lark is not materialistic, thank goodness. All he wants are books, chemicals, and knowledge. But giving him more money might—give him more temptations."

"Hmm, what about giving him more books? We could give him money that can only be spent on books. I've heard of that kind of money-configuring technology from my mom."

"Awesome!" Graham said with delight. "When do you want to get that device?"

"Tomorrow, as soon as we have time."

___

1. **Calendar Days, Months, and Years**

It takes Drell 25 hours (12.5 cores) to spin around once, which means that one day is 25 hours. One month is 30 days, as the closest moon, Iyis ("eye-yis"), takes 30 days to orbit Drell. Finally, one year is made up of 13 months, since Drell takes 13 months to orbit its sun.

To convert a Drellian age to an Earth one, first of all, one Drellian year is 13 months = 390 days = 9750 hours. One Earth year (assuming it's not a leap year) is 12 months = 365 days = 8760 hours. Thus, one Drellian year is 9750/ 8760 = 1.113 (approximately 1 and 1/9) times an Earth year.

The legal "adult" age is 20 Drellian years, which is 20(9750/8760) = 22.3 Earth years old. So you could say that Drellian adolescence lasts longer than ours.

NINE
RAOUL FAYA AND THE FONDAL

W hen school was over on the next day, Lark was looking forward to going to Haus's hideout again. Unfortunately, Karrin Treek popped up beside him and proceeded in his usual asking of "how do you do?" And Lark proceeded in his usual ignoring of this meaningless social convention. However, this time Karrin followed him as if he wanted to escort him home.

"Please go away," Lark was obliged to say. Be aware that Lark was not a polite person. He only used "please" when he thought that there was a greater chance of the other person complying with his request.

Karrin looked at him wistfully, but he didn't know what to say because he wasn't supposed to tell Lark that he needed to keep a watch on him. Instead, Karrin invented a lame excuse. "Oh, I was just thinking of inviting you to my house to play—"

"As I have told you many times in the past, I am not interested in going to your house. So please, I implore you, leave me alone."

That left Karrin feeling very glum. But then he tried something else. "Lark, I know you really like reading books. Why don't we go buy books together? I can pay for you."

This indeed tempted Lark, but he quickly regained his cool. "I am sorry, but I already have a great number of books. Now if you excuse me." Lark tried to rush past Karrin. But Karrin hurried after him. "Go away!" Lark cried.

Karrin was quite hurt at this loud rejection, even though he was used to these situations with Lark. Karrin was about to say something when he saw Eeera approaching them. Not another friend to comfort? Karrin thought grimly.

Thankfully, she wasn't. It turned out that Eeera only wanted to chat and accompany him home. Karrin was pleased partly because of this display of friendship, and partly because Eeera could help him prevent Lark from leaving. Now Lark tried to flee again but Karrin again overtook him, with a puzzled Eeera close behind. This time Lark did not pause for breath and kept running, as extremely tired as he already was after just a short distance. Not that this was a problem for Karrin and Eeera, because Lark really was that unbelievably slow when it came to running.

In despair, Lark let his two classmates walk him home. Eeera's house was closest to school, so she left first. But Karrin's house was farther than Lark's, so Lark had no way of abandoning him first to run off by himself. Along the way, Karrin tried hard to engage him in conversation but obviously he was met with no response from the silent and sulking Lark.

When they arrived at Lark's door, he said to Karrin, "Look, I am home now. You can stop looking at me and leave now." What Lark said was reasonable, thought Karrin. Lark was indeed home now, and had no more chance of getting into any mischief. So Karrin left for his home contented. He couldn't wait to tell his dad what a great job he did in seeing Lark home without his encountering any odd friends this time.

Lark opened his house's door. Surprisingly, it was silent. His parents were not home yet. They were out to buy a money configurator. With glee, Lark slipped out of his house again and sprinted, i.e. moved as fast as he could, towards the Dillois branch that was also Haus's shop. He glanced surreptitiously all around him to make sure pesky Karrin Treek wasn't around to spy on him.

"Lark!" an enthusiastic Haus cried out when he saw him. "You're back! Marius and I were hoping you would come today."

"Let us skip these preliminaries. Show me more of the Rarerus," Lark said.

Haus laughed. "Always so impatient. Wait, let me get Marius." He disappeared through the door to the brachiorsor room. When he returned, Marius accompanied him with a wide grin on his face.

"The branch closest to here that is a lot bigger than our Dillois one, is the Breemil branch." Which Lark took to mean that there wasn't much more to their Dillois branch than what he had already seen. Marius added, "Lark, are you excited to see it?"

Lark shrugged. He didn't care whether he was excited or not. He just needed to see more of Rarerus to see if he would indeed like to join their society. In all honesty, he wanted to join no matter what, because, though he adored his daily study of science, he also had a surprising hunger for adventure that he had never been aware of.

It was true that even natural obsessors could be interested in something other than their obsession. And Lark, no matter how eccentric he was, was still a kid inside who thirsted for thrill and possible danger. Well, maybe not danger, but something very new and challenging that was a complete break away from his normal life. Plus, the main reason why he wanted to join was probably because, though he enjoyed learning about science, he secretly yearned to apply his knowledge somewhere too, and here was his chance. He was not even afraid of the Arach, antimattering, or possible death.

When Haus and Marius were about to go with Lark outside, Haus got out a spray and made Lark invisible. "To keep you safe, we don't want anyone to see you with us. If the Arach see you, they might want to kill you." Lark was less alarmed by this threat to his life than about how Haus could procure the invisibility spray.

For ethical reasons, like the possibility of spying on people in private places or in their private homes, all Drellian civilians were forbidden from possessing such sprays. Anyone found carrying such an item could be arrested or even incarcerated. Lark was so shocked that he couldn't say anything. But after a few seconds, he unfroze and said, "You are carrying an illegal item. Are you not afraid of getting caught?"

Here Haus smiled. "Don't worry about it. To tell you the truth, the Order knows about our organization, so they sanction our use of this very nifty tool." He looked very proud of himself and his organization when he said that. "Let's go, dudes."

Lark furrowed his brow at being called a "dude." Drellians had a word that roughly corresponded to "dude"; it was also a colloquial and friendly way to refer to someone, whether young or old.

At this moment, Lark was worried that the three of them would be away for so long that his parents would come back home, know that he was missing, and start guessing his whereabouts. He told the two Scythes this, and also that his parents were already questioning him about his two "friends." At this, Marius beamed, "So we are your friends?"

Lark smirked. "No. I said that merely to delude my parents into thinking that I have finally made friends, in the hope that this temporary burst of happiness would throw them off my tracks."

Marius shrugged. He knew that the boy had not developed any real affection for the two older men. They were just old cronies, right? Well, Marius didn't care. Haus didn't care either. They got to do what they wanted, and they got to work for an intersectally important organization. What more could they ask for?

Haus said in reply to Lark's concerns that they would try to be as fast as possible in coming back, and that he understood what pressure it was on Lark to have to hide this from his parents, but he would just have to find ways to circumvent the obstacles and keep his operations a secret. Haus said this all without even looking at Lark. Lark was not one who cared about eye contact, but he still felt the inadequacy of Haus's answer.

Marius, however, said, "Are there any extracurricular activities you could say you're joining when you're out with us?" He chuckled nervously to himself as he knew that the Rarerus missions were in themselves extracurricular—out-of-school—activities.

Lark did not reply, until he said, "That may work. But I have never joined any 'extracurricular activities' before, so I will have to come up with a clever story to deceive my parents." It was true that he had never joined any activities in his life. His parents never forced him to, because they did not believe in coercing a child to do what he did not want to do. And also, while there were some science clubs, Lark so despised the teachers, supervisors, and students there because he had a lot more experience, knowledge, and understanding of science than any of them did. It would simply not be worth his while to associate with such inferiors. Even if he were not slowed by their dim minds during group investigation or learning activities, it was stupid to learn science in a room with others around him. He felt much more at ease and comfortable learning science at home all alone with his door tightly shut from all intruders.

On the topic of Lark's "superior mind," I want to point out that there was no such thing as being inherently "slower" or "quicker" minded than others. Speed of thinking depended on how much experience and knowledge you had on the topic you were thinking about. So it was perfectly logical that Lark would be the swiftest thinker because he had accumulated so many crystals of knowledge—so many little islands of ideas he could connect to help him solve problems.

The puzzles and problems in his class were always too easy and unstimulating, so he excelled in those with barely any effort. The teachers would often thus give him additional, more challenging problems to solve, which he liked better. Yet, even those more advanced problems were rather dry and unexciting compared to all the real fascinating problems that he discovered on his own while reading up on science, chemistry, and math.

Thus, the more knowledge you had in a given domain, the more mental elements you had to make associations between, to create new thoughts, insights, and ingenious solutions to problems in that particular domain.

Apart from a lack of domain-specific knowledge, the other kinds of possible "mental slowness" were fatigue and mental illness. For the former, thankfully, Drellian society was so advanced that they discovered a chemical means of increasing thinking speed to its optimum without any side-effects. By optimum, I mean that a person's thoughts wouldn't become too fast either as to make it hard for them to concentrate on anything. (See "Thinking Speed Restorers" and "Permanent Thinking Speed Enhancement Surgery for Mental Illnesses" for more details.)

When Lark said that he needed to think of a convincing reason to fool his parents into believing that he had finally taken up an extracurricular, it made both Scythes pause to think. Lark also explained how and why he refused to join any science groups. Marius said, "You couldn't say that you suddenly felt the need to join a science group, after all your past rejection of them?"

"What reason?" Lark asked, or rather demanded.

Marius was not at all annoyed at this boy's constant belligerence.

Haus, however, thought otherwise. Haus wasn't resentful of Lark or anything, but he did wish that the boy would get a grip one day and adopt a more cooperative tone; it was true that not all members of the Rarerus were sociable or approachable, but it was much easier to get along with those who were.

"Hmm," Marius mused, "can't you say something like: since you've found these two new friends, you're convinced that you've been lacking something in life, and that you have now decided you should go and connect with other people more, and possibly find like-minded peers?"

"That sounds likely," Lark said sarcastically.

Marius frowned. "It may not make sense to you, because, honestly, you don't understand the concept of social connection. But it will make sense to anyone with a normal social life. Your parents will definitely understand and be pleased with you."

Lark nodded, though not at all convinced. "Say I really do follow your...tactic. What do I do if my parents demand proof that I was really involved in a science club? What if they demand to see the club organizers and the club itself?"

Now Haus smiled. "Why, that's very easily taken care of. I could just ask our members to erect a science club here. And I'll find some innocent-looking faces so that they won't look like your two sketchy 'friends'."

But Lark still frowned. "Yet, since all your members, apart from the two Beams and Liara, are adults, my parents might get suspicious. If they want to see a science club, then it will have to be filled with many other children, preferably many of my age."

"Hmm, do they have to be your age?" Haus said ponderingly.

"Actually, Haus," said Marius, "we don't need to erect a science club from scratch. We already do have those science training centers for future recruits."

"But they are training centers, so they'll look too serious, too real. They won't look like science clubs. Plus, the closest one is so far from here," Haus said.

Marius looked annoyed. "Then you think of something. We could easily set up a 'science club' nearby, I suppose."

Then Haus really did have an idea. "Why don't we set up a science club, and then advertise for other children, maybe even Lark's classmates, to come join us? I know there are many science enthusiasts here," he said as he gave a sideways glance at Lark, implying: you're not the only one here, you know.

"What if my parents ask the other children if I come here often, to check if I have really been at the club?" asked Lark.

"Are your parents really the prying type?" Marius smiled. "I don't know how they're like, but from how indulgent they are to you to let you pursue your science and chemistry, how they buy you tons of toy chemicals and books, and how they never force you to do any extracurricular activities you don't like, they sound like pretty permissive parents, in a good way." You could say that Marius was kind of trying to praise his parents, to gain Lark's favor. But of course flattering his parents did nothing to please Lark as he did not care about how his parents were seen by others.

"They are not exactly prying, but they are intrusive. Every so often, they would knock on my bedroom door and demand that I come out to 'talk' to them; and every so often they would physically force me to go with them on their pointless trips and sports expeditions. But recently, yes, they have been abnormally and obnoxiously prying, constantly asking me about where I have been and what 'friends' I have been associating with."

"Your parents are just concerned about your safety, Lark," Marius said. Lark shrugged, nonchalant. "So what do we do?"

"Why don't we bribe the children?" suggested Marius.

Haus sniggered. "Really? Oh come on, couldn't you have thought of a more moral way of doing this?"

"Then do you have a better idea?" Marius said. To his satisfaction, Haus was speechless.

Lark was not amused at this incessant unhelpfulness. Of course, Haus and Marius were quite helpful so far, but we are apt to skew our perceptions to the wholly negative if things are not going completely our way.

The boy stared off into the distance. He wasn't thinking about arbitrary science things, for once. He was really trying to come up with a brilliant plan, and he was confident that he would find something.

"Are you sure we would not be able to ask your members' children— for the few who do have children—to join this forged science club? It would be easy to ask their children to report that I am frequently at the science club, and that I have been actively participating in those...social conversations," Lark grimaced at that idea. "Although it would be more convincing if those children also reported that I was socially awkward, and reluctant to speak at first, but that I gradually became friendlier and more willing to talk."

Marius marveled that Lark seemed to be more aware of his behavior than Marius would have thought. Yet, this self-awareness was not that remarkable; Lark had simply been parroting what his parents said to him about how he acted, and how they envisioned he would slowly change for the better one day.

Haus nodded. "Sounds like a sensible plan. I thought at first that any plan involving the other members' children would endanger them, but now I can see that they should not come to harm if this was merely staged as a science club." He thought some more. "If the Arach see that these children still have no knowledge about them or the Rarerus, they should not come after these children. And though this science club will be staged, we should make this genuinely a science club with all the proper facilities, books, science teachers, group discussions, and the like. This could be a chance for the parents to expose their children to science more and hopefully make them appreciate it more."

When he saw that questioning look on Marius's face, Haus anticipated what he was wondering, and added, "If there are some children who are completely averse to learning about science, then their parents could offer more pocket money or something, or think of some other incentive."

As the other two thought of no more flaws to this plan, for now, the trio walked with a greater peace of mind than before. Marius and Haus would discuss the logistics on how to open this science club. They would need to erect it as soon as possible.

———

THEY TOOK A HYURE FOR SOME DISTANCE. LARK WAS SILENT during the whole journey, as he had lost interest in talking to the two adults; instead, he delved back into his daydreams and ponderings about science and chemistry.

When they arrived, Haus told him that they were now at a place called Breemil; this was still in the Fartha sector where Lark and all his classmates lived. Lark nodded without caring in the least, though he whispered to his computer and electronic map to record this place in case he had to come here himself someday. Hearing Lark do so pleased Marius, as this was a sign that the boy had already decided to join the Rarerus.

Breemil was a place coated with a pleasant, verdant landscape of bluish-green grass. There were some buildings, but they were placed in quite aesthetically pleasing ways. Not that Lark could appreciate any of these aesthetics, though. He didn't even appreciate the loveliness of the blue-green lawn; it was simply the color of the general landscape, a neutral fact.

At length, they came to a little building, so little that it resembled a small shop. It was shaped in a regular rectangular prism, looking absolutely ordinary and unremarkable, except that its walls were all white. But this was not that peculiar either, because there was a good number of small buildings on Drell that were pure white. Lark assumed that the plainness of the shop-like building was to avoid attracting any unwelcome attention.

"Come in," Haus said, gesturing to Lark, before Haus disappeared through the doorway.

Lark frowned as he didn't need to be told. He would do so whether he was asked or not.

It was a regular bookstore, with the books shown via computer projections; like on Earth, they were displayed using book covers, some more beautiful, some less so, depending on your taste in covers.

A lady in her early thirties glanced up at them from her book. She looked only slightly older than Lark's mother. Haus and Marius quickly explained to the lady who Lark was, and their desire to see the Rarerus Breemil branch. The lady smiled at Lark, thinking, like all adults initially thought, that he was just the typical adorable child, until they were faced with his constant sulkiness and antisocial behavior.

"My name is Pree, nice to meet you." And she stuck out a hand, expecting him to shake it. He didn't want to shake it, but he wasn't stupid either. If she was a member of the Rarerus, she might have the power to

take revenge on his impoliteness in some way, so he had better not antago-
nize her—too much. Yet.

After a few more preliminaries, where Marius and Haus chatted with
Pree for a few more seconds, which felt like a few more cores to Lark,
Marius and Haus guided Lark through a hidden doorway. This resembled
what he had seen at Haus's chemistry shop.

As soon as he went in, he was surrounded by an overwhelming pink-
ness. It wasn't exactly pink; it was crimson and lilac, the flush of the
sunset. But of course Lark didn't much appreciate the beauty of sunsets
either, though he did appreciate the chemistry behind them. He understood the chemistry and physics behind aurorae too.

But honestly, thought Lark, was it just him, or were these Rarerus
people, or at least Haus and Marius, obsessed with the color lilac? Lilac
was much too close to pink.

(See paragraph on the lack of gender differences for favorite colors in
"Gender Expectations[1]," under "Gender Issues" and "Drellian Society.")

And once again, to Lark's dismay and displeasure, there were those
strange gel or plastic-looking curls all over the floor. They swam uncom-
fortably around his feet like bubbles. Well, they weren't as dense as
bubbles in a bubble bath, but they were still bouncing around and
touching him unpleasantly.

There were also emotographs on the walls, but to Lark's secret relief,
the picture of the man in fear or despair was not here. There were different
emotions of emotographs here, a real heterogeneity; but most of them
were in yellow and other happy and optimistic colors.

Lark also saw some...human beings sitting at panels, their faces either
lowered or looking straight ahead in a vacant gaze. It struck Lark that they
looked...defeated, or...faded. He grew suspicious, and then he was
surprised when one of these "faded" human beings, a tall, slender young
man in his mid-twenties, with brown hair and eyes, glanced up, saw him,
and broke into a bright smile of genuine pleasure.

"Lark! Marius and Haus have been telling us about you! Come here!
I'll show you what we've been doing."

Warily, Lark walked over, pushing through the annoying gel or plastic-
looking things on the floor. The panels were fenced by shields to prevent
outsiders from seeing what the people were doing, and when this young

man showed Lark what was behind his shields, Lark was struck with puzzlement.

Slightly above this panel floated a complex structure made up of broken mirror shards. In fact, the shards of mirror seemed to be held in place by some kind of magnetic force, though it was odd because mirrors were not made of magnetic materials. The shards were suspended in that ball-like formation as if they were little bubbles in the liquid of a potion, or little beads in a gel. Lark glanced around at the other people's panels, but was disappointed that they were all blocked from his view.

Lark was about to ask what the other people were making or doing, when he shook himself to his senses and asked what this young man was doing and what the mirror shard complex was.

The young man, who actually had a healthy complexion and energetic eyes, both of which must have been concealed by the panel shields, grinned down at the little boy. "Do you recognize the shape of this complex? Its arrangement?"

These questions were intended to be friendly and to invite responses, but Lark interpreted them as challenges. So the boy narrowed his eyes and fled through the wild jungle of his mind to find something in his memories that would match what he was currently seeing. To his relief, his mind did manage to hit something.

With a pompous and flaunting air, Lark said, "This is one of the newly invented crystal forms in synthetic chemistry. At first glance it looks like it is in complete disorder, but once one understands its patterns and equations, one can see a definite, perfect organization in how all the individual components protrude and arrange themselves. I also seem to recall that this peculiar crystal form is named...Fondal."

The young man seemed to be pleased at his answer. "And how is this Fondal form useful?"

Lark furrowed his brows again and then spoke without thinking, letting his precious knowledge flow out of him. "The Fondal is useful for a number of things, including the making of explosives and flames of certain colors and shapes." In Drell, they had discovered a way to synthesize flames of different shapes as well, including both the ordinary triangles, circles, squares, stars; and the fancier human and laminae shapes. These fancy-shaped flames were mainly used for entertainment purposes.

"Very good," said the young man. "But apart from this function of explosives and fire, do you remember any other major functions?"

"Yes, of course," Lark said, for the first time in his life feeling stressed because an adult actually asked him a question that was at the peak of his knowledge level, and about his favorite thing in the world at the same time. He felt that he had to prove his competence and knowledge once and for all, or else he would scorn himself for the rest of his life.

So Lark continued, "The Fondal, strangely, can also be used to make water, but an odd kind of water, containing a special mineral that inexplicably boosts one's vitality to a significant extent." Lark anticipated that the young man would ask him what he meant by vitality, so he defined it. "By vitality, I mean physical vigour: speed, stamina, strength, and suppleness. In short, a dramatic increase in all crucial athletic qualities."

Lark really need not feel so stressed because though the young man was delighted at Lark's knowledge, he would not think any less of Lark either if the boy happened to not know; because one, Lark was only five; and two, there was just so much science knowledge in the world that even with the memoria, one could not possibly know everything there was to know.

(See "The Rapidity and Stunning Number of Scientific Discoveries[2]" under "Drellian Society" and "The State of Science.")

The young man was actually thrilled that Lark knew so much: this boy was either extraordinarily lucky, or just amazing; the young man had no doubt that Lark was either the latter, or both.

So, as you can see, this young man was someone who tended to believe in the best side of people; he was a very cheerful and positive person indeed. His strong belief in others also made him a very attractive and popular person in the Rarerus. He might then remind you of Mr Karrin Treek; but Karrin, though optimistic about people in general, never had this much faith in other people. Karrin was more of the normal believer in others; whilst this young man, whose name was Raoul—Raoul Faya—was the fervent, as well as stubborn, believer.

Lark wondered what on Drell the Rarerus folk were going to do with this Fondal. He had an idea but he wasn't sure. Raoul said, "Come with me, please." He strode out with Lark following beside him, past the long rows of people bent down at their work, until they arrived below a doorway half-concealed by a vapor-like veil a quarter of a qwort above them. He introduced his name to the boy as they walked. Raoul invited Lark to climb onto a levitating panel which took them up to the doorway, and within a second, they were through.

Lark marveled at the blue and metallic-grey room, some of his favorite colors and not anything to do with pink at last. There were a few machines of dark green that soared through the air, though most only hovered, stationary, above them. Some looked very triangular or at least angular; others were smooth and round, but not circular or spherical.

Before Lark could ask what those green machines were, Raoul said, "Those are Teeleopes. They do a number of functions including the recording of the products and projects we make and do, and the processing of this information into the larger picture of what the Rarerus will do against the Arach."

Lark wondered whether a regular computer would be able to do all this anyway, and he was not afraid to ask this.

Raoul was not at all offended, and replied, "Your enquiry is a sensible one. Indeed the average computer would be able to process, organize, and analyze information; but such average machines cannot possibly process this amount of information with such speed. The processing is faster than human thought; it's almost instantaneous." Then he added, "But there are also other functions that our machines here can do that the average computer cannot do at all, but that will be another story to tell."

With an ordinary adult, Lark would have insisted on his telling him immediately, but something about Raoul made him hesitate. It wasn't exactly respect he felt; but Lark seemed to have no, or at least less, disparagement towards him. Raoul was not aware of the effect he had on the little boy, however.

Just then, Lark noticed a huge emotograph half a qwort high and a quarter of a qwort across on the wall opposite him and Raoul. A figure was clad in all yellow; he glowed yellow too, and was standing in a green landscape. He was bending over, holding a long item that looked like a weapon, and swinging it back as if he were about to throw it, or drive it, into the enemy's face. "What is this?" Lark asked, before correcting himself and saying, "Who is this?"

His companion smiled and did not answer. But after a moment he replied, his smile disappearing, "One of our seniors—he was an advisor and combatant—who died in battle ten years ago."

"What was his name?"

"Bulwark," Raoul said, but he seemed unwilling to say more. He made an anticlockwise turn of about thirty degrees, and hurried to a place where there was a human-sized pit full of something that looked like soil, but was evidently not soil. "Lark, guess what this is."

The boy stared and contemplated for a while. "Freet minerals? The nutrients used to feed most laminae?"

"Correct. Now let me take you to the laminae concerned." One reason why Lark seemed to feel more comfortable around Raoul than around most human beings was that Raoul had adjusted his style of speech to a more formal, sometimes even scientific style. This young man had heard from Marius and Haus that Lark tended to speak more formally, so he set off to speak in such a manner as well.

"Computer, take us to the Ramisen enclosure."

Immediately, there was a flash, and the two were teleported to a huge meadow.

"This is also within the Breemil Rarerus branch?" Lark asked.

Raoul nodded the affirmative, then trotted briskly about ten degrees clockwise. Lark huffed a bit as he tried to keep up with his pace; Raoul noticed this and slowed down. If Lark were an ordinary boy, he would have felt grateful, but Lark was simply relieved. Presently, he caught sight of brown specks in the distance. As they drew a bit closer, Lark said, "Urlassens."

These laminae were indeed urlassens. They had four legs, and plump round bodies of brown, glossy fur. Their legs were strange in how the upper part was large, but that this part tapered to a mere ballerina-sized foot, a tiny paw, at the bottom. It was a wonder that these laminae could support themselves at all, let alone move. Their ears were like two wrinkled pieces of thick cloth, which probably wouldn't appeal to us Earthlings; their eyes were round and blue; they had a conical muzzle with a shape similar to their tapering legs; and they sported a tail that looked like several pieces of rags pasted together.

All in all, the urlassen was not a very attractive-looking creature by our

Earthly standards. Despite their miniscule paws and huge body mass, they were quick runners, though they were not very strong.

Now, contrary to what he was used to do, Lark waited for Raoul to introduce him to the urlassens. Yet, contrary to what he expected, Raoul didn't. Instead, Raoul trotted over to one of the urlassens, patted its broad but round back—it was the height of a pony—and asked Lark to ride on it.

The boy was taken aback as he had never ridden on a lamina before. He didn't really want to get on, but Raoul had already lifted and placed him on the lamina's back. "Ready?" asked Raoul rather playfully.

Lark was now rather scared, but he nodded to avoid looking like a coward. He bit his tongue to resist screaming as the urlassen rushed forward and charged through the meadow. Close behind him was another urlassen with Raoul riding on its back. "We will travel a bit of a distance, if you don't mind. The urlassens need a bit of exercise." Lark felt sick already at the mention of "a bit of a distance."

Along the way through the great, seemingly never-ending meadow, they eventually came upon a tall barrier. Lark gasped and held his breath as the urlassen leapt as high as it could—the boy dearly hoped that it would make it—then its feet hit the top of the barrier; it kicked off, and landed safely on the other side. Raoul and his urlassen landed shortly after, but Lark's urlassen had already started running again.

This meadow, or the "Ramisen enclosure," as Raoul had called it, was not completely meadow. There were reams and rays of dark green trees here and there—if I may be allowed to use such an expression—which enriched and enlivened the view. Not that Lark really noticed any of these displays; he was so overwhelmed by the speed of the urlassen and the sick feeling in his stomach.

The trees they passed were called auna, which meant "island in the snow." The auna were commonly used for decorative purposes, because of their wispy, mist-like cloak of leaves and their appealingly green-grey trunks—most trees' were just plain brown. There was also something "silver" in the aunas' air. They were graceful but even the word "grace" did not quite capture the kind of beauty and dignity they exuded.

"We're almost there," said Raoul.

Lark sure hoped they were. He soon saw a purple and black speck in the distance. Finally, something urban in the midst of this deluge of nature. The closer they got to the speck, the more Lark relaxed. It was a building, and he felt most comfortable in buildings. He didn't mind nature; he just preferred being indoors.

Gradually, their urlassens slowed. Raoul hopped off his urlassen and helped Lark off of his. The urlassens bowed and galloped away after Raoul thanked them. Lark stared at their receding silhouettes; the boy rarely got to see laminae, let alone laminae of that size. But he quickly refocused on the building, as he saw that Raoul was walking away. Again, Raoul was walking too fast, and again he slowed to accommodate Lark, which not a little annoyed the boy.

The floors were all light blue, but a very flat and plain-looking blue; and they shone. The walls were a similar color. So a kind of cyber-, machine-, or tile-looking blue. Lark glanced around, but couldn't look around too much because he had to avoid losing sight of Raoul, who was again walking too quickly.

There were machines everywhere, including another purple and pink one with a shiny glass cover. It was taller than Lark and it seemed to be whirring. He wondered why there were so many purple and pink things associated with the Rarerus. But this was probably just his misperception, because we tend to think that the thing we notice is a lot more common than it really is.

After a while, Raoul stopped abruptly and pointed to the black, rectangular hole in front of him. "Ready, Lark?"

"Ready." While he said that, the boy was feeling rather uncomfortable that—he was not interacting as he normally would with a person. He was being so...cooperative, and compliant.

They walked into that rectangular hole. Lark gasped inwardly as he felt a powerful suction from above and they shot—glided—through the air. As Lark was not very used to suction soarers, he felt like he was tied to a rocket. To his credit though, he did not once show his fear.

After what seemed like cores to him—during which he was mighty glad that Raoul did not try to engage him in conversation during the soar, for he was feeling sick—they gradually saw light; and Lark was happy when his feet were finally allowed to touch solid ground.

When they came into the new space, Lark was dismayed that it was once again a purplish-pink color all around. He much preferred the dull cyber-blue room. He turned to see what Raoul would do next—Lark didn't like the feeling of constantly looking to what another person did, but it didn't seem like he had any choice.

"All right, we are here," Raoul said, opening an innocent-looking white door. Immediately, white smoke erupted from the doorway, engulfing and choking Lark before he could make a run for it, not that he would have been able to get far. Raoul laughed good-naturedly when Lark coughed. "It's cleaning gas. It removes all dirt and hidden microbes on you. Although of course it will leave the benign microbes on and in you alone." Lark was not amused, especially when Raoul laughed.

After the smoke cleared, Lark saw a group of young people about Raoul's age standing around a large panel. All four of them beamed when they saw them. "Lark?" One of the girls said. There were two girls and two boys in this group of young adults. The girl who spoke had long black hair tied back with strings. Some people liked to wear something reminiscent of music, so what better than a string from their instrument? Drell did indeed have musical instruments involving strings.

This girl also seemed to have glowing sky-blue eyes that scared him. He was mighty ashamed of himself that he felt such a weak emotion at all. It was uncharacteristic of him to feel so. Yet, Lark was indeed quite frightened when she tried to pick him up. He backed away fearfully.

"Deana, stop it," said the other girl who had light orange hair and green eyes. The other two young adults were a boy with black hair, grey eyes; and another boy with black hair, brown eyes. "Anyway," said the orange-haired girl, "let's introduce ourselves. I'm Glia, she's Deana, he (the boy with black hair, grey eyes) is Topps and he (boy with the black hair and brown eyes) is Ace."

Lark couldn't believe that the girl had named herself after a kind of brain cell, but it was actually not that unusual for Drellians to name their children after scientific molecules, chemicals, biological structures, and the like.

"Anyway, Lark," Glia continued, "want to see what we've been working on?" she asked amicably.

Again, Lark was displeased that everybody was treating him like a little kid. He nodded, but failed to erase the annoyed look on his face. When

Deana saw this, she laughed. "I don't think Lark liked the suction soarer much, or the cleaning gas." Raoul and the others laughed too.

Lark didn't see anything funny about that. He now had a strange desire to go back home. He had the even stranger thought that he might even be happier being back with his parents than with these mocking, jeering people. He didn't understand that these people were just being friendly. But of course, Lark was not one to back out. He had chosen to be here, and they wanted to recruit him for his skills and knowledge. So he would see what they had got.

Deana wanted to pick him up again, but when Lark skidded away, she made a face, and Glia sighed at her. He was now standing next to Topps, who looked at him with only the hint of a smile.

Glia said, "I'm sure Raoul has already told you about the fondal structure with our mirror shards that we've been making." So this was all a pre-planned tour, Lark thought. She picked up a sheet of ice-white substance from the middle of the panel with a protective transparent glove. In Drell, apart from using the robotic hand to pick up and feel chemicals, one could also wear protective barriers—barrier gloves—and handle the chemicals directly; but only if the chemicals were not dangerous.

Glia lowered the piece of ice-white substance to Lark's eye level so he could see. There were the exact same patterns he saw with the mirror shards, the same fondal structure. Then she said something that took him aback, "So, would you like to be our first test subject?"

"What?" he couldn't help saying.

Deana chastised Glia. "You shouldn't have put it in that way. You're scaring him."

Glia just gave a repentant little smile but Lark still had that horrified look on his face. She said, "I was just scaring you; and I apologize for that. All I meant was that, if it pleases you, you could be one of our first test subjects on drinking a bit of the fondal-made water. It isn't that much of a big deal because we're just replicating past results. Many other past research studies have shown that fondal water minerals can enhance your athletic capacities. We just wanted to see for ourselves what these minerals can help our members do."

"But why did you choose me to be one of your first subjects?" he asked, with no small amount of anxiety.

She calmly replied, "Because you are the littlest of our members—ah, members and potential members. As you know—"

"—chemicals may have a more potent effect on individuals with a smaller body mass, which means young children." Lark felt a bit better now that he was arrogantly interrupting an adult like he was used to do. But at the same time he was feeling uneasy about interrupting in this situation, with this group of people.

It didn't seem to matter, though, because Glia smiled. "Good job. That's exactly why we would like to see if you will get an even more substantial boost in your athletic abilities."

Lark thought about his athletic abilities and wondered what would happen too. He asked, "How long will the effects of the fondal minerals last? How many cores, or days?"

"Or how many hexa- or decaweeks." Glia shrugged. "Or it's probably much longer than that. Maybe even a whole year."

That wasn't very reassuring to the little boy. "Do you have an ethics committee?" he wanted to know.

All of the four junior researchers seemed to look sheepish. "Of course we do," said Glia.

"They do," Raoul confirmed. "The ethics committee approved this experiment because there have already been numerous reports of successful tests on human beings, such that there is no reason for us to not succeed."

"But did those past research reports include any studies with five-year-old children?" Lark asked.

Once again, the four junior researchers appeared sheepish, but Raoul answered for them, "I recall that there were a few done on young children, but they were a bit older. Aged eight to ten."

"But there were none on five-year-olds or younger."

"No," said Raoul, not looking at all flustered.

Lark tensed his lips and gave them a hard stare. "Since your experiment does carry its risks, as we do not know what will happen to children of my age, do I get a compensation?"

His query made everyone smile. "Yes, you definitely do," said Raoul. "Name your prize and we'll see if it is suitable."

At this, Lark faltered. There were many chemicals that he wanted, but there wasn't any he particularly wanted or needed. Same thing with books. And with machines, gadgets, and devices. There wasn't anything else in the world that he was interested in either.

"If you can't decide now, you can always tell us after the experiment," Raoul said.

Here, Lark was smelling something very fishy. "Why do you so eagerly desire me to be your test subject?" He eyed them all with suspicion, and secretly with fright too. For a bizarre moment, he wished that his parents were there to protect him and to take him back home. It was one of those very rare moments—if not the very first moment in his life—that he actually wanted his parents to be there.

All of them looked tremendously fishy indeed, but again, Raoul was the first one to speak. "I understand how you feel, but this is for the good of all. If we could arm one small child with better athletic abilities, we could easily arm many more children with the same advantages, to help us fight the Arach."

"Do you mean that you want to recruit more children of my age?" Lark asked.

"Not necessarily, though that is always a possibility. So, will you volunteer for us?"

Lark thought that these Rarerus people seemed to be forever asking him to accept their "invitations," and this annoyed him. "Give me some time to think about this," he said, unwilling to give in so soon. Despite his anxious doubts about their intentions, Lark was genuinely curious to see what the fondal minerals would do for him.

"Fair enough," Raoul said. "And we did promise not to keep you too long away from home, didn't we? So let's take you back before your parents get too worried."

This time they used a teleporter to transport them directly back to the original lab with those gel or plastic-like curling tubes on the floor. As if expecting Lark's question, Raoul said that they took the slower and longer way through last time so he could show Lark more of their compound.

Another reason was that teleporters consumed a tremendous amount of energy to work, so the Rarerus didn't use them too often, and only teleported over short distances. That was why they rode on Hyures, Coasters, and other vehicles to travel to farther places.

Though energy was technically "free" indoors, such a huge consumer of energy as the teleporter needed a special device to capture and hold this gigantic amount. This device was highly expensive and would overload and break if you tried to transport people over excessively great distances. Also, though no one could ever teleport far due to the limits of this energy-holding device, nobody knew if such a gargantuan energy absorption into the teleportation machine would permanently damage the environment somehow.

When Lark and Raoul were back inside the main building, Haus and Marius grinned and told Raoul about their plan for the science club. "Oh, then I could go back with Lark and say that I'm escorting him home from his new science club," said Raoul.

"It isn't really that late, though," Haus said. "He could go home by himself after we drop him off at my store. You going with him might— alarm his parents, you know?"

"Hmm, but if I go with him, then his parents will see that this science club's supervisors are responsible people who care about the children's safety." He shrugged.

Lark seemed to be given no say in this. "I can go home by myself."

"Oh okay, let's drop you off at my store."

"No, I meant that I can go home all by myself, without any help at all," Lark said.

He was met with three mystified stares. "I'd advise you not to," said Haus. "We came a long way, and the Hyure are likely not going to listen to a five-year-old child, no offense."

Lark scowled. He just wanted to go alone anyway, so he stayed there stubbornly. "Thank you for your generous offers, but I really am able to return home without any aid," he said drily.

But Raoul decisively shook his head. "No, I'm sorry. We can't be so irresponsible as to let you have your way. I'll come with you too, if that would make your journey back more pleasant." Lark had no idea how Raoul came to believe that Lark would appreciate his company.

"Do what you like," Lark said, tapping into his logical side again as going with the adults would more likely grant him a swifter return home. One must not give in to whims, after all.

1. **Gender Expectations**

   Males are not pressured to hide their emotions anymore. Men on Drell can be very emotionally expressive, even of "weak" feelings, without being labeled "weird." That's why there was a rise of males like Karrin Treek and Graham Arias who are quite "girlish"—their "inner female" can at last be released!

   In this gender liberation of males, there are also no longer any "girl" or "boy" colors. There are thus many males who have pink, lilac, or purple as their favorite colors.

2. **The Rapidity and Stunning Number of Scientific Discoveries**

   Even with the memoria to help the Drellians, there are countless more scientific discoveries made every single day on Drell than on Earth. It was already impossible to keep up with everything on Earth. So on Drell, think of how much more impossible it is to keep up, even for the top scientists in a specialized field.

   So, even though there are some "more major than usual" discoveries, there will always be a portion of even the top scientists in that field who have not heard of some of these major findings, because there are too many "more major than usual" discoveries made so often.

TEN
LIARA GRAE

When Lark was back at Haus's chemistry shop, Raoul was about to hug him goodbye but Lark backed away hastily. "Thank you for your escort. I will now leave." And he hurried home.

His parents were, again, extremely worried that their son came home late. This was very irritating, but Lark decided to get it over with and told them about the recent science club that he had joined, describing how he had now realized the importance of social communication between great scientists like himself.

At first, Kreesha and Graham beamed in delight, believing that a miracle had fallen upon them. But then they grew suspicious. "Really?" Kreesha asked.

"Do you not believe me?" Lark asked.

"I do, honey, it's just that this is so unexpected, so sudden," she said.

Lark shrugged. "Not all things happen gradually. Some things strike us without warning," he quoted word for word a story that he had read for class. Not that he liked the platitudes or the wordings of these stories, but he found that quoting platitudes seemed to appease adults and convince them he was right.

Kreesha and Graham exchanged glances. Graham extended an arm to pull Lark to them, but Lark hurriedly evaded that attempt, frightened and aversive to any contact. So that didn't change, thought Graham with disappointment. "Well, son, if you have found a club that makes you happy, we'll be happy for you too," he said.

His son gave a curt nod, and marched towards his room again.

"Son?"

"Yes?"

"Your mother and I want to suggest something to you." Not another suggestion, thought Lark. "If you promise to not meet up with those 'friends' of yours anymore and to get rid of that par-the-air, then we can give you extra money to buy your books." A wondering expression appeared on Lark's face, and he paid a little more attention. "But this money can only be used to buy books, because we have configured it. So what do you think?" Graham asked cheerfully.

Why was everyone suddenly giving him strange offers? Lark thought, notwithstanding that this offer was an unquestionable gain for him, and fooling his parents to continue seeing his "two friends" should be easy. "All right. I accept your offer and its accompanying conditions," Lark said. He stayed one moment more, unsure if his parents would give him the money straight away, or if they would voice their doubt that he could truly adhere to their rules; but when they didn't do either, he turned to go to his room again.

His parents watched him with worry. When he had locked the door, Kreesha whispered to Graham, "Do you think this is going to work?"

"The boy did promise," her elemen said. "We should trust him, right?"

On the subsequent day, Lark strode back to Haus's chemistry shop, and was ready with an answer. (He had run away from school before Karrin had a chance to accost him.) Haus looked up cheerfully, greeting him. Lark glanced once at the floor, then he decisively raised his eyes and said, "I will volunteer to be a subject for your experiment."

Haus didn't expect such a quick decision. "Oh, that's fantastic! Thank you."

"But you promised a compensation for my participation, correct?"

"Yes, of course."

"Then I request that you give me my own supply of fondal structures, as much as I want."

Haus thought that was an odd request and he wasn't sure if the Rarerus would allow a child to have his own supply. Haus would have to discuss this with Marius and Raoul, so he quickly contacted them (Marius was at the Breemil branch). Marius seemed amused at Lark's proposal but Raoul was worried.

"Lark," the latter said, "I understand your desire to learn about this amazing structure in your own time, but as you are already aware, apart from the minerals, the fondal can also be used to make explosives and fire, and it is not an easy chemical to inoculate. We don't want you to get hurt."

Of course Raoul would say that, Lark thought. But he had something to say too. "If you cannot grant that request, then I regret to say that I no longer wish to join your Rarerus, and I may, in my childish carelessness, accidentally tell my parents about the Arach."

That got them. Raoul nervously said, "Lark, please don't tell anyone about the Arach. This is dangerous, and anybody who finds out about the Arach may be targeted to be their next victims. You don't want any harm to come to your parents, do you?"

Though Lark did not feel any particular fondness towards his parents, he certainly did not wish to harm them either, so he said, "Of course not. But as I am a mere five-year-old child, who knows if I will one day forget about my promise and tell the world?"

Haus had a look on his face that said: are you threatening us? Lark also had a look on his face, which said—yes. The three adults frowned at him. "Do you want your own supply of fondal structures so badly?" asked Raoul.

"They would be a very welcome addition to my collection of chemicals," Lark said. "If you are so concerned about my safety, perhaps you can upgrade my computer and enhance its lab protection facilities. And perhaps allow me the use of some of your barrier gloves." He had barrier gloves of his own, but they were only kiddy ones. There was no telling what might happen if he handled a more unstable chemical with those weaker gloves.

"How about an upgrade on all your chemical handling equipment, but not the fondal?" Raoul tried one more time.

Lark shook his head. "It is either all or nothing."

The three adults looked at each other glumly. "All right," Raoul said. "You will get your reward."

"When?" asked Lark. "As I am a mere five-year-old, and I do not know any of you very well, I have the right to be cautious. Please fulfill your promise first before I participate in your experiment, or else I will again drop away from your organization and accidentally tell everyone I see about the Arach."

Raoul and co. looked quite pained, but they desperately wanted Lark as a participant, as well as a recruit, so they agreed. "Please come over to the Breemil branch again and we will give you what you want," Raoul said.

When they had updated Lark's computer and given him some fondal structures that the three Rarerus members seemed loath to part with, Lark was finally satisfied. The fondal structures were carefully protected by the new equipment they had installed onto Lark's computer. Lark couldn't wait to perform experiments with these "dangerous" new chemicals, and no, he wasn't afraid of dying.

But now that that was done, it was rather disconcerting to see how eager Raoul and his cohorts were for him to participate in their experiment. Lark, for a brief second, wondered if what he would participate in would indeed kill him; and for a moment, he was about to go back on his word—in spite of Lark's earlier conviction that he did not fear death. But he wasn't one to break promises, and he said, "Let us get this finished."

Haus, Marius, and Raoul were delighted at his new alacrity, but Raoul said, "Not yet, though. We'll have to ask you to go to the Rarerus Center with us in Vénus. Would you mind going? All our test subjects will go there for the big experiment."

"That is illogical. Is it not a lot more time efficient if we gave the fondal minerals to each test member in their home sector? What is the point of this...congress?" It was indeed shocking that even five-year-olds knew what congresses were. It was the wonder of the memoria again: hyper-accelerated factual learning.

To Lark's displeasure but not surprise, the adults looked uncomfortable and none of them seemed to want to answer him. Again, it was Raoul who said, "It is a sort of congress, a ceremony. We just want to make sure we all manage to give our test subjects the same amount of fondal minerals at the same time."

"That is also illogical. You could very easily do this by careful instructions to the computer for the correct measurements administered at the same time. If you wish to see all test subjects simultaneously, you may also contact the researchers concerned and watch them via holograms."

Raoul smiled. "There's another reason why we would want all the test subjects to go there. Miss Liara wishes to witness this operation personally."

At the sound of Liara Grae's name, Lark fell silent. He knit his brows together, but after a while, he said, "I see."

"Then you will come with us?"

"I seem to have no other choice."

"Thanks, Lark. We will tell you when we are ready for the experiment."

So from that day on, Raoul, and sometimes Marius and Haus, showed Lark around even more places in their Breemil branch, and showed him their many operations, and many chemical projects. They hadn't yet shown him any of their military equipment, but Lark was in no hurry; he was already wholly absorbed by the cutting edge chemical creations that he now got to see firsthand every day. There seemed to be no limit to the things he could see in the Rarerus, and he became increasingly fascinated with this society, at least the chemistry side of it.

And during this time, Lark would always tell his parents that he had been in the science club. His parents did gradually believe him because he had lately acquired a new glow in his complexion and demeanor. They had never seen Lark so happy before, and sometimes Graham or Kreesha would smile and say, "Larky, what makes you so happy these days?"

Lark, not ceasing to smile—to himself, not to his parents—would reply, "The science club."

His parents were thus overjoyed that something was at last changing in their previously stony son. He had finally found friends! He had reached out to other science enthusiasts at last as they had advised him so many times to do. They were so delighted that once, they asked Lark if he could take them to his wonderful science club and show them around. At this, Lark looked very unwilling and doubtful.

So Graham said, "You don't have to if you don't want to, son. We won't force you."

But to his great surprise and elation, Lark said, "I will show you. Tomorrow."

When Kreesha and Graham got to the "science club" with their son, they found that the building looked legitimate, professional, appealing, but also friendly and inviting. They loved the atmosphere inside the labs, though they did not fancy science themselves: the kids were all so studious, so eager, yet very amicable and warm. This was just the perfect place for their darling Lark.

Kreesha embraced her son from behind and kissed him on the cheek. He immediately wrestled from her grasp in disgust, especially as a few of the other kids were staring at him, and an amused Raoul was holding back his smile at this incident. He caught Raoul's eye and shot a warning glare at him. Raoul pretended not to see him and looked away, going back to his own business.

It seemed like Haus and Marius did quite a good job. This science club was a genuine one, after all; and thankfully many of the members' children were already rather interested in science, so there wasn't too much trouble asking them to come play and learn.

In the profuseness of their joy, Graham and Kreesha became convinced as well that this science club must have impressed their son so much, that he lost all desire to hang out with those sketchy "friends" or to meddle with that "par-the-air."

The Arias's told the Treeks this too, and though neither Hlen nor Ella were a hundred percent sure that Lark was now all right, this was the Arias's private family matter, so they could not intrude. The Treeks could only ask Karrin to report back to them if he found Lark doing anything suspicious.

And about the configured money, Graham and Kreesha gave Lark a bit of this in addition to his weekly allowance. Lark was satisfied by this arrangement and went to buy more and more books, learning all that material with as much intensity as ever.

He had always been a happy and satisfied boy, with all his science around him. But now, his joy had soared up to an even higher level, as he was suddenly granted access to a whole new world of the most advanced chemistry and science.

It felt so different learning about rare chemicals by seeing and manipulating them in real life, than by merely reading about them in books. It was fantastic to read about them, but it was even more exciting to touch and fiddle with them in person.

Thus, at this point, Kreesha, Graham, and Lark had all risen to a new height of satisfaction in their lives, though they were originally very happy people already.

Whilst the three of them were thus trundling blissfully along their path of life, the big day came. Lark was to travel to Vénus with Raoul. Haus and Marius would stay behind to look after the Breemil branch. The trip wasn't much of a big deal, actually, because in Drell, travelling to another sector on the Coaster didn't take very long; it only took about one and a half cores to get to Vénus. Of course, this still took up some time, so Raoul and Marius created this "Trip to Vénus form" for Lark's parents to read and give their permission for his "science club" trip. It would take less than a day, but they would definitely escort all the children back home in case the trip finished too late.

Kreesha and Graham were excited that their Larky was getting increasingly involved in a social life; their son finally had a social life! They shouted for joy and gave their permission without a second thought; then they both tried to hug their son but he had slipped away from them just in time.

Drellian "forms" were not paper forms; they were digital documents, as you might have already guessed. And as for signatures, they didn't need those. All they needed to do was to hold out their finger for the computer to scan their finger prints and say yes for the computer to confirm on the document that they gave their consent or agreement.

On the Coaster with Raoul, Lark was all tremulous with excitement and anticipation, but he controlled himself and tried not to let his feelings show, for it was unseemly for someone like himself to reveal such childish emotions.

Raoul could guess what Lark was thinking, however, as he was already so used to this little boy's personality and antics. Lark wasn't that unpredictable, after all. Eccentric, but not erratic. Thus, Raoul simply minded his own business and read his book. He had come to learn that Lark felt more comfortable around others when they were not talking to him, unless he himself wanted to talk to them about some matter, great or small.

Like some of the few people in this world, Raoul had gradually learned to like the little boy; antisocial as he was, he really was an extraordinary five-year-old. Raoul had heard a lot of stories about "natural obsessors" and read about them, but this was the very first time he got to know one personally. He was amazed at Lark's innate mad drive to learn about science, and he respected Lark for this. But it was unfortunately not as easy to interact with the boy as he had thought, since Lark really was quite unconquerable—as Karrin had already discovered—and unwilling to chat; but occasionally Raoul could get Lark to say a few science-unrelated things.

At long last, they arrived at Vénus.

Lark had changed into a Dracana that was much thinner than his dark Iminis, as Vénus was warmer than Fartha. Raoul was wearing a Vrillion (pronounced "Vrill-lee-inn"), a garment known for its cool, refreshing fabric that was especially suitable for moderate temperatures.

The two passed by a stream of trees that were called acaijas, willowy trees with a crisp bright green. Very healthy and vital-looking trees. There was yellow sand where they were walking. Lark paid no attention to any of this, however, and neither did Raoul. They said nothing on their way to the Center, because Raoul understood that basically, the less you talked to Lark, the less he repulsed you.

Soon, it was nightfall. It wasn't night in Fartha, but it was in Vénus because they were in different time zones. They trotted along a path that was bordered by dark purple gravel. It might not have been dark purple originally, but this was the color that appeared in this lack of light. There were only a few floating lights around here. Drellians used floating, hovering lights instead of our streetlamps.

In this darkness, Lark was not at all afraid, only exhilarated and curious. The path curved, and curved. Then at last, a black jagged building came into sight. It was possible that it looked black only because it was night time. Regardless, Lark did not care very much about its color.

Raoul gave Lark a smile which was not reciprocated and raised his finger for the computer to check his identity. The door opened. The dark hallway inside lit up immediately and Lark could see that the floor was red. Not scarlet red or any provocative, dangerous red. Just plain red. Maybe even dull red. The walls were a very light blue and grey. This reminded Lark of the time when he went into the building at Phuore to find Marius with his par-the-air. He wondered why they never went back there again. Were there any interesting mysteries in that place? He had always intended to ask, but had never remembered to, absorbed as he was by all the scientific stimulation.

Without a sound, Raoul beckoned and led them through this long corridor until they came to a room with an orange-yellow faded floor, and white walls. The next room they went to was the same color, and so was the next. In these rooms, there were some rather interesting-looking things, most of them machines; but there were also emotographs, paint-ings, sculptures, and decorations. Drellians did have things like paintings and sculptures too, but artists did not necessarily use the same kinds of tools that artists from our world did.

They drifted into yet another new room, and this time it was an aquarium blue, or rather the blue of copper salts. You might have wondered for a while now why buildings on Drell often had such vivid colors on their outer and inner surfaces. The fact of the matter was, Drellian designers, artists, and many others enjoyed playing with the emotional effects of colors on people. Different hues affect us differently.

For example, red feels exciting and intense; orange cheerful and invigo-rating; blue feels calm and tranquil, though also cool and chilly in certain contexts; green is relaxing, soothing, and restful; purple sophisticated, royal, mysterious, or contemplative; pink warm, loving, and nurturing; grey can be de-energizing and suppressive, no offense to those who love grey; black heavy, serious, even intimidating and aggressive; white pure, clean, spacious, or sterile; and brown gives off a sense of reliability, solidity, and quiet seriousness.

At the same time, individual differences factored into how a particular color stimulated one emotionally, due to personal experiences and past associations with that color.

In this room suffused with that copper-salt blue, Lark felt a strong sense of laminae, though he could not see any.

And then, without warning, a girl appeared in front of them. Lark stared at her, expecting her to speak to him and Raoul, but she didn't; she looked away, and padded past them. Raoul looked at her until she slipped through the door and disappeared, and then Raoul glanced back to where they were going. The girl seemed quite young, dressed in a deep green Iminis; her golden-orange and yellow long hair flowed down her shoulders and back. She had eyes that were a luminous blend of blue and green. Her face had an impression of being angular and her skin was quite pale. She was also rather tall. She was probably one of those junior researchers like the ones in the Breemil labs, like Deana and Glia, perhaps.

None of this mattered, though, because they were making their way to an important place. Soon they heard voices; then male and female faces appeared and greeted Raoul. Many of these faces looked at Lark and made admiring little sounds that many adults made when they saw small children. Lark, of course, took no notice of them.

"Are you ready for the grand ceremony, Lark?" Raoul asked.

He nodded, wondering why Raoul even bothered asking as Lark had already pointedly told them that he would keep his promise and come with him here to be tested. The "grand ceremony" was the great event that celebrated the big incident of the fondal testing. There would be food. There would be refreshments. And there would be various entertainments. Lark just wanted them to get it over with as soon as possible.

Raoul led Lark to a room lit with a white-yellow and very bright light, where several people sat on stretch seats and glanced at him. "Just wait here with the other test subjects until we come for you. It won't take long," Raoul said, and smiled. "Later you can eat with us too. Thank you all for volunteering." And with that, he left.

The other test subjects stared at Lark and at each other. Then they all started talking to each other and some tried to talk to Lark, but the boy would obviously not respond. There were seven other test subjects in total, and they were all adults, from those in their twenties to those in their forties. There was one adult who was in his sixties.

When they found that Lark was no good chitchat company, the few adults who had attempted to engage him in conversation gave up and chatted amongst themselves instead. That suited Lark and he simply took out his electrospace to read. A couple of the test subjects asked to see what he was reading, but when they were rebuffed by Lark's unfriendly frown, they backed off, wondering why the little boy was being so antisocial; but later they deduced that it was because the little boy was very upset from being separated from his parents, and was thus feeling very lonely and missing home.

It was not long before Raoul and a few other researchers appeared. Raoul beckoned to them with a smile, then went to Lark as if to give him especial attention. Lark did not appreciate this "especial attention" and he looked away.

But Raoul hadn't come for friendly chatter; he just needed to keep a close eye on this little five-year-old. He did ask a nearby colleague to watch over Lark while he was gone, but Raoul felt more at ease with the boy in his sight, in case anything should happen.

Of course, he could have brought Lark with him just then, but he needed to talk to the other researchers and facilitators for a while to make sure everyone understood what they were about to do; it would be awkward for him and irritating for Lark if anyone assumed that Lark was his son.

THE STADIUM, WHICH THE TWO SOON REACHED, WAS HUGE, with dark blue and black walls and pillars, swept across by beams of white light. So many people were there, flooding the whole place; they made so much noise, and Lark was perturbed by this massive number of roaming human beings. Yet, he made himself stay calm and keep his cool. He was not one to go into hysterics when he felt agitated. Raoul offered him some food and refreshments. Lark only took what he needed to fill his stomach, which was tiny, and then he stopped, staring at that roiling mass of people with continued alarm.

Raoul noticed Lark's expression and laughed inwardly in amusement. He had truly grown to like this little boy and his ways, and he was quite content to be his babysitter for the day. He was relieved that Lark at least did not object to his company. Lark didn't seem to care because he just took out his electrospace again and read. The other scientists were relieved too, because nobody wanted to take care of a hyper-antisocial five-year-old. "You're the one who knows him best," they thought to Raoul.

Still, very often there would be one or more people who would stop for a moment and stare at Lark. Lark tried his best to keep his attention fixed on his book and wait for them to look away. But one could not blame these people as there really was no other child as young as he was in the Rarerus. The youngest was their eight-year-old Beam leader Eventii, and he wasn't here.

Not long after, a voice announced that the experiment would now begin. Finally, thought Lark. He and the other seven test subjects mounted a tall panel; tall probably for no other reason but to show them off to as many spectators as possible. And as he prepared for the fondal mineral administration, the wall that he had been gazing at opened, and in stepped a girl onto a violet platform to face their panel. She was the girl they had seen earlier in the copper salt colored room.

She no longer had the hurried, anxious look about her when she had rushed past them without exchanging a word of greeting; she was now smiling, dazzling, casting her eyes all around her to the admiring spectators, and taking in all their praise and declarations of love; for this girl, was Liara Grae.

She made a gesture with her hands. The talking stopped. She beamed at all the test subjects on the panel, especially Lark, as he was the only child. Then she thanked them all for volunteering, and said what an honor it was for the Rarerus to have such volunteers. She didn't say anything about the compensations they got or would get, though.

Very soon, eight researchers, including Raoul, stepped onto the stage, each carrying vials of what could only be fondal water. Liara watched this all calmly, as if she saw these things every day. Lark looked up at Raoul, who was smiling at him with that vial. Hurry up and get on with it, Lark grumbled inwardly. Then they administered the chemical.

Lark and the other seven test subjects gulped down the fondal water. Lark felt Liara's eyes on them, especially on him, because he, the child, was expected to receive the greatest effect from the minerals. Lark didn't feel anything from the minerals, though, to his disappointment. The other seven participants smiled at each other, and smiled at Liara. They probably already knew her, Lark thought.

———

"ALL RIGHT," SHE SAID. "LET'S SEE WHAT YOU CAN ALL DO now." She gestured to the researchers standing on the tall panel beside the test subjects. "Take them to the training rooms, please."

Just before he was ushered away, Lark glanced at this strange creature who was called Liara, and it happened that she was looking at him too. They stared at each other until one of the researchers blocked Lark's view and he had to glance away.

In the training rooms, before the training, the seven participants excitedly told each other how they already felt enhanced. "My muscles are rippling, man!" said one man enthusiastically to another. Lark naturally ignored such immaturities.

Raoul, always by Lark's side, guided him to an area with a pinkish-purple semi-transparent machine. Why were nearly all Rarerus things pink, purple, or both? "Lark, try to launch yourself onto this propeller."

Lark frowned at being told what to do, even though Raoul had only said "try to launch," not "launch." Nevertheless, Lark jumped. He bounded up so high into the air and landed neatly onto the platform of the propeller. The landing wasn't just neat. It was perfect. No stiffness. No awkwardness. No stumbling. Lark was more stunned than delighted.

But Raoul was clearly delighted. "Excellent. Now, if you please, run on this propeller. Let's see how fast you can go."

As usual, Lark was annoyed that he was being asked to do something, even if it was said politely. Yet, he did promise to go through their experiment, so he would temporarily comply. The propeller was a strange Drellian machine that generated reams and reams of virtual reality paths for the person to run on. It was basically the same as being in a virtual, but propellers specifically made an endless path that enabled the user to keep running for as long as they wanted.

The propeller was not a treadmill, however, because one was really covering distance and moving to different places, albeit virtual places. Fitness trainers used propellers to check how fast or for how long their trainee could run. People who wanted to train themselves simply went on propellers to have a fun run, as these were fun. You could even create your own virtual path, by specifying the surroundings, path texture, colors, and other things.

And thus Lark ran. He had no preference for any particular environment as he simply disliked running. So he got the default yellow, dusty, and sandy path with the sun shining overhead. To his surprise, he was much faster than he usually was, judging by how quickly the trees and other plants beside him whisked by. He was even faster than the average five-year-old. He was not pleased, however, when he heard Raoul clapping.

Raoul stopped clapping when he remembered that Lark did not like social approval, any more than he liked social reprimands or slights. He was happiest when people gave no reaction to him at all, positive or negative.

They proceeded to the various other tests, including strength, stamina, and suppleness. His coordination had dramatically improved too. Lark was increasingly amazed as he did these exercises, and saw that his performance consistently exceeded that of most five-year-olds. He was especially taken aback by his strength and speed. As you already know, he was used to being slower than everyone else at sprinting, which brought him a lot of embarrassment as well as disadvantages. He was also always the weakling of the class who had to be helped in many things.

But now, he basked in self-admiration at what he was able to do. He had never been interested in improving himself in physical health or fitness, yet now that he had improved, he felt unusually pleased; he was even surprised at how pleased he was.

"Okay, thank you, Lark," Raoul said as he held out a hand to help Lark down, but Raoul realized that he was a fool to do so because Lark was physically enhanced already and moreover did not like receiving others' help. Raoul was still smiling, however, and Lark, though used to this young man's perpetual sunniness, was still annoyed when he saw this expression of joy. He didn't mind people expressing their joy per se; he just —maybe he just didn't like it when people had any emotional reaction to him at all, as Raoul had already surmised. "Let's go now and meet Liara," said Raoul.

At her name, Lark perked up and followed the rest of the enhanced subjects out the door. Liara, leader of the Rarerus, was a very interesting person, wasn't she?

THEY SAW LIARA IN A GREEN ROOM, SITTING ON A REGAL-looking stri seat (stri rhymes with dry). Stri seats were fancy stretch seats with more elaborate structures built on them, for decorative or other purposes. Liara's stri seat was gold, a darker and more intense gold than her pale, light hair. Shapes of scary-looking laminae snarled and flew at the sides of the seat's back, as if they were symbolically guarding Liara; parts of these laminae were the color of jade, and parts of them a faded red. The seat's back itself, which was also gold and shining, was a solid, undecorated color; the back also changed its shape to let the Rarerus leader sit as comfortably as she wanted.

Lark Arias felt the intensity around her: the tension, the air that did not dare move. This was a very strange sensation to him as he was never sensitive to social atmospheres. But maybe the idea that she was the great leader of Rarerus managed to strike fear, or at least caution, into him. Whatever it was, it made him uncomfortable to be once again put out of his habitual self-confidence. And though only less than five seconds had elapsed since they entered this room, Lark already felt that this was an eternity; he wished that this Liara would say what she wanted to say and let them go home. He was fascinated by this person, but at the same time she made him very uneasy.

Perhaps it was his imagination, but Liara's eyes seemed to pause on his face for the longest time compared to his fellow participants'. What did she want?

At long last, the leader of the Rarerus rose from her splendid stri (short for stri seat) and smiled at them all, before saying, "You have all exceeded my expectations, congratulations. If you do not mind, might I request your further company to stay a few days longer in the Rarerus Center, for us to observe the development of your changes?"

"No," Lark immediately said. All eyes turned to him; Liara's eyes widened in curiosity. "I must go home today." He felt a lot better about himself now that he managed to express himself and re-assert his independence from them. He had already fulfilled his promise of taking their fondal minerals. Now he was free to go home and investigate the fondal structures and other scientific intrigues in the comfort of his room.

Yet, instead of replying to him, Liara continued to look at him expectantly, even defiantly, as if challenging him. Lark did not like that look at all and he narrowed his eyes, challenging her back, but at the same time remembering that she was the leader of this society he so much wanted to join. So Lark continued, "My parents will be worried if I do not make it back home in time."

Liara smiled. "What filial devotion. Of course, you have my permission to leave whenever you desire, Mr Arias."

That was it? She must have seen the astonishment on his face because she laughed and said, "I am not an unreasonable person, Mr Arias. All our test subjects are free human agents who have the right to refuse our request." Her laugh was not like a regular girl's. It was not a bit like his mother's, or even Alyssha's. It was a kind of laugh that communicated mirth without disrupting for one moment the calmness of her demeanor. She seemed neither relaxed nor nervous.

After one more moment in this tense air, Lark unfroze himself and nodded to Raoul to take him away. Raoul smiled and did so. But before he left, Raoul threw a quick glance at Liara; but it was not one of admiration.

WHEN THEY LEFT THE CENTER—LARK COULDN'T BELIEVE THAT they had finally left; the place inside was so momentous, so powerful, that it left a huge imprint on his mind—Raoul, probably forgetting Lark's preferences, started to try to engage him in conversation. When answered by the usual unresponsiveness of Lark, instead of shutting up as he should, Raoul began talking about whatever he wanted, as if he were chatting for the sake of having something to fill up the silence; as if the silence daunted him. True, it was now very late at night, but surely Raoul couldn't be afraid. There was nothing to be afraid of in this darkness, right?

Of course not. They made it to the Coaster and both were relieved when they sat down. They were going home.

As promised, Raoul escorted Lark back to his parents; Raoul couldn't really have let Liara make Lark stay on Vénus for several days, could he?

Evening had only just touched Fartha, as Vénus's time zone was two cores faster than Fartha's. When they arrived at the Arias's house door, his parents were overjoyed, as usual, to see their darling son return, and they thanked Raoul for taking care of him on his way back, and told Raoul to take care too.

After that, as soon as they went back into the house, Graham and Kreesha bombarded Lark with questions about how the trip was like, what he did, what he saw, etc. etc. He made up all his answers, which, to his immense gratification, was laughably easy. All he had to do was to pull out some arbitrary chemical from his memory and bemuse his parents with the description of its peculiarities; he would tell them about chemical after chemical, and device after device; his parents would understand nothing anyway. Non-scientists were easy to fool. (Not very kind of him to think, I know.)

Nevertheless, he wished his parents would stop gazing at him so fondly already. Then, in a flash of memory, he recalled how...secretly fearful he was when Liara was staring at him. Her gaze was not... unfriendly per se, but it disconcerted him. He also did not understand why she had moved past him and Raoul so quickly, without even a greeting, when they had first met.

Though Lark did not genuinely understand politeness, he was aware that adults who knew each other would at least acknowledge each other's presence by a nod or a "hello," but she just brushed past them without saying anything. It was that sense of mystery that enthralled him yet again. If he did not control himself, he would keep thinking about this mysterious incident for a very long time.

But after he thought about Liara's disquieting stare, he suddenly realized how much less threatening his parents' gazes were. As much as he despised them, as he despised all human beings in general, he at least knew that they would never harm him. He didn't exactly think that Liara would do him any harm, especially not if she was the leader of such an organization, but—she still put him on his guard.

Perhaps his parents noticed the slight perturbation that had come over his features as he went through these thoughts, because they looked at him with worry, and Kreesha said, "Larky, what's wrong? Is everything all right?"

"Yes, everything is all right," Lark said, and wanted, as usual, to walk back into his room where he could be alone again to think. To his amazement, his parents did not stop him this time, and he even glanced back to see if there was some ruse. He was met only with their concerned stares.

"You sure you're all right, Larky?" his father asked.

Lark nodded impatiently, and slammed his door.

ELEVEN
AIRA DANCING

W hen Lark awoke, the first thing he thought of was whether last night's physical enhancement was still there. He stretched his arms and felt that they were filled with strength. He tried to lift something heavy in his room and managed it without any difficulty. He was elated.

When he was all prepared, he wondered whimsically, for a split second, whether he should run to school instead of walking, as running for a long period of time should probably not tire him anymore. Graham and Kreesha were looking at him with concern again just like yesterday, and Kreesha said, "Darling, whatever it is...take it easy, all right?"

Again, Lark gave them a brisk nod and went out.

His parents glanced out and were stunned at the sight of their son running to school. He was actually running, and much faster than he used to!

"LARK, ARE YOU OKAY?" THAT WAS KARRIN TREEK. WHEN they were in the classroom, he deliberately sat closer to Lark because he felt that he didn't get to try chatting with Lark lately.

Karrin's face fell when Lark turned away, as usual, and pretended he didn't hear Karrin. Eeera was sitting nearby and shook her head at Karrin, gesturing for him to give up. But Karrin didn't want to. He tried again and again to get Lark to talk, until Lark sighed and covered his ears. That really hurt Karrin, despite it being nothing out of the ordinary. Karrin glanced at Eeera, who invited him to come to where his other friends were waiting for him.

When Lark was finally left alone, he smiled at the article he was reading. They were the news reports on the fondal:

Fondal Mineral Experiments with Seven Adults and One Five-Year-Old Child Successful

How overjoyed they sounded, thought Lark, still reading. It was then that he came upon a passage that made him pause.

Liara Grae, leader of this investigation (narrator's note: reporters did not know their Rarerus identity), *informed the reporters that she and her team had expected something more from the five-year-old—more than just a significant athletic boost. When asked what exactly she meant, she smiled and refused to reveal her thoughts. But when asked again, she finally said, "We thought there might be some dramatic extra change in him, not as in a change in bodily strength, speed, or endurance, but some kind of additional, interesting change." When asked to elaborate, she again refused, but this time would not yield to further questioning.*

Lark frowned. Liara Grae. Someone was peeking over Lark's shoulder; Lark jolted forward in surprise.

"What are you reading?" asked Karrin.

Couldn't this boy just go away? Lark thought rather morosely. But Karrin sat next to him and continued to try to peek. In great irritation, Lark closed the screen of his article and strutted away.

AFTER SCHOOL, LARK TRAVELLED WITH HAUS BACK TO THE lab at the Breemil branch. The cool and purified smell of the lab greeted them like the breeze, and they sat down in orb chairs that were smooth with the colors of moonlight. Haus and the little five-year-old chemist faced Raoul and Marius, who were opposite them, across a wide and currently bare floating panel.

Lark immediately asked his companions what they thought of Liara's comment that he might have had some extra enhancements from the fondal. Haus lifted his eyebrows. "Who knows?" he uttered. Marius made an almost sheepish smile.

Raoul was the only one who appeared to be genuinely interested in this topic, while the two older men were perhaps too absorbed in their own experiments to care that much about other people's. Raoul said, "How do you feel yourself? Apart from your athletic changes, do you sense anything else different about your body or physical condition?"

"Not anything in particular." Lark pursed his lips. "Could you not contact Liara to ask her?"

A trace of what looked like discontent flickered across Raoul's face, and Haus and Marius tensed when they gave Raoul a glance. But thankfully, Raoul said, "Okay. She's bound to be busy, though, so let's not bother her for too long." He sounded rather hasty.

Before long, Lark, Raoul, Haus, and Marius beheld a glorious projection of the Rarerus leader, who currently stood in a dark purple room. Liara Grae smiled at everyone and cast Lark a curious gaze.

Though Lark had originally wanted Raoul to talk for him, he afterwards felt ashamed at his silliness and cowardice, and so he steeled himself now to ask, "Liara, what did you mean when you said to the reporters that you suspect the fondal might have additional effects on me?"

The leader of the Rarerus arched her eyebrows at him, as though amused, and, oddly enough, delighted at his enquiry. She replied, "Our team were discussing the results after the fondal test yesterday, and Alia (pronounced "ah-lye-ah"), one of our scientists and combat mission leaders, pointed out that the fondal enhancement for you was roughly similar to the physical enhancement shown by the adult participants, which was strange as we thought you would gain a larger boost. We then tossed around ideas, and agreed that the fondal must have given you something more too, though we don't know what."

Lark fidgeted a bit in annoyance but also discomfort. He protested nevertheless, "That is nothing more than what you told the news reporters. What ideas have you and the other scientists 'tossed about'?"

At this moment, someone said in the background, "Liara, why don't I explain?"

Liara glanced to her right, nodded with a smile, and shifted to let a Rarerus member who appeared to be in their early twenties join the conversation. This newcomer was short and slight, but in a pleasant, almost engaging way. Liara put a hand on their shoulder in a gesture of warmth, before letting go and saying, "Lark, this is Alia."

Alia Lyreal (pronounced "lee-ree-oll") was clothed in shades of sea blue, and had soft, dainty facial features that were earnest in their demeanor. "Hello, Mr Arias. First of all, I'm neutrois and androgynous, so please refer to me using the pronoun 'they.' "

Lark nodded. Individuals who had a nonbinary gender identity (i.e. neither exclusively "male" nor exclusively "female") were in the minority of the Drellian population, but Lark had met a few adults and classmates of this identity before, so Alia didn't surprise him. "Neutrois" is a kind of neutral gender while "androgynous" is a combination of male and female. Many nonbinary individuals, though not all, go by pronouns like "they" or "ze" instead of "he" or "she." (For more details, see "Nonbinary gender identities[1]" under "Drellian Society" and "Gender Issues.")

Alia continued, "If the fondal didn't give you an extra athletic improvement, maybe it improved your mental and creative abilities. Do you feel any changes in those areas, Lark?"

Lark scowled at them and said, "As if I need any enhancement in those areas."

Alia seemed to hide a smile. "I wasn't implying that you needed anything. I was just saying, your mental and creative capacities must be outstanding for Haus, Marius, and Raoul to invite you to the Rarerus, particularly at such a young age. But perhaps the fondal increased your intellectual and imaginative powers to an even more impressive height. One can never stop surpassing oneself, you know?"

That appeased Lark somewhat. "Other than that, what other possibilities for the fondal have you thought of?" he questioned.

Alia gave him a little smile. "There could possibly be a—development in your emotional maturity or social skills."

Lark furrowed his brows and his mouth grew tight. "Even if the fondal gave me that, I do not need those emotional or social 'improvements.' "

To Lark's exasperation, Alia shrugged. "It was just a guess."

"What about other types of—more useful abilities?" Lark quipped.

"Like superhuman ones?" Alia asked. "Who knows? That might be possible, and they would be nice, since with our current level of technology on Drell, superhuman powers are still unattainable."

(See "Superpowers" under "Technology.")

Lark peered at Alia, as he could tell from their facial expression and tone of voice that they didn't actually think Lark's idea of superpowers was possible for the fondal. So he said, irritated, "If not superhuman powers, creative, mental, emotional, or social capacities, what else could it be?"

At his question, Alia perked up again, and a light in their eyes seemed to be doing a wild dance. "Oh, it could be anything, like giving you the ability to read other people's minds. Not in the telepathic way, but in an intuitive way; so you have a more acute perception of what others are thinking, which will most definitely be helpful, especially if you're facing off against enemies."

Lark grudgingly agreed with that last point.

Alia went on, "Or, the fondal could make you more eloquent; you'll be able to express yourself more clearly and concisely to others. That goes for written communication too, not just for spoken words. Goodness knows that would be a great advantage when you tell others about your scientific ideas and discoveries."

Lark had to admit that verbal eloquence wouldn't be a bad thing to have either.

Then Alia said, "Or, another thing we thought of, is that the fondal could make you more adept at lying, which would truly come in handy when you want to trick the Arach or any other people."

Liara Grae, who was still standing beside Alia, smiled at this. Alia probably sensed their leader's shift in facial expression because they gave Liara a sheepish look, then turned back to face Lark. "Uh, I don't mean to say that you should use your newfound competence in lying to dupe others regularly. I was really mostly thinking about the Arach."

"Of course," Lark said matter-of-factly. "But only if I do get such a boost in my deceptive abilities." He added, "Yet, it is also possible that different children—if you should experiment on any others of my age—could gain different extra fondal enhancements."

"Yeah," Alia said, looking glad that Lark pointed this out. "There are so many possible things that might have happened with the fondal, so many plausible speculations." They gave Lark a warm smile. "Isn't that what makes science so intriguing?"

Lark would have smiled back if he had a different personality or were a parallel universe version of himself. Instead, he just nodded his agreement and said, "Indeed. But that is only one of the many reasons why science is the most spellbinding and transcendental pursuit in existence."

That was probably the greatest extent of positive emotion Raoul, Haus, and Marius had ever heard Lark express.

AFTER THIS TALK WITH ALIA THAT PROVIDED NO CERTAIN answers, Lark busied himself in the meantime with his daily learning of science. It made him very happy to keep expanding his knowledge and understanding, of course, but very soon, he was curious to see more of Rarerus again. If he really were an accepted member now, he had the right to understand a bit more about their operations. He still had not formally accepted the membership, however, and so the next time he came to the Breemil branch, he announced straight to Raoul and the others that he would today, so please would they show him more of Rarerus.

This abrupt acceptance caught the Breemil Rarerus team off guard; but they beamed. "Finally," Marius said. "What would you like to know about first?"

Lark thought he had nothing to lose by asking directly what he most wanted to know aside from the fondal extra enhancements. "Tell me about Liara Grae."

The others stared. Lark wondered if Liara was so terrifying a leader that they didn't dare complain about her even in her absence. But then Raoul said, "She's a great leader. She only just settled into her new station a few months ago, but she's already led several successful missions to save a lot of victims who were about to be antimattered."

"I still do not understand this," said Lark. "How does Rarerus, or Liara herself, find out who the victims are before they go to the chambers?"

"Ah, when an Arach virus lays its web egg, and the egg starts to spread its web on a person's body, the egg emits a special kind of radiation that we can detect. We have one detector in every branch and the Center, but the Center's detector can sense them at a farther radius than the other branches'. And since we have at least one branch in every sector, we have multitudes of these detectors all over Drell.

"But since detection sensitivity is of limited radius within each huge sector, we unfortunately miss out on many Arach victims and that's why Liara predicts that we only manage to find ten percent of those victims— and we don't even manage to save all of them," said Raoul. There were seventy sectors on Drell.

Lark gave him a "why didn't you tell me all of this before" look, which Raoul got and thus replied, "Sorry we didn't tell you this earlier, because we didn't want you to know too much if you weren't an honorary member of the Rarerus yet." Lark frowned. Perhaps. Then Raoul said, "But did you want to know more about Liara?"

"Yes, please."

"She was recruited into the Rarerus from the age of fifteen, but she had been such a quick learner, that she already gained the favor of our former leader Jax, which explains how she became the next leader. She definitely is a remarkable fighter, scientist, and leader of many Arach combating and victim rescue teams; I myself was often in a team led by her, as were many other members," he said. "Our leader is definitely one to admire." While Haus and Marius nodded their agreement, Raoul looked strangely less enthusiastic.

Marius then told Lark about all the amazing and benevolent things she did, which showed that she was not only a hero in the missions and investigations, but was also a wonderful person who deserved the greatest esteem and love from all the members she led.

Unfortunately, Lark did not actually pay that much attention to what Marius said. He got the general picture of how Liara was like, or at least, how she appeared to be according to her most devoted followers. But this wasn't quite what Lark wanted to know. Maybe Raoul's answers would be more informative if he were willing to tell Lark more, but he probably wouldn't.

Nevertheless, when Raoul escorted him back home, as it was past evening already, Lark asked bluntly what Raoul really thought of Liara, and to tell him anything he should know the next time Lark confronted her in person.

To his surprise, Raoul did not look too taken aback by his questions, as if he were expecting Lark to ask him sooner or later. Raoul smiled. "You noticed, huh?" Lark tightened his lips together, as he didn't want to answer. Raoul said, "Well—I don't plan to tell you any time soon, if you don't mind." Of course Lark minded, but he saw that trying to pry more would not work; still, he believed that Raoul would reveal something sometime or later.

KREESHA RETURNED HOME ONE DAY CARRYING A BUNCH OF fluttering flowers, of blue, violet, and lilac. She showed them enthusiastically to Graham and Lark. She had to knock many times, quite hard, for Lark to come out of his room. He really had no desire to see whatever antics his mother was getting into this time; but her knocking disrupted his reading so much, that he had to come out and glare at her. Kreesha was in too good of a mood to be discouraged by her son's usual moodiness, however. She said, "Grae Grae, Larky, I have a great new plan. We are going to plant these chrystacias everywhere around our front and backyards."

Yes, Drellian houses also had front and backyards where they could decorate as much or as little as they liked. But tenants could choose whether they wanted fences around these places. Graham and Kreesha had already planted numerous things in both the front and backyard, most of them to yield interesting vegetables and fruit for them to experiment with for their cooking, but some were mere embellishments of their home.

"Aren't they beautiful?" Kreesha continued with a beam. "We can take these lovely things to encircle our house so that it's like we're protected by a ring of these purple beauties. What do you say?"

Graham was happy that she was happy and he asked, "What made you suddenly want to get chrystacias?"

Kreesha shrugged. "I don't know. I just really felt like it today, I thought it might be a good idea. It's like how we suddenly have ideas for new dishes." Graham understood her analogy immediately. She then said to Lark, "It's like how you suddenly have ideas for what new science books to buy."

Her son cocked an eyebrow at his mother's attempt to garner his sympathy. He didn't care what she wanted to do to their front and back-yards; as long as she didn't do anything to his room. So, seeing that his parents were chatting with such animation about this new project, he slipped back into the house, not noticing that they were glancing with disappointment at his so-soon retreating figure.

Ever since Lark declared that he would officially join their society, Raoul, Marius, and Haus had been explaining more about the intricacies of Rarerus and told him about the many past missions they had.

"How do you recruit the combaters and rescuers?" Lark had asked. He himself was not particularly interested in being involved in a mission, but he was nevertheless curious about the members who were involved in them.

"Hmm, often it's just a hunch about which people look like they would be strong and resourceful during dangerous missions. But if we can, we do like to observe what they do regularly, to get a feel of their abilities. Just like how we got a feel of your abilities by how regularly and discerningly you ordered your chemicals from Haus's store," Raoul said. "We also have some physical combat training centers, that really do train young and old people how to fight in self-defense or during crucial situations. In those centers, we may find some who particularly stand out, and seem suitable for working in an organization like Rarerus. Then we approach them privately and ask them, like we asked you, if they would like to join."

Here, Lark wondered whether Raoul had ever been one of those combat recruits. Raoul was definitely a scientist, and when he said that he was in many of Liara's mission groups, he could mean that he participated as a scientist, but could it be possible that he worked as a fighter as well? A field agent? Once, Lark had asked him whether he was one of the Scythes like Haus and Marius. When Raoul replied no, he asked what his position was. But Raoul just smiled and didn't answer.

Kreesha and Graham were still decorating their front and backyards with those chrystacia flowers; Lark tossed them a casual glance, and then strode outside to do some field experiments. He wanted to see if he could extract a certain chemical from the quimemoris plant that grew near his house. This was also the plant he had been examining the day he ran into Karrin on his journey to Phuore.

During all this time, Lark had been studying this curious fondal structure with great fervor. It was exceedingly difficult to understand its order, because it was in such a disorder that if one did not know that it was a fondal beforehand, one would have simply given up in ever finding any organization within this haphazard mess. He tried as many equations as he could think of on it, many of these equations he acquired from visiting the Rarerus labs and asking the researchers and mathematicians. He managed to understand a bit of the fondal structure, but there was frustratingly so much left of it that he could not puzzle out at all.

Good-natured Raoul had offered to show Lark his and the other researchers' understandings of the fondal and their worked out equations so far; but prideful Lark thanked him and said he would try to work them out himself. He could probably figure out a lot more than all of those scientists put together anyway, he thought.

So it was curious how Lark could not muster much respect for even scientists at that elite level. Well, to some degree, he did genuinely respect and admire them, and want to emulate them; but at the same time, he had such supreme confidence in his abilities that he thought he could surpass them given a bit more time. Nobody put as much time in science and chemistry as he did, after all. Lark forgot how there were so many areas and fields in science, that even if you were a natural obsessor, there was no way you could be superior to another elite scientist in every realm of science, because inevitably they would be far more versed in the knowledge of certain realms than you were.

Lark also found the chance to ask Liara, via a hologram talk, how she had come up with the number ten percent for how much of the total

Arach activity the Rarerus sensors could detect. Liara seemed intrigued, though not entirely surprised, at Lark's interest in this matter.

She asked nevertheless, "Are you sure you want to know? It's a very complex mathematical situation."

Lark nodded with a firm determination that revealed just a hint of his disbelief that Liara would even doubt his abilities of comprehension.

And so, Liara went through a rather long conversation with Lark, explaining all the variables, equations, amongst many other things. Lark took a while to understand it all, as even he was not accustomed to such complex calculations, his diligent study of the fondal notwithstanding; but after some time, he understood how Liara had inferred that ten percent value.

Liara was honestly impressed by his speed of comprehension, especially given his age and unfamiliarity with Rarerus affairs. Raoul was just astonished that Liara was willing to spend so much time explaining all this to Lark, even as the busy leader of the Rarerus. But Raoul guessed that Liara was eager to train up the child members of the Rarerus in particular; she had always been enthusiastically supportive of the child Beams, Amber and Eventii.

PRESENTLY, LARK HEARD A CRY FROM THE FRONT YARD. IT WAS Kreesha. "Grae Grae, come look at this." Lark at first did not want to care, but curiosity got the better of him and he rushed out—with his newfound speed—to the front yard where his mother was. He knew he should make a better effort to conceal his fondal-enhanced capabilities, but he at times still couldn't resist the urge to dash with that satisfying swiftness.

Kreesha glanced up in amazement at her son's arrival, but she nonetheless said to him, "Look at the petal of this one." She pointed to one of the chrystacia's purple petals that was stained with a yellowish tint. Some other chrystacia petals nearby were stained with a similar color.

"Oh no, have we been taking care of them right?" Graham asked with worry.

His parents went on for some length of time about the possible problems of their plant care, while Lark thought about other possibilities.

"Mother, father, if you do not mind, I will take one of these petals with me and examine it."

"You will? Thank you, son!" Kreesha reached out to hug him, but Lark dodged it, and plucked out a yellowed petal with a robotic arm that he had summoned from the computer and strutted off to his room.

"At least our boy is participating in a family event," Graham said optimistically.

In his room, aka his lab, Lark added many chemicals and solvents to try to isolate whatever was wreaking havoc in this petal. He identified the usual chemical patterns of a plant's petal, though some were specific to chrystacias, and then saw some very interesting other patterns.

Some of the petal cells had a larger-than-normal nucleus, and inside those nuclei, were a few extra chromosomes than chrystacia cells should have. There were also extra ribosomes. Some unexpected cell receptors and cell signalers were found on the membrane too. There was a tiny rupture in the cell wall and membrane of many of these abnormal cells, like they were channels through which strange chemicals could go.

Lark gripped his fists harder in his concentration and fury to understand this abnormality. He used the robotic hand to check the texture of the petal—he dared not use his new barrier gloves, in case it was something very dangerous. The texture was smooth and silky just as a normal petal should be. It later struck him that this cell abnormality reminded him of a brain abnormality he was reading about recently.

The latter was called fetalysis, where the brain cells also had expanded nuclei, more chromosomes, and channel-like ruptures in their membranes. He at first thought these were tumor cells by the way they aggregated. But it was clear afterwards that they could not be tumor cells because they never divided or expanded their territory. Scientists were unsure what this phenomenon meant. They only found that individuals with severe fetalysis seemed to be completely shut off from their external world; they stared into space and could not see you even if you shook them vigorously or screamed their name. They probably became only responsive to their internal stimuli, locked up in the prison of their own mind.

The curious thing about this fetalysis, was that though the person was permanently absent, they did not seem "dead." In fact, after brain scans, scientists found that there was intense and very rapid communication between the brain cells (both neurons and glial cells) in the regions with a high density of those abnormal cells. One hypothesized that these cells were aligning their little channels to do some abnormal extra communication; the cells did occasionally touch their channels for a while, but quickly detached from each other afterwards.

One expected that there would be new kinds of proteins generated from the extra chromosomes; yet, there were none. There were a lot of cell signalers, cell receptors, and other tiny molecules that were transferred from one cell to the other. This kind of channeling reminded one disconcertingly of the process of bacterial conjugation—where bacterial cells connected to each other via a bridge and delivered genetic material from one to the other. Could these fetalysis cells be a form of bacterial cell?

Scientists were unsure about this too. Anyhow, with this super, rapid-fire communication between fetalysis cells and a few surrounding normal cells, it appeared that the fetalytic person was in a frenzy of thoughts. Perhaps it was precisely because the person was so overwhelmed by their internal stimuli that their brain shut down from receiving any external stimuli.

Yet, some scientists argued that this explanation didn't make sense, as taking in external stimuli would often calm down the mind instead; so wouldn't their brains want to open up to external stimuli to slow down those feverish thoughts? But whatever the true explanation was, researchers were still clueless as to what the person was thinking, feeling, or experiencing precisely.

Fetalysis was called so because the person was like a fetus: they had almost no awareness of external stimuli and were only sensitive to the stimuli inside the "womb," i.e. the person's mind. "Lysis" derived from how the abnormal cells were partially broken down to form channels.

After reading about this vast mystery, Lark yearned to discover something about it. He pored through countless articles on this phenomenon and anything tangentially related to it. But he found nothing. It was a shame that he didn't have an actual fetalysis patient in front of him to do tests on.

Right now, this similarity to fetalysis in the petals of the chrystacia fascinated and riveted Lark to no end. He later heard a gentle knock on his door, followed by Kreesha's voice, "How is it?"

"Have you found anything?" Graham asked as well.

"Nothing yet," Lark lied, because if he told them he found something, his parents would demand that he tell them; but it was impossible to explain such complex scientific phenomena to the lay community.

His parents made disappointed noises. Graham said, "Well, take your time, son. We really appreciate your efforts in helping us figure this out!" Lark did not respond.

On his trip to the Breemil Rarerus lab the day after, Lark brought the strange petals and explained to Haus, Marius, and Raoul what had happened and that he suspected it had something to do with fetalysis.

Like Lark, Raoul was quickly intrigued by this mystery. "Fetalysis!" Raoul cried. "We have several of these patients in our labs right now. Liara's been wondering if these patients have anything to do with Arach affairs. They appear not to be Arach clones, as they are clearly unlike their normal selves, and we found no traces of bluamine or zanyliline in their cells. Just extra chromosomes but no strange proteins produced." Raoul and Lark talked about this matter for a while longer.

If Lark were a normal person, he would like Raoul a lot as the latter engaged him in such enjoyable chatter on his favorite subject in the world, science. But as Lark was anything but normal, though he did not dislike Raoul, Lark did not particularly like him either. The boy simply felt more comfortable with Raoul and more certain that he could talk about what-ever science topic he liked without being met with a blank stare, for Raoul was a very well-informed scientist. There were obviously times when Raoul had not heard of something that Lark brought up, but those were problems easily solved, as Raoul could call up his computer right away and read the articles that Lark did, or simply ask Lark to fill him in on the details instead.

Since Raoul was an actual expert scientist, Lark did not mind explain-ing, as he knew he would be very swiftly understood, and Raoul often had questions and thoughts on the topic as soon as Lark finished explaining too. So, whilst a normal person would take great delight in talking to such a companion, Lark only felt more at ease with and less condescension towards him compared to with other people; Raoul's company was just more tolerable.

Haus and Marius soon joined the conversation on these petals. "Are you sure it's not just a coincidence? You sure it must be related to the fetalysis epidemic?" Marius asked, peering at the purple and yellow hues that flowed and criss-crossed on the chrystacia sample.

Lark shot him an annoyed look, because he didn't like having his opinions questioned. This happened a lot in the Rarerus, though; all scientists, if they were real scientists, constantly had their opinions and theories challenged. "If not, then what do you suggest?" Lark said.

Marius shrugged. "It could be anything."

"Then have you encountered a similar phenomenon in your experience of plant biochemistry?"

"Not really," Marius admitted, and continued in his reflections.

All of a sudden, Haus said, "Hey, what about the green substance? You know, the green stuff that contained troptomyces in your room that made you sick? Maybe there's still some of this green substance left in your house, and it somehow affected those chrystacia petals?"

Lark had told them about this incident in an attempt to elicit some explanation of par-the-air's functions, but without success, as Marius and Haus, and even Raoul, were so tight-lipped.

Lark really had not thought about the troptomyces in a while. He mused, "That is a possible factor in our equation. I wonder if what my parents made on that day had anything to do with the troptomyces, or even with this petal situation." Lark explained about the Ruminence his parents made when prompted to elaborate.

Marius said, "Why didn't you tell us about this earlier?"

The boy shrugged and simply said, "It did not seem to be relevant to any of our past discussions."

Haus ignored this trifling issue and said, "Well, I suggest we get our par-the-air and some amosti and do some experimenting!" Raoul smiled at his enthusiasm. Lark wondered why Haus would risk getting them sick again, though Lark himself would do the same thing. Anything to solve this chemical conundrum.

Haus then said that perhaps Lark could ask his parents to make the Ruminence again.

Lark was open-mouthed at the suggestion that he should ask his parents a favor.

Haus immediately understood what he was thinking, and said, "Come on, it's easy. And it would be a great help in our understanding of this strange chemical riddle."

With much reluctance, Lark mustered up the self-control to nod, albeit with a very grouchy expression on his face.

THAT NIGHT BACK AT HOME, LARK MADE HIS REQUEST AND HIS parents just stared at him. "Make Ruminence again?" Kreesha said. "Why of course we can, honey!" She was delighted.

But Graham said, "Are you sure though? Last time it made you sick—"

"That was because of my own chemical tampering, father, and for that I am again very sorry. But this time I desire you two to make me this Ruminence for me to study in my science club," Lark said.

Graham silenced, and acquiesced. His parents were both smiling, and they beamed at each other. So Lark left them alone to do their work.

The new Ruminence was glistening, green, and wobbly when it was done. It really looked like some kind of jelly, although on closer examination, it was clearly a lot more sophisticated than that. Still, an ordinary mortal on Earth would have drooled at it. An ordinary mortal on Drell would have drooled at it too.

In contrast, Lark grimaced when he picked up the Ruminence with his barrier gloves. His parents asked him where he got those gloves from. Lark curtly answered that they were free gifts from his science club, a response which thankfully already satisfied his parents.

"Here it is," said Lark, and set down the green Ruminence on one of the lab's ivory-brown panels. Raoul had accompanied Lark to the Breemil Rarerus branch as had become their habit.

"It looks beautiful!" remarked Marius. "Would you mind if I tasted a bit of the Ruminence?" He got stares from the other three. He shrugged. "What? It was intended for dessert, right?"

"Taste it if that pleases you," Lark said, disgusted. "But be quick with it."

So, with both gratitude and joy, Marius scooped a bit of it into a container and slurped it up. "Oh my gosh, this is so delicious! Lark, you're so lucky to have such parents! And you said they make things like these for you very often?" Lark nodded, making a face again. "How wonderful!" Marius exclaimed. "Ahem. But now I must leave this marvelous dessert to you for investigation." He said that as though he were incredulous that such an innocuous and charming delicacy could have anything to do with troptomyces or fetalysis, let alone with the chrystacia's petals. Lark and the others thought otherwise, of course.

"Ready to test it, Lark? I'll let you decide how to investigate this," said Raoul generously.

Lark accepted this generosity without a thought, as he had fully expected Raoul to make such an offer. Lark commanded the computer to scan the Ruminence as well as the carefully boiled mixture of par-the-air and amosti. He had cautiously kept the spring-green product formed by the par-the-air and amosti reaction in a tightly sealed expanding container. This container was to hold in all steam and pressure while it expanded; it was like a balloon that could be inflated indefinitely without popping.

As it turned out, there was not a trace of similarity between the green substance and the Ruminence. The Ruminence was, as predicted, a harmless green dessert that coincidentally looked like the green substance in both texture and color. Looking at this dessert probably triggered Lark's memories of the green substance, and sometimes the mere memory of things could jolt up physiological reactions inside a person.

Even now, Lark felt a kind of nausea mounting to his throat, but he brushed that off as silly. He must be imagining it. Nonetheless, he glanced away from the experiment panel to the pristine, soothing blue wall opposite him until the sick feeling faded away.

Marius glanced at him. "Are you all right?" Lark gave him a curt nod and refocused on viewing those molecules.

"The green substance molecules remind me of a neuronal pattern," said Raoul.

When Lark and the other two asked him to explain, he said, "Maybe I'm just being inappropriately imaginative, but it looks like that the way these molecules, these atoms arrange themselves, the way they move—doesn't it remind you of how a neuron moves?" Yes, Drellian scientists had discovered that neurons could actually move and migrate, at certain times.

Upon closer observation, Lark and the other two indeed recognized the motion that Raoul had noticed. The ability to draw connections in science was highly dependent on having a wayward imagination, after all. Lark then started to make inferences everywhere. "Perhaps this green substance—or the troptomyces inside it—are linked to brain function, and the petals are also linked to brain function, which in turn is linked to fetalysis."

"You draw conclusions too quickly," Raoul smiled. "How do you know that the culprit chemical in the chrystacia petals is troptomyces—or the green substance—for sure? Let's scan these petals again." Without even waiting for Lark's approval, Raoul commanded the computer to start scanning. The computer announced that it was indeed troptomyces as well as the particles surrounding the troptomyces in the green substance. But something did not add up. Raoul tapped his chin. Lark racked his brain for ideas. Could it have been something similar to the green substance or troptomyces instead?

"Let's compare all of these samples," said Haus, breaking up their reveries. In a moment, the Ruminence, the green substance, the petals, and a sample of a fetalytic patient's brain cells were compared. The latter was obtained by non-intrusively copying a 3D image of the brain cells. It was like a brain scan, but with separate cells visible and in a 3D holographic image, complete with the recordings of its physical texture; so you could touch this hologram if you liked.

Immediately, with much excitement, Lark exclaimed, "I see a pattern! The petal and fetalytic cells, the Ruminence and green substance molecules, are all shaped and move about in a certain manner that reminds me of the Aira dance!"

The Aira dance was a kind of motion pattern that cells and molecules sometimes engaged in when they were under a certain kind of stimulation. They could be chemically or electrically stimulated to "dance." But at times, some molecules or cells could be seen "dancing" in this way even in the absence of stimulation, which baffled scientists.

It was called "Aira" precisely because the style of dance implied a kind of airy feeling. You see, scientists were permitted to be a bit artistic and vague in their expressions as well; vagueness of expression was not the prerogative of artists. Aira dancing was like dancing in the air, involving air spirits, or something of that sort.

Raoul, Marius, and Haus fixed their eyes on the scenes of those cells and molecules moving. The more they looked, the more Lark appeared to be right. How come they had never thought of it before? It was so simple! It was one of those times when hindsight bias occurred. When you know the answer, everything seems so simple. But before you know the answer, it's so hard to figure it out. Raoul beamed and was about to pat Lark on the back, but Raoul withdrew his hand when he remembered that Lark did not like physical displays of affection or even approbation.

Right now, Lark looked up at them. "Since we finally know a bit about what is happening, can we figure out more? I know that we do not know very much about the Aira dance, as it is a recently discovered phenomenon, but can we use this present knowledge to deduce further knowledge?"

Raoul tapped his chin again, deep in thought. Then Haus said, "They are probably being stimulated by some source. You know," he added, "I've always had a theory that when molecules do the Aira dance 'in the absence of stimulation,' they actually are stimulated by something, but it's just that our current scientific technology cannot permit us to see what that source of stimulation is—we can't even see the stimulation itself."

"You are suggesting that the stimulator and the stimulation are invisible?" asked Lark.

"Uh—that could be possible, but not necessarily," Haus answered, shaking his head with a smile that looked both blithe and earnest. "It could simply be a physically visible thing that we cannot yet detect with our instruments. It's like how in the very ancient times, people couldn't detect bacteria because they did not have the instruments to see such small things, but the bacteria were by no means invisible."

"You mean whatever the stimulator and stimulation are, they could be too small for our instruments to see?" Lark asked, intrigued.

"Not necessarily," Haus said again. "I—it could also be something like a different wavelength. You know how the naked eye can't see UV rays? So whatever the stimulator and stimulation are, they could be in a different wavelength, or a different dimension, or different code, or something like that—something that we haven't thought of detecting before because we were never aware of its existence."

"Until now," said Lark, actually smiling at the idea.

"If my hypothesis is correct," said Haus, chuckling but maintaining his scientist's skepticism. But he was pleased that Lark seemed to be quite taken with his idea already.

"Why don't we assume that your theory is true, and see what we can deduce from that," suggested Raoul.

Marius nodded, entertained by and interested in their discussion.

Lark said, "All right. So, the Aira dance links the Ruminence, green substance, chrystacia petals, and fetalysis cells together, even if they do not all look alike. And the green substance molecules' atomic movements resemble the movements of a neuron. Possibly they are all stimulated by some unknown source that current science cannot detect." He thought and thought, getting increasingly excited.

In the midst of this feverish intellectual wandering, Marius said, "Um, sorry to spoil your fun, but what are we doing this for?" He instantly received a glare from Lark, and a reproachful look from Raoul. Haus gave Marius a smile. Marius continued, "I mean, it's fun intellectually and all, and I would like to speculate on this more myself, but what's the point in this? What will we gain by studying these mysterious things that seem to be connected by the Aira dance?"

Before Lark could reply, Raoul said, "On the surface it doesn't look at all useful, and I understand your concern that we might be wasting valuable time and energy investigating this, but my intuition tells me that we may be coming across something that may be useful for future missions."

Marius didn't at all believe him, as he knew that Raoul habitually

THE BOY WHO LOVED SCIENCE TOO MUCH

went on such intellectual adventures, just because his intuition told him it would lead somewhere. Even if it did not lead anywhere useful, Raoul ardently believed that what he discovered and learned so far, would be useful in the future anyway. He was one of those who firmly believed in the vast interconnectedness of science, where knowing about one chemical would be a pathway to learning about another, and another, and another, until you came to the great important chemical.

Marius shook his head inwardly. Youngsters were all like this. They weren't as careful with their time and resources like older people were. Nevertheless, Marius wanted to indulge these young people; he enjoyed indulging young people and seeing the happiness on their faces because it made him feel young too.

While they delved into their task of constant speculation, Lark Arias thought about all the other plants in his parents' front and backyards, and wondered if he should test them all. Now even he thought that his whim was unreasonable and would likely take up too much time. It was great to forge a network of chemical knowledge, but when one was with the Rarerus, one should choose something more practical to study.

After a much longer time of staring at the chemicals and magnifying different parts of those molecules and cells, Lark and Raoul decided to give up for the day and rest. They would more likely think of a solution after they had dipped their heads into some other things; exposing oneself to other stimuli often gave one new ideas to solve the original problem. So they left these four chemical samples behind with a complacent confidence in their hearts.

---

1. **Nonbinary gender identities**
    People who are nonbinary identify as neither exclusively "male" nor exclusively "female." Gender identity is one's inner sense of what gender one has, which can be the same as, or different from, the gender one was assigned to at birth. Gender expression, on the other hand, refers to one's behavior, personality, interests, and self-presentation that display a degree of masculinity and femininity; gender expression doesn't always match up with gender identity, however. For instance, one can act and present oneself in a mostly masculine way, yet identify as female.
    Some nonbinary gender identities include: neutrois (a type of neutral gender), androgynous (a mix of both male and female), gender fluid (gender varies over time), genderqueer (a different term for "nonbinary"), agender (no gender), demigirl (partially

female), and demiguy (partially male). Many of these individuals, though not all, use nonbinary pronouns such as "they" or "ze" instead of "he" or "she."

Although nonbinary individuals are in the minority on Drell (like on Earth), they are fully accepted by the Drellian society. Lark himself has a number of nonbinary acquaintances and classmates, so Alia (Liara's neutrois and androgynous friend) is not a surprise to him.

TWELVE
THE FIRST MISSION

When Lark met up with Raoul, Haus, and Marius again, they continued to examine the green substance and the other three chemicals. Lark had told his parents that he brought their yellowed chrystacia petals to the science club to study, where the scientists had found nothing really wrong with them; some plants simply went through a yellowing stage that, even if it lasted an indefinite amount of time, would not likely harm the plant itself.

And indeed, Kreesha and Graham's chrystacias seemed to have nothing out of the ordinary about them, save the yellow stains on some of the petals on a few chrystacias. Mr and Mrs Arias still felt a bit apprehensive, but since even the scientists at Lark's club said that it was no cause for alarm, there was no reason for Kreesha or Graham to doubt this. And thus, Lark successfully deflected his parents' suspicions once again.

At the Breemil labs, sometime during the scientists' intense focus on their work, Haus announced, "Attention, members. I have just received a message from our leader." He proceeded to distribute the sounds and images of the message to everyone's computers.

Soon, a life-sized hologram of Liara's head and shoulders appeared in front of every person in the lab. "Honored members," she said. "My research team here in Vénus have been investigating plants and drinking liquids that have mysteriously changed colors. We have found that all cells and molecules involved in these abnormalities are performing the rare Aira dance. In addition, several branches across Drell have reported similar Aira dance incidents with abnormal plants and chemicals. We believe that this co-occurrence of Aira dancing molecules in recently found affected life forms and substances may be related to Arach activities."

Lark was surprised that Liara had already unearthed this discovery he just made yesterday. He was also a little disappointed that he was not the only scientist who had figured out that it was Aira dancing.

Liara continued, "More specifically, we speculate that this simultaneous eruption of Aira dancing is a vibratory network generated by the Arach. Perhaps they are trying to communicate their next target locations for their victims. My team is currently investigating this possibility. Good day, members." And she was off.

Lark took in all of this with a kind of awe, wonder, and terror too. So he was at last joining them in the fight against the Arach?

KARRIN WAS, FOR ONCE, DOING SOMETHING WITHOUT HIS parents knowing. It had started off innocently, when a friend called Criva (pronounced "Kree-vah") said he found this fun new club somewhere close to school that could train you in the skills of combat.

As Karrin was both a curious and a people-pleasing kid, he started going with his friend to this club. It proved to be a great delight and magnificent fun for Karrin too, all those physical maneuvers, those punches, kicks, jumps, sprints, cuts, all those cool things. He in addition felt quite at home in this activity because he found that fighting was very similar to dancing. Both were about moving in an elegant and coordinated way to achieve some purpose. He didn't know why, but he just really enjoyed trying out his physical abilities and challenging himself.

Yet, though this fighting had a lot in common with dancing, Karrin felt that his parents would disapprove of such a violent sport. He thought that fighting need not be violent, though. Friendly matches were non-violent. But on the other hand, if one needed to act in self-defense, one had to be violent anyway or risk being killed.

It was also unbelievably fun when he was taught how to use weapons. There were elastoropes that could stretch as long as one wanted when one threw them. There were guns that did not need reloading: their beams were generated by electricity that was recharged by ordinary indoor sources. They could be charged by portable chargers when outdoors too. But what Karrin liked most were the epics. These were long, sharp blades with edges that glowed gold, orange, or yellow. If one pushed a button on an epic, the blade would divide into a series of short golden flashes that slashed the enemy at a long distance.

Karrin and Criva now marched into a yellow and black battle room that seemed to thrum with energy, and they grinned. "Ready?" Karrin asked.

"Ready!" Criva said, and they both raised their epics. "Go!"

The two children had tremendous fun jumping around, slicing at each other with these epics, stabbing, wheeling, and doing any move possible. It really was no different from dancing. It was also as harmless as dancing, as this combat club's weapons were inoculated in that they would immediately pause just an inch away from the victim's skin, therefore never hurting them. So the only way to get hurt was to be punched, kicked, or the like. But since these fights were always closely supervised, nobody ever experienced anything serious. And even if anyone acquired any bruises, there were machines that automatically healed damaged tissue.

In a happy frenzy, Karrin and Criva lunged at each other with those epics. Karrin pressed the button—he loved pressing it—and ambushed his friend with thousands of flashing golden pieces. Criva shrieked but in a fury brandished out his golden pieces too with a press of his button. After a while, the two boys got enough of the good fight and retired from the arena, laughing with each other as they did so.

Raoul, who was supervising the two boys, smiled.

So every day, Karrin, Criva, and many other little boys and girls they befriended had frequent matches against each other and everyone had so much fun. Karrin especially enjoyed it because he felt more and more that this sport was so like dancing. It was all about being nimble and agile, having quick reflexes. It was more about being fast than being strong. The power of weapons that did not make direct contact with the adversary's skin was independent of the user's strength, of course; but close combat like punching and kicking did.

Still, Karrin was able to dodge most of these kicks and punches with ease; and thus, unlike most of his four to six-year-old peers, he was able to compete with the bigger and stronger boys and girls without any fear, and beat them almost effortlessly. It wasn't completely effortless because he had to concentrate to get his timing right, as fighting was not just about speed; it was about rhythm too. The rhythm had to be both accurate and fluid. Without fluidity you would likely become too rigid in your movements and not be able to respond to surprises.

This little Mr Treek was usually a modest person, but when he saw his unexpected success in this combat club, he couldn't help feeling rather delighted and proud of his fighting skills. One day while he was lifting weights, as many of the trainers had insisted that he become decent in strength too, Raoul, who was his current supervisor, came up to him. Karrin looked up.

"Karrin, you know you don't really need to be that strong."

The boy was confused.

Raoul continued, "In these arenas, you need to be able to punch and kick hard, but in real life, as you know, speed and agility count a lot more than strength."

Karrin was still befuddled and asked his supervisor to elaborate.

Raoul smiled, and since no one was listening to them, he explained to the little boy about the Arach. Karrin was scared, and like Lark, he asked what antimattering did to the victims. But Raoul's explanation was just as vague as Marius's was to Lark; because they really didn't know.

"So," said the boy, "what do you want me to do?"

"I am from an organization that resists and fights the Arach. We are called the Rarerus. We have been observing all of you, and you are among the five we have singled out for exceptional performance to help us fight the Arach. You are fast, Karrin, very fast for your age, and you are one of the few who understand that quick reactions are the key to winning, not strength. And now we humbly ask if you would like to join our society."

Poor Karrin was open-mouthed. "Who are the other four kids?"

"They are kids who you don't often talk to, and they are all older than you: eight, ten, eleven, and twelve-year-olds."

"But why pick a five-year-old like me?" Karrin asked, quite daunted.

"Because you have potential, and for two other reasons."

"What are they?"

"Let me show you something." Raoul took out two small metal contraptions. "These are hand beams. When you attach them to your wrists, you can fire energy blasts from them whenever you give them the thought command. All you have to do is will them to fire."

So these 'hand beams' were even more convenient than the guns that didn't require reloading, Karrin thought.

Raoul smiled, and continued, "This is why I said that the strength of your punches and kicks don't matter that much in our real world. And secondly, have you heard of the fondal structure?"

The boy shook his head truthfully.

Raoul remembered in embarrassment that Karrin was not a scientist like Lark; Karrin was a fighter. "The fondal is a chemical that can produce water, and in its water there are minerals that will make you stronger, faster, more flexible, and greater in your stamina. Strength doesn't matter much in your fights, but an extra boost would not hurt. And if we boost your already high speed and flexibility, and increase your endurance, you will be even more ready to combat the Arach."

Little Karrin wanted to say that he needed to ask his parents first, but he knew that they would never approve; so instead he said, "But what exactly will we need to battle against? The Arach clones?"

"Yes, the Arached humans. But the Arach have also been known to antimatter and Arach-clone laminae as well, clearly because many laminae have better physical and combat abilities than humans do. The Arached humans will have weapons like we do too, and some even with hand beams like these. But we also have shields, specifically gel body armor against physical attacks, and ray reflectors against such energy beams."

"So when their rays hit us, the rays will bounce back at them?"

"That is the idea, but some Arach clones have good enough reflexes to dodge these reflected rays, depending on how agile the original human is. But, there are times when their hand beams or physical attacks will be so strong that they will penetrate your armor and ray reflectors and hurt you —but still, your shielding will absorb a good amount of the blow."

"But we will get to heal ourselves when we do get hurt, right?"

"Yes, but only after the fight. During the fight you won't have time to open your healing equipment. And it would be dangerous to heal during combat because to heal, your wounds have to be opened wider for the healing chemicals to go in and do their job. Widening your wounds while you're battling would be dangerous because it makes those wounded places even more vulnerable to further attack," Raoul said. "Now during these missions, your task is not just to save the victims and fight against the Arached clones. You have to protect the scientists who go with you as well."

Karrin widened his eyes and waited for Raoul to explain.

Raoul continued, "We need the scientists to pour in just enough octamethyst to digest the webs on the victim, and on the right areas. It's not that we don't trust the combaters to do it themselves; it's just that the precision of the areas is very important. The scientists are trained to calculate the exact amount of octamethyst to apply to the particular victim and the exact areas of the body to apply it to. They then tell their computers the precise volumes and coordinates of the application."

Mental calculations were quite easy for Drellian scientists, actually, because they could speak out or think all the steps, formulae, equations, and operations needed, and let the computer check that there were no careless mistakes. Karrin was going to ask another question, but Raoul anticipated it and said, "If you were wondering, the scientists do wear ray reflectors and gel armor too, but frequently the blows will be strong enough to hurt them if the combaters are not careful in protecting them."

"Okay, but could we sometimes take the victims back to the branches for the scientists to use octamethyst, so that we don't have to put the scientists in danger in the first place?"

"We've thought of that too. But we never know when the web actually started forming—the Arach eggs only release a small amount of radiation at the start, so it's difficult to detect the egg when it's first laid. We very likely only start detecting their web-making after the eggs have made a good amount of the radiation. And the more web already made, the longer the octamethyst will take to finish digesting the web. So we want the web to be gone from the victim as soon as possible before anything else happens. That's why we need scientists to be there, ready to take immediate action.

"Also, since there is always the chance that the Arach will successfully take the victim away from us, we have to hurry to let the octamethyst start work on the victim. If we do lose our victim to the Arach, they might lay a new web egg. With two webs forming, the octamethyst will only slow down the webs' progress but not stop it, because the octamethyst won't act fast enough to beat the speed of two enlarging webs.

"Yet, this slowing down of the webs will still buy us time. Sometimes the Arach do succeed in taking the body away from us; and from past experience, applying the octamethyst beforehand indeed gave us enough extra time to ultimately save those victims." As an additional note, the Arach, for some inexplicable reason, preferred to have only one egg on the victim at any one time, and only lay an extra egg if the octamethyst was about to consume the old egg.

This was all so much to take in and Karrin was quite frightened, yet excited at the same time. "Okay," Karrin said. "When will the four other kids and I meet?"

"Very soon. But we have to see if the other four want to join us first."

It turned out that one girl and one boy, the eleven-year-old and ten-year-old respectively, decided not to join, for various reasons. So the eight-year-old girl, twelve-year-old boy, and Karrin were invited to meet in the combat club on a day where the club was normally closed.

Karrin Treek glanced around the peach and orange colored meeting room; pale yellow light glimmered down on everything and everyone inside, with warmth but also with concentration. The eight-year-old girl Yearlie (pronounced Year-lee) was staring straight ahead in a kind of frozen fear. The twelve-year-old boy Gastra looked calm, but it was evident that he was only acting so. Karrin didn't know how he looked like, but it was certainly not one of perfect composure either.

Raoul and the other supervisors sat down opposite the three nervous children, comforting them and saying that they need not be scared. Raoul elaborated to them many more details about the Rarerus and how they worked, and what they were currently doing. When Raoul saw that the children were considerably calmer after getting things straight in their minds, he asked their permission to give them fondal water. At this, Yearlie and Gastra looked clearly panicked; but Karrin gave a determined nod.

Lark marveled at the vehicle that Raoul Faya, Haus, and Marius drove, in which Lark and the other scientists from the Breemil branch now sat. It was pale green and sleek, streamlined to ensure maximum flying speed yet large enough to accommodate the thirty or so Rarerus members. "Why did you not use such a vehicle to transport us from your chemistry store to the Breemil branch?" Lark asked Haus. "That would have been a lot more efficient."

The group of scientists had taken off from the Breemil labs to go to the Larence ("Lair-rins") branch in response to Liara's request. Larence was a place located in Oftonoss, a sector that was relatively close to Fartha.

"Well, there wasn't any place to park such a big vehicle at the chemical store, and such a large Rarerus vehicle would attract too much attention and questions from ordinary Drellians. Not to mention that invisibility sprays are expensive so we couldn't waste it on hiding these big machines every time we go to the labs. It's a lot less wasteful just to spray a few human beings."

After hearing Haus's explanation, Lark kicked himself inwardly for asking such an obvious question. "How long will we take to get to the Larence branch?" he asked, trying to cover the previous stupidity with a more intelligent question. The Larence branch had reported the highest number of abnormal Aira dancing molecules out of all the branches, and it had coincidentally detected recent Arach activity.

Arach activity normally erupted in multiple sectors in Drell at once, not just one, so the branch or branches closest to these sites would work against the Arach by themselves without aid from other Rarerus teams; but for this Larence incident, since the Aira dance was a special phenomenon, Liara herself led the mission and invited twenty other branches closest to Larence to join. The Vénus Center was temporarily left to the seniors' care.

"We'll take about thirteen minutes to get there. Our Streeto (Stree-toe) is much faster than the Coaster, let alone the Coaster plus a few Hyure trips." To be more precise, the Streeto, at maximum speed, was about one and a half times faster than the inter-super-sector Coaster.

While they traveled, Lark studied the controls and all the physical features of the Streeto, and analyzed them with complicated equations in his head.

Before embarking on this mission, the Rarerus had again told Lark's parents about another science club trip that might last a few days, depending on how much they found to learn and explore in the Oftonoss sector. Food and extra change of clothing would be provided. Graham and Kreesha were simply glad that their son now had so many chances to socialize and connect with like-minded children instead of staying in his room. But they were worried that Lark might miss a lot of his studies.

"Do not worry, mother," Lark had said. "I can catch up again very quickly. You know I always do whenever I fall sick and miss classes."

So the Arias gave their permission, and told their Larky to have fun.

But even as Lark returned to the Rarerus with triumph, he wondered anxiously if his parents would still find out the truth one day.

LIARA GRAE GREETED LARK AND HIS COLLEAGUES WHEN THEY arrived at the Larence branch; it was hidden under an innocent-looking shop just as the Breemil branch was, except that this shop sold decorations instead of books. "You are the second branch to arrive," Liara said. "Thank you for responding with such rapidity. Now let me show you around the branch to familiarize you with the facilities while we wait for the others."

Marius, Haus, Lark, Raoul, and the others followed suit. But with puzzlement, Lark noticed that whilst all of the team's eyes followed Liara with an almost obsequious and intense eagerness, Raoul was glancing all about him, his expression blank, as if he didn't really care where Liara was guiding them. Lark noted to himself to ask Marius and Haus about this later in secret. Lark may be a natural obsessor and only interested in science, but strangely, these kinds of mysteries intrigued him too. During moments like these, one sees that there was a streak of humanity in Lark, after all.

At length, they came to a large room with fake blue-green grass for the floor. A room large enough to fit all of the Breemil branch. Liara turned around with a smile. "Here you see the energy dispenser, which would be useful for recharging ourselves after missions. For those of you who are new to Rarerus," here she glanced at Lark, but she quickly looked away to everyone else, "our energy dispensers generate liquids to replenish our energy, while imbuing this liquid with the taste of one of your favorite foods." She paused to let the new members make their sounds of awe. Lark was the only one who kept silent because he had no favorite food. Liara seemed to notice his silence, but she pretended to be oblivious.

She showed them around various other rooms and facilities of the Larence branch, and it turned out that different branches had different focuses of function: Larence was more into combat and missions; Breemil more into science and research. After this tour, Liara invited them all into a large, bright, and comfortable room to relax and eat with the first arrived branch, Miha, which was in the Darra sector. Liara offered them another gracious smile and went out to meet the next arriving branches.

The other eighteen branches eventually came too and everybody got busy discussing their assignments for the different missions. Raoul went over to talk to some of the leaders in the other branches; and while Raoul was thus occupied, Lark took this chance to pull Haus and Marius aside; he asked them quietly, "Please tell me truthfully. What is going on between Raoul and Liara?"

This question took the two aback, and they exchanged a nervous glance. Lark shot them a look of displeasure and said, "By your reactions, I can tell that you do indeed know something about this, so tell me."

Haus said to Marius, "I guess it's okay to tell him if he doesn't tell Raoul," and then to Lark, "you will keep this a secret, won't you?"

"Of course," Lark said.

Haus cleared his throat. "Not many of the Rarerus members know this, but Raoul and Liara are half-siblings."

Lark stared at him in amazement. "Please expand on that."

"Well, Raoul's father, Phinn Faya, died when Raoul was only eight. His mother Ustella soon married another man, Orlen Grae, who was very kind to her and Raoul, and the new couple soon had Liara. Raoul never liked his stepfather or half-sister because he was very close to his own father. And he was angry at his mother for falling in love with and marrying another man so quickly, as if she had completely forgotten about his father already. Plus, his mother and stepfather had Liara so quickly."

Marius wanted to jump into this narrative too and he said, "Yeah, the few of us who know this story feel really sorry for Liara, because it was obviously not her fault for being born from the second man and there was nothing wrong with being the second man's daughter either. Raoul was very cold to Liara all her life, and still is. And although on the surface, he follows her commands and goes on her missions like everyone else, it's very clear to us that he doesn't follow her in his heart. There might even have been some sibling rivalry between them.

"You know, Jax, our former leader? He appreciated and praised both Raoul and Liara, but especially Liara because she was more well-rounded. You see, Raoul was an out-and-out scientist, but he wasn't very interested in combat or strategizing. Yet, Liara was a good scientist, strategist, and fighter; she excelled in leading missions and her missions were so often successful and efficient; whilst Raoul wasn't that into leading missions and only led when nobody else could take the spot. He liked leading scientific investigations and research, but he really preferred someone else to do the actual combat missions." Marius smiled and shrugged. "So you can guess why Jax chose Liara to be his successor rather than Raoul. Raoul doesn't show it but we all think that he wanted to be the leader."

Lark shrugged. "But perhaps Raoul really does not want to be the Rarerus leader, especially since he does not enjoy leading battle missions. Being the Rarerus leader necessitates the leading of such battle missions from time to time, if I am not mistaken."

Marius still didn't look convinced, and was about to bicker on when Haus gestured for him to shush, as this was unimportant. Then they hastily left Lark for now and went back to check on the rest of the Rarerus members; Haus and Marius were two of the Scythes, after all, so many people were waiting for them.

Meanwhile, Lark took off by himself to an obscure corner where no one would bother him so he could contemplate those equations he had about the fondal. Could he ever solve those puzzles? He fiddled around with a million numbers, facts, and figures in his head, hoping that some connection would result.

Marius and Haus went off to look for Lark after the Rarerus had finished discussing their plans. The two had expected the boy to come with them to take part in the discussion, if not to contribute, then to at least listen. But they should have known better than to believe that Lark would suddenly become a proactive member of the society. "Where is that boy?" Marius asked, scratching his head.

Haus frowned. "He was here last time I saw him." He pointed to a corner.

"Maybe we'll ask Raoul to help us. He seems to know Lark best out of the three of us," said Marius.

"But he's busy now," Haus said. Raoul seemed to be discussing a very important topic with an approximately fifty-year-old woman. She was making faces and obviously disagreeing with what he said. Liara was close by talking to some other members, but Marius and Haus could see her eyes darting towards Raoul from time to time with some anxiety.

"Want to go and see what's wrong?" asked Marius.

"No. Let's let them deal with whatever it is themselves."

Raoul Faya was arguing intently, but civilly, with one of the three Spikes, Monna ("mawn-nah"), that the Arach operation could not be done without a certain member of the Rarerus. This member was a rather old man of about seventy, who was a decent scientist and an ex-combatant. Due to his old age, he had to do some of the less strenuous jobs. He could help with the science investigations, but he told Raoul that he really missed the old days of the Arach missions. He said that he would like to at least follow along and give the youngsters some advice on the sidelines. Raoul sympathized with him and said that he would try to let him join a team, and ask the mission members to give him extra protection.

So Raoul went to ask several members to see what they thought. Many were in favor of his proposal; the remainder just nodded, seeming to agree, so he assumed they did. He, in his satisfaction, was just about to ask one of the mission leaders to take care of the old man—he was called Centuri— when Monna the Spike cut in and said that he was being ridiculous. "Centuri is old and fragile! We can't send him off on a dangerous mission like that just to satisfy his whims."

In Drell, they had conquered Alzheimer's, but physical deterioration still happened, though thanks to medicine, the deterioration only went to a certain point before it stopped; and it would stay at this level until the person died. The person usually died at around a hundred years old. They could always opt for longevity, but not all Drellians chose that. Many wanted to find peace and rest after living for so long, especially as many on

Drell believed in an afterlife. Those who did choose to live longer were the ones who wanted to keep helping as many people as they could, thinking that going to rest after only a hundred years was selfish. Still, the longevity pills did not last any longer than fifty more years, for ethical reasons.

Raoul argued politely that the old man needed a little spark in his life, a little more flavor and excitement. It would not take that much effort to brighten up an old man's day just this once.

"You young men are so unreasonable," said Monna. "When I said no, I mean no. I understand that you are being kind to him, but he really does not need to put his life in danger like that."

As he fumed inside, Raoul was about to reply when Monna's eyes widened and she said, "Liara."

His half-sister now stood beside him, smiling. He shifted a bit farther from her as inconspicuously as possible. Liara noticed, but she was used to it. She was still smiling when she said, "Monna, Raoul, I think we can find a solution that will make Centuri happy and keep him safe at the same time."

Raoul looked at her defiantly, seeing what kind of ingenious solution she would provide for them.

Liara calmly said, "If you recall, our scientists in Vénus have been developing the design of a new vehicle—the Silver. It has not yet been improved to our satisfaction, but it should be adequate for a mission. The vehicle will be thin enough to fit through house doors, but just thick enough to fit one rider. Centuri could be our first to test drive the Silver for an actual mission, and he will be able to witness the Arach mission firsthand while still in the full protection of the Silver."

"Perfect. Thank you for your wonderful solution, Liara," said Raoul, with a deliberate slowness and graciousness. He was annoyed that she had come up with a solution so quickly, but his goal was to help Centuri, after all, not to best her.

Liara cast a warm, soft look at her half-brother. "I am very happy that you like my suggestion." She ordered her attendants to get the Silver ready. Then she turned toward Raoul again. "I'd advise you to put Centuri in Renore's ("Rin-nore"—rhymes with "pour") group." And with those words, she left them to help other Rarerus members.

Renore was a lady in her mid-thirties. Raoul guessed that the reason why Liara wanted Centuri to be in her group was that Renore was one of the members who were more adept at interacting with and understanding older members. Yet another reason might be that Renore was one of the leaders who were closer to Liara, as if Liara wanted Renore to keep watch on Centuri and to report back to her what happened. In short, Liara did not trust Centuri.

This thought made Raoul angry, and he sought to put Centuri in Braiven (Brye-vin)'s group, where he knew Braiven, a man of about Raoul's age, would treat Centuri more like an equal. Braiven was a rather affable, free-spirited, and somewhat boisterous kind of fellow. But his boisterousness was what made Raoul especially like and trust him; moreover, Braiven's large-heartedness was likely what would make Centuri feel most comfortable and accepted. So as soon as Liara's attendant showed Raoul the room where the Silver was situated, he nodded and went off to find both Centuri and Braiven to discuss his plans.

"LARK! THERE YOU ARE!" MARIUS CRIED AND ATTEMPTED TO grasp Lark's arm to drag him back to the main room. Lark's new reflexes let him escape this grasp, however.

The boy said, "There is no need to use force. I am a reasonable person and will come of my own accord. Has it finally been decided where we should all go? These operations are surprisingly slow and I would not be shocked if we are too late for whatever is happening."

Marius ignored this biting last comment and said, "Yes, yes, come with us, and let's go."

Marius and Haus were intending to take Lark with them in either Marius or Haus's group, when they bumped into Raoul. Raoul brightened when he saw them.

"Lark! I would like you to come with me to join my friend's group."

Lark wondered who this friend was but walked away with Raoul. The latter cast an apologetic glance at Marius and Haus, in case the two had wanted the boy in their group.

Lark and Raoul eventually reached an oblong room with a few Teeleopes twirling in the air; nobody paid attention to these machines, as they were a familiar sight. Beside a pearly-blue floating panel that held a tube of pink flowers immersed in clear water, stood a young, tall, and stout-looking man with an older man. Raoul said, "Lark, I would like you to meet your group leader, Braiven, and a group member, Centuri."

"Good to meet you, Lark," said Braiven, hand extended for Lark to press. In Drell, a hand greeting between people could involve either pressing hands or shaking them, whichever was preferred. Lark didn't want to press his hand, but he wanted to be in the mission to put his octamethyst knowledge to use, so he pressed it, and pressed Centuri's too. Raoul explained to the two that Lark was their five-year-old genius scientist who would be helping them on their mission.

Braiven and Centuri were both astounded, and Centuri even looked a little jealous. Then when Centuri caught Lark staring at the Silver, he explained to the boy what it was and how it worked.

Lark's eyes widened in fascination and he asked whether he could try it during the mission. Raoul, Braiven, and Centuri all glanced at each other in consternation.

Centuri said, "Maybe not during the mission, but after the mission's over, I am sure Liara would not object to your trying it out. She is such a kind leader." Raoul rolled his eyes at the "kind" part.

Very soon, with Raoul's help, the rest of Braiven's group assembled in the room. Lark surveyed this group of twenty or so people, until his eyes alighted on one of them and he opened his mouth in shock.

"Oh my gosh, Lark, I can't believe you're in the Rarerus too!" Karrin cried, and rushed forward to hug the bewildered scientist boy. Lark twisted around with his new reflexes to avoid it, but unfortunately Karrin was fondal-enhanced too; and since Karrin was originally much faster than Lark, he managed to catch Lark and embrace him anyway, much to the latter's disgust.

Though Karrin was a very new recruit, the Rarerus believed in exposing new combaters to real Arach situations as early as possible, yet they would be closely protected by experienced combaters: new combaters would just stay in the background and observe most of the time. Raoul had split the three children Karrin, Yearlie, and Gastra up into three different groups so that the veterans could more easily protect each young fighter.

"Wow, I never would have thought that you already knew Lark," said Raoul to Karrin, pleased. Karrin grinned at him, and at Lark, delighted that he had now found another familiar face and possible friend. Lark just couldn't believe that this was happening to him and he tried not to look at his classmate.

When it came to the twenty or so members, including Raoul, Lark, and Karrin, to ride in a Streeto, Karrin rushed up to Lark, as the latter had strategically wandered away, and said, "I want to sit next to Lark."

Lark's automatic reaction was of course, "No, I will sit alone."

But Raoul, the traitor, came over and said, "Oh, but we have too many people. Everybody will have to sit beside someone, and it would be good to put you two friends together so you can watch over each other." He smiled and went away to his own seat. Raoul liked pleasing Lark, as he liked pleasing others in general, but there were occasions like these when he wanted to tease him instead. After all, it would not hurt Lark to have a bit more social interaction in his life.

On the drive towards one of the houses where Arach activity was found, Karrin Treek chatted nonstop to Lark and asked him a million questions which the latter never bothered to answer. Karrin did not seem to find anything wrong with this, though, because Lark was always so unresponsive anyway and many of the other Rarerus members were chatting with their seat mates too. Plus, Karrin was still feeling overexcited about going on his first mission and seeing his good old classmate in the Rarerus.

Meanwhile, Braiven was chatting with Centuri, and Raoul saw to his satisfaction that the old man was indeed made quite comfortable and happy by Braiven's candor, and that Braiven really did treat him as an equal, not as an old man. Raoul sat back and relaxed as he in turn talked with his neighbor, or rather, his neighbor was talking to him, as the former was quite a loquacious fellow. But Raoul did not mind listening to this random chatter because he was in a good mood. And he never minded listening to what others had to say.

WHILE ALL THESE LIVELY EXCHANGES WERE HAPPENING, LIARA and her current attendant Fabil ("fae-bil"), a woman in her early twenties, were riding some distance away from Raoul and company in the leader's vehicle, the Glass: Supple rose-colored seats filled the interior, and the walls around the seats were a smooth, almost translucent white.

The Glass was designed to be the fastest of all Rarerus's current vehicles (at maximum speed, it was two times the speed of an inter-super-sector Coaster), and its surface was immaculately polished. The color of it could be changed to whatever Liara felt like.

Liara was not a capricious person and she would choose whatever color was most suitable if they could be camouflaged; if not, she did not care what color it was. The creator of the Glass had simply sought to please her by adding this freedom of color choice. But though Liara never cared about the color, she knew that her attendants did, so she often let her friends—her attendants were all her good friends—choose their daily preference.

Earlier, before mounting the vehicle, Fabil had asked if she could have purple. Liara of course accepted this suggestion and gladly changed it for her.

In the Glass, Liara drove and followed a few of her groups to their assigned destinations.

(See "Driving[1]" under "Transportation.")

"Liara," Fabil spoke up, "did you know that Raoul put Centuri in Braiven's group instead of Renore's? He disobeyed you again!"

Liara smiled. "I actually expected that." She held a feeling of equanimity through her facial features.

Fabil looked at her quizzically.

"Who knows?" Liara said, with an even and collected voice. "Maybe he did choose the right group leader for Centuri. You know Raoul always had a knack for knowing and understanding people."

"Except when it comes to you and your father," remarked Fabil.

Liara didn't reply. But afterwards she said, "Don't blame Raoul. He lost his father, so it's only natural that he would dislike my father and I."

"You're too kind to him," said Fabil. "Let him know who's boss for once."

"That's all right. Raoul is a good and competent member of the Rare-rus, and is always a great help to us."

"But, as I said to you many times before, don't you think that his constant coldness towards you is unreasonable? I mean, yes, he is a poor boy for losing his father when he was just eight, but that wasn't your or your father's fault. Especially not yours. He is your half older brother, after all; he should protect and be kind to you, not be hostile to you."

A nearly imperceptible furrow touched the smooth skin between Liara's brows. Yet, she said, "Don't worry, Fabil. He's never hostile to me. He is very civil."

"Civil but cold," persisted Fabil. But she sensed her leader's wish to drop this topic, and talked about something else instead.

---

1. **Driving**
   Just tell the computer where exactly (in coordinates) you want to go and it will drive for you. But you still have to stay alert to help the computer dodge possible obstacles in the air.

THIRTEEN
THE FIGHT AND STRUGGLE

Very soon, Lark and co. descended upon a dark street with gray roads. Some roads in Drell were paved with a color, like the purple gravel road leading to the Rarerus Center in Vénus. But this road was an undecorated, plain grey; and they weren't in Vénus. They were in Oftonoss, not too far away from the Larence branch where they flew from. They could see a house that was faintly lit up, but this was probably just a nightlight. Drellians who were afraid of the dark when they went to bed used small lights too.

The troop of Rarerus members advanced cautiously towards the house.

(See "How they hide their operations from civilians[1]" under "The Rarerus.")

Raoul rapped on the door.

They waited only a short while before they heard the pattering of feet, and then a gruff voice asking, "Who on Drell are you?"

Raoul answered calmly, "We are the Order, and we were informed that a criminal suspect is hiding in your house."

"Why should I believe you?" the voice asked.

Raoul smiled and took out an Order identity pad; this was secretly handed to the Rarerus by the Order for these types of missions.

They heard a gasp from inside the house, and the door finally creaked open.

Standing in the doorway, was a tall, broad-shouldered man with a messy beard, who looked as though he had been rudely woken up from bed. He growled, "If you have to search, hurry up."

Raoul bowed in thanks, and waved the rest of the Rarerus troop in.

The man grumbled, "I doubt you'll find anybody, but I'm going back to sleep." He stifled a yawn and turned around to walk away.

Just as the man turned his back, Braiven hissed, "Yes, go back to sleep." Braiven sprayed the man with a misty powder, and before the man could react, his eyes closed, and he collapsed to the floor in slumber.

Centuri, who was right behind Braiven, winced. "Poor guy."

"All the more reason we should get the web off him. Now," Braiven said. The Arach detector Braiven brought had informed him that this man was the victim they were trying to find.

The living room they were standing in had very little furniture, only a stretch seat here and a panel there.

They carried the man and placed him on a stretch seat in the far back corner of the living room. "Good, bring the scientists," Braiven said.

On Rarerus missions, there were usually about three to five scientists, though one of them would usually suffice to do the job. But they needed extra scientists in case one fell from an attack.

Raoul pushed Lark towards the man. "Now's your chance to try."

Lark stepped forward cautiously and squatted down at the victim man's side. He used the computer to find the exact whereabouts of the web, and detected a vast concentration on the man's neck, shoulders, and chest. Fortunately that was all. So far. Quickly, he recalled all those equations needed and spun through the calculation with speed, while the computer verified that he made no careless mistakes. Even more quickly, Lark ordered the computer to apply the amount of octamethyst on the man. Now it was just a matter of waiting, thought Lark. Karrin stood by his side, curious to see what would happen.

Just then they heard an eerie noise. The main door had swung open. At the threshold was the very man Lark had at his feet, and a woman beside him who looked like his sister. As they entered, the Rarerus crew saw that there were a number of other men and women, some quite tall; and they were about twenty in total. Karrin felt cold and scared. The Arach clones were finally here.

"Now!" cried Braiven, and the twenty something combaters rushed towards the door.

Karrin wanted to follow but he didn't want to leave Lark alone and unprotected. Raoul approved of his loyalty and asked four of the veteran combaters to stay with the two children. He also told Karrin that he could use his hand beams when he felt ready, and to not be scared.

After that, Raoul smiled at Lark. "Watch over the progress of the octamethyst for us, Lark." And he swept towards the door as well.

To both Karrin and Lark's surprise, Raoul began shooting bright gold energy beams. He was wearing hand beams as well! "I didn't know Raoul was a fighter too," said Karrin to Lark. Lark didn't reply, but it was obvious he thought the same thing. In the combat club, though Raoul often supervised Karrin and the other young fighters, he himself had never fought, and he told them that he was simply one who was familiar with watching combat moves but did not try them out himself; he was a scientist who analyzed moves. Karrin had always found it rather odd that the trainers would assign a scientist to supervise them, even if he were an adept analyst of combat strategies. But now it all made sense.

The Arach clone version of the victim man rushed forward and grasped hold of a man in a Rarerus dark suit, for that was what they dressed themselves in—a black suit with a band of fluorescence for Rarerus members to see each other in the dark.

Braiven immediately dashed at the Arach clone's head with his epic, but the clone dodged the blow and swung the Rarerus man at Braiven. Now the Arach clone took out his own weapon, a gun, and aimed it at Braiven's face. The latter sneered and batted the gun away with his epic.

Unfortunately, the Arach clone held on adamantly to the weapon and swung the gun back to fire at Braiven again. Then out of nowhere, the Arach clone was smacked in the face and knocked onto the floor by a beam of golden yellow.

Braiven looked up to see young Karrin Treek, and grinned. Karrin grinned back, proud, glad, and relieved that all his training at the combat club had paid off. Accuracy was just as important as speed. Greatly encouraged, Karrin swept his eyes around the room to see who else he could shoot.

Lark was trying not to pay attention to the mania around him and to keep his eyes focused on the trail of octamethyst. The computer had magnified an image of what was happening to the web on the man's body. It was unbelievably slow. At length, even Lark lost patience and started watching the battles raging all around. He was gripped by fear, though he fought to deny it, because he had never seen such danger before. Perhaps a part of him was glad that Karrin, and the other four fighters, were there to protect him.

Just then, an Arach clone managed to wrest free from Braiven and the others, and charged towards Lark, Karrin, and the Arach webbed man. The five fighters with Lark cried out and shot their hand beams at this Arach clone and a cluster of other clones coming towards them. But the Arach clones were wearing ray reflectors and the energy beams bounced harmlessly off them, and harmlessly off the Rarerus, until the beams disappeared. Though the Arach clones were clearly armed with hand beams of their own, they did not use them, and instead took out their epics, elastoropes, and a host of other weapons.

At this mass menace, Lark shrunk back as far as possible in terror. He couldn't deny that he was scared anymore and all he wanted to do was to get away, to be safe again. An elastorope suddenly flicked towards him and he cried out, but Karrin rushed forward with his epic and smacked the elastorope down. "Don't worry, Lark, I'll protect you."

Lark was very embarrassed at this and though his classmate had just saved him, he did not have it in him to feel grateful. Yet, he edged back behind Karrin in case any more weapons should fly towards him. And indeed there were. Something like burned bones tore through the air in an arc and fell towards him. Lark had his back against the wall and tried to move out of the way, hoping his enhanced reflexes would be enough. It was, but only just. The burned bones dug into the floor just an inch behind him. Lark needn't have felt so afraid, however, because he had his gel armor to protect him from most of the potential hurt.

Now Karrin was busy fighting an Arach warrior, and their battle was quite a sight to see. An adult, tall man, fighting with a little five-year-old. Karrin was certainly fast enough to dodge all the Arach man's blows, but the man was also fast enough to dodge Karrin's epic. It was such a shame that the hand beams were of no use. Karrin had not expected that the Arach would be wearing ray reflectors of their own. But he couldn't give up, so he lunged with his epic and pressed the button to let the golden shards fly.

To his joy, one of the shards hit the man on the head. But since there was something like gel armor on the Arach clone, the man was merely distracted. He lunged towards Karrin too and the boy shrieked and rolled away, aiming a kick as he did so. His kick only made contact with a soft material, and he knew with despair that the man was covered all over with gel armor. Raoul and the other Rarerus members had not told him what to do in such a hopeless circumstance. Fear was gaining on him more and more and he wondered what would happen to him after he died.

Then all of a sudden, the man fighting Karrin was knocked down to the floor. A particularly big fighter from the Rarerus team who was guarding the children had shoved him. He picked up the knocked down man and threw him towards the house exit. But this effort took up a lot of his time, and another Arach clone hit him on the waist. The gel armor only cushioned a bit of this force, so the big man, even with his size, was hurled back, towards Lark.

"Lark!" Karrin cried, and ran towards the big man. But he was too late and Lark was crushed under the big man's weight. Lark mumbled something incoherent like "the octamethyst..." Karrin quickly helped the man up and Lark peeled himself away. Lark resented having to rely on the fighters around him for protection, while he was supposed to watch the progress of the octamethyst.

And clearly the fighters were not doing an efficient enough job. There were many fighters still crowded near the house exit door, dealing with about thirteen clones. The chance of victory seemed bleak, and again and again, an Arach clone would claw towards the man with octamethyst in his veins; but they were always blocked off by a Rarerus fighter.

The battle raged on for some time more, and Lark became increasingly anxious as the octamethyst was truly taking a long time, when they heard a rumbling. Lark's eyes were still focused on the computer's display of the octamethyst when he heard Karrin cry, "Lark, look!"

Reluctantly, Lark tore himself from the screen and followed his gaze. He gasped. The door, which had swung shut after the last clone entered, was now open again, and more people poured in. Not Rarerus people.

"More Arach clones!" Karrin screamed, and Lark wished he wouldn't scream because that scared him too. Lark wanted to shut the little boy up by punching him or something, but that wouldn't be too smart as Karrin was supposed to be his protector. There was a total of about twenty more Arach clones. This house was so big that sixty something people could stand in it. Drellian homes were usually quite big, but this house was extra big.

Lark heard Raoul cry out, "Call for backup!" Raoul was facing Centuri, the only person who wasn't occupied in either fighting or in watching the octamethyst with Lark. Centuri returned to his senses—he had been so wrapped up in watching everyone fight—and commanded the computer to reach the nearest Rarerus members outside of this house. In his desperation, he called Liara too.

The situation was so grim that the Rarerus members looked like they were going to die with all these Arach clones tramping into and flooding the room. Lark and Karrin could barely see the heads of Raoul or Braiven anymore, so consumed were they in their self-defense—but it was notable that Raoul and Braiven still did not fall. Karrin and Lark were again amazed that Raoul, a scientist, was a good fighter. Perhaps he trained in secret.

But many other Rarerus members were knocked down onto the ground and hurt; some were bleeding even with the gel armor, because some of the clones were just too strong. Karrin, feeling tremendously helpless, kept firing his hand beam here and there. Fortunately, he never hit any of his team mates, but unfortunately, his beams only occasionally hit an Arach clone.

To make the situation even worse, since there were now so many Arach clones, many more of them pushed through the group of five fighters to grab the man that Lark was watching. The few Rarerus members left guarding the man couldn't defeat the clones, but they still managed to prevent the man from falling into their hands. Several times, the Arach clones would reach for the man, or even claw for Lark. Lark would leap away in fright—thankfully his fondal-enhanced reflexes helped him do that, or he would have been a goner a long time ago.

Karrin wasn't doing a great job trying to defend Lark either. Lark really wished that he had a weapon too, so he could defend himself and the man. Hurry up, octamethyst...Not that it would help if the octamethyst finished, though, because if the Arach recaptured the man, they would lay another egg on him. And once the octamethyst completed its work, it would break down into useless components and be washed away to be excreted by the body. If there was, however, still a little octamethyst working on the web, that little bit of octamethyst would be able to slow down the formation of the new web too, when the Arach laid that second egg. Lark gripped his fists in both annoyance and panic.

Then out of the blue, an Arach clone fell from above towards Lark. The boy had no time to scream before the Arach clone had landed on him and snatched his legs. Now Lark was really screaming. "Unhand me, you filthy specimen!" But the Arach clone held onto his legs. At the same time, as it happened, another Arach clone held Karrin captive. Karrin, with his amazing reflexes due to his natural speed and the fondal enhancement, should have escaped, but the back corner of the room where they fought was getting too crowded for him to move freely.

"Let go of them!" yelled a Rarerus fighter near them. The Rarerus members tried to attack the two captors but they were disrupted in their efforts by other Arach clones attacking them.

Lark wrestled to move his legs but they were held in a vice-like grip. His captor soon grabbed his whole body and lifted him. Karrin was lifted up too and he kept trying to attack his captor with his epic and his hand beams, but the Arach clone's ray reflector and gel armor protected him. "Help!" Karrin cried. Lark didn't cry for help because he was both too petrified and unwilling to do so.

"Hold on, Lark, Karrin! Help is on the way!" That was Raoul.

"Why are they taking so long?" asked Centuri.

"Patience," said Braiven. It wasn't the first time that the Rarerus were outnumbered. This was why they would always call for help nearby. There were of course a few times in the past where there really were no Rarerus members nearby, and they had ended up captured, or horribly injured, by the Arach, so that they had to wait till the far-off Rarerus members came to the rescue.

Centuri shook with panic and agitation in his Silver, and his eyes darted forwards and back.

"Submit," said the Arach clone that held Lark captive. "Surrender to us or else we will kill these two children."

"But they are just children! How can you be so cruel?" cried Centuri. Nobody told him that the Arach wouldn't even care whether they were children or not.

The clone said, "That is your fault for bringing children into your mission in the first place. Now, we command you to stop fighting, and let us take this man away with us."

"Not a chance!" cried Raoul.

"Do you want these children killed?" the Arach clone said.

Raoul fell silent. And soon, all the Rarerus members stopped fighting. It had been a foolish plan to involve two five-year-old children, after all. They thought they had enough people to protect those children, but they had clearly underestimated their enemy. They didn't think that they would be outnumbered, on this day, on this mission. Arach outnumbering rarely happened. There had been times before when a Rarerus member had been thus held captive too, but the member had always been at least a twenty-year-old, or near twenty years old, so there was less panic.

"All right, everybody, don't move," said the Arach clone. He signaled with his head to his team mates and they picked up the man who still had octamethyst in him. The Rarerus members could only follow the Arach clones with their eyes.

Lark's captor gestured with his head again, and they all filed out the door, with the man, Lark, and Karrin.

"Give us back the boys!" yelled Raoul.

"Be quiet," said the Arach clone with Lark. "Or else we'll kill them immediately." And they continued streaming out the door.

"Oh my gosh, what are we going to do, what are we going to do?" Centuri whimpered softly.

Just then, they heard a whistling sound in the air outside. Centuri declared in a quiet but relieved voice, "Finally!"

It was indeed the other Rarerus members. By the looks of it, there were at least sixty members. But the Arach clones were not hurried. Instead, they stood their ground with an arrogant calm. They had the captives, after all. And they could always kill the man if they could not kill the children.

When the sixty or so Rarerus members alighted, they immediately began shooting hand beams, which knocked down a number of the Arach clones. They rushed out and stabbed, roped, and slashed at the Arach clones, when they heard the yell, "Stop! If you keep fighting us, these two children will die!"

Everyone stopped. Now everyone was staring at Lark and Karrin. Lark really wanted to say something at this moment but he was speechless. Karrin, on the other hand, cried out, "Help us!" Lark wanted to hit him because obviously the Rarerus members would help them whether he yelled for their aid or not. But Lark hated himself, and hated everyone on his side, for not being able to think of anything to save them. Now, seeing that everyone had indeed stopped, Karrin and Lark's captors sauntered leisurely with the rest of their gang.

"Don't even think of following us either," said the Arach clone carrying Lark; we shall now call Lark's captor the leader clone.

Everyone from the Rarerus was looking at each other with the utmost panic. The Arach clones were really getting away. There was already a vehicle, which was a faded red, waiting for the Arach clones to get on.

Suddenly Raoul cried out, "Lark! Karrin! Catch!" He threw something that looked like a small yellow ball—which to us might even look like a ball of egg yolk—high over and towards the children. The children reached out to catch it, but of course, the Arach clones caught it instead, and threw it back at Raoul. Before long, they were all inside the vehicle, and flew away.

"They're really gone now, what should we do?" wailed Centuri. Braiven looked at the distraught old man with sympathy.

But Raoul said calmly, "Don't worry. I just threw them our latest technology, the soft bomb. I didn't intend for the children to catch it; I expected the Arach to catch it instead and throw it back. But when I threw it, I let the soft bomb release its tracking dust—the dust is invisible to the naked eye—whatever life form the tracking dust falls onto will be tracked. Fortunately it managed to fly above the heads of the two children before the soft bomb was caught and knocked away. We'll be able to follow the children wherever they go now. The soft bomb can identify the different life forms tracked for us by sending back a 3D image of the life form being tracked, so we can tell between Lark and Karrin." He signaled to Braiven and the other members. "Now let's follow them."

1. **How they hide their operations from civilians**

   Now when the Rarerus enter a house, it would be considered burglary if they don't use their detector to confirm that there is Arach activity inside first. And in case they bump into anyone in the house, they have forged Order identity pads they can call up on their computer.

   The Order issued these ID pads to the Rarerus because they agreed that the Rarerus should operate unknown to as many people as possible. Order members are also told not to tell their friends or family about the Arach or the Rarerus, lest this knowledge should harm them.

   Also, as neighbors and passerby will hear the commotion whenever the Rarerus members fight against the Arach, the Order and the government made up this cover story: the Rarerus members are Order agents cracking down on criminals or criminal organizations and their overlords. This is actually believable as everyone on Drell knows that organized crime and formidable evildoers exist, and the Order and the government military have to protect Drellian citizens from these villains. Children involved in the Rarerus missions are easily explained, because some undercover operations require the assistance of such young recruits.

   Of course, there will always be people within the civilian population who doubt the veracity of this cover story. But that can't be helped. There are conspiracy theorists in the world who are sometimes right too.

   The reason why the Order and the Drellian government don't directly battle the Arach, is because the Rarerus alone have the forces, power, resources, and knowledge to deal with these unpredictable and unknown viruses.

FOURTEEN
CHRYSTACIENCE

Lark had never been this frightened in his life. And his classmate screaming his head off beside him was not helping in the least. Lark wanted to scream too, but perhaps he was too scared to scream. He thought about a million things; a million pictures, words, and numbers spun around in his head. Among those many things, he wanted to know how the octamethyst in the man was doing. Surprisingly, he thought about his parents too. How they would react, how they would look if they saw what he was in now. I'm not saying that he missed them or anything. Just saying that he at least had a passing thought for them.

While Lark was simply frozen in space, Karrin wasn't just yelling, he was crying; and those tears were streaming down his face. Lark was very embarrassed to hear the boy cry out for his mommy and daddy; why, Lark would never call for his parents, no matter how dire the situation, or how close he was to possible death. To Lark's disbelief, however, the Arach clones did nothing to stop Karrin from his bawling. It was as if they were all deaf. Lark supposed that since they were Arach clones, these childish sounds made no difference to them, as long as they were not heard by other humans; and since they were inside this red vehicle, the little boy's cries were completely insulated from the rest of the world. Lark just wondered when they would land, not that he looked forward to it.

When they did touch the ground, Lark noticed how dark everything was. There were fewer floating lights than usual here. He could only see five from where he was. Now like a battalion, the Arach clones tromped towards a dark building, still carrying the two boys; Karrin had finally stopped wailing, his eyes dreadfully red. As they entered, Lark heard a whirring sound and then the place filled with white smoke. He wasn't too shocked because he was familiar with the cleaning gas. He smirked to himself, because weren't the Arach themselves microbes that could be cleaned off? Or perhaps they were special microbes that did not want the interference of other microbes.

Quite dispassionately, Lark thought that maybe the Arach clones would now take him and Karrin to the Arach chambers to be antimattered. But when it struck him that they were going to be antimattered, he was choked with fear. He glanced at Karrin, whose head was hung dejectedly. The poor boy was probably unaware of what they were going to be up against. But what could they do to get out of here?

After a while, the Arach clones came to a brightly lit room with several stretch seats all painted in gold. They bound up Lark and Karrin with elastoropes so that they could not move and placed them on the seats. Half of the clones went off with the man, probably to the antimattering chamber. The other half kept a tight watch on Lark and Karrin. Karrin was lying on his side, sobbing quietly now. Obviously his hand beams would be of no use, thought Lark bitterly. Lark peered around, for anything, anything they could use to escape. But this room was astonishingly bare of everything but stretch seats. It was like a prison devoid of anything for the captive to use or even to entertain themselves with.

Eventually, the clone that had carried Lark took out a container of a strange-smelling liquid. It was transparent, and the clone sloshed it about. He forced open Lark's mouth, though Lark fought to keep it shut, and poured in a little bit of the liquid. Lark tried to spit it out, but the clone forced him to look up, so gravity eventually won the war and the liquid slid down his throat. He immediately felt a tingling feeling and very soon after, his eyelids drooped and he fell asleep.

Upon awaking, Lark gasped at something sharp that was stinging his elbow. He was also shocked upon remembering what had happened to him and Karrin. The sharp thing turned out to be a protrusion from the stretch seat he was sitting on, and the protrusion seemed to be some sort of bizarre and distorted ornament, some kind of monstrous pattern that the Arach fancied. As he pulled himself up, he peered around and spotted Karrin on a stretch seat near his. The boy was still sound asleep, curled up, with pain clearly etched onto his face.

Lark was glad that he was now free of those elastoropes, but he wasn't so naïve as to believe that the two of them were safe. He wondered whether he should awake Karrin, though it would probably not do any good—and Karrin would make too much noise anyway. Instead, Lark tiptoed around the bare white and brightly lit room. There really was nothing here except for the few stretch seats. There were two doors opposite each other but both were locked. The ceiling looked as featureless as the walls.

Lark racked his brains to come up with a plan. He tried to call up his computer to contact Raoul and the others, but of course his computer was taken from him.

(See "How to Carry Around Computers[1]" and "How Someone Can Take Your Computer Away From You, and How You Can Get It Back[2]" under "Technology.")

He fumed, but there didn't seem to be anything he could do, so he trotted up to Karrin and shook him. "Wake up."

Karrin opened his eyes with labor. "Lark!" he said, surprised that the boy who had always hated him was now staring at him, albeit with his usual scowl. Then Karrin remembered where he was and was instantly very distressed. "What should we do?" he asked.

"You do not have your computer with you either?" Lark asked him back.

"Wha—oh, I don't usually bring computers with me—" said Karrin; Lark stared at him with incredulity. Karrin checked his hand beams. They were still there. This was because hand beams were securely locked into the skin and nobody could take them off except for the Rarerus. "Here goes nothing." Before Lark could stop him, Karrin fired several shots at each of the two doors.

"What do you think you are doing?" said Lark through gritted teeth.

"It's not like there's anything else we could do, right?" said Karrin.

"The Arach clones will come back for us anyway, and we would have a chance to escape if we broke out of this room."

Though Lark knew Karrin was right, he still crossed his arms and looked away with disapproval. Indeed, they very soon heard footsteps and one of the doors opened. An Arach clone stepped inside with a huge frown on his face. "I guess it's time for you two to come out." He gestured towards the door. "You can try to escape but it will be in vain." And he just left the door open like that as if he had not a care in the world.

With caution, the two boys walked out; Lark peered warily at the Arach clone as he exited. This clone led the two to a brown and white room that was unpleasantly warm and humid; more Arach clones awaited them on hard-looking stretch seats.

The clone that had first captured Lark smiled. "Did you have a nice sleep?" The boys did not reply. So he said, "Now, boys, we would like you two to relax and go through that teleporter yonder." He pointed to a dazzling silver machine some distance in front of him. Lark gave him a look, but Karrin just nodded fearfully, not even daring to use his hand beams at the clone. They were just two inexperienced children against so many captors, after all. "Now hurry along, kids."

Lark gazed in disbelief when Karrin strode dutifully towards the teleporter. But Lark stayed put and waited to see what they would do to him. His former captor smiled at him. "A rebel here, huh? I understand. You're scared, aren't you?"

"I am not scared," Lark responded reflexively.

But the clone was smug. "Would you like me to walk through the teleporter with you?" By this time, Karrin had already teleported; Lark narrowed his eyes.

"Where are your leaders? Where are the Arach viruses themselves? You are just clones controlled by the Arach's DNA."

The clone laughed. "You're right. But that doesn't matter, does it? You are still in the Arach's control whether directly or indirectly. And you do not need to know where the 'real' Arach are. All you need to do is to walk through that teleporter there." He grabbed Lark's hand and proceeded to move toward the teleporter. Lark tried to resist and stay put, but his enhanced physical strength was clearly still inferior to this big man's. Then the clone threw him into the teleporter.

In a moment, the world flashed away before his eyes; and when it reappeared, Lark was staring at a very huge green field that was fenced around. The field had a diameter of several qworts.

"Lark!" It was Karrin, who was grateful that he wasn't alone anymore. Karrin's presence did not give Lark any comfort, however. "So what's going to happen?" Karrin asked. Right after he posed that question, they heard a loud scuffling. The boys turned and saw a large quadruped lamina with white and yellow fur, and long pointed ears. It bore its teeth as soon as it saw them and extended its claws. "Um," Karrin looked from Lark to the lamina—a velocip. Karrin wanted to say: What have we done to offend it? But instead, he took the more sensible route and fired several hand beams at it.

The velocip screeched in pain when they struck its legs and this only incensed it even more. It snarled a warning at Karrin and at once leapt towards him. Karrin sprung out of the way in fright. Thankfully, his escape was not too hard, as he was naturally swift as well as fondal-enhanced.

Frustrated at its failed attempt, the velocip next glanced at Lark and made its pounce again. Lark was not as fast as Karrin but the enhancement let him move quickly enough to just dodge the blow; its claws then flashed at him but he managed to escape that too. Lark ran as far as he could from the velocip, whilst fully aware that it could overtake him anywhere he went. The velocip soon figured out that Lark was the weaker boy and bounded towards him in a great chase. Lark ran for his life. And miraculously he was still not caught.

Meanwhile, Karrin fired carefully with his hand beams and occasionally succeeded in singeing a bit of fur here and there, but nothing major enough to deter the velocip from pursuing his companion. The hand beams were not even distracting enough to turn it towards Karrin instead, which he was trying to make it do, as he had a much better chance at evading the lamina than Lark did. It was too bad that the Arach clones had taken away his epic, elastorope, and other weapons as well because maybe they would hit harder, Karrin thought. Though the hand beams were supposed to be equally strong.

The lamina ran round and round, snapping at Lark's heels, whilst Karrin kept trying to shoot it without any success. The situation seemed hopeless and Lark was soon tiring. At this point, Karrin decided to spring out closer to the velocip to distract it, and then realized he was close enough to hit it full on with his beam. He shot it and the lamina screamed; its torso was burned. Karrin wondered why he had just been aiming at it from a distance when he should have run as close as he could and fired from there instead.

But the shot was far from debilitating for the velocip, and it recovered and jumped towards Karrin. This time, since he was already so close to it and had to turn around to run, he only narrowly escaped its clutch and frantically moved away. Yet, the velocip was no longer chasing him and was on Lark's tail again. In desperation, Karrin ran towards it once more and fired furiously. The lamina swung around to bat at Karrin every time he hit it, but he used his dancing skills to spin out of the way, though his evasions were not easy. If only Lark had a weapon too.

Then suddenly, Karrin thought of something. He sprinted as close to the velocip as possible and launched himself into the air. He landed on its back. Now he thought with remorse already at what he was about to do, before he fired a solid blast into its back.

The creature cried out in intense agony and began to thrash about, not caring about Lark anymore and just trying to shake Karrin off. After releasing that shot, Karrin didn't want to fire anymore because it seemed so wrong, so inhumane. Instead, he simply clutched onto the lamina with all his strength and kicked it whenever he could. Then without warning, the velocip threw itself onto its back, and before Karrin could scream and release his grip, he was crushed under its vast body.

Lark watched this all with supreme horror. He wished he could do something but he was a scientist, not a warrior. He was suddenly angry at himself because all that knowledge of science and chemistry amounted to nothing here. And when he saw Karrin crushed under the velocip's body, he gasped and ran as quickly as he could towards the fences.

When he reached them, he began climbing up, as they were high, even higher than the velocip's head. Feverishly, he scaled the fence for his dear life. Maybe you would think that Lark was heartless in completely abandoning Karrin, even though he had never liked his classmate; but Lark's reasoning was: what could he do? Running to save Karrin would only get both of them killed. But he could at least save himself.

A second later, he heard the lamina dash towards him and he scrabbled even faster up the fence. He heard it grasp the fence as well and climb towards him, with a speed much quicker than Lark's. When he turned around, knowing that he would never make it up in time and hoping that he could at least jump off to avoid its jaws, he saw Karrin clutched between its teeth. The boy lay limp and battered, but he was moaning. It was a great relief to see that he was still alive, but Lark had no time to think about this. He leapt off from the fence, and the ground shot towards him, ready to smash him into bits.

It was then that Karrin, the velocip, and the whole world disappeared and he reappeared in a place flooded with golden light. The light ran down from the various tall buildings around him, and there were beautiful trees and streams interspersed between them. He heard footsteps and not to his surprise, he saw the Arach clones approaching him. "What do you want now?" he said.

His ex-captor grinned. "Nothing, except for you to run along to where that lady and young man are sitting. I'm sure that after all that exercise and thrill, you would like a little rest."

Lark narrowed his eyes and again refused to comply. He dug in his heels.

The clone sighed and said, "Do I have to take you there myself again?"

Lark ignored him and wandered off in another direction; he ran. But the big man was much faster than him and caught the struggling boy in his arms. He marched with Lark towards the aforementioned lady and young man, who were smiling amicably, and he placed Lark between them.

When Lark tried to escape again, the young man and lady grasped him, but gently, and both entreated him to relax and take it easy; they were not going to hurt him. As even he could see that he could not escape these clones no matter how hard he tried, Lark stopped struggling and glared at their faces to see what they would do.

AT THE SAME TIME THAT LARK WAS TELEPORTED TO THAT grand place, Karrin Treek was teleported to a place of white, with islands of glistening, pristine pools curving around this vast white floor. Though he was still in much pain, Karrin forced himself to get up with a groan. At once, a female Arach clone came up to him, smiled, and commanded the computer to heal all his wounds. The boy looked warily and fearfully at her, waiting to see what she would do next. The female clone was still smiling and she gestured to a stretch seat for Karrin to sit on. He did so cautiously, expecting a wild lamina to come thrashing its way towards him again. And he wondered where Lark was.

"Now Karrin," she said, "Please wait here while my friend comes." And she left.

He immediately glanced around to see if there was any way to escape. But the room was completely walled in just like the room he and Lark had woken up in. And before he knew it, another Arach clone trotted towards him and asked him to get up and walk with her.

Karrin was creeped out that these clones were so much like real human ladies. It was as if all this Arach business was just a dream. Yet, he wanted to see his parents again and he started to cry. The Arach clone, as wrong as it sounded, seemed to take pity on him and patted his shoulder. He shrunk away in fright and she sighed. "Now, please step through this doorway," she said, gesturing courteously with her arm. He slowly walked inside.

To his marvelous surprise, he saw Eeera. "What are you doing here?" Karrin cried in both delight and fear for his friend.

She smiled sadly. "What are you doing here?"

Now without any thought of keeping the Rarerus or the Arach affairs a secret anymore, Karrin told her everything that had happened to him, from the combat center to the mission to here. Her eyes widened as he told his story. "And what about you?" he asked.

"I don't know. I was just teleported here and there were just these people wandering around telling me to go this way and that until I got here. Am I in a dream?" she asked.

He shook his head. "This is all real, and what's more—" But he was interrupted by the shuffling of footsteps and another female clone appeared. She beamed at the two children and politely asked them to follow her through another doorway.

Emboldened by his friend's presence, Karrin followed. He still wondered and worried about where Lark was. When they entered through the doorway, both he and Eeera were struck with a huge surprise when they saw Criva and many of the other friends they regularly played with.

"What are you all doing here?" Karrin cried. It turned out that they had all ended up in this place the same way Eeera did, and none of them had ever heard of the Rarerus or the Arach. Karrin soon, finally, remembered that he was not supposed to tell anyone about the Rarerus or the Arach, but what did it matter anymore since they were all in the Arach's clutches now?

"Hey Karrin," said one of the boys named Snizis. "While we were all waiting here for something to happen, look what we found?" He trotted over to a panel, jumped on it, and immediately it turned pink and played a pleasing musical note. There were several panels here, all close to the ground. The other boys and girls, and later Eeera, were bouncing on the panels, and soon they were all laughing.

Karrin stared in disbelief at how they could laugh even in such a situation, but maybe his friends were just trying their hardest to ward off their fears. So soon, he joined them as well in leaping, dancing, and laughing. He did honestly feel a lot better, now that he was dancing; and he was with his friends.

———

THE YOUNG MAN AND WOMAN LED LARK TO A LARGE ROOM lined with velvety material. It was immaculately clean. And before he knew it, the two clones had left him too. But unlike what he had feared, the door that they went through did not shut when the clones exited. He was free to leave. So he waited at that doorway for the two clones to walk far enough for him to escape. Yet, the young man saw him and laughed. "Come on, Lark, be kind. We only wanted to show you an interesting place. Just look at what's in there."

Lark furrowed his eyebrows because there wasn't anything in that room, but then he heard a sound, he turned, and to his dismay saw a computer—its silvery network splayed out. There was a protection screen and many chemicals of all colors surrounded him. There was even a pair of barrier gloves beside him on a panel. As he peered at the chemicals around him, he saw that they each had a label indicating what they were. Amongst these, he could see amosti and par-the-air. He tensed. Something must be up. He was about to command the computer to examine these two chemicals when he heard a voice behind him.

"Lark." He swung around. He gaped when he saw Raoul standing beside him.

"How did you—but there are no doors—"

"I managed to teleport here into the Arach compound without them knowing, so keep your voice down," he whispered. "You see all these chemicals here? We have to find the specific chemicals to create the concoction that will destroy all the Arach clones we meet later when we go to save your friend Karrin."

"He is not my friend—"

"Lark, really. He's at least your comrade," Raoul reproached. "I see you've already found the amosti and par-the-air. That's good, because all we need now are the trichloroes, octamethyst, and the brachiorsor."

Lark gasped. "So I will finally find out what these chemicals do."

"Yes, finally," beamed Raoul. "I'm sorry that we've kept this information from you for so long. Now if you mix the octamethyst, par-the-air, trichloroes, and brachiorsor together, you will form a virtually impenetrable barrier. The barrier will protect against almost all physical and energy attacks, unless the blows are excessively powerful. And later, we will mix the par-the-air and amosti to create the green substance again." He smiled. "I had a secret hunch that this green substance didn't contain troptomyces all along, and I recently proved it in my lab that it didn't."

"If the green substance truly has nothing to do with troptomyces, then what is it?" asked Lark.

"I haven't given it a name yet. Would you like to christen it for me?"

Lark thought for a while. "Chrystacience. A blend of chrystacias and Ruminence."

"Excellent, we will go with that name. Now after we make this chrystacience, we have to elevate its density as much as possible and hide behind the brachiorsor barrier as we do so to protect ourselves. Then we will put the chrystacience into these two guns I brought." He took them out and gave one to Lark. "When this beam of green hits an Arach clone, they will be struck with disease and die immediately."

Lark was shocked at how rapidly Raoul and the other Rarerus scientists had developed this new weapon; Lark was even a bit awed. Nevertheless, he quickly got to work, using a chemical compressor to force the chrystacience particles to pack more closely together.

(See "Chemical compressor[3]" under "Chemicals" and "Chemical Apparatus and Other Things.")

He peered around the very numerous flasks of chemicals in the room. At one point, he asked Raoul, "But why did the Arach clones leave all these chemicals for us, when we can use these chemicals to destroy them?"

"They don't know I'm in here with you. They think it's just you here, and they want to be entertained by what you can make by randomly mixing chemicals. And they want to get their entertainment from you before they antimatter you," Raoul said bluntly.

Very soon, the two found their chemicals, created the brachiorsor barrier and prepared their chrystacience guns. Lark felt his hope rising as they finally had a chance to escape. He asked, "After we rescue Karrin, will we be able to teleport out of here?"

"Yes. All we have to do is go back into this room, which shouldn't be hard after all the Arach clones are down. It took a long time for us to dig in a teleporting portal in that room from our labs."

Something didn't sound right to Lark when Raoul said that, but Lark ignored this for now and went with him to shoot down those Arach clones once and for all.

WHEN KARRIN AND LARK AWOKE, THEY WERE BOTH ALARMED. Staring down at them were the Arach clones, all smiling. The two five-year-olds had returned to the brown and white, and warm and humid room. The air felt heavy and sticky as well.

"Have you both enjoyed your dreams?" grinned Karrin's former captor. "Now since you are both going to be antimattered very soon and have your bodies cloned, we might as well tell you what we were doing.

Lark," he said, turning to the boy who glowered at the mention of his name, "you remember what Liara said in the news report about possible extra enhancements in fondal-treated five-year-olds?"

"Yes, of course I do." Lark tensed inside as all the possibilities Alia had mentioned whirled through his mind. And what if it really was about gaining the gift of deception?

"Smart boy," the Arach clone said with an amused laugh. "We ourselves are just as curious as you are about what those extra enhancements may be, and so we ran several tests on you two while you were asleep, but none of them produced any physical response from you. So we lighted upon the idea that something might happen if we arouse your emotions."

Lark widened his eyes, and his fury rose up to an even greater level. "So you put us into a situation to generate our intense fear, and then into another situation to generate joy and hope." His voice was barbed and bitter, and he fixed a sharp glare on his enemies.

"You really are the scientist, aren't you? Yes, indeed. And to our joy, during these two situations, we detected unusual changes in your body biochemistry and genetic activity. We are so curious about what this means that, happily for you two, we will keep you unharmed and alive until we find out exactly what it is that produced those reactions, and what advantages—or disadvantages," he smiled, "this may have conferred on you."

Lark clenched his jaw and hardened the expression in his eyes even more.

Karrin darted a glance from Lark to the clones and back again; Karrin was terrified but didn't want to lose his cool here while his companion was holding his own against the Arach. The little Rarerus combatant desperately thought about what they could do to save themselves.

---

1. **How to Carry Around Computers**
   Drellians who want to take their computers out of their house wear a special wristband. This wristband has a small glass capsule that stores a few of the person's skin cells; these cells have the person's DNA that the computer can track and follow.
   An electromagnetic tag on the wristband attracts and directs the computer's attention to the skin cells inside the glass capsule. This capsule contains nutrients that sustain the cells like an agar jelly petri dish, and the glass cover of this capsule is well aerated.

The reason why Drellians use such wristbands instead of directly letting the computer track their body cells, is simply because it's better safe than sorry. Having the computer laser-scan your skin cells (with an invisible laser) almost every moment of your every day, is not a risk computer designers or medics want anyone to take. It's true that cancer treatments are easy on Drell, but getting that much direct daily radiation from the computer that frequently, might cause unforeseen or even unknown health problems. So it's much safer to have the computer keep track of the skin cells in the wristband instead.

Thankfully, ordinary computer use on Drell will not release any radiation.

2. **How Someone Can Take Your Computer Away From You, and How You Can Get It Back**

If someone wants to remove your computer from you, for confiscation or more sinister reasons, they can simply pull off and steal away your wristband. These confiscators or thieves can't use your computer, however, because your computer will only recognize and react to your voice, thoughts, touch, and body movements.

Having your wristband taken from you simply means that your computer won't know where you are, and will stay put where it was the last time you were wearing your wristband. Once you recover that wristband or get a new one (it's cheap to buy and the wristband automatically absorbs some of your skin cells into it the first time you wear it), your computer will soon find and rejoin you.

One may ask why Drellian scientists didn't find a way to make these computer wristbands non-detachable by everyone except by the wear themselves. Yet, the only way that could happen, is if the wristbands were embedded into the skin. Both Drellian scientists and the Drellian public, were generally opposed to the idea of embedding anything inorganic into the body, for fear of unknown consequences, as everybody knew that there was much about the universe that scientists still did not know. Drellians didn't require things like prosthetic limbs or cochlear implants anymore either. Medical technology was advanced enough to easily fix any physical defects, with stem cells and other materials and equipment.

So it was better to take no risks and wear the wristbands like our watches. And Drellians obviously didn't want to bind the wristbands on too tight, as that would be uncomfortable as well as bad for the wrist's blood circulation.

Nevertheless, as in all societies, there were some rebellious scientists who did research studies that involved inserting or embedding inorganic things into the body anyway. Even the Rarerus used technology to attach hand beams securely into the fighters' skin.

3. **Chemical compressor**

A device you can use to press the particles in a chemical closer to each other, thus elevating its density. Lark and company used a chemical compressor to greatly heighten the density of chrystacience, which made the chrystacience into a one-hit killing weapon.

FIFTEEN
THE DISCOVERY

At the Vénus Rarerus center, Liara, Amber, and Eventii all sat down in a room graced with hues of peach and orange. Calm and serenity reigned in this space despite the crisis that had just hit them. The Rarerus leader smiled and said, "So, how are my Beams doing today?"

Eventii smiled but his sister cut in and said, "Liara, come on, get to the point. What's on your mind?"

Liara widened her eyes. "You haven't heard that the two five-year-olds have been captured?"

Ever since these two five-year-olds, the eight-year-old Yearlie, and the twelve-year-old Gastra entered Rarerus, the two Beams didn't feel so unique anymore. On the one hand, they were glad that there were more young people now, aside from Liara; but on the other hand, they were rather resentful that they were no longer the special ones. Or at least, Amber seemed a bit upset at this. Eventii seemed less visibly discomforted, or he was just quieter about it.

"Yes—and what do you think we should do?" asked Amber, whose questions to Liara, as she knew that Liara was very fond of her and her brother, tended to be sharper and more direct. Eventii was a milder speaker, and didn't like to raise his voice that much, but he was still generally audible.

Their leader sighed. "What do you propose we do about it?"

It both flattered and annoyed Amber that Liara frequently encouraged her and Eventii to think of strategies for their Arach missions, and now she thought and thought. "We can't just blast into the Arach compound with our explosives—I mean our most powerful guns?"

"What do you think?" smiled Liara.

Amber pressed her lips together into a tight line. She nudged her brother. "What about you?"

Eventii blinked and said, "Oh, um, since we're recording Lark and Karrin's whereabouts, how about we dig tunnels right under them and then take them out of there?"

His sister frowned. "But you think the Arach compound wouldn't be fortified against obvious attacks like that?" Eventii sighed at this disapproval and stared at the ground. Liara looked at him sympathetically.

Then she turned to Amber again. "About your initial plan of blasting into the compound, do you have a similar alternative?"

The little girl was thoughtful again.

Liara said, "What else could you do instead of blasting that would also be an attack?"

"Oh, we could use fire," Amber said delightedly. "We can surround them with fire so they can't get out. So they would have to surrender to us if they want to escape."

Liara nodded. "But couldn't the Arach clones just put out the fire with their water?"

Amber scowled. "We could use brachiorsor barriers over the fires so that the clones can't put them out." The Rarerus could leave many tiny holes in the barriers to let oxygen through and keep the flames alive.

"Very good," her leader said. "But the Brachiorsor would just protect the Arach clones from the fire, wouldn't it? And can't the clones simply fly out of their compound?"

This time Eventii answered, "If they do that, we can use our soarrows to drop stones on their flying vehicles." Soarrows (pronounced so-arrows) were laminae with velvet blackish-purple feathers and wings. They had bright eyes and were small as our sparrows. Their saliva hardened almost as soon as it made contact with the air, and after hardening, they became hard stones. The soarrows readily produced saliva and thus could be used as flying weapons to drop stones on enemies from above.

"Okay, but the Arach clones could just dig out to escape the fire, right?" Liara said.

Both children were stumped.

So Liara said, "What is related to fire?"

"Smoke," Eventii said when that answer immediately popped into his head.

His sister continued, "We can fill their compound with smoke and smoke them out. No matter how fast they dig, the smoke will very quickly follow them into their tunnels and suffocate them. And they wouldn't dare leave the two five-year-olds and the almost antimattered man behind because they can't antimatter dead people."

"Good," Liara said calmly. "Then let's do it."

But just at that moment, Liara's half-brother burst into the room. "Liara, I will offer myself as a hostage in exchange for the two children. All we have to say is that we treasure young children, especially children this young, so that we want to get them out of there no matter what. The Arach clones should believe us because they know how much the Rarerus values children." Raoul said this with both resolution and firmness, as if he knew that his sister couldn't refuse his request.

The two Beams looked at Liara to see how she would respond. Surely they couldn't endanger an important member of the Rarerus. Yet, Liara nodded. "Good plan."

Raoul bowed grimly and headed out to make preparations for this offer. When Raoul left, Eventii asked, "Why did you let him sacrifice himself like that? You know how much the Rarerus needs him."

But Liara smiled at the little boy. "Don't worry. He knows what he's doing."

RAOUL WAS SWEATING NERVOUSLY AS HE SET UP, WITH THE other Rarerus scientists and fighters watching, his communication with the Arach clones. Drellians could sometimes communicate with people without knowing their contact codes, as long as they could reach into the particular place they wanted to contact and if that place was set to welcome outside communication.

Fortunately, the Arach clone compound did, which Raoul did not expect, but he was simply relieved that he did not have to do any complex hacking to break in.

Once the connection was established, he found himself face to face with Lark's former captor. Raoul knit his eyebrows together but he reminded himself to stay calm and tell them about his offer. The Arach clone was surprised when he heard what Raoul proposed, but also clearly delighted. "I see that you are desperate," said the clone. "Very well, we will grant your request. But in order to see that you are not lying, we need you to enter our compound first and be held captive before we release the two boys."

The scientists, combaters, and other Rarerus members in the big room with Raoul stared at him and some shook their heads at this dangerous suggestion. From the crowd, Alia Lyreal stepped out, their brows heavily furrowed. "Raoul, don't do this. You'll regret your decision."

Raoul shot a glance at the nonbinary scientist and combatant. "Alia, I know you mean well, but I'll be fine."

"Raoul!" Alia said in protest.

Yet, Raoul ignored them, and nodded at the Arach clone. "I will come with you, as long as you do let the children come back to us. They are only five. They cannot be antimattered at such a young age."

"True," nodded the clone with mock sympathy. "You are a very kind man, Raoul."

"The Rarerus is a very kind society," corrected Raoul.

When Raoul strode out towards the Arach clones to be transported to their compound, his friends and followers entreated him not to go, not to fall into this obvious trap. But he ignored them and smiled with reassurance. The members were equally baffled by Liara's permission to let Raoul go. With a discontented frown, Alia said, "You can't be sure that the Arach will honor their promise."

"I will save the boys and get out of there," Raoul replied. "Don't worry so much."

Alia crossed their arms across their chest.

As soon as Raoul was strapped down in the Arach vehicle, he smirked. An Arach clone said, "You better not try anything funny, Faya."

"Of course not. I wouldn't dare. I need to get the boys back no matter what it takes."

"I suppose so," the clone said.

When they arrived, two of the strongest clones each grasped one of Raoul's arms and marched towards the door. Though Raoul was tall, he was rather slender and definitely not strong enough to break free. The clones watched him closely to ensure that he really did not play any tricks on them before they could have him locked and bound inside their building.

"All right, Faya, we now need you to lie down and take this." The Arach clones pressed him down onto a stretch seat—he didn't struggle at all—and another clone poured a bit of transparent liquid down his throat. Almost immediately, Raoul Faya fell asleep.

LARK AND KARRIN WERE NOW FENCED INTO ANOTHER environment. The Arach clones exposed them to all sorts of unpleasant and pleasant virtual situations, hoping to activate something spectacular in the boys; the Arach had so much faith in the powers of the fondal. Lark tried with all his might to command his cells and genes not to react to any of these emotion-inducing situations, but of course, his attempts were in vain.

During these tests, Karrin and Lark indeed had some kinds of genetic and biochemical changes in their bodies, but only a little bit at a time. The boys were so sick of being thrown emotionally from one extreme to the other so many times, that they were both collapsing from exhaustion. The clone who took the place of Lark's ex-captor in coordinating these experiments ordered the other clones to let the boys rest. They would resume the tests the next day.

"LARK?" KARRIN ASKED IN THE DARKNESS.

The room where they were locked in to sleep was bare, save the two beds set half a qwort away from each other. Lark was glad for this distance, though he suspected that it was meant to make communication between them more difficult. Supposedly.

"What is it?" Lark snapped. His mind had been occupied by thoughts on how to escape, and the other boy's interruption was highly unwelcome.

"Do you think we'll ever get out? What if we never do and get anti-mattered? How do you think being antimattered would feel like?"

"Why would you want to find out?" Lark said with irritation.

"Well, I just—"

"Please can you be quiet and let me sleep?"

"Okay." But a second later, Karrin spoke again, "What do you think our extra physical enhancements might be? Do you think they'll help us escape?"

This now made Lark think, as he had only ever thought about their current resources for how to break free, but it surprisingly never occurred to him that those physical enhancements may prove a valuable resource not just to the Arach, but to them as well. "Please elaborate," he said.

Karrin was grateful that for once, he was not being ignored. "You know, whatever it is, it'll probably give us some extra power."

"Extra-human power?" said Lark. "I have already had this conversation with Alia—a scientist in the Rarerus. There is a possibility but the question is, will it be powerful enough to help us break out of this compound, as well as the question of whether we will discover this new power or ability in time. Now, as you have no more to say, let me sleep."

Karrin was still up, though, and still thinking. "Then what do you think those extra enhancements have to do with our emotions?"

"How would I know?"

"Because you're the scientist," Karrin said matter-of-factly, without any resentment.

Lark felt ashamed that Karrin was right and that he really didn't know what was going on, so he replied, "I am still pondering this question. Now if you do not let me sleep, I will never be able to figure this out." And finally Karrin shut up once and for all that night, to Lark's enormous relief.

"Liara?" A head peeked into the room. Liara Grae had been pacing around in one of her usual resting rooms, one with walls painted a dark blue like the tide; and Liara had asked everyone to leave her alone for the rest of the evening. Presently, she raised her head at the familiar voice and gave her friend a beam. "Alia."

Alia shot her a warm look in return; they sauntered in and closed the door after them. The neutrois and androgynous Rarerus member stuffed their hands into their dracana pockets, and their brows creased with concern. "So, your brother—"

Liara nodded. "I know. But he'll be all right."

Alia didn't seem convinced, and said, "How long do you plan to wait for him and the kids to come out?"

Liara pressed her lips together; she gazed at the ground before raising her eyes again. "They'll be out as soon as possible. By the end of tomorrow at the latest."

Her nonbinary friend sent her a worried glance. "Yet, what if that doesn't happen and they're still trapped by the end of tomorrow?"

"Then we'll get them out of there ourselves," Liara replied in a stiff but determined tone.

Alia stepped in closer, taking a hand out from its place of security in one of their Dracana pockets, and touched her arm with a quiet softness. "Liara, you know I'll always have your back no matter what you decide, and not only because you're my leader. But I just have to ask—what if Raoul doesn't make it out of there?"

The leader of the Rarerus stared at her companion. Sympathy shadowed the eyes of the nonbinary scientist and combatant, but the evident toughness in Alia's lips held a hint of reproach as well. Liara reached to pull out her friend's other hand from its pocket, and squeezed it with affection. She said, "Alia, my brother has been through so many life-and-death situations before. He will be okay."

This time it was Alia who stared, or rather glared, at the ground with a dissatisfied look on their face. "Yeah, Raoul is definitely competent, but if anything does go wrong, and it doesn't even have to be about Raoul, you can always talk to me, all right? I'll be there." They sounded both grim and awkward when they said that, and Liara chuckled.

"Alia, we've known each other for years before I became the leader of the Rarerus. There's no need to be shy around me." Before her androgynous and neutrois friend could argue, Liara added, "But thanks."

A silence stretched between them, until Alia let go of Liara and said, "Well, I won't bother you any longer. I'll—let you think about it all."

"You never bother me," Liara murmured. Alia gave her a faint smile before uttering a "goodbye for now," and traipsed back out of the room. Liara sighed with a feeling of dejection. She didn't want to appear clingy or needy, especially as she was the leader of the Rarerus now, but in all honesty, she wished Alia could have stayed with her for just a bit longer; their presence had always been a deep, sweet comfort, like a scintillating fire.

Then Liara thought back to her brother. What if Raoul really didn't return? But she told herself not to be silly. Of course Raoul would escape unscathed, and he would bring the children out with him too. Her faith in her half-brother rose back up in her heart.

IN ANOTHER ROOM, RAOUL FAYA WAS ROUSED BY A SHARP PAIN in his head. He found that he was in a strange transparent room; but for some reason, he could see nothing through its transparency. Just picture yourself being surrounded by water but without any blueness, greenness, or any color in it. This water-like surrounding also resembled thick gel, as this "water" did not move. It did not even wobble. In addition to this, all was completely silent. The silence was eerily disturbing and soon he discovered that he couldn't feel his hands, his face, or any part of his body and that he couldn't even see his body.

There was also absolutely no smell in the room at all. It didn't smell mint fresh; it just smelled like nothing; try to imagine that. The only thing in the world he could perceive was the transparent oozy but frozen gel all around him. And so Raoul knew he was locked up in a sensory deprivation chamber. He smiled to himself. This was no surprise to him at all.

Back in the orange and peach meeting room the next morning, Eventii asked Liara whether he and his sister could still carry out their original plan of smoking out the enemy, because after so many moments of waiting, the Arach clones had still not given Lark or Karrin back to them. Liara wanted the children back as well, but she wasn't too happy about this suggestion of using the smoke.

"I know Raoul and the two kids are in there, but we just need to threaten the Arach clones enough so that they'll do as we wish and release everyone," Amber said confidently.

"Do you really believe that the Arach clones will give in that quickly? They'll eventually surrender, but what will happen to our members still left in the smoke in the meantime?" Liara asked.

Amber frowned. "What's the matter with this plan, though? You originally approved our smoking out method, and we agreed that the Arach would definitely save the victims' lives because they can't antimatter them if they're dead, right? How does including Raoul this time make any difference?" And she couldn't resist adding, "You love Raoul, don't you?"

It was a matter of embarrassment that many of the members who did not know that Liara and Raoul were half-siblings, thought that they were clandestine lovers, especially in how Liara seemed to be more permissive and indulgent of Raoul's decisions than of the usual member's. Those who were a little more astute noticed that Raoul showed no such favor towards Liara, so they believed that it was unrequited love on the part of their leader; and these members, as they loved her so, wished that Raoul would love her back one day.

Liara thought with chagrin and bemusement how nobody seemed to notice that she and her brother looked a bit alike. Their physical resemblance was not striking, as they only shared one parent, but it was still there for those who were careful enough to observe it.

Nevertheless, because of such a belief that Liara loved him romantically, the Rarerus members were generally more respectful or even reverent to Raoul. Raoul, of course, was aware of these rumors, but he did nothing to prevent them from spreading. He simply could not care less. And it would be better to be seen as Liara's beloved than as her brother because the latter would make him more irrevocably related to her, partic-

ularly if he were the indifferent beloved who wanted no relationship whatsoever. He just wanted as little to do with her as possible.

But sometimes these beliefs annoyed him so much, that he told other
people that there was nothing between them, that they were not in love, etc.
etc. Yet, it was hard to convince them because Liara so clearly showed an
unusual amount of favor towards him. He did ask her in private to stop
showing such a preference towards him, but she would just shoot him a disconsolate glance, smile, and then say, "How can I help it? You're my brother."

The reason why the siblings had to keep this secret from the members,
and ask those who happened to know to not tell others, was mainly
because of Raoul. He didn't want anyone to know that he was related by
blood to Liara, or to know how his mother had betrayed his father by
marrying another man so soon after his death.

Phinn Faya had passed away when Raoul was just eight, and Raoul
was simply upset that his father was forgotten so soon. But when he grew
older, he couldn't help but suspect that his mother had already had a kind
of relationship with this Orlen Grae; or at least she already had thoughts
of straying, and Orlen thoughts of stealing her for his own.

Perhaps his mother and Orlen had plotted to murder his father in
order to get together in a shameless, public union. And Liara was the
embodiment of his mother's adultery.

So as you can see, he had already assumed that adultery was the absolute truth of the matter, even though he had not a single shred of evidence.
Raoul had openly accused his mother and Orlen of this, many times; but
they would just look at him in sorrow, and ask why he could not believe in
their innocence.

Liara knew of her brother's accusation as well because he had
mentioned it to her a few times when they were alone. On those occasions,
he did not shout; he spoke softly but with much venom. Little Liara,
when she was then twelve-years-old, cried when he had first told her this,
because this defiled the perfect image of her mama and papa who loved
each other so; and she did not believe a word of what he said.

Neither did she believe it now. Sometimes, when they were alone, she
would tell him that her parents had never done such a thing, that they had
simply fallen in love with each other very soon after his father died,

without any prior romantic desires for one another. Not that Raoul ever listened to her.

Still, she wanted to treat him specially well partly because he was her brother; partly because she may someday move him enough to believe in their parents' innocence; and partly because she cared about him in spite of how coldly he treated them.

She thought to herself many times that if it were not for these groundless suspicions, he would have made a fairly good brother. They could even have been close friends, as they resembled one another not just in looks (though many could not tell), but in personality as well. Both had an unusual intuition in understanding people and sensing what they liked and needed; both had an instinctual urge to act in a way to make people feel appreciated and respected; and both were simultaneously competent and well-loved leaders.

Liara smiled now at the older Beam. "Of course I love Raoul. Don't we all? He is such a valuable and selfless member of the Rarerus."

Amber sighed. Eventii said, "But if we don't smoke them out, then how can we save Raoul and the two kids? I'm not sure Raoul can make it out alive alone."

To be honest, Liara wasn't completely sure herself. She only let him go because she had a lot of confidence in his abilities to fight it out and save the children, regardless of how doubtful Alia had been the night before. But now she wondered if her former great confidence was just due to her sisterly faith in him, whether she had unwittingly sent her brother off to die.

This was one of those times when Liara was disappointed in herself for making such gross mistakes, particularly as the leader of the Rarerus. It was also one of those times when she felt that the love and trust from most of her followers were misplaced. She had an especial fear of letting Alia and Raoul down, though the latter already didn't harbor much fondness towards her.

As Liara didn't respond, Eventii continued, "If not, we could try to dig into the compound to save them." He paused. "I know that's a dangerous option because we have no idea what the Arach have waiting inside that building, or worse yet, what the Arach have inside the earth beneath the building in case someone tries to burrow through. But—since you don't want to use the smoking method—"

"Let's use the smoking method," Liara said with resolution, while trying to hide the tremor in her heart. There was a chance that the Arach did want to keep Raoul alive, if not for antimattering, then for other reasons. If they actually wanted to torture her brother to his eventual death, then killing him by smoke would be a much quicker and more merciful death. Her head felt warm and vehement, but she steeled herself, got up, and commanded her Beams to make arrangements for this operation.

RAOUL FAYA WONDERED WHAT THE ARACH CLONES WOULD try on him next. Some instrument of physical torture? Or was this sensory deprivation tank all they had? He laughed to himself. A normal person would have been terrified at this point, but Raoul felt a strange courage in the midst of this, a queer confidence that he could brave this, find Lark and Karrin, and escape. As wandering around in this boundlessly transparent chamber would be fruitless, he simply sat there and waited for the Arach clones to move him elsewhere.

DURING THIS SAME MORNING, THE CLONES TOOK LARK AND Karrin out to their experimental chambers again. More emotion-inducing experiments, Lark thought. But to his surprise, they wanted to try something new this time. They put the two of them on a grey platform that was apparently a cliff, and shoved.

The boys plummeted down to the obscurity below.

The fall seemed to never end and while Karrin's screams were deafening his ears, Lark's screams were choked inside him, which was just as well because he didn't want to lose his dignity by bawling like a baby, not even during this life-or-death situation. Then something like color was emerging down below. Something green. The green grew increasingly vivid until they realized they were about to hit it. Lark shut his eyes, ready for the worst; Karrin's eyes were still open, horrified as he was. But all of a sudden the green floor struck them. Except it didn't strike them. They went through it. An illusion, of course, thought Lark.

From then on, he became more suspicious of floors that came at them, however solid they seemed. And surely, the Arach clones would not really let them die, would they? This was all somehow happening in their minds? Lark was discomforted by how unsure he was about all of this.

While they were still in a terrifying free fall, the darkness around them grew lighter, and the walls became lit up by stars. Even Karrin stopped screeching for a moment to behold them. Without thinking, Karrin shot a hand beam at one of the stars and he stopped falling. Lark stared at him, dismayed, as he continued to drop. Why? Karrin likewise gazed down at Lark, frightened at what was happening, yet also confused.

Lark resented that he didn't have any weapon with him like Karrin did. He stared at all those stars whisking by and vaguely imagined what he would do if he did have a weapon, and what weapon that would be.

It was then that something very, very strange happened that would become one of the greatest turning points in his life.

Unbeknownst to him, his feet began to change. They became spiked, heavily spiked, and metallic. His hands transformed in the same way. When Lark realized what had happened, he gasped in both horror and wonder; then, upon realizing what he had to do, he threw his hands and feet at the walls. The spikes sunk in deeply into the surprisingly soft starred walls, and after a few moments of slowing down, he was secure.

He glanced down below him and sighted a blue illusory platform surging upwards; it stopped at his feet. This blue platform appeared to be solid, but he didn't trust it enough to release his grasp on the wall.

"Lark! It's all right. You're safe now," said an Arach clone.

Lark ignored him, and began to scale the wall. He mentally shut out the Arach clone's increasingly loud demands and pressed on with his climb. As he ascended, he noticed a tickling in his back. Before long, his back grew heavy too; he twisted around to see what was happening, and was struck dumb when he saw a pair of thick, feathery wings!

Distrustful, Lark only let go of the wall when he was sure the wings could support him. Then he flapped upwards as quickly as he could. The boy noticed that his body was considerably lighter than it normally was. But he didn't notice that his bones had become hollow as well.

"Lark!" This time it was Karrin. He stared with an open mouth at his flying companion. "How did you—"

Lark shook his head and wanted to keep flying upwards. But then something like conscience tugged at Lark; he remembered what the illusion Raoul had said, and so he offered Karrin his hand.

"Hurry up. Hold on tight and I will fly you up." Karrin took it in surprise and delight. Lark rolled his eyes at that childishly brightened face and dragged him. But to both the boys' fear, it became apparent that the two were too heavy for the wings, especially as Karrin's bones were still human and not hollow—and Lark was getting too tired of flapping.

"Maybe I can blast a star again," said Karrin, and he tried to do so. But this time, though it hit, Karrin did not stop in mid-air. "How did you manage to get those wings?" Karrin cried.

"I do not know," said Lark with irritation, especially as he was trying to pull his deadweight of a classmate up with him. Then he mumbled, not really paying attention to what he was saying, "I thought about what I needed."

Karrin did hear his words, however, and very soon, to his amazement, his back started tickling too; it grew heavy and he was flapping wings! "Yay, I can fly too! And I feel so light!" he squealed, released Lark's hand and shot up through the air above him.

Lark was not a competitive person, but he too wanted to escape from this eerie tunnel-like pit as soon as possible, so up he zipped. The Arach clone was still shouting at them to come back down; but Lark realized that the clones were not actually doing anything to stop them. He frowned, thinking that perhaps he and Karrin had walked, or rather flew, into yet another trap.

"There's the exit!" cried Karrin, and soared out into the glory of the day—though they were still indoors. Gleeful, the boy landed with all the natural Karrin agility he always had, but he was astonished to see that no Arach clones were waiting around. Where did they all go?

Very soon, Lark arrived too. He felt the spikes on his hands and feet disappearing and his wings shrinking back into nothingness. His normal weight also returned as his bones became human again. So this was their extra physical enhancement? He was still very suspicious about how their enemies didn't take any action to pursue them, as if they had expected them to escape that free-fall tunnel. Part of him wanted to fly back down that tunnel to see what was amiss, but he waved that thought off as silly because that in itself could be a trap.

"Hey Lark," said Karrin, "want to walk over there?" He pointed to a set of transparent doors opposite them a short distance away.

Lark honestly didn't want to follow Karrin or to keep enduring the bubbly boy's relentless chatter, but that same conscience urged him not to abandon his classmate, much as he would really like to. The transparent doors opened immediately upon the children's approach. Karrin jolted at this, but proceeded to walk in.

Lark halted to see if the doors would shut and lock after his classmate; but they didn't, and he reasoned that he was probably no safer staying in the current room anyway, so he followed Karrin.

The new room had a pale green soft floor, made of synthetic fur. Opposite them was a large square door, which was a soft orange. Without even thinking, Karrin made his way towards that door. Lark just watched him go to see what would happen. To Karrin's joy, the square door broke apart like an egg to reveal a path he could go through, and he crept inside. Lark looked around to see if there were any oddities—though all things were oddities around here—before he trudged in after Karrin.

They were in a dark, narrow corridor, where they could only see their way by a red light that was shining from the end of this room. Not surprisingly, this red light was on a door. Karrin poked at the door with his foot and it opened. The boys were blasted with glaring sunlight.

SIXTEEN
THE CHILDREN'S ADVENTURE

I t seemed like a century, or maybe it was just a second, before a door miraculously appeared in the transparent gel and opened; there was an Arach clone right in front of him. Raoul wondered if he was invisible to the clone. As if reading his thoughts, the clone said, "Yes, Mr Faya, I can see you. Now, I'm sure you've had enough of this chamber, so come on out, you deserve it." He handed Raoul a pack of dry but nourishing food, and a large bottle of water.

Raoul took the pack and bottle, as he needed the energy to both survive and find Lark and Karrin. The food and water could possibly be poisoned, but starving and thirsting for so long would definitely make him too weak to save or protect anybody. Yet, right now, Raoul just wanted to laugh at this Arach clone's feigned friendliness. They really didn't need to bother being affable to their guests, but perhaps they were bored and wanted to see how amiability would make Raoul react. "So where am I going now?" he asked.

"Not yet." This particular Arach clone happened to be a young boy of about sixteen. Antimattered at such an early age, because the Rarerus had failed to save him, or to detect him, even. "Please step this way, Mr Faya." The youth—or rather the clone youth—even extended his arm through the door in a very courteous gesture. Raoul shook his head inwardly with pity as he stepped outside.

After a journey through multiple corridors and rooms, the teenage boy clone finally led him to a small room with orange-yellow lights, where three adult Arach clone men sat on stretch seats close together, with a red machine, an orange machine, and a yellow machine placed nearby.

"Welcome, Mr Faya," smiled one of the seated clones as he invited Raoul to a seat. This clone was an amicable-looking old man; again, what a shame. "Here, we just need your help with something, if it would be your pleasure to lend us your assistance."

This degree of courtesy made Raoul want to laugh, as this was absurd; he didn't know what mind games the Arach were trying to play with him. Yet, Raoul decided to play along for now. "I will see what it is and what I can do," he said, giving them the standard answer.

So the old man clone pointed to the red machine. "There seems to be something wrong with its computer system. It can't record information anymore, like it was attacked by viruses." This statement was strange in two ways. One, the Arach themselves were viruses; and two, computers on Drell were supposed to be so indestructible that virtually no virus could ever harm them. There were only very few viruses in the world that managed to infect some computers, but even these strong bugs were very easily gotten rid of by computer experts. And though Raoul was more of a chemist, scientists on Drell had a basic knowledge of computers, which included how to delete a virus, should one of those rare incidences occur.

The old man clone mumbled a few incoherent words and instantly, the silvery-white network of a computer flashed up above the red machine. The familiar sight of a computer network solaced Raoul somewhat, though he knew he was in enemy territory and could be killed or even antimattered at any moment, if they didn't want to torture him first—and with more than a mere sensory deprivation tank.

With a deliberate calmness, Raoul whispered to the computer and tapped keys here and there, as if he were talking to a child.

"Is it all right?" asked the old man clone, looking quite worried as if that "child" were his grandchild and he were not an Arach clone.

Raoul nodded. "Please wait. I haven't finished checking yet."

It turned out that there was a bug in the center of the computer's virtual disk, and it was generating false data into the computer and preventing it from recording real information. Raoul thought that maybe he should make it even worse. But as he couldn't see how that would get him anywhere, except closer to his doom, he decided to fix it and see what would happen.

A short while later, the computer reverted to normal, and the old man clone was exceedingly pleased; he even looked like he wanted to hug Raoul. Aside from feeling unsettled by how cordial the Arach clones were being, Raoul also thought with poignancy that this clone reminded him of Centuri. Nevertheless, Raoul mimicked the clones' impeccable manners and asked, "Is there anything else I can help you with?"

The old man clone thought for a bit, before he smiled and said, "Nope, that's all. Thank you."

Afterwards, the man clone who was sitting next to him, a man in his thirties, not much older than Raoul himself, started to speak. "If you please, could you help me fix this lil' machine as well?" He pointed to the bright yellow one, which wasn't "little" at all. He snapped his fingers, and a computer appeared above the machine like a white mist.

Raoul smiled graciously. "Is it infected by a virus too?" He made sure he didn't pronounce the word "virus" in a mocking tone.

"Uh-uh," the clone said with a shake of his head. "There's something wrong with it. It's generating gibberish instead of ordinary language to communicate with me when I'm bored, but I'm sure there's no virus. Right, guys?" He looked at the other two clones, the old man and the middle-aged man in his fifties; these two nodded without seeming to really agree or care.

This made Raoul frown inside. Whatever the Arach had up their sleeves, he hoped it would be fast. He would rather get the torture over with sooner than later, and then he would think of a plan to find the two children and escape. "Let me see," Raoul said, as he checked the computer network all over for bugs. He was incredulous when he found that there were indeed no viruses. When he announced this to the thirty-year-old clone, he shrugged.

"I told you so."

Raoul racked his brains to figure out the problem. But before he even got onto the remotest hint, the third clone, the middle-aged one, said, "Here, let me have a look."

Weren't they the ones who had asked him to help them in the first place? Raoul thought. Nevertheless, he let the middle-aged clone peer through the machine. After just a moment, the clone beamed. "I know why now. Bobby," he glanced at the thirty-year-old, "the problem was actually quite simple. You entered the wrong equation—you accidentally put the imaginary number in the wrong place."

Raoul couldn't help gaping when he heard this. That was so simple! How come he didn't figure that out? That kind of problem was as obvious and common as our Earth one of having the machine unplugged.

"Thank you so much, though," Bobby and the middle-aged clone said to Raoul, even bowing their heads slightly as if to communicate respect. Their deferential behavior baffled Raoul more and more.

"Now, um," said the middle-aged clone, "would you mind helping me with this baby?" He pointed to the orange machine, the one between the red and the yellow ones. Yes, many Drellians liked to use affectionate names when referring to their machines and electronics. They believed that machines deserved as much kindness and respect as human beings did, because nobody had proven that machines did not have a living, feeling, and sentient consciousness like we did.

"So not a virus, nor an incorrectly set equation?" Raoul asked, smiling.

"No, no," the middle-aged clone said, reciprocating the smile. "I just —I don't know why, but you know how computers, even an average one like this, should have a virtually unlimited memory? Well, for some odd reason, this computer said that it had only memory left to store one book." He shrugged.

Raoul was truly befuddled now. Never had he encountered a computer whose memory was almost all used up. That was supposed to be impossible on Drell. He couldn't help asking, "Are you sure there was no virus involved?"

"No," the clone said; he even looked a bit offended by Raoul's doubt.

With a deep furrow on his brow, Raoul watched the man call up the computer for his orange machine, and then Raoul delved into the fortress of its systems to check. But before he could find anything, they were interrupted by a loud cry.

"Clones, run! Smoke is flooding our entire building!"

AMBER AND EVENTII PEERED OUT WITH GLEE AT THE ARACH building through the Glass's windows. Liara was driving the vehicle as usual, and she had asked her attendants to leave her alone with her two young Beams for this journey. "It'll be any moment now," Eventii said.

Liara thought with anxiety that it would probably not be any moment soon. All they saw was a flood of smoke that poured in and out of the building. Eventually, to the Beams' relief, they saw Arach clone men and women come out—they all looked like ordinary human beings; no one would have guessed otherwise. But where were the five-year-olds and Raoul?

The clones that had come out rushed towards Liara's Glass; its strikingly aesthetic and strong appearance might have indicated that it was the leader's vehicle. These clones raged and shouted at her. Liara gathered up a calm facial expression, and spoke as if she were soothing them. "Worry not. We do not intend to harm you. We merely want our members safely returned to us." Though the Arach were their enemies, Liara was naturally soft and diplomatic in her speech, so she preferred to speak politely even to her adversaries.

An Arach clone that was a man with blue and white hair said, "But we were about to give you back your dear child members right after we finished doing a little experiment with them. Why did you have to smoke us out?"

"You took a bit too long, Mister," said Eventii. Eventii was usually quite gentle in both face and manner, and even when he grew gutsy, he would still look so sweet and endearing. He was a picture of adorableness everywhere he went. He was only eight, after all.

"Yeah, even kids like us can tell you were all lying," said his sister. So yes, the Beams were fully aware that they were little children, but instead of being ashamed of being so young, they used their littleness to their advantage, even if it was just to charge up a cheeky retort.

"And what experiments did you want to do, anyway?" Eventii asked.

The blue and white haired clone smirked. "Nothing to do with anti-mattering if that's what you're worried about. It's something very simple. Just a physical examination."

"A physical examination?" said Liara, her eyes narrowing. "Please do elaborate." She chose this moment to alight from her vehicle; the Arach clones automatically backed away a few steps. It was clear that even if Liara were not wearing her armor, these clones would be intimidated by the mere aura that the Rarerus leader exuded. The Beams stayed inside the Glass at Liara's behest. All this time, she kept an eye on the entrances and exits of the building; Lark, Karrin, or Raoul could come out at any instant.

"Uh—can't tell you what exactly, though. Confidential information. Anyway, I'm too low ranked to even know what was going on myself. But I can assure you that no harm has come to your two treasures," he said in a mocking tone.

Liara's consternation deepened at every turn. Where was Raoul? Where were the five-year-olds? If she were not the leader of Rarerus, she would now grab her Glass, fly right above the building and blast water at it so that she could ensure her brother and her two little members' safety. But as the leader, she could not be so rash. They may yet be coming out.

"Leader," said a voice by her side. It was Braiven. "If they do not bring anyone out, do we have your permission to send in a rescue team?" With his rescue team, he would use gas screens to protect the members for a short period of time, and use lights to penetrate through as much of the smoke as possible. But the gas screens could only last so long before the oxygen supply ran out and the members suffocated. So she shook her head.

"I'm sorry, Braiven. I know you really want to help, but I can't risk your lives here. The smoke is too thick, and the Arach compound too unknown." Braiven bowed with disappointment, but he respected her decision.

A moment later, a short and slender Rarerus combatant swathed in blue and black gel armor strode to her side. Liara's body thrummed with emotion.

This combatant in question was Alia, and they asked in an urgent voice, "Liara, why don't my team and I put out the smoke with our gas vacuum (this sucks out the smoke and excretes it back outdoors) and then find the captives?"

Liara's gaze lingered gently on her friend's face, but still she had to shake her head and reply quietly, "I'm afraid if we do that, the Arach clones will recover their forces and hide our captives in an even more obscure place. And it is too dangerous to wander deep into Arach territory even if we took in a large number of people. A clever trap could kill a hundred people in a single blow."

The forlorn look in Alia's eyes tugged at Liara's heart. She spoke a few soft words with Alia, hoping to comfort them, but Alia just gave her a tight smile, and then trotted away. Liara stared at their retreating figure, and was overcome by sorrow and longing.

LARK AND KARRIN WERE STANDING IN A ROOM WHERE THE SUN blazed down on them with a strangely natural heat and brightness. There was too much nature in such an unnatural place. Nevertheless, Lark thought of a need and immediately, to his smug satisfaction, a thin semitransparent film spread over his eyes, and the sunlight didn't sting anymore. His clothes and skin turned white to reflect off the sun's heat as well. Lark was amazed. Even his clothes could change! Not just his body.

Karrin, who looked exactly the same as Lark with his whitened exterior and translucent extra-eyelids, grinned at Lark. "This is awesome, isn't it?"

Lark was excited too, but the sight of Karrin's enthusiasm dampened Lark's own bright spirits. Perhaps Lark's superiority complex and general arrogance would never go away.

Thus armored, the two children trotted through this narrow passageway that was at once the outdoors as well as a path that led outdoors. When they reached the end of this path, it was as if a tributary had reached the mouth of the ocean. The passageway widened to include the world, and the two boys felt overwhelmed. There were the trees they saw outside the Arach compound, and the brown cobbled ground.

With hesitation, they trotted on to see if any Arach clone was hiding and waiting for them. To their constant surprise, especially Lark's, there really were none. It seemed as though they were truly safe. Free. Soon, they moved around the building until they were near the entrance of the Arach compound. Why did they even come here? Lark thought, shuddering. "Karrin, let us go," he hissed.

"But where do we go?" Karrin asked.

Lark wanted to punch him in the head for being so thick. "Anywhere. Just go anywhere as far as possible from the Arach compound. If you do not move now, I am going without you."

That got Karrin following. "But," here was that annoying boy's soft voice again, Lark thought; Karrin said, "Don't you think they'll be able to spot us really easily out here in the open?"

"Do you think we would be less easy to spot right outside the compound?" Lark asked back through gritted teeth. Karrin had nothing to say to that, and that was a relief to Lark; it gave him a bit more silence to concentrate on what he was doing.

They soon came across a metallic crater, which was literally a metal that people shaped to mimic real craters on Drell. Nobody knew what these were for. Some people just enjoyed wasting their time and money on useless things. Without even thinking, Lark scrambled up the metal to hop inside the crater—"What are you doing?" Karrin hissed, pulling him back. "Are you crazy?"

Now this was a reversal. Never had Karrin expressed any negativity towards him before and that made him gape, for just a while. Then he realized that Karrin was right. He had lost his mind temporarily, perhaps in his desperation to do something, and almost killed himself—a crater was high enough to kill someone who fell off the rim, but not high enough to allow Lark time to "need" his wings out in time. For once, he did feel grateful towards Karrin because this boy had just saved his life, and there was a flash of a smile on Lark's face before it was back to normal again. Nevertheless, Karrin caught that positive social gesture that was so rare, nay, never-before-seen in Lark, at least when towards Karrin, that he darted forward to hug him.

"Un. Hand. Me," said Lark. Karrin really should have known that his classmate was dreadfully afraid of such effusive expressions of affection; but Karrin was such a spontaneous person that he never paused to think before running to embrace people. Lark was immensely relieved when the overfriendly boy released him. "You have wasted time," Lark said. "Every second we dawdle is another chance for the Arach clones to spot us."

"Oh," Karrin said glumly. "Sorry."

Lark shrugged off his apology because it was of no consequence, especially in these life-and-death situations. Then he turned to Karrin. "Tell your body that you need invisibility!"

It was theatrical how wide Karrin's mouth opened. "Invisibility!"

"Yes. I am not sure if this will work, but we must try to save our lives." He closed his eyes and willed for the change.

"Lark," Karrin whispered. "I can still see you."

Indeed, Lark looked the same as he usually did, except for the lightened skin mentioned earlier for reflecting off any excess sun rays. Still, to vent his annoyance, he shot back, "I can still see you too."

Karrin wasn't bothered by this jibe, however. "So what else should we try?" he asked.

"Why do you not try to use your own brain?" asked Lark.

The other boy was disappointed that Lark was so thoroughly antisocial again. Then Karrin said, "Do you think we can try to give ourselves claws and stuff to dig?"

Now it was Lark's turn to drop his jaw. "Dig!"

"Yes, dig!" Karrin closed his eyes, and sure enough, he was growing claws on his hands and feet.

It could be imagined how outraged Lark felt that Karrin's idea worked whilst his didn't. Nevertheless, as Lark told himself, great people never let loose any petty feelings, so he silenced his bitterness and made himself grow claws too.

They dug and dug for who knew how long, and for who knew how far. Apart from the claws, the two boys also grew special respiratory structures to prevent them from suffocating underground. Very soon, they came to a place where there was a pipe. Drellians still used these cylindrical vessels for transporting water, other liquids, and materials, except their pipes were always kept clean, unlike ours. They also used anti-rusting agents on their surfaces. In fact, these Drellian pipes were usually quite lovely to behold.

Karrin couldn't help throwing a glance at his classmate, believing for a moment that he would try to break and get inside the pipe in his desperation to hide from the Arach clones. Fortunately, Lark had the presence of mind not to do anything as embarrassing as that this time. Instead, he simply tapped at it.

Karrin asked, "What do you think's inside?"

"Would you want to find out?" Lark said. "It would be unwise to do so as puncturing the pipe would flood the tunnel immediately and drown us."

"True," Karrin said. "Do you think we can use some kind of x-ray vision?" Without waiting for a response, he focused on this need, but nothing turned transparent for him. He sighed. "Maybe things like x-ray vision and invisibility are too unnatural for us to get."

"Perhaps," Lark said. He hadn't thought of that. It was true that all the things they managed to change their bodies into so far were natural physical features. Invisibility and the ability to see through opaque things were only ever artificial human inventions. They probably wouldn't be able to make anything like Karrin's hand beams either; because in nature, generating such intense energy could kill the firer. Regardless, it was not useful to dwell on their limitations right now, Lark thought. They should only think about what they could do. "Let us ignore this pipe," he said, and continued digging someplace else.

But he couldn't believe it when he found that there were even more pipes, and he soon discovered that their path was completely obstructed by pipes. When Lark tried digging at the sides, he realized that apart from the way they had come, all ways were blocked by pipes.

"Let's dig downwards, then," Karrin said.

"I am not sure if that is advisable," Lark said. "Going too deep may put our lives into more danger if the ceiling collapses."

Karrin gave him a wistful look. Lark frowned and said, "Do whatever you like." With glee, Karrin instantly started digging down. Lark expected to see more pipes, but instead they came across reservoirs of water, or at least, it looked like water, and probably wasn't water.

"What do you think this is?" asked Karrin.

"I could tell you if I had my computer."

"Sorry."

Lark did not bother answering. If they dug upwards, they would be out in the open again. Yet, maybe they could risk going back outside if they could run a distance, escape the pipes, and dig at a different spot? He told Karrin precisely this new plan and the boy agreed.

"Be careful, Lark."

"I know."

He glanced furtively all around him for signs of Arach clones when he poked his head out. Then he pushed himself out of the hole and shook off the dirt that had gotten onto his hair and face.

He really wished that invisibility would work for them, but there was no point whining about something they couldn't have. Flying would not be wise either as the Arach clones had flying vehicles that could overtake them very quickly. Plus, a flying organism, especially due to its greater speed, was invariably more eye-catching than a walking one.

Nonetheless, he wondered if they should fly anyway, just to escape from the Arach compound faster. The building in question was quite a distance away already—it was only a speck to him now.

"So, you want to fly?" Karrin asked. This boy was sometimes more astute than one would think, Lark admitted grudgingly.

Nevertheless, he didn't bother answering Karrin and simply closed his eyes to make those wings appear. At the same time, his claws receded back into nonexistence.

"Hey Lark," Karrin said, "I just thought of something. If we can't turn invisible because it's an unnatural thing, maybe we could try camouflage."

Lark stared at him, astonished and amazed that he himself had not thought of that.

Karrin looked a bit embarrassed, and shrugged. "I just suddenly thought of this idea because we managed to change our skin and clothing colors earlier."

Of course. So Lark desired for his body and clothes to camouflage with his surroundings as he lifted off with his wings. Karrin followed suit. And to the children's delight, they blended perfectly with their environment's colors.

"Lark, do you think we could also get the ability to navigate? We have no idea where the nearest Rarerus branch is, or even where the other members are."

"We could try."

When they fervently wished for a strong sense of direction, they felt something; but whatever it was, it was futile because the boys didn't even remember the directions they came from: in the Arach vehicle when they came, Karrin had been busy crying and Lark had been busy trying to ignore his crying. If we only had a map, Lark thought, still not used to vocalizing his thoughts.

"Do you think we can find a Hyure to take us back home? I know this is a really deserted place with no other buildings around anywhere, but maybe there's hope if we fly fast enough. And can we will ourselves to have the strength to fly faster?" Karrin said, and tried to summon more strength into his wings, but to no avail. It seemed that their new ability only let them grow physical features, but did nothing to increase their athletic capacities.

The two children flew on in the same direction, North-East, hoping to find something in this vast place. They, especially Lark, were soon beginning to tire. "You want to stop and rest?" asked Karrin. Lark simply landed to rest without even answering. So the two started walking again, and their wings gradually disappeared. They could have run instead, but all that flying had exhausted their bodies that it was a miracle they could still move.

"Hey, what's that?" Karrin pointed in the distance at a blue and red box. He wanted to fire a hand beam at it, but resisted the urge. When he raced towards it, Lark issued a word of warning but Karrin ignored him. As soon as Karrin arrived, he stared at the box in disbelief. "Look! There's a mirror here!"

When Lark arrived as well, he saw a liquid mirror inside the box. The mirror wasn't water, because water only gave dim reflections, nothing as clear or sharp as the images reflected on this surface. Liquid mirrors were literally silvery mirrors in a liquid state, bound into the shape of a looking glass by strange, electromagnetic forces; liquid mirrors were not uncommon in Drell.

Karrin stared at his reflection in this mirror, trying to make sense of it. Lark, on the other hand, did not see the point of staring at himself. He might be full of self-love, but he had never been vain. Instead, Lark peered at the edges of the mirror. They were ordinary liquid walls. Karrin said, "What do you think this is for?"

But before Lark could answer, Karrin's stomach abruptly growled.

"Oh gosh, I didn't realize that I was hungry," he said, embarrassed. Lark's stomach hadn't growled yet but he was actually starving too. Karrin said, "Do you think we can will ourselves to have stronger stomachs so we can survive without food for a longer while?"

Lark thought that Karrin's wishes were getting ridiculous and he told him so. Nevertheless, Karrin tried to pull up the ability to withstand starvation; but as Lark had predicted, nothing happened. And along with their hunger, their strength flagged so that they really wanted to stop and rest.

During their break, Lark found that his mind was flooded with thoughts about science, chemistry, and mathematics. For once, he resented his habit of constant scientific reverie. It was much more important to think of strategies to survive the current situation. He didn't realize that perhaps he was unconsciously turning to science, something that felt familiar and safe, to evade the fear that was creeping up on him.

"Do you think that if I fire some hand beams, they'll eventually hit something and something will happen?" asked Karrin.

"Do you think that if you fire a hand beam at this liquid mirror, it will bounce back off and something will happen?" said Lark.

But far from taking this as a bitter remark springing from hunger, fatigue, and frustration, Karrin brightened up and said, "Oh, I forgot about the reflection thing. Let's try it." The boy immediately picked himself up and approached the liquid mirror.

"What are you doing?" said Lark. "You are going to burn yourself the instant you fire that beam and it bounces right back at you."

"But I could just fire at an angle so that it bounces off away from me," said Karrin.

Again, here, Lark gaped. He couldn't believe that at these crucial moments, Karrin was turning out to be the more resourceful one, the thinking person who kept coming up with workable solutions; whilst Lark himself was spinning around in circles trying to come up with something, anything, but kept getting distracted by his almost compulsive thoughts of science.

Lark was too harsh on himself, however, because though his thoughts turned quite naturally to science again and again, Lark had given a number of useful suggestions earlier, as you saw before. But we human beings are apt to forget about what we did right, and only remember what we did wrong.

Without another word, Karrin fired his hand beam at an angle. The boys beheld the beam with a measure of wonder as it shot out; it was such a pretty sight. A beam of bright gold sailed and sliced through the air as if drawing a picture.

"Yes!" Karrin whispered when they heard a boom in the distance. But his whispered cry of exultation turned to dread when they heard a low rumbling and the heavy trampling of feet. His eyes were wide with complete terror when he turned to look at Lark. "Arach clones?" He started running for his life even though Lark told him not to because moving objects, though camouflaged, would be instantly spotted. And while the two boys either ran or walked, they heard more clearly that it was not exactly the pattering of feet, or at least not human feet. Even Karrin spun around to look.

They beheld a huge herd of spixota, a brown and red quadruped lamina, with round brown eyes, and ears so flat that they seemed to have no ears at all. Their mouths were muzzles and their paws were huge and steady. Their tails were a big broad brush which they swept around. These spixota were the height of a tall adult. Even Karrin had stopped running now because he was frozen by the sight. He urged himself to run but his legs would not budge.

One of the spixota sniffed the air; it seemed to catch the boys' scent. Then without warning, it charged towards them. With a scream, Karrin fled, and Lark fled too. Along the way, Lark hurried to form wings. Karrin, on the other hand, stretched his legs until they became ridiculously long.

Soon enough, Lark soared safely above the herd, and he watched and shook his head at how foolish Karrin was to want to run faster when he could save his neck by becoming airborne. Lark shouted, "Karrin, wings!"

He wasn't sure if the boy heard him, but probably not, as the boy kept running and started shooting hand beams at the herd, which was even more foolish, of course, because it only infuriated the spixota and made them run even faster. Lark tried again, "Wings, Karrin, wings!" And he added, "Fly!"

The fear-filled boy finally heard his shout and Lark could see little structures forming on his back. Just before the spixota could pounce on Karrin, he leapt up into the air and zoomed towards Lark. "Good, let us go," Lark commanded, flying away from this herd.

When the two thought they were finally safe, they heard a squawking coming towards them. It was a flock of gray-green feathered laminae flying nearer: the crima (pronounced kree-ma). Their beaks opened with menace and they looked as if they were going to bite the two boys' heads off.

If only Lark and Karrin could induce their bodies to have no scent; yet, this clearly wasn't an ability that occurred in nature, so they couldn't make use of it. Karrin and Lark hurriedly veered around to fly away again; but from the increasingly loud cries behind them, they knew that they were outrun—outflown.

"Want to dig again?" asked Karrin.

Firstly, Lark thought, there would likely be more creatures attacking them underground, in which there would be no escape for them anymore; and secondly, how were they going to dig up so much earth in time before the crima or spixota got to them?

Again, though Karrin knew it was probably no use, he shot at their pursuers with his hand beams; and again, it only exacerbated their situation. Now the crima were getting closer and closer, and Lark pushed himself to grow spikes all over his body so that he wouldn't be eaten, while Karrin urged his skin to erect a layer of armor. But both knew that their change would be too late. The crima closed in on them.

THE ARACH CLONES CLAPPED THEIR HANDS. "GOOD JOB, GOOD job," said one of the clones who was originally a medium height woman. Lark and Karrin exchanged a glance of despair. They had been tricked by an illusion again.

"You see," explained the woman clone, "we have been testing you via different scenario simulations to stimulate your physical enhancements. It turns out that perhaps you did not need any emotional arousal, after all, just life-threatening situations; unless you count fear as an emotion. We are very happy for you to discover your newfound abilities and will support you with all our efforts in cultivating them—when you become our clones."

The children screamed—Lark inwardly—as two buff-looking Arach clones scooped up the two struggling boys and marched off underground.

SEVENTEEN
OUT OF THE SMOKE

eanwhile, in the midst of the chaos and confusion from the smoke, Raoul Faya took his chance and fled the room. The Arach clones seemed so frightened that they were themselves fleeing; and they thought Raoul was fleeing from the smoke too. It was much faster to have him dash on his own legs than for them to carry him and run anyway.

Eventually, Raoul turned a corner and found himself alone. He did not have much time, as the smoke was slowly engulfing more air; but due to his many experiences and training, Raoul was calmer than the average person during these crises, and he kept in mind the goal of saving the children and escaping the compound.

At length, he caught sight of a pair of Arach clones scurrying past; they did not see Raoul, presumably because he was in the shadows. Instinctively, Raoul slinked after them, keeping his body in that obscurity.

Yet, instead of rushing out of the building as they should, this pair of clones—both originally young men his age—disappeared through a hole. Raoul waited a little while before he too climbed down. But it was actually a slope, so he walked down instead.

He almost gasped when he saw light again, but it was an eerie green light that lit up the room only faintly. Raoul crept in silence some distance behind them, and then stopped to hide behind a machine—there were a few machines around—when he sighted a few Arach clones on guard. But he had already glimpsed what was up ahead, and knew what it was. The antimattering chamber.

As if to confirm this, he heard to both his distress and joy the screams of Karrin. He peeped from behind the machine and sure enough, it was the boy. Lark was carried by another Arach clone beside him, and the clones placed the boys on a panel and bound them up with metallic ropes. One of the Arach clones laughed. "That Liara was so stupid to try to 'smoke us out,' when we could just come down here in our underground chamber for a very good length of time safe from the smoke. Now we'll just wait for them to surrender when they see that none of our three captives are coming out."

"But wouldn't those Rarerus people just assume that their three members are already dead by this time and leave?" asked another clone.

The first clone made a dismissive gesture and said, "Don't be stupid. As dumb as those Rarerus people are, they are loyal to the last in saving and protecting their members. They won't give up till they see their dead bodies."

Raoul clenched his fists at this. He was also mad at Liara for using the smoking method before he could do anything. He believed that he was so close to accomplishing his task before the smoke flooded in. As much as he disliked Liara, he thought that when she gave him permission to offer himself to the Arach for the two five-year-olds, it meant that she trusted him at that moment and believed in his abilities. He thought she had understood what he was trying to do and was capable of doing, but he was wrong. But there was no point going on this diatribe against his half-sister and leader right now, because he needed a plan to rescue those two strapped boys and leave, somehow.

Honestly, though, he had no idea how to do this as all his weapons (except for his hand beams, which were securely bound into his skin), armor, and computer, obviously, had been removed from him the moment he had fallen asleep under their sleep concoction.

"Karrin, please be quiet."

Raoul recognized that this was Lark's voice, and couldn't help but be impressed by the calmness of this five-year-old scientist in the face of a doom worse than death. Raoul didn't know that Lark was just remarkably good at hiding his true feelings. Now Raoul peered around. There was elastorope dangling from the ceiling above the boys, presumably to restrain the victims lest they somehow break out of the metallic ropes. By the way, metallic ropes were not chains. These ropes were far stronger than chains, and they had no holes either.

"Let the ceremony begin," grinned the first Arach clone. Raoul could not see a thing, but he could imagine a pair of Arach viruses entering the boys' bodies and starting to lay their web eggs. The Arach clone went on, "Let's make clones of them while we're at it. They could be valuable material with those powers!"

Powers? thought Raoul. Then he realized that they meant the extra physical enhancements from the fondal—he had thought a lot about what these enhancements could be ever since Lark talked about them. He noticed a third body lying on a panel a little farther away. It was the body of the man they had tried to save that night on their mission. Raoul's heart sank as he thought that perhaps his web was almost done, or that it was already done and was solidifying. What should he do—then it hit him, and he was proud of himself for thinking of this new plan.

Carefully, he shot a bit of his hand beam, at a very low intensity, towards the ceiling. As he expected, the beam activated an Arach computer down here, and he could see little wisps of its silvery network appearing. But not too much appeared so that it was virtually invisible to anyone not paying attention. Then, mustering all his knowledge, Raoul whispered and prodded with his beam to hack into this computer. Since it was an Arach computer, it was very difficult to hack into, but Raoul was trained by the Rarerus, after all, and he was soon granted access.

Immediately, he planted false information into the computer, saying from the security recorders that Raoul was spotted escaping the Arach compound. He also feared that the recorders had registered his current location so he erased that memory, and turned off the recorders in this underground region. He was in fact quite surprised that no Arach clone had come after him, since he might have been watched by recorders all the way down here. Perhaps they were too panicked by the smoke that nobody bothered to check the recorders for any escaping prisoners.

In a moment, after planting that false information—Raoul was glad that his earlier episode with the three men clones and the three machines had given him the idea of planting false information and preventing the recording of real information into computers—there was a loud ringing announcing to all the clones that Raoul Faya was making his way to one of the Arach compound escapes.

Many of the Arach clones outdoors were contacted to watch all the exits (though this was very difficult, because there were a lot of exits and the compound was, in an understatement, humongous), and most of the Arach clones down here hurried up back to the main floor, carrying their gas screens and lights to search for Raoul where the recorder had declared him to be.

THERE WAS A COMMOTION OUTSIDE THE ARACH COMPOUND and all the Rarerus members became as restless and anxious as the clones were. Liara overheard one of the clones saying with worry that Raoul Faya had escaped. Liara's heart leapt.

With speed, she dispatched her many Rarerus members to go around the compound to watch when Raoul would come out; or rather, to follow those clones wherever they went because it was those clones who knew where the exits were. She made sure she ordered enough members to follow them for the fight that would come after. Thankfully there were really a lot of Rarerus members here, more than six hundred from twenty-one of the branches and a number from the Vénus Center. She herself stood some distance before the main entrance. Come on, Raoul.

Before long, some of the clones grew impatient; they opened the doors and went in with their gas screens and lights to peer around. These clones here thought that Raoul Faya was exceedingly cunning; he must have hidden from them as soon as he heard their announcement to block all exits. He was probably hiding until the clones would go away. But the clones were not too worried, because they knew that Raoul would not live long without a gas screen or oxygen supply, and would eventually have to surrender himself to them before ever seeing his leader again.

While the Arach clones were in such a frenzy, Raoul twiddled around to see what other things he could do with their computer. He at length found something useful, and gleefully ordered the computer to spray sleeping gas into the antimattering chamber. As he listened to the sound of dropping bodies, he commanded the computer to send him a sleeping gas mask. That arrived quickly enough, and he strode bravely, but still cautiously, into that antimattering chamber.

Raoul checked that the clones were all asleep and collapsed onto the floor before slipping in. Karrin, Lark, and the soon-to-be antimattered man were asleep as well. The two five-year-olds he could carry quite easily, but the man was a bit difficult—Raoul was only a man of average strength. He picked up the two children and strapped the man with an elastorope onto his back. But he had to drag the man's feet on the floor as he really was too heavy.

He fiddled with an Arach computer again and found that it could make him and what he was carrying invisible; he even found a map to guide him out of the compound. But the exits were all blocked by Arach clones, according to the security recordings; yet, there were Rarerus members waiting at those exits too.

After scanning the map a bit more, he spotted his half-sister at the main entrance. His first thought was to go there, but he decided to target an exit nearby instead. Thus, he asked the computer to make them invisible, soundless, protected by gas screens and oxygen supplies, and to give them a map they could follow as they went along.

Liara waited with increasing agitation. Then suddenly, she heard a cry from both Rarerus members and Arach clones. "Raoul!" said the former; "Faya!" said the latter.

Without a second's hesitation, Liara ran towards the source of the cry, as did everyone else who heard it. "Raoul!" she called out when she saw him; he was clutching the two kids and half-carrying, half-dragging the man they had been trying to save. The Arach clones endeavored to seize them, but the Rarerus members attacked these clones so that Raoul could run away.

He saw Liara first, and for a second, he wanted to hand her Lark and Karrin, but then he thought better of it. She was their Rarerus leader whom should not be burdened during such an important time. But perhaps Liara read that initial intention in his eyes, because she ran after him and said, "Raoul, hand me the children."

He didn't really want to, for a multitude of reasons, but since she was his leader and they were out in the open where everyone could see them, he obeyed her command and placed the two boys gently in her arms. "Be careful with them," he whispered almost with warning. "They're my friends."

And with that, he went off to join the rest of the Rarerus, where they helped to take the rescued man off his back. As the over six hundred Rarerus members here vastly outnumbered the approximately one hundred Arach clones, the latter didn't dare fight. The Rarerus members, seeing their clear victory, simply turned away and flew off in their vehicles with their reclaimed members.

Liara put Lark and Karrin in her Glass with her, and requested that Raoul ride with them in the Glass too. These three would be her companions in the Glass this time.

After Raoul placed the children securely in their seats, he incidentally asked, "Is Alia riding with us?"

Liara's senses and awareness spiked up at the mention of her friend's name, and simultaneously, nervousness filled her heart. She said softly, "No, they left on their own vehicle already."

Raoul frowned, but shrugged. "Okay."

Liara anxiously waited to see if her brother would say any more. He did, but it seemed to be an innocuous statement. "Alia doesn't seem to spend as much time with you as they did before."

"Yeah," Liara replied, endeavoring to not reveal too much feeling.

Raoul continued, "Being the leader isn't always so good, is it?"

What he just said also sounded so incidental, and he probably just meant that Alia had grown distant from Liara since she became the leader of the Rarerus; but was Raoul implying something else as well?

Liara asked directly, "Raoul, do you want to be the leader of the Rarerus?"

At first, Raoul looked surprised, but then he frowned at her. "No, I don't. Didn't I make that crystal clear already?"

Liara sighed in response to her brother's habitual animosity. "Yes, you did. Otherwise, Jax would have at least considered you as a candidate for the position."

Raoul regarded her for a second, before replying, "Even if I did want to be the leader, which I don't, Jax would have chosen you. You're more qualified, and you've always been a lot more enthusiastic about and interested in how the Rarerus as a whole runs. Whilst I've always been a lot more interested in the details of how to handle the chemicals, the technology, and how to fight the Arach."

Liara pressed her lips together. "Maybe, but you definitely have leadership qualities."

Raoul said, "But I've never wanted to lead in a role as enormous as the Rarerus leader's. That's too overwhelming to me, too much responsibility, too many things I would need to oversee and pay attention to."

Liara was silent for a moment. "I see."

The siblings said nothing else to one another for the rest of the way.

When Raoul woke Lark and Karrin, the two boys jolted back at the sight of him. Raoul was going to ask, "Missed me?" but recalled just in time that Lark did not like little social emptinesses like this. Instead, he smiled and explained to them all that had happened.

After he was done, and the boys were rapt in wonderment, Liara, who was talking to the Beams and some other members, excused herself when she saw them awake, and came over to the stretch seats where the children were sitting. Raoul, who was standing in front of the five-year-olds, shuffled away from her and subtly put the children between them. Liara peered at Lark and Karrin. "Are you both feeling all right now?"

"I'm hungry!" Karrin cried truthfully.

Liara laughed and ordered an attendant to come back with some refreshments from the energy dispenser. She proceeded to ask them about what happened when they were inside the Arach compound. She had expected both boys to eagerly tell them all that had transpired, but to her surprise, Lark stayed silent and let Karrin do all the talking; Lark also looked away as if uninterested.

Raoul wanted to ask Liara not to give the children so much stress by asking them to talk so much right after their incident at the compound; but little Karrin was so enthusiastic in telling her everything, and recounting these details seemed to be putting the boy more at ease, so he let him be. But the other boy, he observed, seemed very beat up and tired.

"Lark?" Raoul said. "Do you want to come with me to rest over there?" He gestured towards a soft green stretch seat at the far end of the room. "Nobody will bother you or make you talk." He didn't consciously mean to make a jibe at Liara, but she heard it; she reminded herself to let Karrin rest as soon as he was too tired to keep talking, and she inwardly thanked her brother for this albeit cutting reminder.

Lark was so drained that he nodded instantly at Raoul's suggestion and rose from his seat. He mumbled, "Raoul, remember to apply the octamethyst on us."

Raoul did so, and was relieved that he had told Lark and Karrin's parents that the science or combat club trips would last a few days, so they wouldn't suspect anything.

EIGHTEEN
NEW TROUBLE

The day after Liara learned about Lark and Karrin's body-altering abilities, she was eager to ask Gastra and Yearlie, the two children who came with Karrin, to see if they could shapeshift under illusions of dangerous situations—the two were told about this beforehand, of course. Yearlie and Gastra's heart rates shot up even with the awareness that the dangers were illusory; yet, when they thought hard about what they needed to save their lives, no part of them changed. Liara was disappointed at this because she thought more shapeshifting members would help her in some trouble she recently found out about.

This trouble was related to her hurried wandering through the Vénus rooms the day Lark had first met her. Some time ago, a friend of Liara's outside the Rarerus told her about something peculiar. This friend, Carla, worked at a place that managed and sold land to tenants. One day, a pack of ten men and women seemed to be trespassing onto some property that a tenant had bought recently. Unsure of their intentions, Carla followed them to see if they were her tenant's invitees or otherwise.

Soon, the tenant did come and greet them, so Carla thought she could leave with a peace of mind when she heard them mention "Liara." They said something about devastating the Rarerus and sneaking into the Vénus Center, using sleeping powders and potions to drug certain members, and then replace them with Arach clones.

Liara had listened to this all with widening eyes.

"Liara, what does this all mean?"

She shook her head. "I'm really sorry, Carla, I can't tell you. But I promise that I have good reasons not to tell."

"You're always so secretive," Carla sighed, but she respected Liara's wishes. "And oh, I remember one of the men had a scar on his left ear. A pretty big scar, or else I wouldn't have seen it."

Liara instantly recognized that this must be Dras, a member of the Rarerus.

The next time she went back to her Rarerus headquarters in Vénus, she closely observed Dras while she was in a crowd of some other members. When she saw Dras leaving and glancing surreptitiously around him, she excused herself, darted into a hidden place some distance away from him, and put on some invisibility spray. She followed him and as she expected, he turned and went into a meeting room. She managed to slip inside just before he closed the door.

Seated there were nine other members: Martha, Osso, Scrimen, Ussaz, and five others. They murmured about the next victims, Irri ("ee-ree") and Traeph.

After that meeting, Liara hurried out silently. She went and told Irri and Traeph to be careful, to refuse any food or drink offered to them by anyone, and to put up gas screens when they slept. Irri asked her, "What's all this about?"

But Liara refused to tell her or Traeph anything, because she sensed that if they knew Dras's plan, they would be put into even more danger.

The second time she followed one of the traitor members into their meeting room, a man hissed, "I can't believe we couldn't gas Traeph and Irri. It's as if someone knew about our plan and stopped us! Unless one of you is a traitor and secretly supports Liara."

But as nobody said anything to that, the speaker seemed to assume that all here were innocent. He continued, "So in the future, we will use this formula to tell us who we'll target next. We'll be safe this time because nobody knows how to decode this formula except for the Arach and us; the Arach themselves gave me this formula when I told them about how somebody ruined our plan."

When the formula was shown, Liara glanced at it and quickly

recorded it onto her computer. She used her thoughts to command it and obviously the computer was set to invisible.

Then, that day when Lark saw her hurrying through the rooms without so much as a side glance at him or Raoul, she had told her members that she was going to visit a friend to help her with something and would be back very soon, definitely in time for the fondal ceremony. When she saw Raoul with Lark in that copper-blue room, she was extra avoidant of Raoul because she was not sure if her brother was one of those who were already cloned.

Perhaps her extra avoidance made Raoul or clone Raoul suspicious, but she couldn't help it; she was too apprehensive. Besides, her brother was used to her evasive behavior outside of formal settings, so it wouldn't have seemed too out of the ordinary to him, she thought.

Liara went straight to find her most trusted and competent professional decoder, who worked outside the Rarerus. She gave the decoder her formula and he sold her a decoding machine. It reliably generated all those names that were cloned before and to her great relief, her brother was not one of them.

Nor was Alia. Liara could have confided in the nonbinary combatant and scientist about all this, but Liara didn't want to put her friend's life at risk with this knowledge.

When Liara went back to the Rarerus Center to witness the fondal ceremony, her hopes rose again, especially when the five-year-old Lark stepped up onto the platform. She was already convinced that this youngest subject would have extra physical enhancements, and surely the traitors would not target this very young new recruit; she observed Lark closely for any extra physical changes. He and possibly some future recruits could help her solve this traitor problem. Of course, Liara could have simply exposed the traitor members, but she wanted to find out what this was all about first, and why they had decided to side with the Arach against her.

Yet, unbeknownst to Liara, Dras and the other traitors had kept close tabs on that professional decoder, because he was the one the Rarerus members most liked to go to. After failing to drug Irri and Traeph, they figured that someone had been eavesdropping on their meeting. So they contacted each other with their computers, using silent verbal messages to arrange another meeting like they did last time, and talk about the formula.

Before the meeting, each traitor member made their furtiveness more obvious than usual, hoping that whoever it was would sneak after them. Whoever that person was would take their formula to this decoder. So imagine their shock when they discovered that the person who found out their plan was no other than their leader Liara herself! Dras and the others immediately told each other via computer messages that they couldn't keep their leader around any longer.

Liara was in danger.

As Raoul and Centuri had promised, they let Lark try out the Silver vehicle. Lark was amused by and liked driving the Silver, but when he was reminded that he couldn't keep the Silver for himself, that the most he could do was to drive it occasionally under the close watch of some adult Rarerus members, Lark hmphed and crossed his arms across his chest. "Really? I cannot even study it from time to time?"

Raoul replied, "You can, but some fellow Rarerus scientists will supervise you while you do so."

Lark was still disgruntled, and disappointed that they could not trust him, even after all he had endured for their sake. He expressed this thought, and Raoul held up his hands in an appeasing gesture.

"I'm so sorry, Lark. But new scientists to the Rarerus do need supervision when working with newly designed Rarerus technology. If it makes you feel any better, even I couldn't study new devices and vehicles alone when I first came to Rarerus."

Lark was still displeased, but being supervised while trying out the Silver, was better than not being able to drive the Silver anymore.

In the meantime, Lark delved back into his ambition to unravel the mysteries of the fondal.

He observed his arms when they shapeshifted to spikes, or to anything else, and found that fondal minerals were self-assembling molecules. They moved their atoms and electrons about in a free yet non-arbitrary way; they changed their conformation and shape however they liked, without being mobilized by any external force. They also combined and reacted with several of his body's biomolecules as well as genes to create the changes in his body.

All this was very well and interesting to him, but he still didn't understand why this extra physical enhancement only worked with five-year-olds but not eight-year-olds—Liara had announced this curious finding with Gastra and Yearlie to all Rarerus members. Lark furrowed his brows and dove deep into his formulas and equations, digging for a way to explain this.

Raoul offered to help him seek this solution, but Lark insisted that he work alone. Yet, Raoul petulantly said that he himself would investigate this fondal mystery as well, no matter what Lark said, and they would see who came up with the solution first. Lark didn't mind. Perhaps some competition would be good for him to reach this answer more quickly.

Nine days after the children's escape from the Arach compound, Lark went to a regular meeting with Marius, Haus, and Raoul at the Breemil branch. Raoul took all three of them into a private meeting room with white seats, and said he had something important to tell them. Haus, Marius, and to some extent, Lark, were curious to hear it. "Guys," Raoul said, "Liara's been acting strangely lately."

"Strange? Liara's always strange to you, Raoul," chuckled Marius.

Raoul gave him a look. "I'm serious." He went on to tell them that, once, when he went to see her alone on some important Rarerus affairs, there was something different about her looks, expressions, and gestures that struck him. He wanted to ask her what was wrong, but there was something so off about her demeanor and the way she interacted with him, that he believed she was hiding some secret.

Haus and Marius exchanged a glance, while Lark said, "I will help you investigate this matter." Ever since joining the Rarerus, Lark had become more interested than before in mysteries beyond those of science. He had always been intrigued even by nonscientific mysteries, but he never dwelt on them for long before he put his focus back on science. And despite himself, he had become engrossed by the Rarerus and was fascinated by the many Rarerus and Arach enigmas.

However, about Liara's strangeness, nobody understood what Raoul was saying, because they could not see anything extraordinary about his most recent interaction with her. Yet, it was Lark who said, "Perhaps she is an Arach clone."

That shocked them all. Haus and Marius were angry that Lark could even suggest such a thing. Raoul was just bewildered and said, "That's impossible, though. Liara is our leader, so she is highly guarded by her attendants and bodyguards. If there was any Arach web forming, it would have been detected at once as she lives in the Vénus Center where the most powerful detector is."

"But the Arach do not need to spread any web on her to create a clone, correct?" asked Lark.

Raoul frowned and admitted that he was right, though they had never heard of a case where clones were made without webbing and abducting the victim to their Arach chambers first. It was of course possible that the victim was simply abducted without being webbed first, and then webbed later.

However, that was implausible too, because they would have to transport the body a great distance before they could be out of range of the Vénus detectors. And such a long absence would arouse the suspicion of some other members who expected this member to be working with them. Even if it didn't, another branch's detector would sense this webbing and when all the Rarerus members came, they would know that it was their fellow member.

"That is silly," Lark replied. "The Arach could easily steal a sample of hair from one of the Rarerus members when they are out on an errand, create a clone, and then usher in the clone whilst abducting the real Rarerus member away. Nobody would notice anything."

Raoul objected and said, "Nobody can sneak in without being noticed for long. In the Rarerus, from time to time, we get all members to take out a sample of their DNA—to shake off some flakes of skin, for instance, and we tell them to do so in our sight so they can't hide; and our computers automatically analyze the DNA on the spot. So any Arach clones would show up as having bluamine and zanyliline DNA bases."

Lark thought a while, and then asked, "Could not Rarerus members hack into these computers and program them to input false data as soon as it is their turn to provide a DNA sample?"

Raoul shook his head and smiled good-naturedly. "We're talking about Rarerus computers. Even a Rarerus member wouldn't be able to hack into our computers. I myself wouldn't be able to do so either."

"Are you sure you do not have any members who are particularly good at hacking, who could likely succeed?"

"There are many brilliant hackers in the Rarerus, and they often managed to hack into Arach computers," as did I, thought Raoul. "But Rarerus computers are so much more difficult to hack into than Arach ones. Ours are so much more advanced."

Lark pressed his lips together. "When you say there are DNA checks in the Rarerus 'from time to time,' how long exactly is it between the checking times? I have been in the Rarerus for a month now since I officially joined, and still have not experienced a DNA check of this nature. Nor has anyone ever informed me of these checks until now."

Raoul exchanged an embarrassed look with Haus and Marius. Raoul said, "We do these checks every two decaweeks, but we didn't want to burden you with this formality until sometime later on."

Lark folded his arms. "Because I am still an impressionable child?"

Raoul gave him an awkward smile. "If that's how you see it." He quickly changed the topic. "The last time we did a DNA check in the Vénus center, was two days after you and Karrin came out from the Arach compound, on Walketh the 13th. Liara obviously passed the test."

(See "Names of Calendar Months[1]" under "Quantitative Measures" and "Time" in the glossary.)

"But when did you first notice that her behavior was unusual?" Lark asked.

A solid furrow appeared between Raoul's brows. "Yesterday, on Walketh the 19th." Yet, he added defensively, "Though it's true that I haven't seen Liara between the 13th and 19th, something might have happened during those five days that bothered her a lot, hence her strange behavior. Don't you think that's a reasonable explanation?"

Lark shook his head honestly, and replied, "Unless you mean abduction and cloning happened to her during those five days."

Raoul groaned and wiped a hand over his face. "You're insufferable, Lark. What can I say to make you believe me?"

"I will believe you when a test confirms that our leader is not an Arach clone," Lark said.

Liara's half-brother crossed his arms in frustration; but he also worried that Lark might be right.

THEY ARRANGED FOR RAOUL TO FALL SICK. As EXPERT chemists, Marius, Haus, and Lark administered various little tricks for Raoul to have all the signs and semblances of being dreadfully ill without being truly so. Then, Marius got to work and contacted Liara that her brother was unwell.

As they expected, she arrived at Raoul's house, which was situated in the Breemil area, to visit him. Haus, Marius, and Lark were supposedly there to take care of Raoul, as they were closest to him. After exchanging a few pleasantries and questions, they let her into Raoul's room where her brother lay sick in bed. Before leaving the room, Haus activated the sleeping gas system in the room, smiled, and shut the door.

The computer monitors soon showed them that both Raoul and Liara had fallen asleep thanks to the sleeping gas. Marius commanded the computer to reabsorb all the sleeping gas in the room before they entered it again. They woke Raoul up and took Liara's body to the physical examination room. Now was the moment of truth.

Raoul looked nervously at Lark. They had given Lark the position of honour of being the one who got to test Liara's DNA, as he was the one who doubted and wanted to see with his own eyes if Liara was not an Arach clone. Raoul still thought that Lark's idea was too far-fetched.

When he saw the boy's eyes widen and look up at him, Raoul smiled. "I told you she's not an Arach clone."

"On the contrary, I have found bluamine and zanyliline in her genome."

AFTER THE INITIAL SHOCK, RAOUL SAID, "WE HAVE TO DO something with this clone then. We can't let her run Rarerus."

Haus nodded. "So we have to lock her up somewhere." He glanced at Raoul. "Here at your house?"

Raoul immediately furrowed his brows. "I understand why we can't lock her up in our branch, because others will discover her and the clone will say that we have committed treason against her. But why my home? Why not—"

"If not you, then who else?" said Haus. "Not your parents' home, surely? They wouldn't understand why you would want your sister held captive—" while he was saying this, Raoul flicked an anxious glance at Lark and then back at Haus, hinting: don't mention Liara's relationship to me. He doesn't know yet and doesn't need to know.

But Marius said, quite honestly, "Raoul, we already told him, sorry. The boy really wanted to know, and we just couldn't refuse him."

Raoul stared at him in disbelief.

"Sorry," Marius said again.

Haus bowed in apology too.

"Well—Lark, since you know, please don't tell anyone else, okay?" Lark nodded, indifferent.

Haus continued, "So since we can't put Liara's clone in your parents' home because they don't know about the Arach, and can't put it in the branch, then where else can we put her, if not at your place? We're already at your place anyway. I know you don't like your sister, Raoul, but you're the only suitable choice we have here. And remember, you're doing this for Rarerus, not for yourself."

"I guess you're right," said Raoul dejectedly.

"I would offer to take in this clone myself, if my nosy parents did not live with me," said Lark.

"Thanks," said Raoul, grateful that at least one person sympathized, assuming that was an expression of sympathy on Lark's part.

"But what do we do about the Rarerus finding out that Liara's no longer there?" asked Haus. "Won't they suspect that we had something to do with her disappearance, since we were the last ones who saw her? Not everyone knows you're family to her, Raoul. And as much as I hate to rub this in, a lot of people think she's your unrequited lover, so they might think that you've done something to her so that she won't bother you again or something. I know that sounds ugly, but—"

Raoul Faya frowned. "Can we make up an excuse then? Say that she caught my disease when she was visiting me? And that we've sent her back to her parents' home to recover?"

"What do you think?" Haus said. "That might work unless somebody becomes very suspicious—as our leader rarely ever gets sick—and checks on your mother and stepfather."

"Then what do you suggest?" asked Raoul.

Marius cut in, "I know. Why don't we just say that Liara's off to visit some special friend in need? You know she sometimes does that, though never to the neglect of her duties as a leader."

"Maybe. I just don't know how long that pretense can last. We don't know how long it will take for us to get the real Liara back," said Raoul, his brows creasing in frustration.

It was then that Lark said, "I do not understand why none of you are willing to tell the Rarerus members that their leader has been Arach cloned."

The other three whipped their heads around to look at him.

Lark added, "She will be found out anyway at the next DNA check."

"Um, Lark," said Marius, "the knowledge that our leader is gone will drive the Rarerus nuts. You know how crazy we are about her. We don't want to know that our great Liara herself is in danger. So we have to find our real leader before the DNA check happens too."

"But no human being can avoid being in danger all the time," Lark countered. "Especially not in the Rarerus. Moreover, the leader of such an organization, despite all her bodyguard protection, is bound to always be the most at risk for her life and safety, due to her rank and importance. I say we should simply publicize Liara's cloning to Rarerus, which would also give us more resources and fighters to help us get the real Liara back."

"This all sounds sensible," said Raoul, "but haven't you thought of the people or person who helped the Arach clone and kidnapped the real Liara? It's possible that she was abducted somewhere outside the Rarerus while she was going on a solitary trip, even though she always disguises herself as someone else for safety when not traveling with her bodyguards. But it's also possible that she was kidnapped while she was in the Rarerus

Center, by someone in the Rarerus! If we announce this knowledge to the members, then whoever these traitors are will know that we found out the truth and will think that we might even know their whole plan. That would put all of us in great danger, which would not help Liara at all."

At this, Lark lowered his eyes.

"I'm sorry, Lark, I know you want to help, but I'm afraid we won't be able to depend on the Rarerus forces this time," Raoul said. "We will have to act in secret. Although," he added, "you don't have to come with us. This mission, without the other members, will be very dangerous, and I don't want to—make your parents upset over anything that happens to you."

"I am coming, Raoul," said Lark with determination. "I also have an interest in Liara's safety, since she is my leader as well as yours."

Raoul wanted to object but at the same time he was delighted that Lark could come with them, and before Raoul could say anything, Marius chipped in, "Great! So it'll just be the four of us. What should we do now?"

They tied elastorope around "Liara's" arms and legs, and hid her Glass in an underground parking space below Raoul's house. Most people only used the parking spaces above ground, as subterranean parking was usually not open to visitors unless the house owner allowed it. Therefore, any other Rarerus members who happened to come over were unlikely to discover the Glass.

When the clone awoke, Raoul had already plopped her onto a black and silver stretch seat in a spare room. Marius, Haus, and Lark waited in the living room, ready to intervene if anything went wrong; they had left Raoul alone with her so that she would let her guard down to some extent. The clone of Liara now exclaimed, "Brother, what are you doing tying me all up like this?"

"So that you won't hurt yourself."

"Speaking of hurt, why aren't you in bed resting?"

"I got better," Raoul said and shrugged, wondering when he could stop talking to his sister's clone.

"Well, that was quick. But really, brother, I don't understand why you've tied me up right now because there is evidently nothing wrong with me; and you must be aware that I have my other duties to attend to—"

"Are you sure nothing's wrong? I am convinced that there definitely is something wrong with you, in the head, and I'm going to keep you at my place to rest until you become normal again."

The Liara clone was silent for a while before she said, "I honestly don't know what you're playing at, because I am clearly sane—"

"You're not."

"Raoul, please. I know you dislike me, but that doesn't mean you should restrain me in elastoropes like this."

Raoul shrugged again and averted his eyes. "Be a good girl and stay there. I will come back to feed you."

"Really, what are you doing?" the clone said.

He ignored her and left the room. After a while, Raoul returned with some heated food. "Now eat." He couldn't believe he had to personally feed a clone, a clone of his sister, no less.

After a few bites of the food, the Liara clone said, "Are you sure you don't want to untie me?"

"I told you, no. I have discovered that you have caught a mental illness which will make you subject to all sorts of violent impulses, including self-harm. As your brother, I have a duty to take care of you and make sure you don't get hurt."

"I assure you that I am all right," said the Liara clone.

"I assure you that you are not," said Raoul. "Now if you excuse me, I have some duties of my own to perform. I will tell the members that you are sick."

"There you are," Marius grinned when he saw Raoul hurrying back into the living room after he put the clone back to sleep. "So what do we do now? How do we find the real Liara? We haven't detected any Arach activity."

"We should soon," Raoul said in a firm voice.

Haus let out a big sigh. "If the Arach clone her, then they are bound to antimatter her."

"How do you know that for sure, though?" asked Marius.

"Because there's nothing worse than being antimattered," said Raoul.

Lark sank himself deep in thought. "Are you sure that being antimattered is truly the worst fate one could go through?"

"Yes, unless you count any torture before the antimattering."

Raoul could tell that Lark, again, wasn't convinced. "Anything could happen to her," the boy said.

"Like?"

Lark listed some possibilities.

----

1. **Names of Calendar Months**
   These months, from the first in the year to the last, are named Lighteth, Drellieth, Lamineth, Seallien, Skyrus, Falleth, Raineth, Soareth, Dynamel, Walketh, Grasseth, Pinketh, and Lifeien ("Lye-fee-inn").

NINETEEN
WASHING HER HAIR

At an Arach compound in the Eirloe sector, female Arach clones were assiduously washing Liara's hair. Pink and blue bubbles foamed and drifted down her golden strands. "What do you intend to do?" she asked.

"We just think that as the leader of Rarerus, you deserve to be treated with more care than any other of our—clients," said one of the clones, notwithstanding that Liara had been stiffened with a paralysis potion and forced to lie inside a big tub. The tub was pearl-colored and cool as marble. "Your hair is beautiful," the clone continued. "I wish I had hair like this."

"You could easily get hair like this by altering your genes," Liara said flatly.

"True, but I want something natural. If it's not natural, then it's nothing of worth."

How ridiculous it was to be talking about hair with an Arach clone.

"We prize beauty above all else in the Eirloe sector," the clone added with a measure of pride. "And we all strive to look our best."

"Yes, the Eirloe sector. The land that manufactures beauty and is all about beauty," Liara said. "How kind it is for you to take me here, out of all places."

The clone smiled. "I'm happy that you realize your privilege. And if you stay relaxed, I will show you more beautiful things made in Eirloe."

"That would be my pleasure," Liara said, still playing along with this amused clone.

"Good girl. We never expected that the leader of the Rarerus, our long-standing enemy, would be such a pleasant and agreeable person."

"I thank you for your compliment, though whether I deserve it is a matter of opinion."

After some time more of this ludicrous exchange of false pleasantries, the Arach clones finished with her hair and proceeded to give her a bath. Liara could have done it herself had they not paralyzed her limbs. Though they said that they wanted to "treat the Rarerus leader with extra respect and honor," it was still quite comical that they were giving her a wash. And despite herself, she slowly became calmer and more relaxed. A number of times, she was even tempted to close her eyes and enjoy the pleasant sensation of her scalp being rubbed, but she woke herself up and berated herself for letting her guard down in Arach territory.

Raoul had reported to the Beams and the rest of the Rarerus that Liara had caught an illness from him and was now resting, so that she would not be able to attend to her duties for a while. He was in the Breemil branch when he reported this. And now the Beams, who were at the Vénus center, called up an urgent meeting with the members living in Vénus. They settled down in a huge room at the Rarerus center filled with stretch seats and orb chairs; the Beam siblings sat at the front on two silver and blue stri seats.

"Good members," Amber said, "my brother and I want to express our concern that something might be amiss in our leader's presumed illness. It is to our knowledge that she has rarely suffered from illnesses, and had never suffered so much that she needed to stay in bed."

Eventii nodded and added, "We suspect that someone has stolen our leader from us, or is faking her sickness."

The Rarerus members looked at each other, and glanced at the two children. One member said, "Do you mean to say that Raoul was lying?"

"Not necessarily," said Eventii. "It's possible that somebody told Raoul that she's sick, so he has no idea that she isn't."

"But Raoul himself saw her get sick, right?" another member asked.

"We are not sure. Raoul did not specify," Eventii said.

"But whatever it is," Jax of the seniors and the former Rarerus leader, spoke up. "I have absolute confidence in Raoul that he would not betray the Rarerus."

Alia, who was sitting at some distance from Jax, nodded tentatively.

The two Beams clearly had less faith in Raoul than Jax did. Amber said, "As we are not certain, we must contact Raoul to inquire into the details of this event."

Very soon after, Raoul was contacted via hologram communication, and he confirmed that he himself had seen Liara get very sick a few days after her first visit to him.

"Raoul, what illness did you suffer from?" asked Amber.

Raoul made something up in response, "Krutcher's." Krutcher's was an illness where all the person's limbs became flaccid; it was very hard for the person to sit up, let alone walk, and their thinking speed slowed down dramatically. Their mind became almost blank.

The Rarerus members gasped when they heard Krutcher's. "Liara has been afflicted by Krutcher's?"

"Yes, I'm afraid so," replied Raoul.

"Will you allow us to see her?" asked Amber, testily.

Raoul kept his expression neutral as he said, "Yes, of course. When would you like to visit? I have put her at my house for resting for the time being."

There shouldn't be anything surprising about a Rarerus member offering to let another member, the leader no less, rest and recover at their house. But when this offer came from Raoul, it made several minds spin with possibilities, especially as many believed Raoul to be Liara's lover. Amber and Eventii certainly felt this discomfort, but they were also aware of how it was expected that a Rarerus member should provide help to another in need.

So Raoul made his preparations before the Beams, Spikes, Scythes, and Drills could come. The Scythes, of course, included Haus and Marius. Raoul used another sleeping potion on the Liara clone that would last one and a half days, and took some chemical tints (harmless ones) to color her face and make her look pale, haggard, and suffering. Then he untied her and placed her on a bed in a guestroom.

After the Beams, Spikes, Scythes, and Drills satisfied themselves from seeing Liara resting safely in Raoul's house, and indeed sleeping and suffering, the Beams decided to let this go, though Amber still thought it strange that their leader should catch this illness so easily, with her strong body.

Amber also wanted to ask how Raoul had recovered from his Krutcher's so quickly, but resisted asking because different people recovered at different rates. Thus, she just said, "Raoul, I trust you are giving Liara the proper medications?"

"Yes, don't worry about that." He showed her the Krutcher's medication that he had bought just a short while before the Rarerus members came.

So Amber, Eventii, and the others could only believe Raoul for now.

Alia frowned at all this, but said nothing.

Thus, Raoul was let off, and he, Marius, and Haus were relieved. But Lark said, "I still wonder whether it would be better to risk being endangered and get the whole force of Rarerus to help us find and rescue Liara. And you believe that 'finding Liara sick' would make you less of a target to the Rarerus traitors?"

"Yes, of course. They would feel that this is just a natural occurrence. People do easily catch illnesses no matter how strong their bodies are," Raoul argued.

"Perhaps," said Lark. "If they do not think about the coincidence that she falls ill a short while after she is cloned."

"Let's not think about that and just try to focus on what we can do to find the real Liara," said Raoul, irritated.

DESPITE ALL HER STRUGGLING, LIARA GRADUALLY FELL UNDER the trance of the washing, and began to think that all felt surprisingly wonderful. She was so clean, her hair so beautiful, she was so comfortable, and the women (though clones) who were serving her were so kind, gentle, and polite. She fought against these thoughts, but her strength was fading.

After closing her eyes and reopening them, she saw two men and one woman gazing down at her with smiling eyes. Radiant sunshine shone behind them, dazzling, yet gentle and soft.

With a shock, Liara recognized that they were some of the fetalysis patients she experimented on and took care of in the Vénus sector. The patients talked to her gently; their voices were so soothing. They spoke of how lovely life was, how kind the Arach were beneath all their struggles with the Rarerus.

Despite what Liara truly believed, she found herself agreeing with them. She suddenly felt as if she had been taught all her life that the Arach were evil, but she was now hearing the truth that they were on the good side, after all. This was all utter absurdity but Liara's mind was beginning to believe it and take up these positive messages about the Arach.

One of the fetalysis patients told her that in their fetalysis state, others might think they were undergoing some mental turmoil and unrest, but the opposite was true. In their state, they were actually living in Heaven; they were constantly dreaming wonderful dreams.

Liara smiled. "What dreams?"

The patient blushed. "Oh, good ones."

They told her that the Arach were going to let her choose whether to become a fetalysis patient and live in Heaven, or to be antimattered and get transported to Heaven directly as she died in peace and bliss.

When they mentioned antimattering, her mind instantly conjured up an image, a midnight-blue emotograph of a senior just before he was anti-mattered. He had entreated the Arach to take his emotograph to remind his Rarerus members of him before he went away. The Arach had granted him that and gave this emotograph to the Rarerus members who came too late before this senior was antimattered.

Yet, as soon as this blue image of the man, in his last expression of fear and despair appeared in her head, something happened to wipe that image away. Her mind filled instead with messages, feelings, and thoughts that antimattering was good for her. It was a beautiful and benign way to obtain freedom from life's duties and unhappiness.

But when she thought that she was actually very happy in her life and delighted in her life's duties, these thoughts of contentment were suppressed by other thoughts that told her that she was not at all happy. That she was very sad underneath, like with Raoul and his animosity. Liara froze when Raoul was mentioned.

The thoughts prodded on: and what about Alia? A familiar warmth washed into her at the thought of her nonbinary friend, but this warmth was ringed with uncertainty and perplexity. It was something sweet, charming; yet it was deeply inexpressible and thick with a mysterious tension.

Now, said the fetalysis patients, let us take you to explore the wonders of the Eirloe sector.

In a blink of an eye, Liara found herself on a snowy mountain, where pink and peach flowers grew everywhere. "Liara, come and collect flowers with us; pick your favorites!" The female fetalysis patient laughed and threw her an elegantly shaped container that was rimmed with delicate patterns.

The colors of the container, a light blue, pleased Liara already. "Are you sure I can pick any flower?" Liara asked.

"Yes, any of them," the fetalysis woman said with a good-natured chuckle. "Come on and join the fun!"

As Liara picked the flowers with joy, she forgot all about her troubles and worries; she forgot that she was in the clutches of her enemies—and she even forgot that there was such a thing as the Arach or the Rarerus, or that she was the leader of a very important organization. She just enjoyed this activity of collecting beauty, while feeling the breeze on her cheeks, through her hair, and she breathed in that moist but solacing mist all around her.

Later, they invited Liara to eat the fruits that were growing on the trees, those soft green and yellow fruits, and she luxuriated in their taste. Everything was so relaxed, so in balance; she felt so at peace and happy with these people who treated her like a friend. Soon, they trod through a path laced with silvery leaves and bushes, and at the end of the path, she met with the citizens of Eirloe.

She wandered around with her new friends, and later they even showed her the lovely laminae of the region. She got to pet the thorands, which were tall hooved quadrupeds, with smooth translucent skin, that one could ride on. There were myrtles, another species of quadrupeds, with their thick pink and white fur and bushy tails; these myrtles were the size of dogs and foxes. She even got to watch the drings, small winged laminae with bright red or green feathers soaring through the skies, painting an image of everlasting serenity.

And as she enjoyed these sights, one of the Eirloe citizens walked up to her. "Do you recognize me?"

It took Liara a while; this man looked so familiar. It was then that it struck her. "Mr Phinn Faya!" She had seen his emotograph before at her home when she was still living with her parents. What was he doing here? Was Eirloe actually a Heaven that even spirits of the dead came to?

He smiled. "I am sorry for how coldly my son is treating you. Please tell Raoul that Ustella is innocent. She sincerely loved me and never stopped loving me even when I was dead; she loves me still now. I wanted her to find poor Orlen, your father, so that she wouldn't be lonely without me. He is a good man, Orlen. And though we've never known each other, Orlen is like a brother to me." The way Phinn Faya spoke was so reassuring and pleasing to Liara's ears and she asked him to go on.

Phinn proceeded to tell her about all the times he and Raoul had together. Liara was moved as he told her; she felt her eyes grow hot and watery. "Mr Faya, You and Raoul were so close. No wonder he's always so angry at me—I symbolize your death."

The good man shook his head. "Now, now, don't be so harsh on yourself, child. Raoul just doesn't understand yet that it's not your fault I died. It was an accident."

Liara and Phinn talked for a while longer and she felt comforted. Then he said, "I have to leave now, Liara." She looked at him with a cloud of sadness in her heart. "Tell Raoul all that I've said to you." He smiled. "If he doesn't believe you, tell him about all those times I had with him that I told you about. Then he'll know that you really met me."

And right after they exchanged a goodbye, Liara tearfully as she did so, Phinn and the rest of the world disappeared from her sight. A second later, she saw flowers and fruits; these colorful, graceful things multiplied in front of her eyes. Everything was so plentiful, lovely, soft, and full of joy...then she closed her eyes and sank into oblivion.

While Liara was in this dream, the women clones were still bathing her. One of them explained to the other that this water contained special chemicals that seeped through the pores of Liara's skin. These molecules stimulated her brain to release more endorphins, dopamine, and serotonin, making her relaxed and happy. They entered all her other body cells as well, working to slow down her heart rate. It was a calming effect, the clone said to her companion, and it was mighty kind of the Arach to do this for Liara before her final ceremony.

TWENTY
THE FETALYSIS PATIENTS

As the four of them sat there, pondering for a long time on how to find Liara, Lark, in his fatigue, drifted off to thoughts of science again, and he started doing multiplications in his head. When he mused upon scientific things, it was as though he had several heads, all of which were thinking simultaneously; it was a parallel processing.

He was counting the number of moons discovered so far by Drellian scientists, and he theorized about gravity, and about forces that acted at a distance. He thought about a legend that his mother had told him some time ago: There were once two lovers who lived on different planets. They traveled several moons to reach each other, and even gravity helped them get together. While his parents were sighing at how romantic the story was, Lark was wondering how it was possible that gravity could help them cross several moons.

While the four scientists were all engrossed in their own practical or daydreaming thoughts, a signal went off, a kind of beep, and Raoul was alerted by a message he received. On his computer, he got a long letter. It was from an unknown addressor who wrote to him a legend about trees, tropical islands, laminae, old and young adults, children, males, females, and nonbinary people. Then at the end of this letter was an equation. Raoul pondered for just a little while because this style of code looked so familiar. Then his brain lit up and he found words from the legend to fit into the equation. He beamed at his comrades.

"Guys, Liara's in the Eirloe sector, at these coordinates."

Haus, Marius, and Lark couldn't believe that something could just drop out of the sky like that.

"Um, are you sure that's not a hoax, or a joke?" asked Haus. "And you don't know who's it from?"

"Nope, but this is the only lead we've found so far. This location also corresponds to one of the current Arach activity areas that have been detected recently. Liara must be there!"

"But who would be so kind to give you this location, though? And what are their motives for giving you this information?" asked Haus.

Lark nodded in agreement and looked at Raoul to see what he would say.

"But this is the only clue we have, right?" Raoul said.

"Yet, we need to make sure that this someone isn't just misleading us or luring us into a trap," said Haus firmly.

Raoul tried not to let his annoyance show, and pointed out, "But it is one of the Arach activity sites anyway, so we wouldn't go there for nothing."

"Uh—Raoul," said Marius. "Hate to burst your bubble but the location you got isn't exactly the location detected by the Eirloe sector branches. It's off by quite a lot."

After narrowing his eyes to see the exact coordinates of the Arach activity detection areas, Raoul sighed. "We have to do something, though, don't we? Why can't we just take the chance?"

"Tut tut, Raoul. You young people are so impulsive," said Haus. He ignored the look from Lark when he made such a generalization about young people. "We need to make sure you're not being tricked."

"And how will we be able to do that?" said Raoul.

"It is simple," said Lark impatiently. "All we have to do is to inform the rest of Rarerus and have all members work on this location at once. Four people are easy to deceive, but several hundred are a different story."

"You just have to get the other members involved, don't you?" Raoul asked.

"I am not trying to be stubborn. I am trying to be helpful," Lark shot back.

Raoul Faya paced around the room for a while, when Lark said, "How is the Liara clone?"

"Oh, her? I left her bound up in elastoropes again."

"She still believes that you think she's the real Liara?" asked Marius.

"She probably knows that I know, but she's still playing along. But let's not talk about her, okay? The genuine Liara is troublesome enough."

"True," Haus said.

"But no matter what," said Raoul, "I don't want to get the other Rarerus members involved. Sorry, Lark."

"Fair enough. You may do as you please," the boy said, looking away nonchalantly. He suspected that Raoul had other motives for not wanting the other Rarerus members' help, but right now he couldn't care less. Let them die and fail in this audacious and presumptuous mission, then; he wasn't afraid of death anyway.

If Lark were an ordinary boy, Raoul, at the sight of this gesture, would have repeated his apology; but for Lark, he knew that more apologies would just annoy him because the boy had such a detestation of super-fluities. Instead, Raoul gave Haus and Marius a rueful look. "Well, guys, I agree this is a dangerous mission, so if you don't want to participate, you can say so now."

"Oh, who says I'm backing out? I'm in!" said Marius.

"Guess I'm in too," smiled Haus.

"Lark?" asked Raoul.

"I will come if it pleases you," Lark said, still in his nonchalant tone. Raoul tentatively took that as a yes.

THE THREE MEN AND ONE BOY STRAPPED THEMSELVES INTO their seats in the Streeto and drove as quickly as they could to the Eirloe coordinates.

Before leaving, Raoul, Haus, Marius, and Lark had announced to other Rarerus members that they were off on a special journey to enhance Lark's chemical knowledge. Such "apprenticeship journeys" were common in the Rarerus, and Raoul, Haus, and Marius worked most closely with Lark, so this declaration should not be surprising to anyone.

And once again, Lark had asked his parents to sign a form for his trip.

"Boy, your science club organizes a lot of trips!" Graham said. "Hope you're having fun, son."

"Of course I am, father," Lark said dispassionately.

Normal parents would have taken this for sarcasm, but Graham and Kreesha knew that their son did not like to display his true feelings, so they hugged and kissed him and wished him yet another wonderful time of learning and socializing.

When Lark and his three companions arrived on Eirloe, Raoul, Marius, and Haus recognized some Rarerus members hanging around, so they flew even faster before any of them could recognize their Streeto.

"Told you we should have just taken a Coaster and Hyure," said Marius. Haus and Raoul ignored him. Lark didn't even hear him.

When they arrived at the coordinates, at this presumably Arach building, the four companions found that there was a waterfall at the main entrance.

"Why, that's interesting," said Marius. The other three didn't look that amused, as a waterfall was another obstacle to add onto their already challenging mission. Marius shrugged. "They are in the Eirloe sector, after all. You would expect them to do fancy decorative things."

The other three shot him a "whatever" look and began discussing how to bypass the waterfall.

"Is there not another entrance?" asked Lark.

"Perhaps. Let's wander around and see what we can find," said Raoul.

After wandering anticlockwise around the building, they found what appeared to be another opening. But in front of this opening, was a small garden of trees and bushes lined in a very neat and elegant way. There were green and pink shadows on the ground caused by a source of pink and green lights shining from inside the door.

"Should we go in?" asked Marius.

"Don't you want to make sure it's safe first?" Haus asked.

"If we have to ensure the safety of everything we come to, we'll never get anywhere and Liara will already have been antimattered," protested Raoul.

Marius said, "It's not too much of a problem, really. We didn't detect any Arach activity here specifically, so she's likely still safe. And we still aren't detecting any activity," he said.

Raoul peered around the trees, bushes, and the strangely colored shadows. Then, without another word, he marched through the entrance.

"Wait for us!" cried Marius as he, Lark, and Haus rushed in after him.

When they entered, they came into a dimly lit dark blue hallway. But after they walked a few steps, the hallway slowly lit up. Raoul peered anxiously around him in case anyone had noticed them and purposely turned on the lights. There was no one. It was probably just an automatic body heat sensor that had illuminated this hallway. Now that they could see more clearly, they saw that the walls of this place were chiseled with decorations of swimming laminae. It was as if they had stepped into an aquarium.

In this world of water, there were shopher (pronounced Shoa-fer), streamlined sea laminae with shimmering scales and fins. There were also kaytwirls, creatures with five limbs and smooth bodies. And there was a vast variety of sea laminae surrounding them that made them feel like they were in an ocean. What if they came alive? wondered Lark. As though in answer to his hypothesis, some of these chiseled figures seemed to move just the slightest bit, but he had probably just imagined it.

At the end of the hallway, the four wanderers were dismayed that they faced a dead end: they were fenced in by more blueness and laminae.

"Can we blast our way through?" asked Marius.

"Or we could corrode our way through," suggested Lark.

"There must be some secret door around here," said Raoul, and began tapping around the area with his feet and hands.

"Ah, here's something." Haus found a little purple cube—smaller than a sugar cube—lying on the floor as inconspicuous as a speck of dust. Cautiously, he kicked it. It rolled and hit the wall in front of them. The wall moved an inch. Amused, he kicked the cube again, this time harder. The wall moved several inches. As his companions watched in bewilderment, Haus kicked the little cube again and again until the wall was pushed back far enough to reveal an opening on the right wall. Raoul entered it as soon as it appeared. Haus sighed that young people would never take precautions before wandering into unknown places anymore.

Once they were inside, they stood in a room of pink and lilac. Toy laminae littered the room, but not in a messy way; they were arranged in a rather tasteful fashion that anyone, even those who were not too sensitive to aesthetics, like Lark, could appreciate it.

Lark noticed that further along this toy-riddled room, curled many of those gel and plastic-like tubes. Raoul laughed when he saw what Lark was looking at. "So the Arach use oloe tubes just like we do." When prompted by Lark to explain what these "oloe tubes" were used for, Raoul said, "They comfort and massage your feet. They feel nice."

"Is that their only function?" asked Lark, preparing for disappointment.

"No, of course not. They also provide nourishment for your feet and legs to make them healthier and stronger. If you stand for a long time amongst them, your legs and feet become cleaner as well."

On a whim, Lark marched directly into this pile of oloe tubes and shuffled around. His legs indeed felt quite comfortable and soothed after touching all these interesting structures. He wondered why he had felt so discomforted when he first encountered these at Haus's shop.

"Lark, quit fooling around over there and come look at this."

Lark glared at Marius when he said that, but the latter was gazing intently out a window. Lark trudged over to his side.

Outside that window was an obscure blue figure, or rather, blue object. It blended around with its surroundings with an icy majesty. They could not really make out what it was, but staring at it was so pleasing to the eye. In front of this frosty wonder, was a patch of glowing, light green; it wasn't grass, but it seemed to be some kind of strange green, and it was a delicious-looking material. "Pretty, isn't it?" smiled Marius.

"Is there anything else aside from the aesthetics of this object for one to appreciate?" asked Lark.

"Yes," said Raoul. "Look." He pointed at something farther out in the distance. There was a pink figure, really a figure this time, striding towards the blue object. Haus pushed in to look as well.

All four of them thought that the advancing female figure might be Liara so they pressed against the glass of the window, but it turned out to be a smiling woman that none of them knew.

"Do you think that's an Arach clone?" asked Marius.

"Most likely," said Haus, losing interest and beginning to glance around the room for something more worthwhile to look at. His eyes were especially drawn to the two doorways in the room where yellow light, or just yellow walls, glowed. "Guys, why don't we—"

"Oh no!" cried Marius. "She saw us!"

The female figure stared at them in shock. She ran towards them and at the same time, Raoul and the other three backed away in fright, not knowing what she would do. When she reached the window, the four Rarerus members already had their backs against the wall; then she punched the glass of the window and leaped inside. She rushed towards Lark.

The boy darted swiftly away from her thanks to his fondal enhancement and all four of them fled through the doorway. She shot after them. Now was a wild chase of cat and mouse—though Drellians would not use that expression. Lark, Raoul, Haus, and Marius charged through as many rooms as they could possibly count.

At first, the four sprinted through rooms of different interesting colors, like gold, silver, chocolate brown, grass green, scarlet red, fresh orange, and fruity yellow; but after a while, all the rooms became a single pale red but not quite pink color. Not that Raoul or his companions cared about the color of the rooms. Lark soon wished for a pair of wings, and when they formed, he flew over the heads of his companions, leading the way.

Despite their shock when they saw that Lark was flying, the other three didn't stop running. Eventually, Raoul spun around quickly to shoot a blast from his hand beam. The female dodged it easily, so Raoul whirled back around to catch up with his companions.

Very soon, the four of them got into a room that was finally not a dull red. It was a bright yellow again, and its walls seemed to be made out of dangerous-looking coils. As the Rarerus crew approached the next exit, to their fright, the opening began to close. Lark was about to pass through when the exit coiled up with sudden speed and they were all locked in. The four of them glanced back at the running female figure.

Haus, Marius, and Raoul frantically shot hand beams at her, but none of them hit. Now that her victims were cornered, the female grasped towards Raoul and Marius with her seemingly clawed hands. The two men leaped apart to let her hit the wall, but she didn't. She touched the floor lightly and bounced up to reach for Lark. In fear, the boy swerved away, wishing he could fight back. Claws started erupting from his limbs and his body began to spike. The other three marveled at the sight of the boy becoming sharp all over.

As Lark was now fully spiked, the female gave up on him and jumped maddeningly towards the other three again. They dodged and turned, several times narrowly falling into her hands. At long last, Raoul cried out, "What do you want?"

At this, to his surprise, the lady stopped her pursuit. She replied, "You are intruders. I need to ward you off away from our home."

"Are you an Arach clone?" asked Marius.

She frowned. "How rude. What makes you think that?"

"So you're not?" Marius asked again.

"She could be lying, you know," Haus said.

In reply to both of them, the female said, "I am not saying whether I am or am not an Arach clone. That is for you to judge. Now, may I ask you all to please leave our building. It is very unpleasant for us to get unwelcome visitors."

"I'm afraid we can't do that, lady," said Raoul.

She crossed her arms. "Then what is your business here?"

"We're here to save someone we know," Raoul frankly said, even while his companions stared at him in alarm for admitting this truth so early.

"Hmm...that's a good reason, but do you have any proof that that is your intention rather than a desire to rob us of our riches?"

"You have riches in here?" gasped Marius.

"That is none of your concern, old man," she replied.

"You called me old man!"

She ignored him and said, "Well, where's your proof?"

Raoul smiled grimly. "What kind of proof do you want?"

"Tell me the name of the one whom you seek."

Despite the beseeching eyes of his companions, Raoul said outright, "Liara Grae."

At her name, the woman's expression changed, but to their astonishment, it changed to an expression of awe, wonder, and respect. "Liara Grae! Yes, she is here and we are so happy she came. She doesn't need saving, though, as she is enjoying herself here. Nevertheless, if you are all so desperate to see her, I will gladly lead you to her."

Marius and the others gaped. Marius said, "Really?"

"What? Do you not believe me? If not, then I shall withdraw my help."

"No no," Marius said. "Never mind me. I'm just a silly old man. Please do show us the way."

AND WITH THAT, THE WOMAN LED THEM THROUGH THE rooms, past more pale red rooms and rooms of other different colors. Raoul was mystified that there weren't any metallic or lab-like rooms. One would expect the Arach to have experiment rooms, but perhaps they had not yet come upon those. After what seemed like a century, the woman stopped outside a brown door. "Liara is right behind this door." She gestured towards it. "Well, what are you waiting for?"

Raoul moved towards it carefully, and eyed the woman with suspicion.

She was incensed by his doubtful glance. "If you don't believe me, you can just walk away and try to find your way out of our building."

So Raoul decided to trust her for now, and pushed the door open. And indeed, to his amazement, there was Liara. She was clothed in rich splendor, looking like the wealthiest person in the world, and she sat on an equally splendid and effulgent-looking throne.

When she saw him, she gaped and said, "Raoul."

"Liara," he said. "What are you doing there?"

She smiled. "Sitting, enjoying the atmosphere. You know, it's rather pleasant sitting around doing nothing here. Eirloe is really such a charming sector. I like it here. Call it my holiday away from my Rarerus duties."

"But leader, the Rarerus needs you!" cried Marius.

She looked at him with pity. "You've always been so loyal to me, Marius. I appreciate that. But you must also appreciate that I am a human being. I need my rest from my responsibilities from time to time too. And where better to rest than the Eirloe sector, in this beautiful palace?" When

Drellians said palace, they didn't mean the palaces that we have on Earth. A "palace" for them was a place or building that was breathtakingly beautiful. Therefore, palaces were names subjectively given by the beholder of the place.

"You have got to be joking, Liara," said Raoul. "You have gone out of your mind. You need to get back to Rarerus because they're confused without you."

"They are?" she said in wonder. "No, I have absolute confidence in my Beams. They can reign just as well as I." And that was all she said.

"Leader, please. You cannot be serious," said Haus.

But Liara just answered him again that she was, that she really needed a vacation, and that Amber and Eventii could be her temporary substitutes. Then she glanced at Lark. "Lark, you have not spoken a word yet. What do you think of this predicament?"

The boy frowned at being addressed. "I think this is utter absurdity. There is nothing more for me to say, except that I feel I have wasted my time coming this far and enduring such pursuit," he pointed at the woman standing faithfully outside the door, "when you do not even want to leave. This is also absurd because, as you know, there is an Arach clone that has taken your place in the Rarerus. Do you know that?"

Liara widened her eyes. "Really? Why, then that's convenient. I won't need to worry about the Rarerus for a long time."

"What madness is this?" said Lark, shaking his head. "You are now truly insane, and I agree that you cannot go on reigning anymore. It is time to choose a new leader," he said bluntly.

Raoul, Marius, and Haus stared at him with vapid alarm when he said such a daring thing to their leader. Yet, Liara seemed to be merely amused. "If we should choose a new leader, who do you propose we elect?"

The boy was unprepared for this, as he had only blurted that out in a moment of anger and frustration. "Who do you propose?" he asked back.

"You could reign, my boy," said Liara with an obvious lack of seriousness.

"Stop toying with me if you please, madam."

But now Liara had really tired of toying with him. "Raoul, what about you? How would you like to lead Rarerus in my place? You are my brother and I already have faith in your abilities as well as your perpetual good intentions towards the Rarerus."

Raoul was not too taken aback because he had half expected her to say so. Nevertheless, he shook his head. "I told you already that I don't like that kind of leadership."

Liara shrugged. "Very well, then. Let us allow my clone to take care of our Rarerus affairs for a while, and then I can come back and continue to lead." She glanced at Marius and Haus, the most loyal members of the four in this room. "What do you say?"

"Um," Marius stuttered. "If that gives you pleasure, leader."

She nodded; she looked up at the woman attending her at the door. "Now, Margah, please take these four gentlemen to the next room."

"What do you think you're doing?" cried her brother. "We haven't finished with you yet and you had better come back with us to the Rarerus."

Liara grinned. "Brother, you are so silly. Surely it should have been obvious to you that I wasn't the real Liara."

All blood drained from Raoul's face. "You escaped my house."

She shook her head with amusement. "No, I'm not her. I am another clone. Surely you can't be that slow to realize that the Arach can make additional clones." But here she ran out of patience and she called out, "Margah, take these gentlemen to the next room!"

Marius was protesting against this, but Raoul, seeing that she wasn't his real sister, lost all interest in staying and followed this Margah—there was no reason to try to escape either because they could never hope to get out of this labyrinth of a place by themselves. Lark and Haus also didn't see the point in staying any longer so they all walked after him. Marius cried, "Wait for me!"

THEY SOON CAME TO A GREY ROOM. IT WAS SO DIMLY LIT THAT the grey seemed to be floating in clouds of mist before their eyes, as if the five of them were trapped in a dark sea. But gradually, the greyness cleared and the room became bright enough for them to see what was inside. To their shock, they saw before them rows upon rows of people sitting on stretch seats; but their expressions were clearly vacant as they stared out into nothingness.

Raoul knew immediately what they were. "Fetalysis patients!" He even recognized several from his own lab.

"Look!" Marius cried. "Liara!"

Sure enough, the four companions spotted their leader in the very last row of all these fetalysis patients. They ran to her and discovered to their horror that she was also staring into nothingness. "Liara!" Marius called, trying to rouse her.

"She's gone forever."

"Stop being so pessimistic, Marius," snapped Raoul. "She's Liara, after all."

Lark calmly walked up to her and peered into her eyes. He frowned. "I can understand why you say fetalysis patients look vacant, yet their heads are not at all vacant. I can see from the subtle changes in her eyes that she is thinking about something. Thinking very quickly too."

"It's a shame we didn't think of bringing neuroscans," said Haus.

"No point in lamenting what we have not done," said Lark. He thought aloud, "What can we do to reverse this situation?"

Margah, who was standing behind them, said, "There is nothing you can do." Her smile actually looked sad, as if she felt sorry for Liara.

Raoul ignored her, as the enemy was always trying to make one lose hope, and often unsuccessfully too. "There must be a way, guys, think." Then he turned round and said to Margah, "Do you mind if you leave us?"

"No, I don't. But since I also care about Liara, maybe my ideas, when they occur to me, may be of help."

Marius gaped. "But didn't you just say there was nothing—" He restarted his sentence. "But you're an Arach clone. Why would you care about Liara? Why should we trust you?"

She smiled faintly. "I never said that I was an Arach clone, did I?"

"Then what are you?"

"That is none of your business."

"Whatever," said Haus. "As we admittedly are quite lost ourselves, it would be nice to have another person contribute to the discussion."

"But she might mislead us into killing Liara!" Marius cried.

"No, she won't. We're smart enough to know if she attempts such a thing. We are expert chemists, after all," said Haus.

Raoul wanted to say that highly skilled chemists could blunder too, and that Margah's solution might not even be related to chemistry, but Raoul didn't want to exacerbate his team mate's distress, so he held his tongue.

"I'll give you a clue," said Margah. Everybody glanced at her suspiciously. "Do you remember what you initially found to be strange about fetalysis patients?"

"Their brain cells," Raoul answered immediately. "Those channels between them and their abnormally enlarged genomes."

"Okay...What else?"

They all thought it was quite ridiculous that this woman, who may or may not be an Arach clone, was guiding them like a teacher towards a possible solution. This thought made Haus and Lark frown.

Then Lark said, "The Aira dance."

The woman's eyes brightened. "Yes. Now think about these two answers you have given. I am sure you can work it out by yourselves now." And she started walking away.

"Wait," said Marius. "Is that all you're going to tell us?"

"It was very generous of me to lead you so far already."

"But I thought you said you cared very much about Liara's welfare too."

"So I did. But I already lent you all the assistance I am allowed to give without breaking my mistress's wishes."

Marius widened his eyes. "You mean your mistress, the Liara Arach clone, permitted you—or even ordered you to tell us these hints?"

"Believe what you will," she said, and in a jiffy, she left them alone with Liara and the other fetalysis patients.

Raoul, Haus, and Marius exchanged a bewildered look. Lark stared into space. All of a sudden, Lark said, "Look at the walls."

Everyone had been so focused on the fetalysis patients and the leader of Rarerus that nobody had paid much attention to the walls. They were just plain black with golden patterns on them. But now that Lark pointed them out, the men saw that there was something strange about the patterns. In fact, it was a foreign script: it was not in any of the Drellian tongues but it was definitely a language.

"Anyone know what any of this might mean?" asked Marius.

Nobody answered him.

Then after a while, Lark said, "The language here strangely reminds me of some equations I have seen before." He paused to jot down all those equations onto his computer for everyone to see.

Raoul started. "I recognize this constellation of equations. These represent the orbiting activity and conformation of moons near Drell at specific times. Which means—"

Lark cut in, "Liara and the other fetalysis patients' brain waves may match the gravitational forces and orbiting patterns of these moons."

"Woah, woah, that's jumping way too fast," said Haus. "You two are so intuitive. How do you know that these equations have anything to do with Liara? Aside from that they happen to be written on these walls where the fetalysis patients are?"

"Is it not reason enough that the equations are here with these fetalysis patients?" said Lark and Raoul at the same time. Well, they didn't use the same wording, but that was what they both meant.

Haus frowned. "Okay, whatever you say." He muttered something under his breath about insolent and flighty-minded youngsters.

"All right," said Marius, trying to make peace again. "Let's say that what Lark just deduced is true. Then how do we link this to the Aira dance and brain cell connecting channels?"

Lark peered at those jotted down equations and at the language on the walls, and back again. A look came into his eyes. "I see that the moon's gravitational and orbital activity patterns seem to be approximately the reverse of the Aira dance pattern. How did we and the other scientists neglect this when we were first studying the Aira dance phenomenon?" he cried out in exasperation.

"What?" said Haus.

"Just look," Lark said.

Raoul nodded slowly. "You're very good at finding patterns, Lark. So, if I'm not wrong, the solution to defeating this fetalysis condition in Liara and all these other people, is to generate this moon activity—let's call it the moon dance—in those cells to reverse the Aira dance effect."

Marius exchanged a glance with Haus, and they rolled their eyes at the "youngsters." But Haus decided to be kind and said, "All right. So how should we create this moon dance?"

Lark was about to answer but Haus himself answered first. "Since Aira dancing originated from, for example, the green substance produced from amosti and par-the-air, let's start by getting a lot of those reactants."

"But how do we reverse that activity?" asked Lark.

Haus pressed his lips together. "Hold on. I was getting to that. It's probable that if we get that green substance and force it to re-become its reactants amosti and par-the-air, we will be able to induce such an activity."

"Now you're the one who's being intuitive," smiled Raoul.

"Whatever. Whatever works, right?" Haus said.

"Whatever works," Raoul agreed.

With that straight, the four of them decided to get a great ton of par-the-air and amosti to create a huge amount of green substance first. And then use forceful electrolyzers to make the green substance break down and reform its original reactants.

(See "Forceful Electrolyzer[1]" under "Chemicals" and "Chemical Apparatus and Other Things.")

The amosti would be easy enough to obtain; forceful electrolyzers were common enough to find too. Now for par-the-air, the most abundant supply that they knew and had access to was in Phuore, the place where Lark had first met Marius.

They needed to buy these chemicals because going back to a branch lab to get their supplies would alert other Rarerus members that something was wrong. What was more, Raoul and a lot of other Rarerus scientists didn't keep many chemicals at home, aside from some bare essentials; this was done as a precaution against accidents, and against thieves with outstanding hacking skills who might use the more volatile substances to cause trouble. Consequently, neither Raoul, Haus, nor Marius had any of the above needed chemicals or equipment at home.

Finally, nobody, not even expert chemists, would keep chemicals inside their computer pouches for too many hours; there was no telling what would happen if any chemicals leaked out of their containers while the person was walking around. Some containers for chemicals were highly sturdy and hard to break, but you could never be too careful. Instead, people would keep chemicals inside a large room in the real world, behind a protective barrier where they could be seen; or people only carried the chemicals in computer pouches for a short period of time, say, three hours max.

Marius continued their discussion and said, "But we need someone to guard Liara and the other fetalysis patients just in case the Arach do anything to them."

"Right. In case they take the bodies away or something. And hopefully we can fend off the Arach clones when they come to antimatter them," said Haus. Marius shot him a reproachful look. Haus said, "Well, it's true! Without our other Rarerus comrades, we are unfortunately severely outnumbered no matter what they are going to do."

If Lark were a normal boy, he would have said a "Told you so. You should have listened to me." But he was not a normal boy, so he let this comment pass because he did not care for these trivialities.

"Okay, well, we'll make do with what we have," Marius responded, and tried to look calm. "Let's have two of us guard them, and the other two can get the supplies."

Everyone agreed. In the end, Raoul and Lark went to collect the chemicals, while Haus and Marius looked after the fetalysis patients.

"But how do we find our way out of here in the first place?" Raoul asked, dismayed.

Just then, they heard a footstep. The men and boy were astonished when they beheld Margah back in the room.

Marius said, "Didn't you just—"

"Leave?" said Margah. "Believe what you will, but I overheard your conversation, and I think you will need help navigating out of our palace."

"You heard everything we said and you managed to make us think that you were gone the whole time?" Marius said.

She just ignored him and gestured to Lark and Raoul. "Well, do you two want to complete your mission, or not?"

It was with consternation that they accepted her help; but they were still uneasy about it all. They had no clue what her intentions were.

WHILE LARK, RAOUL, MARIUS, AND HAUS WERE GONE, ALIA had flown on Alia's vehicle to Raoul's house; the nonbinary combatant and scientist had felt uncomfortable throughout the whole incident of Liara's "illness." It wasn't as if Alia didn't trust Raoul, but something felt off, and they experienced only a tiny twinge of guilt about sneaking here in Raoul's absence.

Alia pressed the signal bell to the door, and tapped their fingers on their hip in much nervousness. As they had expected, nobody answered the door. Alia couldn't help but wonder why Raoul had not asked anyone to look after his sister while he, Lark, Marius, and Haus went off on that education trip. It was no news to Alia that Raoul hated his sister, but leaving his leader uncared for like this was downright irresponsible.

With apprehension coiling up in their chest, Alia activated their computer's communication code, and prayed that Liara was still wearing her computer wrist band.

But of course she wasn't. The computer reported that Liara was presently unreachable. Alia gritted their teeth, and tried to contact Raoul's home. This call did connect, but no one spoke on the other side for a long time, and all Alia could see in the hologram projection, was Raoul's living room with all the lights turned off. But a few moments later, a weak voice called out, "Alia?"

Alia's heart pounded in both fear and joy. "Liara, are you okay?"

"Not really. Raoul's gone crazy," Liara's voice said, though her person was still nowhere to be found in the hologram of Raoul's living room. "He tied me up and put me here."

Heat surged through Alia, and they clenched their fists. "Why on Drell would Raoul do that? This is outrageous! You're his leader, not to mention his sister."

Liara said in her usual melodic tone, "He thinks I'm an Arach clone."

Alia widened their eyes; they had to stop themselves from shouting. "What nonsense! What proof does he have? Do Lark, Haus, or Marius know?" Suspicions built up in Alia's mind.

Liara said, "They supposedly found Bluamine and Zanyliline in my DNA." She sighed. "Which is ridiculous, because I am the real Liara. The DNA test must have been botched somehow."

The nonbinary scientist and combatant furrowed their brows. "Okay.

Then to verify, tell me something you know about me, and something about us." Alia's breath hitched a bit when they uttered the latter, and instantly regretted asking that.

Nevertheless, Liara answered. "What do you want me to talk about, more specifically?"

Alia felt abruptly flustered. "Just tell me what only you and I would know," they said quickly.

Liara let out a laugh that was only partially mirthful. Then she sounded grim. "You—had problems growing up, and your uncle who raised you kicked you out of his house when you were only thirteen. He wasn't happy about his 'niece's' gender change."

Alia snorted. "In this day and age, pretty much everyone is accepting towards transgender and nonbinary gender identities."

Liara said, "Yeah. He said he was disappointed because he was ecstatic to have a girl to raise, like you were his daughter. But, according to your uncle, you ruined it by coming out as nonbinary."

"Absolutely eccentric uncle," Alia scoffed.

"But you think that he was masking a much deeper issue," Liara continued. "He, uh, had certain emotional needs that can apparently only be satisfied by close female company." Alia cringed at that memory. Liara added, "You said that your uncle probably saw you as a human tool to aid in some magic spell that requires a female participant. Before your gender transition, he had always been overbearing and excessively affectionate too."

"Excessively indeed," Alia said with a nod they knew Liara wouldn't be able to see.

"So you were kind of glad, actually, that you got to leave your uncle," Liara said.

"That's right," Alia said quietly.

"Mmm hmm," Liara murmured. "You never saw your uncle again, and neither he nor you ever tried to get back in touch."

Alia heaved a sigh. "And then what happened?" they asked.

"And then," Liara began, "on the day you were kicked out, you found me. I was only nine years old at that time, and I was with my parents and Raoul at the Fleming ("fleh-ming") park on Vénus." She chuckled softly. "My brother and I were locked in combat—a practice combat."

"I was watching you two," Alia said.

Liara replied, "That's right. You were sitting on a nearby stretch seat. Later on, I asked you if you wanted to play fight with us. You were shy and hesitant at first, but you got up to join us. Raoul said you should pair up with me to battle him."

Alia smirked. "Such an arrogant older brother."

Liara laughed. "Yeah."

"So who won?" Alia asked.

Liara said, "The fight was close, but...Raoul won." She paused. "You were great, though. Your fighting skills were much better than mine."

Alia smiled. "I was older than you."

"Still," Liara replied with a peculiar tenderness in her voice. She paused again before speaking. "After that, you told us what happened to you. My parents wanted to adopt you—at least for a while, since you didn't have anyone to go to."

Alia Lyreal had refused to be adopted by Liara's parents, or by anyone, but the nonbinary child was willing to visit them from time to time. Raoul was civil towards Alia for the most part, but he was as distant towards them as he was towards his sister. Orlen and Ustella were kind and warm; yet, Alia felt detached from them due to their generational gap.

Even with Liara, who had been ardent in her desire to make Alia feel liked and accepted, the neutrois and androgynous teenager did not fully trust her, though they had sensed that Liara would never hurt them. Alia also disliked the idea of becoming dependent on someone else. Ever since being evicted from their uncle's house, Alia vowed to become completely self-sufficient. They struck out on their own and found their own home: even the Graes never got to discover where Alia lived.

Yet, as the days went by, despite Alia's steadfast independence, they grew to be more comfortable around Liara. Alia came to see Liara's sisterly ministrations, cares, and concerns not as intrusive and strange, but as simply a friendly attentiveness from a naturally affectionate soul, or at least, a soul that had taken to Alia for some reason. And if Alia would ever admit it, they felt drawn to her too, as though Liara were a glowing orb that emanated a soft, inviting warmth. In Liara's presence, even the lights seemed to change into a gentler, more reassuring, and more beautiful hue.

But now Liara and Alia's relationship was different. The lights became less gentle and more mixed with something else, though the lights were no less beautiful than before.

The present Alia hesitated, and then asked, "What happened after, Liara?"

"You sound like you're asking me to read you a bedtime story," Liara said.

Alia was flustered at the softness in her tone. They laughed and replied, "Maybe. But keep telling me this story. I need to be certain that you are indeed my good friend and not an Arach clone."

Liara chuckled. "You honestly don't sound like you need any convincing."

"Just continue with the story!"

"As you wish," Liara said. "One day, when I was fifteen, you asked me and Raoul to meet up at the southern entrance of the Cinta forest ("sintah"). And then there you were, sitting on a flat rock with an adult—Jax—with you." She sighed. "That was when it all began, the recruiting, the training, the Rarerus, and the Arach."

Alia nodded. "It was like discovering a new galaxy, or a new universe." They paused. "And after that?"

Liara laughed. "Are you sure that getting me to retell all of these details can test whether I'm your real friend or not? I'm sure Arach clones can just read the memories stored in their brains."

"True," Alia said, "but believe me, through your storytelling, I'll be able to sense whether you're the real Liara or not." In all honesty, Alia might be lying about why they wanted Liara to recount their past together. Alia went on, "Can you remember any more?"

Liara chuckled. "Whether I'm a clone or not, I would definitely be able to tell you more."

Alia pursed their lips in frustration. "You're right that I don't need much convincing, Liara. But how would I get to you? Raoul's house computers are virtually impenetrable."

"Or, you don't even need to penetrate them," Liara said softly. "As mad as my brother is, he isn't going to harm me, I don't think. I'll just have to be patient until he returns." She was quiet for a second. "But I really appreciate your coming to see me, nevertheless. Your—company means a lot to me."

An energizing warmth flowed through Alia's body and limbs. "I hope you're not just saying that to make me happy."

Liara laughed. "Definitely not. I'm serious, though. Don't worry about me. Raoul will see reason eventually, and he'll release me. It's not like he can detain the leader of the Rarerus forever."

"Yeah...," Alia responded uncertainly.

"It's all right," Liara said. "You're busy, right? Go back to what you were doing. The Rarerus needs you. And please don't tell anyone else that Raoul has me locked up."

Alia's mouth tightened. "There's really no need to keep defending Raoul like this. He's being stupid."

"No, really, please don't mind it," Liara replied. She hesitated for a moment. "I'll be sure that Raoul doesn't involve himself in any such silliness again." She added, "If you want to help me, Alia, you can come chat with me sometimes, until my brother comes back."

Alia's eyebrows gathered together like rain clouds. "I don't like Raoul," they said bluntly.

"I know." Liara laughed, but Alia could hear the despondency and resignation in her voice. Alia yearned to do something to make her feel better.

---

1. **Forceful Electrolyzer**
    An instrument that forces chemicals to return to their original reactants, i.e. force a reaction to reverse itself. This doesn't always work, however.

TWENTY-ONE
THE FINAL VICTORY

I t had been such a long time since Lark had stepped into Marius's hideout in Phuore. Those days of innocence from the knowledge of the Arach and Rarerus were long gone, and Lark was glad. As Raoul was very familiar with the place, the two quickly emerged with the par-the-air that they needed and put it into a container. And after they got a great supply of amosti and forceful electrolyzers from a store, they left back to Eirloe where Margah was waiting to lead them back to Haus and Marius. The supplier of amosti had looked askance at Lark and Raoul when they ordered such a great amount.

In answer to his baffled gaze, Raoul said, "I want to show my son here how exciting chemistry can be." Lark glared at Raoul at the word "son." Raoul pretended not to see the boy's glare, and laughed to himself.

Once they returned to the fetalysis room, Margah excused herself again and left. Marius checked and saw that she had really gone out of the room this time, though there was no telling if she would re-enter through the door later. She was an unpredictable character who did not cease to unnerve them; yet, now was not the time to puzzle her out.

Marius glanced at the huge stock of amosti and par-the-air, and at the forceful electrolyzer. "I can't wait to begin!"

The four chemists stepped back, letting the computer create an extra thick protective screen, before mixing the large amounts of amosti and par-the-air, and heating and cooling them. In a moment, they had an enormous volume of green substance (Chrystacience, as Lark named it). After that, they commanded the computer to use the forceful electrolyzer.

To their joy and relief, the instrument worked as the green chrystacience separated away into two liquid layers: the colorless amosti, and the pink par-the-air. When they used the computer's magnifying viewers, all four scientists were excited that the molecules in both reactants manifested something that looked like Aira dancing, but was clearly its opposite.

"Excellent," said Marius. "Now we just need this to affect Liara and the others." He instructed the computer to pick up small portions of the amosti and par-the-air, and to thinly veil them with a protective covering. "We'll touch the patients' heads with these protected reactants, so that the vibrations of the dance will stimulate their brain cells and make these brain cells imitate the moon dance. But the thin veiling will ensure that none of the reactant will actually touch the patients' heads," he explained. And, as Marius was brave, he commanded the computer to touch Liara's head with the chemicals first. Everybody held their breath. Then something momentous happened.

All their computers broke down.

The four Rarerus scientists gaped like they had never gaped before. But just when they thought that was all, the silvery networks of their computers began to spark with electricity.

"Oh no, back away—" cried Marius, but it was too late. The electricity threw itself around him and shocked him repeatedly until he became paralyzed. The same happened to the other two men, but Lark was safe. He had thought to turn all his skin, hair, and clothes into rubber and was thus insulated from the shocks. The electricity died down right after it had claimed three out of four of its targets. Just then, Lark heard a scurry of footsteps racing towards this room. Instinctively, he threw himself down onto the floor and pretended to be paralyzed as well, whilst willing his skin, hair, and clothes to turn back to normal.

When those who arrived into the room stepped before them, Lark perceived out of the corner of his eye that there were men and women. Probably all Arach clones. He recognized Liara's voice, or rather, clone Liara's. "Tut, tut. You call yourselves great scientists. But you should have known better than to think that the opposite of a curse is always the solution. In fact, opposites often exacerbate the problem. You really are way too intuitive." She paused, and said, "Take them to the antimattering chamber."

Lark willed his limbs to turn as stiff as stone just before an Arach clone picked him up. He was grateful that limb stiffening was a possible part of his shapeshifting abilities.

LIARA GRAE HAD WOKEN FROM HER TRANCE TO YET ANOTHER wonderland, and her mind was filled with endless joy. But while she was peacefully surfing the skies on her new vehicle, she saw someone down below waving frantically at her to land. Puzzled, she did so, and to her surprise and delight, she cried out, "Mr Phinn Faya!"

It was indeed Phinn again and he was also pleased to see her. But he looked at her sadly, and said, "Liara, my son is in trouble. Save my son, please!" And with that, his body began to fade.

"Wait," said Liara. "What do you mean he's in trouble and how do I— wait!" But Phinn Faya had already disappeared, as if he had never been there in the first place. The only thing left of the apparition was the gloom and dread that hung over her.

Nevertheless, Phinn's desperate plea had jolted her out of her happy trance. Even if she were, somehow, and inexplicably, in paradise, this did not mean everybody else was in paradise too. She berated herself for forgetting all about her comrades back home and in the Rarerus. What had happened earlier to put her people out of Liara's mind and make her believe that life was nothing but a Heaven to be enjoyed?

Liara clenched her fists, and re-entered her vehicle, driving it through the skies and looking down at the land everywhere to see if she could find anything that could help Raoul.

What had befallen him? And what about the others? Then pleasant thoughts, about eternal paradise swam towards her again and tried to soothe her, to calm her down, but Liara fought them off as she would not be deluded by their false happiness anymore. She needed to rescue her brother. Those pleasant thoughts asked her why she should believe what Phinn Faya said. But the very questioning by these thoughts just made her believe Phinn and suspect this "Heaven" even more. She squeezed her head with her hands and banished those sweet lies forever. A part of her was sad as she did so, but the other part of her pulled herself together. It was time for thought and action, not for lamenting over departed joy.

Whilst flying around, she saw many people below waving to her. She descended and found that they were the many Eirloe and fetalysis patient friends she had made. She concisely explained the situation Phinn told her about, and asked them whether they knew what was happening to Raoul and what she could do about it.

To her amazement, none of them had any idea what was happening in the "outside world." It was clear that her friends here were still deep in their dreams of intoxicating bliss. Liara wanted to wake them up, to let them see that this paradise was fake, and that they needed to do something to get out here. But at the same time, she didn't want to tear them away from their happiness. After a while, she decided not to disillusion them, as she could not bear to do so, and she set off by herself in search of whatever she needed to look for.

As Lark lay there helpless with Raoul, Haus, and Marius, he watched in despair as the Arach clones brought in more and more paralyzed bodies of the other Rarerus members. The clones dumped them onto the black and white panels inside a grand, hall-like room; the antimattering chamber near the Larence branch was tiny compared to this one. He heard from the clones' talking that these were the "Rarerus scum" found in Eirloe. In the other sectors, they collected more "Rarerus scum," and soon, all of the Rarerus would be antimattered and exterminated from their sight.

Lark remembered from what Haus and Marius had said that the Arach had specific patterns of targeting victims; they weren't just ordinary viruses seeking to infect every single living being in sight. He wondered whether this rule applied anymore. Perhaps the Arach had become so desperate to get rid of the Rarerus, their perpetual enemy, that they just wanted to eliminate them all regardless of whether this fitted into their original plan or not.

Soon enough, a head Arach clone announced to the others that all

Rarerus members from the Eirloe sector were put here, and Arach were placed on them to lay web eggs—that included Lark himself and he shuddered. After the Arach clones got over their exhilaration, they gradually filed out of the antimattering chamber. But Lark didn't dare move even when they were gone, because he suspected that there were security recorders in this chamber.

It was then that he heard a voice. "Lark."

He started when he heard it, and froze in case it was an Arach clone.

But the voice said, "Lark, don't be afraid. I'm from your mind. I am the spirit of Raoul's father, Phinn Faya."

Lark thought that he must be going crazy from all this trauma he experienced today.

The mysterious voice continued, "I know you are incredulous that you are talking to a spirit from the dead, and I understand that. But now is not the time to ponder whether I am indeed a spirit. I now speak to you specifically because you are the only one who escaped the paralysis and can save the other Rarerus members."

Lark listened hard, as it was indeed more important to save the others now than to figure out how the spirit of Phinn Faya came to be here. Besides, Lark had heard of spiritual sightings before in paranormal science news; maybe some of these apparitions were genuinely from the dead.

Regardless of what he thought, the spirit of Phinn Faya was somber and dignified when he said, "Here is what you have to do, Lark."

———

WHILST LIARA GRAE HUNTED AROUND FOR SOMETHING, anything that could tell her what was going on, she was aghast but overjoyed when the figure of Phinn Faya appeared before her once again.

"Finally," she said. "Please tell me what is happening to my brother!"

Phinn grimly explained the predicament to her, including how she was currently under the spell of fetalysis. She widened her eyes.

"Then what can I do to help Raoul?"

"Even though you are fetalyzed, you can still move your body to some small extent." Liara looked at him in dismay but Phinn went on, "Close your eyes and focus on returning to reality."

She thought she might be dreaming, or dreaming within a dream, she wasn't sure, but she closed her eyes nevertheless. To her astonishment, she found herself sitting on a stretch seat, along with rows of people staring into space, and she was in a room with black walls and golden writing.

"Those are the other fetalysis patients." Phinn Faya was no longer in front of her. But a second later, she heard his voice again. "Liara, do you see the chemicals in front of you?" She nodded. "These are par-the-air and amosti. I want you to react these to form a green substance. But before you do that, take from the computer pouches here the octamethyst, trichloroes, and brachiorsor."

After saying that, Phinn Faya slipped a wrist band on Liara's hand so she could control one of the Arach computers in this room. Goodness knew how he managed to procure an Arach wrist band or even touch Liara despite being a nonphysical entity.

At the same time, though the computers had broken down, the computer pouches could thankfully still be opened.

Haus, Marius, Raoul, and Lark had thought to bring the octamethyst, trichloroes, and brachiorsor to set up a brachiorsor barrier to protect themselves lest it came to a big fight with the clones. They didn't set it up beforehand, because these barriers didn't last a very long time; and they didn't want to waste any chemicals before it was absolutely crucial to use them. The Arach clones were also heedless enough to leave these chemicals and other items behind here, as they thought all their enemies were paralyzed and unable to retrieve these chemicals anyway.

Liara knew instantly what Phinn meant, and reacted these three chemicals, along with the par-the-air to form the barrier. She used her thoughts to command the computer in managing this reaction, as she couldn't quite move her limbs.

"Very good," said Phinn. "Surround yourself with the barrier, and mix the par-the-air and amosti together again. Use a chemical compressor stored in their computer pouches to greatly increase the mixture's density."

After she got that done too, Phinn said, "Excellent. Take out the guns from Lark, Raoul, Haus, and Marius's computer pouches, and fill them with green substance."

Liara was grateful that the Arach clones had not thought to remove any of these weapons as well as these chemicals. Once the guns were loaded, Phinn said, "Thanks, Liara. Please wait till Mr Lark Arias comes and then I'll tell you your next step."

In accordance to Phinn's will, Lark called out his wings and formed hard, reflective, and armored skin. Silently, he flew out of the chamber, and followed Phinn's directions to get into the fetalysis room. He flew to the end of the room and found Liara, still in the exact same position as he had found her before.

Phinn spoke up again. "Lark, take up the chrystacience guns."

"Chrystacience guns?" the boy cried.

The apparition smiled. "I know you've made these before, even if it was with my son's illusion." But Phinn didn't explain how he even knew about Raoul's illusion before adding, "Please also take Liara with you, as she, with her fetalysis brain waves, will be able to deparalyze the others."

Lark gaped, and then was about to ask how he was supposed to take hold of so many things at once with only two hands, when he thought to grow extra hands. How slow he could sometimes be. As Liara had the weight of an adult, and Lark was only a child, albeit fondal-enhanced, he half-lifted, half-dragged her by the feet across the ground.

When he reached the antimattering chamber, he turned Liara to face Raoul, Haus, and Marius as Phinn instructed him, and watched the electricity sprint from her head to penetrate into theirs, and in no time, all three could move their limbs again.

"What's happening?" said Raoul.

"Your father asked me to bring Liara here to de-paralyze you all," Lark replied laconically.

"What—"

"Perhaps I am crazy but your father's spirit was speaking in my head. This does not matter as you are all back to normal." He handed each of them a chrystacience gun. "Aim these guns at an Arach clone and they will immediately drop dead by a disease." It amused Lark to see that Raoul did not recognize the chrystacience gun that the Raoul illusion had taught Lark about. "Now let us deparalyze the others."

So, since Lark was really too weak to carry Liara around, and it was not very fitting for Haus and Marius, despite their ages, to carry their female teenage leader around, Raoul had to carry her, albeit reluctantly. And every time they aimed her head at a Rarerus member, Liara, in her dream world, saw the face of that member and delivered sparks of electricity from her head to that of the member's. It was like firing hand beams.

Soon enough, all the Rarerus members in the chamber recovered their ability to move. Lark, Raoul, Marius, Haus, and the other scientists there quickly went around to everybody to administer octamethyst to them before the webs could cover too much of their bodies. Lark was ill at ease because the Arach clones would discover their escape from their paralysis very soon. Liara, in her dreamscape, though she could not see what was happening, worried about the same thing.

The voice of Phinn Faya asked Lark to calm down and to pour in more chrystacience into the other Rarerus members' guns, until no more of the solution remained. And before Lark knew it, he beheld the Arach clones in the doorway.

Carefully, Haus aimed at an unsuspecting Arach clone man. The man convulsed violently; he did not even have the time to gasp. Then he collapsed onto the ground. He didn't move again. Raoul, Lark, the other Rarerus members, and the Arach clones stared at the dead man, amazed and horrified at the same time.

"What are you all looking at?" cried one of the clones. "Raise up your ray reflectors!"

Lark now panicked because none of the Rarerus members, including him, had any ray reflectors on them. If anyone fired at a clone, the beam would bounce back and immediately kill one of them. Then, to his alarm, one of the members—a woman slightly younger than Raoul—shot a ray towards the lead clone. "No!" they all cried.

But instead of bouncing back from the armor, the beam spread out quickly to cover the armor, to coat the body completely in green. The green wrapped more and more tightly around the body, until it was apparent that the ray reflector had been eaten away, as there was a muffled scream from inside. Within a few seconds, the body also fell to the floor; it twitched some more, and grew completely still. The Arach clones that were standing there watching this spectacle seemed to be frozen. Then one of them screamed, "Run!"

Broken out of their trance, the other clones started screaming hysterically as well as they ran after the one who first called out.

Victorious but still cautious, the Rarerus members strode out of the chamber. They encountered no Arach clones as they wandered through the compound, and Lark grew increasingly suspicious. They walked and walked through the endless rooms. Meanwhile, several Rarerus members, using Lark's directions, went to the fetalysis patients' room to retrieve those patients.

When all were freed from that black, language-inscribed room, Phinn Faya, in the fetalysis dreamland, instructed Liara and the other fetalysis patients to concentrate and create images of computers in front of them, and with their hands, draw strands and bands of electricity from these images.

Bit by bit, all the Rarerus computers were restored to their former condition, and the Rarerus crew soon found a stack of computer wrist bands in the compound to use. These wrist bands were locked inside a labeled box, and though the box was made of a very tough material, specialists in the Rarerus used their hand beams to open the lock. It was like picking a lock with a piece of wire, but in this case it was done with laser beams.

"Fantastic!" said Marius. "Let's see if we can hack into their computers to get their maps." To his glee, he succeeded and downloaded a huge 3D map onto his own computer. "Everyone, here are all the exits."

Lark knew something was wrong, but he followed Marius, Haus, and Raoul anyway. It was then that they discovered that all the exits were blocked by a wall of electricity. The Arach clones had fled their compound and locked them in.

Yet, Lark was not at all fearful. He had expected this. While the Rarerus members were lamenting how they didn't have any electricity absorbers with them, and that their supply of brachiorsor barrier ingredients was all used up, Lark spoke. Unfortunately, nobody heard him because they were all talking. Frustrated, Lark pulled at Raoul's sleeve. The latter saw him, and then said in a loud voice, "Everyone, Lark wishes to speak."

As Lark's name was well known from his being the first ever five-year-old scientist in the Rarerus, the members all fell silent and searched for the little boy. Lark located himself for them with his voice. "Members, I have an idea. As you may have already heard, I have gained extra abilities from the fondal to shapeshift and possess any natural body parts that I need. Here, since we have no barriers or absorbers, I can simply dig through this floor to let us all escape." Without even waiting for their response—which was nothing but utter awe—Lark immediately made himself grow long claws. He got to work and in a moment, already dug out a hole large enough to accommodate two adults.

"Way to go, Lark!" said Raoul. Lark said nothing and continued to dig.

The Rarerus members were at first hesitant to go into the hole for fear of any deadly traps underneath the Arach compound floor, but as Lark seemed to be safe, they more confidently followed him.

Raoul, Haus, and Marius had wanted to warn Lark before digging first, but the boy dug with such speed and ferocity that they couldn't intervene—he was deaf to their words. Soon enough, everybody was in a dark underground tunnel, but they all commanded their computers to light up. In an instant, the whole tunnel was flooded and flowing with luminescent and silvery networks. It was like an underground garden of glowing systems.

When they were outside the building, they were all surprised that no Arach clones awaited them. It appeared that they had all fled. The Rarerus crew decided then to go as one team to each sector one at a time lest the Arach clones outnumbered them. Some flew in Haus's Streeto while the rest followed via the Coaster and Hyures.

After saving a good number of Rarerus members from some other sectors, they judged it safe and more efficient to split up and rescue multiple sectors at once.

Not long after, Raoul, Lark, Marius, and Haus's team flew to the Fartha sector.

To Lark and Raoul's surprise, they saw little Karrin Treek wandering around in an Arach compound at Fartha and he flushed in great delight when he saw them. "Lark! Raoul!" When they told each other what had transpired, Karrin beamed. "Wow, Lark. We both had the great idea to turn our skins to rubber just before we got touched by that electricity, and both of us had the sense to stiffen our limbs when the clones picked us up. What a happy coincidence!" Lark was not so amused that he and Karrin had thought alike on this occasion.

Karrin was even more elated when Raoul handed him a chrystacience gun. "Now, please be very careful with this weapon. Only aim if you are absolutely sure you can't miss, because anyone you strike with this will die instantly." Karrin nodded gravely and swore that he would take very good care of his weapon.

After the big rescue, and checking that everyone was safe again, a great number of the Rarerus members now rallied in Vénus, including the Beams. Raoul, along with Amber and Eventii, asked the members whether anybody had any idea how to cure the fetalysis patients and their leader. All were silent, until the men and women who had been assigned to take care of Liara rushed into the room. "Everyone! Liara wrote a message!"

Since they could not fit everyone inside the room where Liara and the other fetalysis patients lay, the person who just shouted read out her message. "Go to the island of Ishiri (pronounced Ish-shee-ree) and find a chemical called lepraun ("luh-prawn"). Let the fetalysis patients and myself drink the lepraun and we will wake up from our trance."

"Excellent!" Marius punched the air.

So a great big band of Rarerus members flew in their Streetos to this Ishiri island. Lark was unaware that Ishiri was next to the sector of Itheris, where his closest friend in the world whom he would meet many years after, lived.

It proved to be easy to obtain the lepraun, as the island inhabitants knew where to find this not too uncommon chemical. The Rarerus team instantly flew back to Vénus and lo and behold, the fetalysis patients were indeed all cured! They stared around at each other and around the room in wonder; they had been disconnected from the real world for so long.

When Liara Grae awoke and saw Haus, Marius, Lark, and Raoul in front of her, she made a little smile at them. "Thank you for saving us all." Then she said, "Raoul, I'd like to speak to you in private, if you please."

Her brother's face darkened with his habitual change of expression every time his sister asked to speak with him alone. Nevertheless, he could not refuse his leader; and so he walked off with her.

"Please, have a seat," she said to him. Cautiously, he did. Undiscouraged by Raoul's usual coldness towards her, she beamed and said, "Raoul, whilst I was in the fetalysis state, I saw your father."

Raoul started, remembering that Lark had said a similar thing to him about hearing Phinn's voice. Regardless, he said, perhaps with pride and an attempt to reassure himself, "All right. But I hope you are aware that that was what your mind conjured during your coma state."

"I'm not so sure about that," she said, still beaming. "He told me that you and he used to go diving to catch shophers, kaytwirls, and many other sea laminae. And once you wanted to challenge yourself and went after an ekleki." Ekleki (Eh-kleck-kee) were bigger than the average fish we eat, and had luminous fins and scales; it could also emit electric shocks. "Then the ekleki shocked you and your father had to resuscitate you with an anti-shock potion, and thankfully you were back to normal again before anyone else noticed." She smiled. "So that your mom—our mom— wouldn't find out and ban you from going diving with your father again."

All through this narrative, Raoul stared at her with an incredulous look on his face. "How did you know—I've never told anyone about this before, and I've never recorded this experience."

Liara shrugged. "I told you your father's spirit came to visit me for real. He told me to tell you about this experience, and some others that no one else knew about in case you didn't believe me. Should I tell you more of these experiences?"

"No, that's all right," Raoul said, thinking of all the other embarrassing things that had happened and he couldn't believe that his sister now knew all. He said with widened eyes, "Then what else happened? What else did he tell you?"

Now her smile shrunk to a small and awkward one. "He said—that our mother and my father are truly innocent. That our mother had loved your father all along till his death, and loves him still. In fact, your father had wanted my father to come and take care of our mother so she wouldn't be lonely in this world after he had gone."

All of this was so sudden that Raoul didn't know what to say. The stubborn part of him didn't believe it, even though he had always been curious and open-minded towards the phenomenon of spirits from the dead visiting the living. He asked, "My father really said this all?"

"Yes. And if you still don't believe me, then I would have to reveal all your other personal stories."

"No, no, please don't," Raoul said, and was forced to conclude, "I believe you."

Lark, Raoul, Liara, Haus, and Marius now had to deal with the Liara clone still tied up at Raoul's place. "What should we do with her?" Haus asked. Nobody answered. They assumed they would make a decision when they got to Raoul's place.

Yet, to everyone's shock, the bed where Raoul had deposited the clone was empty. They searched the whole house, but that particular Liara clone was nowhere in sight.

The real Liara knit her brows. Lark pressed his lips together, and said, "Is there anywhere else she might have escaped to?" He glanced up at the genuine Liara.

The leader of the Rarerus returned his look with a smile. "She could be anywhere out there, but for now, we will just have to be wary of any other—copies of me. If she chooses to reappear, she will definitely come back."

Lark looked askance at her, his expression full of disapproval. "Then how will we know who the true Liara is? Shall we run DNA scans on you every time we meet?"

"If necessary," Liara replied.

Raoul, who was standing opposite his sister, folded his arms across his chest. "Mind if we do a check on you now?"

Haus shot him an indignant look. "Really, Raoul? Our leader was fetalyzed! I'm sure the Arach wouldn't subject even their clones to something like that."

"Yeah," Marius agreed, though he sounded less certain than Haus did.

"It's all right." Liara held out her arms so that she was wide open. "Do the test."

Lark was again the one who administered the test. To his partial surprise, this Liara truly had no bluamine or zanyliline in her DNA. Lark displayed a deep frown. "You are the real one, I suppose."

Liara nodded with a light smile.

THE DAY AFTER THEY DISCOVERED THAT THE CLONE HAD disappeared from Raoul's house, Liara heard a tap on her door in the room she was resting in at the Rarerus center. Liara rose from an orb chair to let her friend in. She grinned with an inexpressible pleasure. "Alia."

Her nonbinary Rarerus ally beamed back at her and even tilted their head in a way that was quite endearing to Liara. Alia was clothed in waves of aqua blue, and looked especially lithe and strong today. They wrapped a hand around Liara's wrist, and whispered, "Let's talk somewhere private."

Liara laughed. "This room isn't private enough for you?"

Alia shook their head. "Anyone can disturb us at any moment. Please, let's go somewhere else. I'll drive you there."

The softness of Alia's voice cast Liara into an aura that was cool and soothing as water; and she assented.

The two slipped into the Glass, and Alia flew them to the Cinta forest; the dark green shapes of the trees gathered together, emanating some unspoken promise into its silent depths.

Alia gestured for Liara to sit down on a rock opposite Alia, just outside the forest.

"Well?" Liara asked.

Alia grinned with a certain elation. "Liara, I know this will sound extremely odd to you, but—I visited your look-alike at Raoul's house."

Liara widened her eyes. A second passed before she spoke again. "Alia, do you know how she escaped?"

Alia avoided her gaze for a moment, and then looked back at her. "Yeah...some friends of hers helped her get out. Goodness knows how they managed to break through Raoul's security systems." Alia's eyes began to shine with an even stronger effulgence. "But that's not the important part. The crucial bit was that she says she knows what the Arach are on about. She—for some reason, does have bluamine and zanyliline in her genome, at least, according to Lark's and the Arach's tests."

Liara furrowed her brows. "That means she is an Arach clone, right?" She had been certain that the Liara who escaped from Raoul's home was the Arach clone of her, but Alia's joyful manner made her doubt her assumption. She also didn't understand why Alia would let that other Liara abscond with her "friends" in the first place, so the original Liara queried her nonbinary friend on this.

Alia said, "First of all, I was outnumbered. They were seven, not including your counterpart, while I was by myself. Second of all, that Liara promised me before her friends came to fetch her that she would give us some secret information from the Arach. I do not think she is an Arach clone, despite any evidence to the contrary; and she doesn't think she is one either. What's interesting is that the Arach believe she is their clone, and thus, they trust her to a certain extent."

"But what secret information would she be willing to provide?" Liara asked with a doubtful expression.

Alia answered, "The Arach are cautious, so they never give any particular clone too much knowledge. But so far, they let her know the Arach's next target locations."

"So this Liara clone—or not clone—let you know using her computer communication system?" Liara enquired, still amazed.

"We exchanged contact codes," Alia confirmed. "Uh, her code is exactly the same as yours, except it has a '2' at the end."

Liara's lips quirked up in amusement. "She's the second me."

"That's a good way to call her, the second Liara," Alia said. They gave the "first Liara" a look. "So are you up for this? We can discover some valuable information."

Liara frowned. "I'm not sure about this."

Alia's face fell a bit, and they sighed. "I knew you wouldn't be willing." They continued, "But we've got to. And even if you don't want to go into this, I'm going to go into it." Alia's gaze was defiant.

Liara smiled. "And I have no right or power to stop you. You're a free person."

"That's right."

The Rarerus leader deliberated for some time, before saying, "Okay. I'll join you on this—quest." Then she fixed a harder stare on her friend. "But the moment it's clear that this is too dangerous for you, I'm pulling you out."

"Ha," Alia said with a laugh. "It can't be any more dangerous than the regular missions we go on."

"Perhaps," Liara conceded. "But you do understand that this is quite extraordinary, right? Nothing of this sort has ever happened before. We should talk to Raoul, the Beams, Jax, and many others too."

Alia Lyreal cast an earnest glance at her, and tightened their lips with a vague displeasure. "Is that really necessary? As you said, this is dangerous, so the fewer people embroiled in this endeavor, the better." They hesitated for a moment. "Most importantly, we shouldn't bring Lark into this."

Liara lifted both her eyebrows. "Why Lark in particular?"

"The second Liara said that the Arach can sense something special about him. They know something momentous will happen with him. His fondal shapeshifting and profound scientific abilities are only the tip of the iceberg," Alia replied.

"I see," Liara said slowly.

Without thinking, Liara reached out and clutched Alia's hands in hers. Alia flushed but didn't try to evade her gaze. A tenderness, but also exhilaration, threatened to bubble out of Liara's being; but she curbed it before that impulse could take over her senses. Instead, she squeezed her friend's hands with a sisterly warmth, and said in a determined voice, "Wherever you go, Alia, there I will be. Let's go get those Arach."

The radiant smile that came over Alia's features touched Liara's heart and soul. "Thanks, dear. We will emerge victorious."

At Alia's words and gaze, Liara's insides hummed even more deeply with an inexplicable, secret tension; she felt hot, cold, cool, and warm all at the same time, as if a cascading chaos were rushing through her entire body. Liara inhaled a large gulp of air, swallowed, and said, "Alia, don't leave me, okay?"

Alia Lyreal widened their eyes and tilted their head at her. "Why would I leave you?"

Liara gave them a smile. "There may come a time when you'll want to."

"That time will never come," Alia promised.

Liara glanced down at their intertwined hands. "I hope you're right." She still couldn't name the strange tide swirling in her, but she didn't want to confront it either. At least not now.

"But Liara," Alia began, and Liara looked up, startled, scared about what misgivings her friend might have with her. Alia said, "Since you consider me a good friend, you shouldn't keep such important things like the Rarerus treasons from me. I know you feel a responsibility as the Rarerus leader to keep everyone safe, including me, but look what your secrecy did to you!" Alia leaned in a bit closer to Liara, while their hands were still joined; a feeling of anticipation surged up inside Liara in addition to that secret tide; it was all so intense and even a little maddening.

The nonbinary scientist and combatant, probably unaware of the delirium they ignited in their friend, went on in a soft voice, "Dras and those other nine traitors might have truly run away for good, but who knows if they'll return one day to seek revenge? I don't like seeing you hurt, Liara, Rarerus leader or not, so even if you don't want to tell anyone else about something like this, please at least tell me." They gave her an urgent look, as if waiting for her to give them that reassurance.

Liara gazed at them with a deep affection, and whispered back, "I will."

Alia smiled, then drew their hands out of Liara's grasp and rose to their feet. At Liara's alarmed eyes, Alia grinned and pulled her up too. They threaded an arm through Liara's and said, "Let's take a walk through the forest like the old times, eh?"

That fantastic thrill and intoxication in Liara's frame were still there, but she was eager to take this trek with Alia. Besides, they were alone with no one to interrupt them.

EPILOGUE

L ark was now aged eighteen. He had been through many more Rarerus missions, so many that he couldn't count. Some were easy, some were much harder, and some were as life-threatening as the first two adventures he had when he was five. The Arach never seemed to give up, and they kept making more and more clones.

What was worse, was that the Rarerus still couldn't fathom the Arach's motives. The Arach could be after world dominion, though Lark doubted they would want something that crass and simple, unless ruling the world was a means to some other end.

Another possibility was that the Arach were simply malicious and enjoyed anti-mattering humans, or that anti-mattering victims was what they were naturally inclined to do, just as it was natural for ordinary viruses to infect living things and make them sick.

Or maybe the Arach wanted to take revenge on human beings for some grudge that wasn't noted down or was wiped out from the historical records.

Alternatively, the Arach could be working for a hidden boss or organization. If so, what would be the motives of this boss behind the scenes?

Or, if the Arach all had individual motives, then what had caused them to band together against the human race on Drell?

Did the Arach target inhabitants of other planets too?

Another grievance of Lark's was that after seeing the immense, one-kill destructive power of the chrystacience guns, the Rarerus voted to ban the use of these guns once and for all, as they were too dangerous to keep around. One could accidentally kill a fellow member—and in such a cruel way—with just one slightly misdirected shot.

Apart from the prohibition of such a powerful weapon, Lark was also frustrated that their Rarerus detectors could not reach most of Drell, and he had asked—though it sounded more like a demand—Liara to set up more stations with Rarerus detectors. They did not need to construct whole new Rarerus branches or recruit more members. They could simply plant these instruments in innocuous places, like the underground. Haus and Marius had asked him what if the detectors were found by Arach clones? Or devoured by burrowing laminae?

Lark replied that that was a chance they could take; the worst that could happen if a clone found it was that the clone would destroy it. No harm done to the Rarerus except for money lost. As for the burrowing laminae issue, detectors were too tough to chew and too big to swallow anyway.

Since Lark's suggestion was reasonable, Liara ordered more Rarerus detectors to be installed in many areas around Drell, and this increased their efficiency in stopping more Arach and saving more people; Liara beamed proudly at this growing boy.

Yet, this boost in detection ability also meant that they needed more Rarerus members, so they went wild to enlist even more people with potential, setting up a rising number of science clubs, combat clubs, and military strategy clubs to scan for those with promise. Lark himself recruited a number of new scientists—he was uninterested in the combat or military strategy clubs; science was still his only real interest.

Though all the new Rarerus scientists gawked inside at how serious, and antisocial this boy was, they all came to respect him, as they learned that even at this young age of eighteen, Lark was already one of the best scientists in the Rarerus, due to his intense and obsessive daily studying. So while some young recruits resented Lark for being so antagonistic and cold towards them (as he was towards most people), the others admired him and aspired to study as fiercely as he did, vowing to become just as great as he was.

To Lark's credit, he had already become a little less antisocial than he was when he was five; being in the Rarerus forced him to learn a bit about cooperating and getting along with other people. But, being Lark, he only learned the bare minimum to cope in the Rarerus; thus, the people who didn't understand him tended to either fear or dislike him, which was quite a shame. It seemed he would never become as popular as people like Karrin, Raoul, and Liara.

Lark still didn't have any friends at the age of eighteen. Raoul, Liara, Haus, Marius, and to some extent Karrin, could be considered his "almost friends." Lark was probably closest to Raoul, as he was the one who most understood and appreciated Lark's scientific meanderings of thought. Liara, Haus, and Marius could appreciate and comprehend these meanderings too, but Liara was the busy Rarerus leader, and Haus and Marius were not nearly as patient or affable as Raoul; and of course, Karrin was not the least bit interested in science.

Now Karrin, as you may have expected, grew up to be one of the most popular members in the Rarerus; he made friends with almost everyone. He was a bit like Raoul in his sociability, except he was bubblier, more childish, and more hyper. Outside of the Rarerus, Karrin became the best of friends with Eeera, and the two were almost always seen together; it was a wonder that he could still keep the Rarerus a secret from her, but he had to do so for the sake of protecting his friend.

The other main children in the Rarerus, Amber and Eventii, were now aged twenty-five and twenty-one respectively. They continued to lead and were well respected by all, though Amber was a little bossy just as she used to be when she was twelve. Eventii was still the milder but shyer one. Together, the siblings balanced each other.

And speaking of siblings, Raoul and Liara, now thirty-nine and thirty respectively, became different towards each other. The truth took some time for Raoul to digest and get used to, but he eventually swallowed his pride, became cognizant of the full impact of his mistake, and apologized and begged dearly for his mother and stepfather's forgiveness, for having doubted and hurt them for so many years. Most of all, he begged for Liara's forgiveness, especially as out of all people, she was the one whom he had hurt the most.

So after all that awkwardness, Raoul gradually changed his attitude; it was hard and strange to get out of his habit at first, but slowly he grew to be more amicable and even good-humored towards her.

The Rarerus members who did not know the siblings' family history before were astonished when Raoul and Liara revealed that they were not lovers, but half-brother and half-sister. Amber was quite disappointed because she couldn't tease Liara anymore. But everyone else laughed and treated Raoul with even more respect than before, being the brother of their most beloved leader.

Going back to Lark, you might be surprised to hear that Lark's parents, as well as Karrin's and the other children's parents, were still cleverly fooled by the science trip or other disguises, such that they never discovered that their children were involved in a perilous cause. Karrin, Lark, and the others also took care not to let their family or acquaintances see their greatly improved speed, stamina, suppleness, or strength.

Despite hiding so much from his parents, Lark had witnessed so many horrors of too-late rescue missions and antimattered victims, that he learned to treasure his parents more, as they too might be captured and antimattered one day without warning. He became less grudging, and grumbled less when Graham and Kreesha dragged him to their sports games, though he still refused to participate.

When it came to the Arias's desserts, instead of finishing them and sprinting immediately back to his room as if the desserts were a mere energy charger, he would say, "That was good. Thank you. May I have some more, please?" Kreesha and Graham were ecstatic that their son had at last seemed to appreciate their capabilities, just as they had always cherished their son's scientific ones.

Lark used his facility in science to the full when he worked with the other Rarerus scientists to make new weapons, shields, healers, vehicles, and all sorts of cool technological items; or to vastly improve current ones.

But the most intriguing project of all, was when Lark and the other scientists found out how to give fifteen-year-olds the power to shapeshift using the fondal, and this maximum age of power acquisition increased every year. It may or may not surprise you as well that these fondal bodily changes, both the physical and extra ones, seemed to be permanent. Karrin and our protagonist retained the ability to transform at will.

And little did Lark know, that by the time he was twenty, he would recruit his own band of young shapeshifters, and they would become his lifelong friends.

———

"I'M HAPPY FOR YOU," ALIA SAID TO LIARA WHEN THE PAIR flew to a lake in the Glass to rest from their Rarerus duties. Alia was referring to Raoul's much ameliorated treatment of her, but Liara couldn't help but wonder if they meant something else as well.

Liara grinned with a lightness of heart. "Yeah, it's great."

A silence ensued where the two sunk into their thoughts.

Then Alia said, "Liara, about the second Liara—"

The first Liara raised her eyebrows. "What about her?"

Alia Lyreal shot her a smile that was almost shy. "She's got new information for us. It's finally something other than more Arach activity predictions."

All throughout the years, though the second Liara maintained a helpful and friendly demeanor towards both Alia and the first Liara, all the second Liara gave them were indeed just forewarnings of Arach attacks, where many of the attacks were aimed at specific Rarerus members. Alia and the first Liara always averted these attacks without arousing anyone's suspicion of how they foresaw the assaults. Liara made it look natural and logical that they would figure out these Arach schemes against these Rarerus members.

This power of foreknowledge could not protect the Rarerus members that the second Liara was not informed about, however, and the second Liara had to keep some of the things the Arach told her a secret, in case the Arach should find the first Liara and Alia's predictive abilities a bit too potent, and suspect that there was a spy in their midst.

The second Liara was also like the vast majority of the Arach clones: she was not informed of the Arach's true purposes behind antimattering people, nor did she know what antimattering would do to living things. Furthermore, the second Liara was utterly clueless about who the central control Arach were.

The original Liara now urged, "What did she say?"

Alia replied, "She told me that the Arach are going to try something different, and this will unfold about two years from now."

Liara gaped. "What thing are they going to unfold?"

Alia looked away for a second. "She didn't say anything more specific. She just said it was a new approach in the way they'll do things. And what's interesting is, we human beings may never find out what this is."

Liara was exasperated. "Why bother telling us if what the Arach will try to implement won't even be detectable to us? Unless the new thing will bring us extra harm, of course."

Alia nodded. "The second Liara thinks it might be harmful, but it might not be. Who knows?" Then their gaze tightened. "But you're not too bothered that the second Liara gives me a lot more information than she gives you, right?"

Liara made a smile. "I'm fine with it as long as you relay everything she says to me."

Alia let out a sigh of relief. "Good."

An awkward silence spanned out between them. Liara shifted her feet on the grass and soil; then she stretched out to hold one of Alia's hands, and stroked it gently. A strange feeling burned deep inside the nonbinary scientist at the caress. Over the years, Liara and Alia had become—more physically affectionate with each other, so that whatever they had between them became even harder to define.

Alia let out a cough. Liara looked up from their clasped hands. The nonbinary scientist and combatant sent her an abashed glance, and turned to stare out into the lake, as if they were determined not to meet Liara's eyes.

Liara couldn't help but start laughing at this all. Without looking back at her, Alia asked, "What's so funny?"

"Nothing," the Rarerus leader said. After a moment's pause, Liara continued, "The second Liara didn't say anything more about Lark, did she?"

Alia's shoulders relaxed, as though they were relieved that Liara didn't talk about the mysterious thing that hung between them. They shook their head. "Nope. As usual." They rubbed a thumb thoughtfully over Liara's fingers, in a flow of natural warmth. Their gesture pleased Liara, but also made her nervous; a current of electricity swam through her veins, profound and absorbing. Liara took a deep breath, and said:

"Alia?"

"Mmm?"

Liara gripped her nonbinary friend's hand more tightly. "You know I'll always love you, right?"

Alia hesitated, then chuckled. "I do. And I love you too. I'm like your second Raoul."

Liara hid a smile. "My love for you is different from my love for my brother, though."

Alia was silent, and gazed down at the ripples closest to them on the lake. "I know. We're—not related, after all, no matter how close we are."

Liara stared out at the lake as well. "Yeah. Of course. But—" She sighed. "I don't know. I guess all I want to say is, you're very important to me, and my life wouldn't be as happy or as meaningful without you in it." She added quickly, "I know I'm being sappy, but—"

Alia laughed. "It's not sappy. It's—sincere. And I appreciate it. I'm thankful that I've got you too, even if my gratitude isn't always apparent."

Liara suppressed a smile at that. But though she was happy with Alia's reply, she wasn't quite satisfied. She didn't understand what that discontent was, but she tugged at Alia's hand and said, "Are you tired?"

Alia's gaze flickered over to hers; the eyes of the nonbinary scientist and combatant harbored a kind of uncertainty, like a liquid moon beam that quivered with emotion. Alia answered quietly, "Not really." Then they sent Liara a certain glance. "But are you?"

Liara's frame suffused with lightness and a heady delirium. "Yeah."

The two of them lay down and rested some distance away from the lake. When their heads touched the soft grass, Liara whispered, "Close your eyes." Alia did so, with a sweet smile. Liara wrapped her arms around Alia and shut her own eyes too. "Sleep tight," she said. Their computers would alert them if any danger came nearby, but for now, Liara just wanted to enjoy this moment.

She vaguely wondered if things might have been different if she were not the leader of the Rarerus. Could she and Alia have been closer? Would this lingering feeling of dissatisfaction in the midst of their happiness be gone? As she thought about these things, Liara kissed her friend's cheek, and caressed their hair with a tender love. They would figure out what they were to each other one day.

GLOSSARY

Warning: Major Spoilers Ahead!
N.B. Word pronunciations will be in brackets.

CHARACTERS

MAIN CHARACTERS

All ages below are in Drellian years. See "Time[1]" under "Quantitative Measures" for how to convert Drellian years to Earth years.

Lark Arias ("Ah—rye—uhs")

Age: 5
Protagonist of the story
Blond hair, blue eyes, average height, and relatively skinny

Karrin Treek ("Care-rin")

Age: 5
Lark's classmate
Brown hair, sea-green eyes, and of average height and weight

Kreesha Blé ("Blay")

Age: 28
Lark's mother and Graham's spouse
Long, red hair and bright green eyes

Graham Arias ("Ah-rye-uhs")

Age: 29
Lark's father and Kreesha's spouse
Reddish-brown hair and blue eyes

Raoul Faya ("Fye-ah")

Age: 26
Liara's half-brother, Ustella and Phinn Faya's son; a lead scientist in the Rarerus, Lark's mentor, and one of Karrin's mentors
Tall and slender with brown hair and brown eyes

Liara Grae

Age: 17
Leader of Rarerus, Raoul's half-sister, Ustella and Orlen Grae's daughter
Rather tall with long, golden-orange and yellow hair. Her eyes are a luminous blend of blue and green, her face has an impression of being angular, and her skin is quite pale

Haus ("Haw-s")

Age: Late 40s or 50s
One of the four Scythes, and Lark's first initiator into Rarerus

Marius

Age: In his 60s
    Also one of the four Scythes and Haus's friend

MINOR OR SECONDARY CHARACTERS

Hlen Treek ("Len Treek")

Karrin's father and Ella's spouse
    Brown hair and sea-green eyes

Ella Treek

    Karrin's mother and Hlen's spouse
    Orange-brown hair and green-gray eyes

Alia Lyreal ("Ah—lie—ah" "Lee-ree-oll")

    A Rarerus scientist and combatant leader, as well as Liara's close friend. Alia identifies as neutrois and androgynous, and goes by the pronoun "they."

Alyssha Juess

Age: 3
Evervessa and Dron Juess's daughter

Evervessa Juess

    Alyssha's mother and Dron's spouse

Dron Juess

    Alyssha's father and Evervessa's spouse

CHARACTERS

Eeera ("ee-rah")

Age: 5
Karrin's friend and classmate
Long chestnut-brown hair in a ponytail, pale green eyes

Amber

Age: 12
One of the two Beams and Eventii's sister

Eventii ("Even-tie")

Age: 8
One of the two Beams and Amber's brother

Phinn Faya ("Fye-ah")

Raoul's father and Ustella's first spouse

Ustella

Raoul and Liara's mother; Phinn's and Orlen's spouse

Orlen Grae

Liara's father and Ustella's second spouse

Lilla Blé ("Blay")

Kreesha's younger sister

Rai Arias ("Rye" "Ah-rye-uhs")

Graham's younger brother by two years

Braiven ("Brye-finn")

Age: about 25
A Rarerus mission leader
Tall and stout

Centuri ("Sen-chew-ree")

Age: about 70
An elder member of the Rarerus

Jax

Age: 30
Previous leader of the Rarerus

Pree

Age: In her 30s
Lady at the bookstore that is the entrance to the Breemil branch of the
Rarerus

Glia ("Glee-ah")

Age: In her 20s
A researcher in the Breemil branch
Light-orange hair and green eyes

Deana

Age: In her 20s
A researcher in the Breemil branch
Black hair and sky-blue eyes

Topps

Age: In his 20s
A researcher in the Breemil branch
Black hair and grey eyes

Ace

Age: In his 20s
A researcher in the Breemil branch
Black hair and brown eyes

Bulwark

A senior, advisor, and combatant in the Rarerus who died ten years ago in battle. There is a large emotograph of him attired in yellow in the Breemil branch.

Yearlie ("Year-lee")

Age: 8
One of the fighters (the girl) selected to be in the Rarerus, along with Karrin and Gastra

Gastra ("Gah-strah")

Age: 12
One of the fighters (the boy) chosen to be in the Rarerus, along with Karrin and Yearlie

Monna ("mawn-nah")

Age: In her 50s
One of the Spikes

CHARACTERS

Fabil ("Fae-bull")

Age: In her early 20s
   One of Liara's attendants

Renore ("Rin-nore"—rhymes with "pour")

Age: In her mid-20s
   A Rarerus mission leader who is relatively close to Liara, and one of the most adept at understanding and interacting with older members

Dras, Martha, Osso, Scrimen, Ussaz, and five others

The ten traitors in the Rarerus
Dras has a prominent scar on his left ear

Carla

Liara's friend who works in selling land to tenants

Irri ("ee-ree") and Traeph

Two members in the Rarerus that the traitors wanted to kidnap

Criva ("Kree-vah")

Age: 5
One of Karrin's male friends; Criva invited him to join the combat club

Snizis ("Snee-zis")

Age: 5
One of Karrin's male friends; Snizis showed him the musical jumping panels in the Arach hideout

1. **Cores**
   1 core = 2 hours

   Calendar Days, Months, and Years
   It takes Drell 25 hours (12.5 cores) to spin around once, which means that one day is 25 hours. One month is 30 days, as the closest moon, Iyis ("eye-yis"), takes 30 days to orbit Drell. Finally, one year is made up of 13 months, since Drell takes 13 months to orbit its sun.
   To convert a Drellian age to an Earth one, first of all, one Drellian year is 13 months = 390 days = 9750 hours. One Earth year (assuming it's not a leap year) is 12 months = 365 days = 8760 hours. Thus, one Drellian year is 9750/ 8760 = 1.113 (approximately 1 and 1/9) times an Earth year.
   The legal "adult" age is 20 Drellian years, which is 20(9750/8760) = 22.3 Earth years old. So you could say that Drellian adolescence lasts longer than ours.

   Names of Calendar Months
   These months, from the first in the year to the last, are named Lighteth, Drellieth, Lamineth, Seallien, Skyrus, Falleth, Raineth, Soareth, Dynamel, Walketh, Grasseth, Pinketh, and Lifeien ("Lye-fee-inn").

   Decaweeks and hexaweeks
   On Drell, instead of a seven-day week, they count in terms of a ten-day week, called a "decaweek," or a six-day one, called a "hexaweek."

PLACES

THE SECTORS

There are 70 sectors on the planet Drell. A sector is like a country, a big piece of land. The term "intersector" means across all sectors, or across more than one sector; intersector is thus a bit like "international" on Earth. Each sector is grouped with several other sectors to make a super-sector. There are 9 super-sectors in all. (See map at the beginning of the book.)

In addition, there are 3 oceans and 7 seas. The "oceans" are only called oceans instead of seas, because they are the main bodies of water surrounding or touching the smallest super-sectors, Jadice, Swirnis, and Bayta ("Jae-dis," "Swer-nis," and "Bae-tah.") Arguably, the Achelée Sea ("Ah-shuh-lay"), or even the Geranian ("Jer-ray-nee-inn"), should be called an "Ocean" as well, because they touch so much of Jadice. But the namers of these waters probably wanted a smaller, more focused center to be the "Oceans" area, so only Plutoria, Cadra, and Dapono ("ploo-tore-ree-ah," "cah-drah," and "dah-poe-noe") were included. Achelée and even Wilophera ("will-oh-fair-ah") were excluded.

Fartha

This is the sector that Lark and Karrin live in, and is about 2 cores (4 hours) slower than Vénus in time zone difference.

Vénus (pronounced "Vae-nis")

Where the Rarerus Center is located, and is about 2 cores (4 hours) faster than Fartha in time zone difference. Many intersector events take place in Vénus. Despite the aura of grandeur and dazzle that surrounds Vénus, especially when viewed through the eyes of outsiders, Vénus itself looks exactly the same as any other place on Drell, with buildings, greenery, soil, etc.

If you take the Coaster from Fartha, it only takes about one and a half cores (3 hours) to get to Vénus.

There is a Fleming Park ("fleh-ming") where Alia, Liara, and Raoul meet for the first time. There's also the Cinta ("sin-tah") forest where Liara and Raoul meet Jax for the first time.

Oftonoss ("Off-tin-noss")

Contains Larence, and the Larence branch of Rarerus. The Larence branch is the one that reported the greatest number of Aira dancing molecules, as well as recent Arach activity at the same time.

Darra ("Darr-rah")

Contains the Miha branch of Rarerus, the first branch to arrive at the Larence branch for the Aira dancing mission.

Eirloe ("Air-loe")

Famous for manufacturing beauty; the best Drellian beauty products are made. Put simply, beauty is valued above all in this sector.

Ishiri ("EE-shee-ree")

The island sector where the Rarerus goes to obtain a chemical called lepraun, which helps Liara and the other fetalysis victims return to normal.

Itheris ("ith (rhymes with "pith") – thur – rus")

The sector next to Ishiri. Itheris is where Lark's closest friend in the world whom he will meet many years later, lives.

PLACES INSIDE THE SECTORS

Phuore ("foo-oar-ray")

In the Fartha sector. Where Lark goes to get par-the-air.

Vermint

Also in Fartha. Alyssha and her parents live here.

Dillois ("Dill—Lwah")

The city in Fartha where Karrin, Lark, and Eeera live.

Bricalo ("Bri (rhymes with "Brit")-cah-low")

A place in Fartha with a water world that Alyssha went to. Water worlds are amusement parks with all sorts of water-related games, rides, and entertainments for Drellians, especially for children.

Breemil

In Fartha. Site of the Breemil Rarerus branch where Haus, Marius, and Raoul work. Raoul's house is in the Breemil area too. Described as a pleasant, verdant landscape covered with bluish-green grass.

Larence ("lair-rens")

In the Oftonoss sector. The Larence Rarerus branch is the one that reported the greatest number of Aira dancing molecules, along with recent Arach activity.

EVERYDAY PLACES

The Houses

Drellian homes are usually quite big, but in the chapter "The Fight and Struggle," the Arach victim's home was especially big: sixty something people could stand in it and fight!

Back and Front yards

In the front and back of your house. You can choose whether or not you want fencing around them.

Water Worlds

Amusement parks with water-related games, rides, entertainments and the like. Children especially love them.

Bookstores

Books are shown via computer projections. Like on Earth, they are displayed by their book covers, some more beautiful, some less so, depending on your taste in covers.

OBJECTS

FOOD

Trooflées ("true-flays")

A bright green, shiny, rubbery, and soap-bar shaped snack. Sweet enough to make you happy, but not too sweet to repulse you. Karrin asked Lark if he wanted one.

Kraeks

A crunchy, brownish-yellow and golden snack. According to Kreesha, Lark seems to "respond relatively favorably" to this.

Ruminence ("roo-min-nens")

A spring-green, gelatinous, semi-liquid and frosty dessert that Kreesha and Graham specially made for Lark—it was their new creation, but it made him nauseous and sick.

Sheavus ("shee-vis")

Yellow food with a strong and strange smell that Kreesha made the day before she and Graham made the Ruminence. Kreesha suspected that the Sheavus may have reacted with Lark's green chemical to make him sick.

Angielle ("ann-gee-yell")

A blue and white creamy and swirly food that Graham made the day Kreesha made her Sheavus.

Apple-like fruits

Drellians don't have apples per se, but they had some similar looking fruits.

Genetically Designed Fruit

Drellians have the technology to design their own fruit using DNA technology.

USEFUL EVERYDAY OBJECTS

Floating Lights

Floating lights are used instead of streetlamps. These lights float independently, like strong hovering bubbles that will never pop.

Liquid Mirrors

Liquid mirrors are literally silvery mirrors in a liquid state, bound into the shape of a looking glass by strange, electromagnetic forces; liquid mirrors are not uncommon in Drell.

Electronic Maps

Electrically powered maps you can carry around. It will show you where you are exactly on the map, and tell you how much distance you still have to cover to get to your destination.

Liquid crystal airborne maps

Haus flashed up such a map from his computer. These maps hover in the air like a sheet of liquid crystal.

Hovering Buttons

Or just "buttons." These buttons exist in the air and you just press them. They are like buttons you can press on the computer, except these buttons are for machines that are not computers.

Elastoropes

Ropes that can be stretched a very long distance.

Metallic ropes

Not chains. Much stronger than chains and with no holes.

HOUSEHOLD OBJECTS AND PLACES

Washroom

Like our own. There's a tub for bathing.

Living room

Also like our own.

The Culinary

Their kitchen.

Beautiful flowers in a tube filled with water

An ornament. You can put this on a floating panel.

Grey Beam

This beam is used to neutralize any excessively acidic or alkaline substances.

Stretch Seats

Can be stretched out onto any surface, to a long length (1, 1/2, or 1/4 qworts, i.e. 4, 2, or 1 meters). They are held up securely in the air by strong magnetic forces.

You can adjust its texture, level of softness or hardness, the location of the armrests and backs, and the lengths and shapes of these armrests and backs. You can also compress the stretch seat into a small enough size for carrying. So furniture is easily transported when you have to move into a new house.

Stri Seats (Stri rhymes with Dry)

Stretch seats with fancy structures designed on them, for decorative or other purposes. Liara has a stri seat.

Orb chairs

These chairs mold themselves perfectly around the sitter's back to ensure maximum comfort, and have armrests as well; but they can't change shape or size like stretch seats can. Nevertheless, orb chairs are beautiful, smooth, and full of grace, just like a tough but supple jelly.

Floating Panels

Floating panels, like stretch seats, are held securely up in the air by strong magnetic forces. These panels can be used as tables, seats, supports, or simply useful surfaces. You can't adjust their texture or softness, and there are no appendages, and thus they are cheaper than stretch seats. But you can compress the floating panels into a portable size just like with the stretch seats.

Nightlights

Like ours. Small lights for those afraid of the dark when they sleep.

MUSICAL INSTRUMENTS

There are some musical instruments involving strings. Some people like to use string from an instrument to tie their hair, to give their hair an "air of music."

MISCELLANEOUS OBJECTS

Shrim strip

At Haus's shop, there is this long, narrow, and flat object gleaming with a bronze color called a shrim strip. Apparently, outsiders have to rub it on their forehead to mark them as "not an intruder" before they can enter the backrooms of Haus's shop.

Metallic Craters

Metal shaped into craters. They are really as tall as craters, enough to kill you if you fall from the top.

Pipes

Still used in Drell to transport liquids. But they are always kept clean and anti-rusting agents are used on them. In fact, pipes in Drell look quite attractive.

Vorte Cup ("vor-tay")

Vorte is one of the sturdiest materials in Drell. Lark once imagined what it would be like to pour lava into a vorte cup.

Bubble balls

Size of a young child's palm; bubble balls are rubbery, bouncy, and range from opaque, translucent, to fully transparent and can be any color. Karrin was juggling a light blue bubble ball.

Chrisjaras ("kris-jair-ruhs")

A toy that Alyssha's mom bought her. She wanted to tell Karrin about this new toy of hers.

Roads

Roads in Drell are sometimes paved with a color, like the purple road leading to the Rarerus Center.

CHEMICALS

· · · • ● ● ● • · · ·

THE DIFFERENT KINDS OF CHEMICALS

Fondal ("fond-dull")

A recently discovered new crystal arrangement. At first glance, this seems like a complete disorder, but once you grasp its pattern and equations, you will find that there is a definite perfect organization to it. It has a number of functions, including:

1. making explosives, and flames of different colors and shapes
2. making water that contains a special mineral. This mineral dramatically boosts your physical traits of stamina, speed, strength, and suppleness.
3. giving one the ability to acquire any type of physical adaptation that exists in nature, for instance, camouflage, wings, armored skin, or claws to burrow underground or attack enemies.

Brachiorsor ("brack-kee-oar-sore")

This chemical looks like a small chrysalis swimming in purple liquid. Haus claims that he and his friends need to use brachiorsor to "seal their loyalty to each other." Specifically, the brachiorsor will convert nitrogen and other strange chemicals in the air into octamethyst and trichloroes.

Nitrogen + Some other chemicals in the air + Brachiorsor Octamethyst + Trichloroes

Octamethyst is a purple pigment "and a fixing agent" (this fixing agent part is not true—Haus was just making this up); trichloroes is a green pigment and an energy generator. Haus said he needed the energy generated by trichloroes to "boost his intellectual abilities," to help him win the "Great Annual Game" against his friends to write the best poetry or draw the best picture. The "prize" was apparently something that looked like a pink ticket.

Yet, to do this chemical reaction, brachiorsor needs a fuel—par-the-air.

As well, you can make a brachiorsor barrier by mixing brachiorsor with octamethyst, trichloroes, and par-the-air.

Octamethyst ("oct-tah-mee-theest")

See "Brachiorsor[1]" under "The Different Kinds of Chemicals"

Octamethyst is also used to digest and destroy Arach webs, but it only works if the web is not fully solidified yet. The octamethyst also takes quite a while to do its job. If the Arach successfully kidnap the victim again before the octamethyst finishes, they will lay a new egg which will start forming another web.

With two webs to handle this time, the octamethyst will now only slow down the progress of the overall web—the overall web will keep spreading. More octamethyst is needed to digest the web faster than the two eggs make the web. (For some reason, the Arach prefer to have only one web egg working at one time, and the reason why they would lay a second one is because the octamethyst is about to consume the old egg anyway.)

After the web is completely digested, the octamethyst will break down and become excreted by the body. So, in a way, it's better to have some web remaining when the victim is kidnapped again, so that there will still be some octamethyst left to slow down a new Arach web.

Additionally, octamethyst can be mixed with trichloroes, brachiorsor, and par-the-air to form a brachiorsor barrier.

Trichloroes ("try-clor-roes")

See "Brachiorsor[2]" under "The Different Kinds of Chemicals."

You can also use trichloroes, with brachiorsor, octamethyst, and par-the-air to create a brachiorsor barrier.

Par-the-air

The chemical Haus asked Lark to get for him. This is a pink liquid with a very high boiling point that fuels the brachiorsor.

Par-the-air can be used to make a brachiorsor barrier, when mixed with trichloroes, octamethyst, and brachiorsor.

As well, par-the-air, when mixed with amosti, can create chrystacience (the green substance). If the chrystacience is made to a high enough concentration using a chemical compressor, the chrystacience can become a weapon that kills the enemy with a disease.

Amosti ("Ah-moss-tee")

Amosti can glow in the dark when it is dipped into ice.

When mixed with par-the-air, it can form chrystacience. If the chrystacience is of a high enough density, it can make whoever is blasted with it die of disease and illness.

Chrystacience (green substance) ("kris-stay-shens")

Produced from amosti and par-the-air. If made to a high enough density using a chemical compressor and put into a gun, anyone blasted with this high-density chrystacience will die immediately of disease.

Brachiorsor ("brah-kee-or-soar") barrier

Use trichloroes, brachiorsor, octamethyst, and par-the-air to make a brachiorsor barrier. This barrier doesn't last very long, though.

These barriers can be used as an abnormally strong shield to protect the user from very dangerous chemicals, for instance, when making a very high concentration and volume of chrystacience, which can kill by touch. These barriers can be used to defend against enemy attacks as well, even against fire.

A group of chemicals: the Troptomyces ("trop-toe-mye-s")

The medics claimed that the green substance (chrystacience) that Lark made was troptomyces, though Raoul disagreed.

These troptomyces chemicals will cause the rare disease charmia, which causes great fatigue, as well as some different symptoms depending on the individual. For instance, Kreesha had migraines and difficulties in breathing; whereas Lark suffered from nausea, uncontrolled crying, and narcolepsy.

Lepraun ("Luh-prawn")

Found on Ishiri. Give this to fetalysis patients to drink and they will wake up from their trance.

CHEMICAL APPARATUS AND OTHER THINGS

Inoculation

A process to make a chemical non-toxic, non-corrosive, non-flammable, non-explosive, non-irritant, etc. This turns the treated chemical into an acceptable "kiddy chemical." However, some chemicals are way too powerful to be inoculated.

Inertizer

Coats a chemical and makes it inert, or as inert as it can get. You could coat a container with inertizer.

Expanding Container

Can expand indefinitely. If you put in a chemical and heat it, its steam will be trapped inside this container, because this container will keep expanding like an endlessly stretching balloon.

Forceful Electrolyzer

An instrument that forces chemicals to return to their original reactants, i.e. force a reaction to reverse itself. This doesn't always work, however.

Chemical compressor

A device you can use to press the particles in a chemical closer to each other, thus elevating its density. Lark and company used a chemical compressor to greatly heighten the density of chrystacience, which made the chrystacience into a one-hit killing weapon.

The Computer

Apart from the many other functions a Drellian computer can do, it can do the following things for a chemist:

- extract a precise amount of any chemical, and place this where you want it to be
- mix and react any chemicals together, heat up chemicals, collect products, and any other chemical manipulations
- erect a transparent shield to protect the user from spills and gases.

It also has a robotic arm and hand, where the user can control it to touch and fiddle around with chemicals however they like in safety. The robotic arm and hand will transfer all tactile sensations to the user's arm and hand, so that it is almost the same as touching the chemical with your own bare hands.

Barrier gloves

Like the computer's robotic hand, except more direct. They are literally gloves but they offer a great amount of protection from the chemical that the user touches.

Containing and carrying around chemicals

Nobody, not even expert chemists, would keep chemicals inside their computer pouches for too many hours; there's no telling what will happen if any chemicals leak out of their containers while the person is walking around. Some containers for chemicals are highly sturdy and hard to break, but you can never be too careful.

Instead, people keep chemicals inside a large room behind a protective barrier where the flasks can be seen, or people only carry the chemicals in computer pouches for a short period of time, say, three hours max.

CHEMICAL PHENOMENA

Aira dancing

This phenomenon is when cells or molecules move in such a way, that they look like they're dancing airily, dancing in the air, or dancing like air spirits.

Aira dancing happens when the cells or molecules are stimulated by something, chemical, or electrical. But sometimes, this dancing happens even in the absence of stimulation. Haus has a theory that in these latter situations, they are still being stimulated; it's just that we don't have the instruments to detect these stimulators or stimulations yet. Perhaps they are of a different wavelength or dimension so we can't see them yet—we're not even aware of their existence.

The Moon Dance

A name Raoul gave to the orbiting activity and gravitational forces of the moons near Drell. This activity happens to be the approximate reverse of the Aira dance.

Neuronal Movement

Drellian scientists discovered that neurons can actually move and migrate at certain times.

---

1. **Brachiorsor ("brack-kee-oar-sore")**
   This chemical looks like a small chrysalis swimming in purple liquid. Haus claims that he and his friends need to use brachiorsor to "seal their loyalty to each other." Specifically, the brachiorsor will convert nitrogen and other strange chemicals in the air into octamethyst and trichloroes.
   Nitrogen + Some other chemicals in the air + Brachiorsor Octamethyst + Trichloroes
   Octamethyst is a purple pigment "and a fixing agent" (this fixing agent part is not true—Haus was just making this up); trichloroes is a green pigment and an energy generator. Haus said he needed the energy generated by trichloroes to "boost his intellectual abilities," to help him win the "Great Annual Game" against his friends to write

the best poetry or draw the best picture. The "prize" was apparently something that looked like a pink ticket.

Yet, to do this chemical reaction, brachiorsor needs a fuel—par-the-air.

As well, you can make a brachiorsor barrier by mixing brachiorsor with octamethyst, trichloroes, and par-the-air.

2. **Brachiorsor ("brack-kee-oar-sore")**

This chemical looks like a small chrysalis swimming in purple liquid. Haus claims that he and his friends need to use brachiorsor to "seal their loyalty to each other." Specifically, the brachiorsor will convert nitrogen and other strange chemicals in the air into octamethyst and trichloroes.

Nitrogen + Some other chemicals in the air + Brachiorsor Octamethyst + Trichloroes

Octamethyst is a purple pigment "and a fixing agent" (this fixing agent part is not true—Haus was just making this up); trichloroes is a green pigment and an energy generator. Haus said he needed the energy generated by trichloroes to "boost his intellectual abilities," to help him win the "Great Annual Game" against his friends to write the best poetry or draw the best picture. The "prize" was apparently something that looked like a pink ticket.

Yet, to do this chemical reaction, brachiorsor needs a fuel—par-the-air.

As well, you can make a brachiorsor barrier by mixing brachiorsor with octamethyst, trichloroes, and par-the-air.

ELECTRICITY

Drellians have invisible power sources installed in their indoor spaces that cost nothing. All the energy comes from nature, including the sun and wind. Thus, all appliances and electronics, when placed indoors, are automatically charged up.

But if you are outdoors, you don't have that electricity power up. Thus, you may fully charge your device indoors, but once you step outdoors, the energy level depletes gradually until there's no more. So you need to bring a portable charger.

THE PORTABLE CHARGER

Karrin's charger is a black blob (warmagotchi-sized) that you can squeeze. Gas comes out, streamlines and thickens into a liquid, which plunges into the device, spreads, and seeps into the device.

TECHNOLOGY

...●●**⬤**●●...

Signal Bell

You press this at the door of a building to announce your arrival to the people inside.

Memoria

This helps in generating a kind of permanent memory. The memoria is a feature in the computer. It's a code that sends electrical signals to your neurons and other brain cells to make your memory permanent. You choose the exact thing (target) you want to remember, which prevents you from remembering any extraneous and unwanted things, like the smell of food wafting into your nostrils at the moment you were learning something new.

However, your brain hurts if you use the memoria too much for an extended period of time. But different people have different levels of stamina. Some people can do one core (two hours) of nonstop memorizing. Some can do only half a core (one hour). Thus, you must rest for a while until your brain stops hurting, before using the memoria again.

You can also delete unwanted memories that were acquired using the memoria. You probably can't delete naturally formed memories, though.

The memoria is how even five-year-olds can know so much already about science and other things. Therefore, people like Lark who spend a disproportionate amount of time studying would be able to become an expert even at the age of five, albeit just a mini-expert who knows more than the average adult does.

Thinking Speed Restorers

If you take the right dose as prescribed, you will boost your thinking speed to the optimum (overly fast thinking will make it hard for you to concentrate on anything) for five hours, which is more than enough for a person, since a brain usually only slows down during the afternoon.

However, these restorers only slightly boost thinking speed for sleep-deprived people. Sleep deprivation restricts the boost to only a tiny increase. So if you're sleep deprived, you will have a lower-than-optimal thinking speed no matter what.

Permanent Thinking Speed Enhancement Surgery for Mental Illnesses

There is a free health service for those born with lower thinking speed to increase it to a "normal" speed of thought. As they can now think as quickly as "normal" people do, they can also function more effectively in society and not suffer the ridicule, teasing, shunning, and prejudice from others for being "slow."

Emotographs ("EE-moe-toe-graphs")

These are like 2D photographs, except there are certain color and graphic effects that can convey the precise emotion you want. This is like a very advanced and precise kind of expressionist painting.

Money Configurators

You can configure an amount of money that can only be spent on a certain thing or type of thing. For instance, you could configure a sum of pocket money to make it only spendable on books.

Graphic Design software

You can press keys, draw or scribble on pads, etc. to create your design electronically. But you can also use your voice to speak to and ask the computer to do things for you. You can even connect to and deliver your mind's images to the computer.

Unfortunately, the mind image communication is not so successful because images from the imagination tend to be very blurry. But the few people with very clear and detailed imaginations tend to do better with this approach to the graphic design software.

Computers in General

A computer is an invisible or transparent air network. It is normally invisible, but when you want it to become visible, it becomes a white, silvery, and transparent network in front of you. These computers can follow you everywhere if you choose to bring them.

They can often be voice commanded, even if you speak softly; just articulate clearly. Computers are quite intelligent at interpreting ambiguous vocal signals, and are usually even better than humans are at interpreting speech. Of course, you can also press buttons, use joysticks, draw or touch things on the computer air panels (airborne keypads) if you wish—or just control everything by voice. But sometimes it's easier to communicate using your hands or visuals instead of by words, so you might want to use these tactile or visual techniques instead.

You can also command the computer using your thoughts and mental images. However, this method can be difficult as thoughts tend to be interrupted very frequently by distractions, which may confuse instructions to the computer, or even lead to the wrong commands.

Computers have such a massive memory that it feels infinite. Apart from their amazing memory, computers are also almost indestructible. Very few viruses and bugs can affect them, but even these are easy to exterminate.

Communication via Computer

The contacting function is built into the computer. You can use holograms, two-dimensional faces, just voices, just words, or just images. More than one person can participate in the conversation, of course, in any of the above forms of communication.

Automatic note-taker

Whenever you want to take a note, you can tell the computer precisely what you want to jot down, and in what file, what subtitle, what category, etc. You can put it in the regular 2D files or the 3D files. When you call up a file, document, or note, it can turn into any color, size, or font you want.

Books and Electrospaces

Drellians still read their books in words (whether by looking or listening to the words), not in direct mental images or any other fancy nonverbal modes of communication—though fancy nonverbal books are available to those who want them. Drellians also think, like some of our Earthly friends, that written words are too beautiful to eradicate, no matter how ambiguous and flawed in expression they are. And often it's because they're so opaque and able to be interpreted in so many ways, that written language is so endlessly attractive and interesting. So Drellians (and the many generations of human beings before them) decided to continue the writing of words in their culture.

Books are electronically stored, so they're like our e-books. There is basically infinite storage space—not literally infinite, but the memory is so massive that it feels infinite for all practical purposes.

Such electronic books can be read directly from the computer, where the computer projects a page of words in front of you like a phantom book; there is also no backlight, so your eyes can read comfortably. Alternatively, you can put the book into an electrospace. Electrospaces are like e-readers, except the shape and size of the screen and device, as well as their thickness, can be changed any time to your liking. You can ask the computer to hold the electrospace for you too, if it ever becomes too tiring to hold up yourself. There is also no backlight on electrospaces, for the same reason as detailed above.

Plus, the books' pages are automatically adjusted to the person's comfort. The word sizes, fonts, and spacing can be controlled either via words or touch panels. If you want to turn the page, you just need to signal to the computer in some way: press a button, touch a screen, make a gesture, nod, tap your hand on your knee, say something, etc. You program the signal you want to use.

3D Recorders

Will record a hologram of whatever object or living thing you want. You can also turn on its smell or touch (or even taste, if applicable); touching this hologram will let you feel the original texture of the thing. 3D recorders can even capture the objects' sounds.

Computer pouches

Computer pouches use space tunnels, space pockets, space wells and the like to carry around physical objects within virtual, electronic space; and computers can easily retrieve these physical objects whole when the user needs them. However, once again, these carried objects must be portable-sized, so you can't carry a house or a large vehicle with you— excessively large objects can damage the computer. Similarly, carrying way too many albeit portable-sized objects can also damage the computer.

Nonetheless, even with these size and number limitations, Drellians rarely have to hand-carry anything they bring anymore, unless they want to, or if they didn't bring their computer. Some people still like to carry bags with them, though.

How to Carry Around Computers

Drellians who want to take their computers out of their house wear a special wristband. This wristband has a small glass capsule that stores a few of the person's skin cells; these cells have the person's DNA that the computer can track and follow.

An electromagnetic tag on the wristband attracts and directs the computer's attention to the skin cells inside the glass capsule. This capsule contains nutrients that sustain the cells like an agar jelly petri dish, and the glass cover of this capsule is well aerated.

The reason why Drellians use such wristbands instead of directly letting the computer track their body cells, is simply because it's better safe than sorry. Having the computer laser-scan your skin cells (with an invisible laser) almost every moment of your every day, is not a risk computer designers or medics want anyone to take. It's true that cancer treatments are easy on Drell, but getting that much direct daily radiation from the computer that frequently, might cause unforeseen or even unknown health problems. So it's much safer to have the computer keep track of the skin cells in the wristband instead.

Thankfully, ordinary computer use on Drell will not release any radiation.

How Someone Can Take Your Computer Away From You, and How You Can Get It Back

If someone wants to remove your computer from you, for confiscation or more sinister reasons, they can simply pull off and steal away your wristband. These confiscators or thieves can't use your computer, however, because your computer will only recognize and react to your voice, thoughts, touch, and body movements.

Having your wristband taken from you simply means that your computer won't know where you are, and will stay put where it was the last time you were wearing your wristband. Once you recover that wristband or get a new one (it's cheap to buy and the wristband automatically absorbs some of your skin cells into it the first time you wear it), your computer will soon find and rejoin you.

One may ask why Drellian scientists didn't find a way to make these computer wristbands non-detachable by everyone except by the wear themselves. Yet, the only way that could happen, is if the wristbands were embedded into the skin. Both Drellian scientists and the Drellian public, were generally opposed to the idea of embedding anything inorganic into the body, for fear of unknown consequences, as everybody knew that there was much about the universe that scientists still did not know. Drellians didn't require things like prosthetic limbs or cochlear implants anymore either. Medical technology was advanced enough to easily fix any physical defects, with stem cells and other materials and equipment.

So it was better to take no risks and wear the wristbands like our watches. And Drellians obviously didn't want to bind the wristbands on too tight, as that would be uncomfortable as well as bad for the wrist's blood circulation.

Nevertheless, as in all societies, there were some rebellious scientists who did research studies that involved inserting or embedding inorganic things into the body anyway. Even the Rarerus used technology to attach hand beams securely into the fighters' skin.

How do Computers Move?

Drellian computers move via virtual space technology that involves complex physics and mathematical models, algorithms, and formulae, including: vectors, matrices, imaginary numbers, and much more.

Magnifying Viewers

Simply a function in the computer to help you magnify something, like a chemical you're studying.

Virtuals

Similar to virtual reality, but are for shows, movies, and the like. You can go inside these virtuals and feel the physical environment (but be protected from e.g. excessive heat or cold) of the show or movie, but the characters and creatures in that show or movie will never be able to touch or see you.

Films and Movies

Drellians have moving pictures as well as virtuals, because people don't always want to immerse themselves bodily into that movie. Sometimes they just want to see it quickly.

Propellers

Not treadmills. Propellers generate virtual reality paths: you can choose what kind of environment to run in, and can actually cover distance because your environment changes. You can thus use a propeller to train yourself physically. A trainer can also watch how fast you're running.

The default running landscape is of a yellow, dusty, and sandy path with the sun shining overhead.

Physical Appearance Change

Parents can choose to genetically alter their baby's physical appearance before they are born. People can also choose to genetically alter their own physical appearance at any time.

Yet, most people don't bother changing how they look, because in Drellian society, it is at last acknowledged that there are an uncountable number of different beauty standards in the world, none of which are more popular than any other, so that overall, everybody is equally beautiful but in their own unique way. This uniqueness of one's beauty standards is clearly involved in spouse selection, as people tend to choose someone who is very beautiful according to *their* ideals of what "beautiful" looks like.

WEAPONS TECHNOLOGY

Elastoropes

Ropes that can stretch to any length when you throw them.

Guns

Guns in Drell don't need reloading. They only need to be charged with electricity.

Epics

Long blades with golden, orange, or yellow glowing edges. When you press a button, the blade becomes a series of short golden flashes that slash the enemy at a distance.

Hand Beams

These are attached to the wrists by being locked into the skin, and are transparent and invisible to the naked eye. Hand beams are the same as guns, except that you only need to *will* them to fire, so they are more efficient than guns. The sensor in this hand beam device will detect your brain cell (neurons and glia) signals, so when you very clearly and unambiguously desire to fire, it will fire.

Inoculation (for weapons)

Makes weapons harmless for practice fights, like for the fights in the Rarerus combat clubs. The weapon will stop just an inch away from the attacked person's skin, so it won't touch or hurt them.

SUPERPOWERS

Flight

Drellians can't create flight, because human beings are simply too heavy, and of course nobody would volunteer to become hollow-boned.

Energy Beams and Eye Lasers

Drellians are also unable to make eye lasers or energy beams, because the human body is just too frail: if you try to create any kind of energy release big enough to shoot out of the body and do damage to opponents, it will inevitably destroy your body tissue; and generating that magnitude of energy would very likely burn and kill too many cells that it ends up killing you.

Invisibility

Invisibility can't work on humans either, because how can you voluntarily make all your cells and proteins turn transparent? And what about your clothes? Drellians have to rely on invisibility sprays to change the configuration of photons around a person to hide them; in short, making it so that the person does not reflect light and thus is not seen, but without creating a shadow of lightlessness either.

Teleportation

As for teleportation, Drellian scientists managed to do an extraordinarily complex mathematical maneuver, to transport all the atoms of a human being, lamina, another life form, or an inanimate object, to another location, using something like space tunnels.

Space tunnel technology is analogous to traveling through the center of the earth from the United States to Mongolia. They are short cuts. These space tunnels and mathematical calculations simply warp a person or a thing to another location in almost an instant, with the person or thing intact.

Yet, to teleport without a machine is unthinkable. How can you diffuse your atoms and access those space tunnels by yourself? Those space tunnels are apparently some kind of mathematical and physics trick. They are something like imaginary numbers and negative numbers where the thing is "not real," yet it works in real life, one of those many strange and miraculous paradoxes in math and physics.

What's more, teleporters consume a tremendous amount of energy to work, so the Rarerus don't use them too often, and only teleport over short distances. That's why they ride on Hyures, Coasters, and other vehicles to travel to farther places.

Though energy is technically "free" indoors, such a huge consumer of energy as the teleporter needs a special device to capture and hold this gigantic amount. This device is very expensive and will overload and break if you try to transport people over excessively large distances. Also, though no one can teleport too far due to the limits of this energy-holding device, nobody knows if such a gargantuan energy absorption into the teleportation machine will permanently damage the environment somehow.

Extra-sensitivity

For extra-sensitivity, scientists can for example tweak the genes coding for eye proteins a little bit to improve eyesight to a small degree; or tweak with the eardrum for better hearing, etc., but all improvements are rather slight. They are noticeable improvements, but they are not so significant as to constitute new abilities; they aren't even substantial enough to produce any improvements in your life.

Physical Speed, Stamina, Strength, and Suppleness

Tweaking with muscle fibre genes improved these athletic abilities a little bit, but nothing big ever came out of it. That is why everybody is so excited about the fondal; nobody understands how this chemical can do it. It seems that the fondal minerals can somehow self-assemble, self-organize, self-replicate, and self-direct in precise ways to affect the body's molecules to substantially enhance physical functions.

Yet, the above explanation is just a vague guess at the operations of the fondal. The fondal minerals do move their atoms and bonds around, have the ability to break and form new bonds without any energy, affect different body molecules to affect other molecules, etc., but the 3D recording of what these minerals do biochemically to these body molecules is not clear.

Scientists can see what exactly is moving when and where in the body under fondal influence, but they don't really understand the interactions and happenings that are going on; they also don't understand how these strange interactions and operations in the body have anything to do with enhanced physical function. So, they can see everything, yet they can't make sense of anything they're seeing.

Telepathy

For other superhuman abilities, telepathy is not yet possible either. Even if you can miraculously brain-scan anyone you meet on the street just by looking at them, you won't be able to read their mind. You might see relative brain activities in specific areas of their brain, or even the activities of specific brain cells, but none of this would mean anything. You could deduce general things, like whether the person is experiencing pleasure in a situation or not, or whether they are actually paying attention, but nothing specific.

Drellians do have handheld neuroscans, where you can aim at a person's head, and in a second or so, be able to have their brain scan; but these neuroscans, as expected, are illegal, and are only permitted to be used by the Order and some authorized organizations like the secret Rarerus. Also, even if you can read a person's thoughts, how can you communicate with the person telepathically? How can you create thoughts and images inside another person's head?

Telekinesis

As for telekinesis, scientists are also clueless. Perhaps if you can control the air particles around a person's arm, you can make the arm move wherever you want it to, but how can you control air particles in the first place? Even a machine would only be able to manipulate some air particles within a certain vicinity, and they can't actually "control" the particles; they can only influence them in some ways, like energize them and make them move faster.

Experiments with magnetic and gravitational forces didn't yield any results either in moving other people's bodies at a distance. Machines can move people, as seen in the suction soarers, using magnetic forces, but they only move the whole body, not the individual parts of bodies. Yet, a person by themselves have no ability to generate any magnetic force big enough to move other people.

Shapeshifting

Shapeshifting is an equally elusive ability: how can you make a whole new set of genes, turn on certain genes, and turn off certain genes by yourself? Even machines can't do it. Machines can only do tiny things with genes, like change eye color, or alter the shapes and sizes of facial features.

Wish Granting, Precognition, and Time Travelling

Wish granting, precognition, and time travelling are simply impossible for Drellian scientists.

COMMUNICATION TECHNOLOGY

Contact Codes

Drellians can communicate with holograms, just voices, just a 2D face, just words, or just images.

Each individual can choose their contact code, which is a combination of letters and numbers, as long as no other person on Drell have this code. When you change your code for whatever reason, you can select the people you want to inform of your code update: this means you can throw off undesired contacts as well.

Sometimes you can communicate with people even without knowing their contact codes, as long as you can reach into that place you want to contact, and that place is set to welcome outside communication.

Signatures and Documents

For signatures to give consent or agreement to documents and terms, you only need to present your finger to the computer to take down your fingerprints, and send it to the person's document to give that consent or agreement.

MEDICAL TECHNOLOGY, DISEASES, AND DISORDERS

Old Age and Longevity—and No More Alzheimer's

Drellians live up to a natural age of a hundred.

They will physically deteriorate, but thanks to medicine, will stop deteriorating at a certain point until death.

Many Drellians choose to die at their natural age, because they want rest and peace after such a long life. Many on Drell believe in an afterlife too.

Yet, some Drellians choose to use longevity pills, which can extend to a maximum of fifty more years (no longer due to some ethical reasons.) These Drellians might want to stay awhile and help others, help society, etc., because they think going to "rest" so soon is selfish.

Cancer treatments

Cancer is now easily treated at a low cost!

Deafness and Blindness

Very cheaply and easily cured

Krutcher's

Arms and legs become limp; it's very hard to sit up, let alone walk. Thinking slows down so much that the mind is almost blank.

Charmia

Rare disease caused by a group of chemicals called troptomyces. Troptomyces's influence is abnormally strong as it can penetrate through any ordinary lab barrier. Charmia manifests itself in different symptoms in different individuals, but it always causes extreme fatigue.

Fetalysis ("fee-till-lye-sis")

Fetalysis patients, like a "fetus," are almost totally locked away from outside stimuli, and the person can usually only react to internal stimuli, like in the uterus. As "lysis" implies, their cells are split so that they have tiny ruptures in their membranes.

But the brains of these patients are not dead. In fact, there is very intense and swift communication between brain cells (both neurons and glial cells) in areas with high densities of fetalysis abnormal cells. Thus, these patients are always in a frenzy of thoughts and feelings, but we don't know what exactly they're thinking or feeling. We can only see their cell activities and brain activations.

Scientists hypothesize that abnormal cells are touching their membrane ruptures together to form channels, to communicate with each other in a special way. Indeed, these cells swing around, align channels, but then swing away again very quickly. And indeed, lots of cell signalers, cell receptors, and molecules are transferred through these channels.

All of this inter-channel activity reminds one of bacterial conjugation, where bacteria make a bridge between each other and transfer DNA. Are abnormal cells like bacteria? Nobody is sure.

Yet, though there are extra chromosomes in these abnormal cells, no strange new proteins are formed.

There were fetalysis patients in the Rarerus labs because Liara believed that fetalysis patients might have something to do with Arach antimattering, though Rarerus scientists found no bluamine or zanyliline in these fetalyzed individuals.

Permanent Thinking Speed Enhancing Surgery for Mentally Illnesses

See "Permanent Thinking Speed Enhancing Surgery for Mentally Illnesses[1]" under "Technology."

Anti-shock potions

You can use this to cure someone who was electrically shocked; for instance, someone who was shocked by an ekleki (a lamina.)

FORBIDDEN OR SECTOR-CONTROLLED TECHNOLOGY

Invisibility sprays

These are forbidden to all except for special organizations like the Order and the Rarerus, so that people don't try to spy on others in private places.

Human Cloning

Human cloning is usually forbidden, for ethical reasons.

Lock picking using lasers

Instead of picking a lock with a piece of wire like on Earth, some Rarerus specialists can use their hand beam lasers to open a lock.

---

1. **Permanent Thinking Speed Enhancement Surgery for Mental Illnesses**
   There is a free health service for those born with lower thinking speed to increase it to a "normal" speed of thought. As they can now think as quickly as "normal" people do, they can also function more effectively in society and not suffer the ridicule, teasing, shunning, and prejudice from others for being "slow."

FASHION

Hair Ties and Strings

Some people like to use strings from their musical instruments to tie their hair, so that the latter would have an "air of music" to it.

CLOTHING

Dracana ("druh-cah-nah")

A loose-fitting garment with long sleeves commonly worn in the fall.

Iminis ("imm-min-nis")

Can be of different textures and thicknesses. Lark's is black, furred, and rough in texture. But most other people prefer wearing smoother and gentler Iminises. The Iminis that Liara wore when Lark first met her was deep green.

Creema ("cree-mah")

A silky and soft one-piece attire. Alyssha and her mother Evervessa Juess were wearing Creemas when Lark met them in the Coaster.

Vrillion ("Vrill-lee-inn")

A garment known for its cool, refreshing fabric that is especially suitable for moderate temperatures.

LAMINAE

Laminae are the non-plant creatures on Drell, analogous to our Earthly animals.

Velocip ("vay-loe-sip")

Four legs and paws, yellowish-white fur; claws, sharp fangs, long pointy ears, with a muzzle. Carnivorous.

There was a painting of a velocip on the ceiling in the building where Lark got his par-the-air.

Chresins ("Kree-sins")

Winged, million-legged (it *looks* like it has a million legs) laminae bugs that are very common on Drell. Graham found some in green slime on the wall outside his house.

Urlassen ("urr-lah-sin")

Brown with glossy fur. Round and plump body. Four legs, with huge thighs and tiny paws—their legs taper from their big thighs to their small paws. Height of a pony. Blue eyes. Tail looks like rags pasted together. Its two ears look like wrinkled thick cloths. Conical muzzle with the kind of taper that reminds you of their legs. Quite fast runners, but not very strong.

Soarrows ("soe-air-rows")

Sparrow-sized. Velvet blackish-purple. Bright eyes. When their saliva hardens, which is about one second after their drool touches the air, this liquid forms rocks. Thus, soarrows can use these saliva rocks to attack their enemies. Soarrows readily produce their saliva too; so combat soarrows are like fighter jets dropping their bombs.

Thorands ("thor–RANs")

Like horses, but with translucent and smooth skin.

Myrtles ("mer-tulls")

Like foxes with pinkish-white fur.

Drings

Like small birds with bright red or green feathers.

Shopher ("show- fer")

Streamlined sea laminae with shimmering scales and fins

Kaytwirls ("kay-twirls")

Five limbs, smooth bodies. Also sea laminae.

Ekleki ("Eh-kleck-kee")

Bigger than the average fish we eat, with luminous fins and scales; it can also emit electric shocks.

BUG CONTROL

Drellians invented technology to keep bugs away from their towns and cities without killing these creatures, as it is unethical to destroy another species without a very good reason.

PLANTS

Quimemoris ("kwi (sounds like "quit" without the "t" sound)-mem-more-is")

The plant that Lark was contemplating while waiting for Alyssha to come out of the washroom.

Auna ("Aw-nah")

Type of tree, mainly used for decorative purposes. There are some in the Ramisen enclosure in the Breemil branch of Rarerus.

These trees are beautiful in their dignity, grace, and something else. They have lovely green-grey trunks, and a cloak of misty, wispy leaves. They have an aura of "silver" as well. Auna means "island in the snow."

Acaija ("Ah-kye-jah")

Willowy trees with crisp, bright-green leaves. Lark and Raoul saw a lot of these in Vénus before entering the Rarerus Center.

Chrystacias ("Kris-stay-shas")

Blue, purple, and lilac flowers that Kreesha bought to plant in their front and backyards to form a protective ring around their house.

DRELLIAN SOCIETY

THE STATE OF SCIENCE

The Rapidity and Stunning Number of Scientific Discoveries

Even with the memoria to help the Drellians, there are countless more scientific discoveries made every single day on Drell than on Earth. It was already impossible to keep up with everything on Earth. So on Drell, think of how much more impossible it is to keep up, even for the top scientists in a specialized field.

So, even though there are some "more major than usual" discoveries, there will always be a portion of even the top scientists in that field who have not heard of some of these major findings, because there are too many "more major than usual" discoveries made so often.

LOVE AND RESPECT FOR MACHINES

Drellians believe that machines deserve kindness and respect too, especially as there is no proof that machines can't feel or have a consciousness just like human beings do. Some Drellians even call their machines by affectionate names.

THE DRELLIAN SCHOOL SYSTEM

Their Assessment Methods

Unlike many of our twenty-first century school systems on Earth, Drellians didn't use any grading systems (e.g. A-F, or 0-100%), because grades were an incomplete, inaccurate, and sometimes even arbitrary measure of one's true ability, not to mention that grades created an unnecessary social hierarchy amongst children.

Instead, in higher education, when school committees decide which applicants to accept into a particular program, the committee would ask applicants to either prepare a project, write a paper, compile a portfolio, or complete another task relevant to the program; for instance, a portfolio of sketches for a specific visual arts program.

The committee reviews these productions, and accepts the applicants who present work of the best quality; the accepted quality level depends on the competitiveness of the school's program, and it must be admitted that judgment was subjective. If your work happened to suit the tastes of the committee members, you would have a higher chance of getting into the school.

Some programs also ask applicants to come in for an interview, to see how the applicant interacts with people (which is especially important for social service programs like teaching); how competent the applicant is at on-the-spot critical thinking; and how they are at other skills that interviews can assess.

When Assessments Happen

School assessments occur during the selection of applicants into institutes of higher education, and again after the student completes their higher ed program, to check if they have an adequate mastery of their field or fields of study. Any further education beyond higher ed is optional. Seeking institutes beyond higher ed, i.e. advanced education, once again requires one to do a school assessment to get into the institution, and another assessment to verify that the student has deeply understood what they learned in their advanced ed program. Higher education itself is optional too, but since higher ed degrees are necessary for many jobs on Drell, most people enroll themselves in higher ed anyway.

Throughout the higher education program and throughout school prior to higher ed, schools regularly give students some assessment tasks and interviews, so that students can gain practice in these, and also get an idea of how well they are doing in their subjects.

However, these mid-program and mid-school assessments are purely to garner practice and self-knowledge; they are not for selecting students, and teachers do not assign any grades, marks, or even "pass/ fail" decisions, though students who did poorly (in the teacher's opinion) would get some extra help and guidance. But even students with satisfactory or distinguished performance would receive feedback on their strengths, weaknesses, and suggestions for improvement, as Drellians believe deeply in the value of constructive critiques.

Assessing Current Ability Rather Than Past Performances

Therefore, school assessments on Drell are arguably more accurate measures than our system of grading, because Drellian assessments test your current level of ability rather than your entire history of high to low performances throughout school. This way, students feel more comfortable making mistakes and "flunking" sometimes: only your present competence at the time of testing matters. Plus, we learn an abundance of lessons from our mistakes.

In this, Drellians are present and future-oriented; the past doesn't matter except in how much it trained you to grow to the skill level you are now at.

How Employers Select Job Applicants

Out in the occupational world, employers also select their applicants using these present-focused methods of evaluation. As well, employers always use interviews, since they clearly want to make sure that the applicant is someone the employer can enjoy working with. Or at least, employers want to hire someone with a personality that is tolerable to them.

How to Motivate Children to Do Their Homework Assignments

Without the grading system, then, teachers and parents motivate their kids to complete homework tasks for the sake of the future, because practice makes perfect. Parents and teachers remind the students that to enter certain schools or jobs, students would benefit from getting as much training in their skills as possible. No one wants to fall behind.

Choosing Subjects

Children don't begin to narrow down their subject choices until their mid-teens, which is similar to what many of our schools do, where we pick our courses for grades 8-9 and then again for grades 11-12. It is not impossible that a child later finds that they want to go into a subject that they have dropped. At first glance, this child may be at a disadvantage compared to their peers who had chosen "the right field" the first time. But, with extra hard work and extra time, the child can catch up.

Children, especially younger kids, may want to skip over or skimp on homework tasks for subjects they don't enjoy, but teachers would still urge them to try their best even for subjects they dislike. This is because the child may realize afterwards that they do like the subject, after all, and regret not having acquired the practice needed for this area of interest.

Or, the child may discover that their field of interest requires skills from subjects they don't particularly like. For example, a child who wants to go into science but hates math, would still need to train up their math skill and understanding to a level sufficient for their specific area of science.

Training Courses in Open Institutes

If one does not get accepted into their program, school, or job of choice, they could either apply elsewhere, or take individual training courses at open institutes, to enhance their skills in those particular subjects, so that they'll have a better chance at getting accepted the next time they apply. And unlike in our society, there is no stigma against taking these open courses. Most people have at least a modicum of respect for those willing to acquire extra training to boost their abilities.

THE NAMES OF ACADEMIC DISCIPLINES

You might have been wondering why Drellians would still use some of our academic categories on Earth, like psychology, chemistry, biology, and physics. Firstly, these terms simply indicate the "level" of complexity for the subject under study. Physics involves the study of fundamental matter, energy, and their interactions; chemistry focuses on the structure, properties, and transformations of substances; biology is about living organisms and their processes; and psychology studies mind and behavior, to name a few examples on this continuum from the most basic to the most complex subjects.

Thus, these names of academic disciplines just mark a certain "level" of study on this continuum; this type of categorization is simply a social convention that most on Drell follow, though others like to use different categories. For example, some like to put what we call "physics" and "chemistry" in the same group, since they both talk about the physical, material world that is not necessarily living.

Next, one reason why Drellians still had professions like "psychologist" and "chemist," was because most people favored certain categories on that continuum of complexity over others: Lark liked the complexity level of chemistry best, for example. Many people were happy to hold more than one title, e.g. both a chemist and a physicist, if they had wider interests. But most professionals would only pick one academic discipline to specialize in, as there was obviously a great deal to learn within any one discipline already.

At the same time, Drellians did not have the danger of overspecialization or developing tunnel vision from these academic divisions, because scientists and other experts regularly talked to those outside their fields, to gain interdisciplinary insights. Even experts as antisocial as Lark was would eventually recognize the value of such inter-field discussions.

NATURAL OBSESSORS

Natural obsessors are people like Lark who are supremely obsessed with one thing, uninterested in everything else, and tended to hate humanity, or at least be astonishingly indifferent to humanity. Some psychologists call these individuals the "natural obsessors," though some experts prefer to use a more pleasant sounding term.

However, some other psychologists think that it's very prejudiced to call a particular personality by a special name; because by doing so, it's like saying they have a mental disorder, that there is something "wrong" with them—but there is clearly nothing wrong with them! They can live very happily and healthily just the way they are, with their one life obsession and their shunning of fellow human beings, and being perfectly content with that.

There are, of course, lots of psychologists who argue that natural obsessors are suffering from a mental disorder, because their condition ("their personality!" the other psychologists correct them) necessitates their having no friends. Absolutely no friends, though some people may still grow to love them and hope that they will one day love them back. And having no friends is obviously impacting their psychological and social sphere.

A lot of debate then raged up about how "having a social life" had become an essential thing in life. Why do you need it? Of course, it's very good for preventing depression, protecting against stress and early death, and it boosts your immune system. Yet for these natural obsessors, their immune system is perfectly fine, and their likelihood of developing trauma, depression, stress-related diseases, etc. is exactly the same as the rest of the normal population's—no different from the average normal person with an average number of friends and social contacts.

So these "natural obsessors" are just a very strange phenomenon. They do seem to be naturally self-sufficient. Their only problem is that they don't fit in with society. The only problem is that other people are bothered by their extreme obsession with one thing, and their perpetual unfriendliness, coldness, and unresponsiveness.

But it is true that some natural obsessors, like Lark, whose realm of obsession does not require a lot of physical activity or much outdoor work, may be physically a bit weaker, and have a weaker immune system than the average person. This is not because they are in this "unhealthy" category of "natural obsessors," though, but because they simply don't spend much time outside, or much time exercising.

Of course, there are some natural obsessors who handle themselves very well by exercising. (Just because they're obsessive doesn't mean they're stupid. They too can acquire knowledge about basic health, and understand that they have to eat well and exercise enough, sleep well, etc.) But then there are some natural obsessors, like Lark, who don't bother exercising. Not because he's lazy, but because he's too drawn to his one great love.

The natural obsessor expectedly finds it extraordinarily hard to disengage from their favorite activity. They have to be literally torn away from their work. Perhaps they would kick and scream, but no matter. And since they have a harder time than most people do in disengaging from tasks, they just have to work extra hard to disengage themselves anyway, because they later learn that to succeed or survive in life, one has to balance oneself a little bit.

People explain to them that if they want to carry on doing the thing they love best, they had better learn to take care of their health, so they do so. But kids like Lark don't quite understand yet, so they don't trouble themselves with exercise. Also, some natural obsessors, just like a lot of "normal" people, understand that they need to exercise, etc., but they still don't anyway! That is why they tend to be physically less fit. However, these natural obsessors are the same in fitness as an average inactive "normal" person.

And when I say Lark was ultra passionate about science, I meant both a) He could not live without science, could not survive without science, could not imagine a world without science; and b) He loved science with an astounding fervour. So what I mean is, he was not just driven by a survival necessity; it was not just a psychological need. He was also driven by a genuine, fanatical pleasure to do and learn about science. It was a sublime, high, and pure pleasure. It was a joy and passion from the head, from the heart, and from the soul. It was a sense of deep, inexplicable connection to that larger realm of that something called science.

SOCIAL CONVENTIONS

Middle and Last Names

Couples typically use one of these two options in passing down last names to their children. The first is to have the child receive their last name from one parent, and their middle name from the other parent. For instance, if the parents were Kate Snow and Joachim Fraser, the child might be called Lezlie Fraser Snow, or Lezlie Snow Fraser.

Alternatively, the child could themselves decide which parents' last names to use when introducing themselves to new people. Since Drellians usually only mention their first and last names for convenience to new acquaintances (or, more commonly, just their first name), Lezlie would either call herself "Lezlie Fraser" or "Lezlie Snow."

Couples with more than one child may choose to name the siblings differently, for instance, "Lezlie Snow Fraser" and "Bonzo Fraser Snow," though couples usually opt to keep the siblings' middle and last names the same. E.g. Lezlie Fraser Snow and Bonzo Fraser Snow. Or, of course, parents can let the children choose which names to use when introducing themselves to new people.

As for the couples' way of addressing themselves, spouses tend to decide on whose surname to stick to, such as Mrs and Mr Snow, or Mrs and Mr Fraser, as well as what titles to use. Mr, Ms, Miss, Mrs, Mx, Misc, and Ind. are common titles. These are approximate English translations of the Drellian titles. However, some other couples do change whose surname to follow from time to time, or some may even wish to switch their titles throughout their life.

The naming conventions for non-monogamous couples are more complex, which I will not go into detail here, but basically it involved a great deal of negotiation for which children get whose surnames, the possibility of multiple middle names, and many other considerations.

In this story, as an example, "Juess" is Evervessa's maiden surname. Her spouse Dron adopts Juess as his surname as well; his original surname was Phelia (pronounced "fee-lee-ah"). They call themselves Mrs and Mr Juess, or Evervessa and Dron Juess. Their daughter's full name was Alyssha Phelia Juess, or just Alyssha Juess for short.

Hand pressing or Handshakes for Greetings

You can choose whichever you prefer.

"Dude"

Drellians also have a word roughly corresponding to this word. It also means a colloquial but friendly way of addressing someone, whether young or old.

"Mom," "Mommy," "Mother

The Drellian language had terms roughly corresponding to mom, mommy, and mother too.

"Palace"

When a Drellian says "palace," this usually doesn't literally mean a palace. It means a place or building that is breathtakingly beautiful for the beholder.

THE LEGAL "ADULT" AGE

The legal "adult" age is 20 Drellian years, which is 20(9750/8760) = 22.3 Earth years old. So you could say that Drellian adolescence lasts longer than ours.

(See "Calendar Days, Months, and Years[1]" under "Quantitative Measures" for details on converting Drellian to Earth years.)

POCKET MONEY

Drellian parents also give their children pocket money.

THE ORDER

The Order on Drell are like our police force; they maintain order in the society. They are a very competent and efficient intersector organization, so Drell was a safe place most of the time: the Order have monitors all over the planet, so it's easy to track criminals who are not careful. Yet, there are some quite deserted or rather unpopulated places that the Order cannot survey. They can't survey indoor places either because of privacy issues.

What's more, due to a debate in the past where people feared that the Order would have too much power over the world, the law also dictates that though the Order can monitor most outdoor places, they aren't allowed to record any of these surveillances.

There is expectedly much controversy over this latter law, as some say that this will render the Order less capable of searching for kidnapped persons trapped indoors, for instance, since there aren't enough Order members to watch over every monitor. Besides, no Order member would want to sit and watch a pretty much uneventful surveillance for even half a core. Regardless, the compromise is still that the Order can monitor most outdoor areas but can't record them on film.

The Coaster Order

The Order at the Coasters.

Order Identity (ID) Pads

Like police identity cards. The Order also issued the Rarerus some forged Order ID pads, so that when they enter a house to seek an Arached person, and they are met with the people inside the house, the Rarerus can pretend that they are the Order on an investigation. This is done because the Order agrees that the Arach and the Rarerus should be kept a secret from the public, to keep people safe.

THE MEDICS

Doctors, healers, or nurses.

CHILDREN'S HOMES

For children who don't have a guardian or can't live with their guardian for whatever reason.

GENDER ISSUES

Gender Expectations

Males are not pressured to hide their emotions anymore. Men on Drell can be very emotionally expressive, even of "weak" feelings, without being labeled "weird." That's why there was a rise of males like Karrin Treek and Graham Arias who are quite "girlish"—their "inner female" can at last be released!

In this gender liberation of males, there are also no longer any "girl" or "boy" colors. There are thus many males who have pink, lilac, or purple as their favorite colors.

Nonbinary gender identities

People who are nonbinary identify as neither exclusively "male" nor exclusively "female." Gender identity is one's inner sense of what gender one has, which can be the same as, or different from, the gender one was assigned to at birth. Gender expression, on the other hand, refers to one's behavior, personality, interests, and self-presentation that display a degree of masculinity and femininity; gender expression doesn't always match up with gender identity, however. For instance, one can act and present oneself in a mostly masculine way, yet identify as female.

Some nonbinary gender identities include: neutrois (a type of neutral gender), androgynous (a mix of both male and female), gender fluid (gender varies over time), genderqueer (a different term for "nonbinary"), agender (no gender), demigirl (partially female), and demiguy (partially male). Many of these individuals, though not all, use nonbinary pronouns such as "they" or "ze" instead of "he" or "she."

Although nonbinary individuals are in the minority on Drell (like on

415

Earth), they are fully accepted by the Drellian society. Lark himself has a number of nonbinary acquaintances and classmates, so Alia (Liara's neutrois and androgynous friend) is not a surprise to him.

COMPLEX AND STIMULATING JOBS FOR EVERYONE

Drellians understand that having enough mental challenge and stimulation every day is crucial to their mental health, so very few jobs on Drell are monotonous.

PHYSICAL ATTRACTIVENESS AND BEAUTY

It is acknowledged on Drell that there are an uncountable number of different beauty standards in the world, none of which are more popular than any other, so that overall, everybody is equally physically beautiful.

During spouse selection, people tend to choose someone who fits their *own* unique ideal of beauty, someone who looks beautiful to *them*. Therefore, few people are dissatisfied with their appearance anymore, such that few are interested in using the available technology to change how they look.

MARRIAGES

The vast majority of couples on Drell enjoy satisfying and lasting marriages. Most couples are happily married and mature enough to maintain and deepen their relationship.

Unhappy marriages are quite rare.

WHY BUILDINGS ON DRELL ARE SO COLORFUL

Drellian designers, artists, and many others enjoy playing with the emotional effects of colors on people. Different hues affect us differently.

For example, red feels exciting and intense; orange cheerful and invigorating; blue feels calm and tranquil, though also cool and chilly in certain contexts; green is relaxing, soothing, and restful; purple sophisticated, royal, mysterious, or contemplative; pink warm, loving, and nurturing;

grey can be de-energizing and suppressive, no offense to those who love grey; black heavy, serious, even intimidating and aggressive; white pure, clean, spacious, or sterile; and brown gives off a sense of reliability, solidity, and quiet seriousness.

At the same time, individual differences factor into how a particular color stimulates one emotionally, due to personal experiences and past associations with that color.

GHOSTS AND SPIRITS, THE PARANORMAL

In Drell, there is a branch of science that investigates the paranormal, and articles on the supernatural are put in the paranormal science news. There have been spiritual sightings reported before, but no one knows for sure if these are apparitions from the dead or something else. Many scientists hold an open mind towards paranormal phenomena as part of something they don't know much about.

---

1. **Calendar Days, Months, and Years**

    It takes Drell 25 hours (12.5 cores) to spin around once, which means that one day is 25 hours. One month is 30 days, as the closest moon, Iyis ("eye-yis"), takes 30 days to orbit Drell. Finally, one year is made up of 13 months, since Drell takes 13 months to orbit its sun.

    To convert a Drellian age to an Earth one, first of all, one Drellian year is 13 months = 390 days = 9750 hours. One Earth year (assuming it's not a leap year) is 12 months = 365 days = 8760 hours. Thus, one Drellian year is 9750/ 8760 = 1.113 (approximately 1 and 1/9) times an Earth year.

    The legal "adult" age is 20 Drellian years, which is 20(9750/8760) = 22.3 Earth years old. So you could say that Drellian adolescence lasts longer than ours.

MYTHS AND LEGENDS

THE MOON TRAVERSING LOVERS

There were two lovers who lived on different planets, who traversed the moons to meet. Even gravity helped them. Lark wondered how exactly gravity could possibly help them.

TRANSPORTATION

Driving

Just tell the computer where exactly (in coordinates) you want to go and it will drive for you. But you still have to stay alert to help the computer dodge possible obstacles in the air.

Parking in residential areas

Most people only use the parking spaces above ground beside the house, as subterranean parking is usually not open to visitors unless the house owner allows it.

Hyure ("high-yoo-rae")

Like our taxis.

The Hyure are sleek and swift flying machines driven by both the computer and a human driver. These machines are long and slender and are available in a variety of colors, including bright pink and lilac for people who want those colors. There are also yellow, blue, green, and orange, mostly bright colors and not so many black or grey—or even white. But white is more common than black or grey.

Coasters

Like our planes and trains. These are large white transports that fly over longer distances than the Hyure, including intersector flights.

However, to be precise, there are different types of Coasters of different speeds. The slowest are the **intra-sector** ones, those that only travel within one sector. Faster ones are the **intra-super-sector** Coasters, which travel within the same super-sector. And the fastest are the **inter-super-sector** Coasters, and these travel across the seas and oceans between super-sectors.

Streeto ("Street-toe")

See "Streeto[1]" under "Rarerus Technology and Items."

The Glass

See "The Glass[2]" under "Rarerus Technology and Items."

The Silver

See "The Silver[3]" under "Rarerus Technology and Items."

---

1. **Streeto ("street-toe")**
   The large Rarerus vehicle: sleek and pale green. Streamlined for speed but can fit a lot of people, e.g. 30 something people from the Breemil branch.
   At maximum speed, the Streeto is 1.5 times faster than the inter-super-sector Coaster. But the Rarerus members usually only take the Streeto for important speed trips, because they would have to keep it invisible to avoid questions from curious passerby, so they'll have to use a lot of invisibility spray. This spray is expensive, so they don't want to use it on this big machine too often. It's better to just use invisibility spray on people.
2. **The Glass**
   Liara's vehicle. The fastest vehicle in the Rarerus: at maximum speed, the Glass is two times faster than an inter-super-sector Coaster. It can change to whatever color the

user prefers (it was purple on Lark's first mission). It's also very shiny, with a highly aesthetic and strong appearance.

3. **The Silver**

Newly made and still in the process of improvement by Vénus scientists in the Rarerus Center. The Silver is small enough to fit through doors, and one person can ride in it. This is the vehicle Liara suggested Centuri ride in, to be the first tester of the Silver.

QUANTITATIVE MEASURES

· · · ● ● ● ● · · · ·

TIME

Cores

1 core = 2 hours

Calendar Days, Months, and Years

It takes Drell 25 hours (12.5 cores) to spin around once, which means that one day is 25 hours. One month is 30 days, as the closest moon, Iyis ("eye-yis"), takes 30 days to orbit Drell. Finally, one year is made up of 13 months, since Drell takes 13 months to orbit its sun.

To convert a Drellian age to an Earth one, first of all, one Drellian year is 13 months = 390 days = 9750 hours. One Earth year (assuming it's not a leap year) is 12 months = 365 days = 8760 hours. Thus, one Drellian year is 9750/ 8760 = 1.113 (approximately 1 and 1/9) times an Earth year.

The legal "adult" age is 20 Drellian years, which is 20(9750/8760) = 22.3 Earth years old. So you could say that Drellian adolescence lasts longer than ours.

Names of Calendar Months

These months, from the first in the year to the last, are named Lighteth, Drellieth, Lamineth, Seallien, Skyrus, Falleth, Raineth, Soareth, Dynamel, Walketh, Grasseth, Pinketh, and Lifeien ("Lye-fee-inn").

Decaweeks and hexaweeks

On Drell, instead of a seven-day week, they count in terms of a ten-day week, called a "decaweek," or a six-day one, called a "hexaweek."

LENGTHS

Qwort

1 qwort = about 4 meters.

TEMPERATURE

Drellians have their own system, but for the sake of simplicity, the temperatures in the story are translated to Earthly equivalents.

THE ARACH ("AH-RACK")

ANTIMATTERING

These Arach, alien viruses from an unknown planet—it is not known whether they are even from the same universe—will lay a web egg on the victim's body (but the victim cannot see or feel the egg); this egg will then erupt and spread its web until it covers the entire body. Next, the Arach will hypnotize the person to make them go to the underground Arach chambers and be exposed to a special gas. After 24 hours, the web will fully solidify and the person will be antimattered.

Nobody knows what antimattering really means. We only know that the victim vanishes completely. There are bits of hair and skin particles left behind—but this is probably only because everyone sheds hair and skin particles everywhere they go.

OCTAMETHYST ("OCT-TAH-MEE-THEEST")

The octamethyst is used to digest and destroy Arach webs, but it only works if the web is not yet fully solidified. The octamethyst also takes quite a while to do its job. If the Arach successfully kidnap the victim again before the octamethyst finishes, they may lay a new egg which will start forming another web.

With two growing webs to handle, the octamethyst will only *slow down* the progress of the overall web—the overall web will keep spreading. More octamethyst needs to be added to digest the web faster than the eggs make the web.

For some reason, the Arach prefer to have only one web egg working at one time, and the reason why they would lay a second one is because the octamethyst is about to consume the old egg.

After the web is completely digested, the octamethyst will break down and become excreted by the body. So, in a way it's better to have some web remaining when the victim is kidnapped again, so that there will still be some octamethyst left to slow down any new Arach webs.

DETECTING THE ARACH VIRUS RADIATION

When an Arach virus lays a web egg on a person, and the egg starts spreading its web, the egg emits a kind of radiation. Each Rarerus branch, as well as the Vénus Center, has a detector to sense these radiations and help find victims. But there are only one or more branches per sector, and each detector has a limited radius in such a huge sector (though the Rarerus Center in Vénus has a stronger detector than the branches' with a larger radius). That's why Liara predicts that they can only detect 10% of the Arach victims.

You also need a good amount of radiation generated first before it can be detected: the egg needs to have spread a good bit of web already before you can detect the Arach's activity.

ARACH CLONES

Before the victim is antimattered, the Arach presumably take a bit of the victim's hair or skin to make a clone. Then the Arach, as retroviruses, reverse transcribe (convert) their RNA into DNA which they insert into the clone to control them.

The Arach also imitate the victim's habits to perfection. The Rarerus members believe this is because the Arach suck out the "essences" of the person's mind and soul—even though this has not yet been achieved by modern science. Modern science can't even *imitate* people's essences in robots yet. (Human cloning is unethical and illegal.)

Yet, Lark insisted that this "essence taking" theory can't be true (perhaps it was too horrifying for him to imagine?) It must simply be that the Arach have found a way to flawlessly imitate the neuronal firing patterns and glial biochemical activities, etc.

To detect Arach clones, the Rarerus just take a bit of their cells to test for DNA, to see if there are any Arach-specific DNA bases. The Arach, in addition to the normal adenine, thymine, cytosine, and guanine, also have bluamine and zanyliline: B and Z.

ARACH INTENTIONS?

The Rarerus know that the Arach's targeting of victims is not random. They are not mindless viruses. They are sentient. There are specific patterns to their targeting, but nobody knows what they are, despite that the Rarerus had been studying the Arach's targeting patterns for over 30 years. Also, according to Liara's estimates, the Rarerus only find about 10% of the Arach victims. This great lack of coverage makes it even harder for the Rarerus to find patterns.

Lark suggested that maybe different *individual* Arach have different intentions, which would explain why you can't see *one* consistent pattern in who they pick to antimatter. Aren't the individual Arach separate individuals, not *one* whole coordinated unit like a mindless beehive?

Some Rarerus members have directly asked the Arach clones for their motives. But none of the clones could give them a real answer, since none but the central control Arach know the Arach's true motives and purposes, as well as the details of what anti-mattering does to their victims. What's more, none of the Arach clones know who these central control Arach are.

Therefore, the Arach are judicious in giving information even to their clones, in case any of the latter are forced to divulge knowledge to enemies. Yet, at the same time, who knows if the Arach clones are lying about their ignorance of the Arach's real motives?

FIGHTING THE ARACH

The Rarerus must battle the Arached human clones and sometimes even Arached laminae clones, because the latter often have physical capabilities superior to that of humans.

The Arach humans are sometimes armed with weapons like the combat club's, or even with hand beams.

The Rarerus arms its fighters with gel armor to cushion physical blows, and ray reflectors to reflect back energy beams at the Arach. But sometimes the blows or energy beams are too strong and they penetrate your armor or reflector and hurt you.

Still, the armor and reflector should absorb a lot of the shock.

Rarerus members can't heal themselves during a fight, because 1) there is no time to open the healing equipment, and 2) it's dangerous to use a healer during a fight, because it opens your wounds wider for the healing chemicals to flow in, so those widened wounds are more vulnerable to further damage.

Combatants of Rarerus need to protect the scientists too, not just save the victims and defeat the Arach. The scientists wear gel armor and ray reflectors as well.

The scientists are on site to calculate the precise amount of octamethyst needed for the specific victim, to work out where precisely to apply the chemical in terms of 3D coordinates, and to communicate a command to the computer to measure out this exact amount and locate these coordinates, and put it onto the victims.

The Rarerus needs scientists to be on site: the detectors only sense Arach web activity when there has been a good amount of web made already, since only a tiny amount of radiation is emitted at start of web making. Plus, the more web already made, the longer the octamethyst will take to finish digesting the web. Thus, you want to put on the octamethyst as quickly as possible to get rid of the web as soon as possible.

Also, if the Arach manage to take the victim's body away with them, you want to already have the octamethyst there, such that if the Arach lays another web egg, the octamethyst will stop the enhanced web from forming too quickly. This buys the Rarerus time to save the victim again.

More Mission Protocols

Normally, Arach activity erupts in several sectors on Drell at once, not just in one sector.

So the branch or branches closest to that area will go to that region and save the victims, without the help of any other branches. (There's only one or a few branches per sector, and there are seventy sectors in Drell.)

But for special Arach incidents, Liara gets involved and leads a big team of several branches to go to the site. For instance, in the Aira dance event, she got twenty branches, not including the Larence branch, to go with her.

Since getting inside someone's house would be like burglary, the Rarerus must use a hand-held detector to ensure that there is indeed Arach activity inside. They would also have Order ID pads ready to say that they are the Order—these identity pads are issued by the Order because they agree that the Arach and Rarerus should be kept a secret from people.

PREVIOUS CONFRONTATIONS WITH THE ARACH

Some Rarerus members did manage to break into an Arach chamber and save the victim, without being killed or antimattered themselves. Some others managed to break into an Arach chamber—with the victim already gone—without being killed or antimattered themselves, so they could live to tell the tale of how the victim seemed to have completely disappeared.

Past times when they were outnumbered—but they were rarely outnumbered—they always called for backup. If there was no backup nearby, they would be caught by the Arach and have to wait for the backup farther away to save them. In the past when a Rarerus member was captured and threatened to be killed, the member was always at least twenty years old or almost twenty.

CHECKING FOR ARACH CLONES AMONGST THE RARERUS

The Rarerus do occasional DNA checkups on their members (e.g. every two decaweeks), asking them to give a DNA sample in front of everyone so nobody can hide. The machine then automatically checks for bluamine and zanyliline.

Lark asked if a clone could just hack into the computer and plant in false information when the computer gets to them; but Raoul replied that Rarerus computers can't be hacked into. Rarerus computers are much too advanced, and are way more advanced than Arach computers. They can hack into Arach computers (like Raoul did), but not Rarerus ones.

ARACH TECHNOLOGY

Sleeping Potion

A transparent, strange-smelling liquid. If you drink it, you will swiftly fall asleep.

Invisibility and Soundlessness

You can use the computer to make you invisible and soundless.

Follow-Along Map

The computer can also bring up a map (say, of the Arach compound) that guides you while you navigate through the place.

Bathing water

Seeps through the pores of your skin, and stimulates your brain to generate more dopamine, serotonin, and endorphins, to make you feel happy and relaxed. Also seeps into other body cells to slow down general metabolism. It has an overall calming effect.

THE RARERUS

Seem to favor children more than adults, though they respect and love the adults too. Amber (aged 12) and Eventii (aged 8) were the only children in the Rarerus so far, until Lark joined.

The Order knows about the Rarerus, and sanctions their use of invisibility sprays.

There is at least one branch in every sector (not much more than one, though.)

As there are seventy sectors on Drell, there are multitudes of branches and detectors for the Arach.

UNIFORM AND CLOTHING

During their first Aira Dance mission near the Larence branch, members wore a black suit with a band of fluorescence to see each other in the dark.

PLACES IN THE RARERUS

Science Training Centers for Future Recruits

To train people who the Rarerus think have the potential or the will to become one of the Rarerus. These people, of course, are later secretly informed about the Arach and Rarerus.

The Science Club in Dillois

Specially built to disguise Lark's expeditions with the Rarerus from his parents. Other than this, it is a genuine science interest club that some Rarerus member children were invited to.

Physical Combat Training Centers for Future Recruits

Real training centers to train anybody interested in improving their combat skills for self-defense. Rarerus staff single out some who are particularly good at fighting or at a particular skill, and tell them secretly about the Rarerus and ask if they want to be a recruit.

These centers use weapons as well, like guns, epics, and elastoropes. But they only showed Karrin and the other chosen children the hand beams *after* the children had been told about the Rarerus.

The fights are closely supervised, so nobody will get any serious injuries. Also, weapons are all inoculated. So blades, ropes, etc. will pause just an inch away from the victim's skin, but won't touch them.

Furthermore, the Rarerus tend to expose new recruits to new missions as soon as possible.

The Ramisen Enclosure ("rah-miss-sin")

In the Breemil branch. A huge meadow, with auna trees. Holds many urlassens.

THE BRANCHES

The Dillois Branch

In the Fartha sector. The closest Rarerus branch to Lark's home. To outsiders, the Dillois branch is just Haus's chemistry shop. This branch is a lot smaller than the Breemil one.

The Breemil Branch

Also in the Fartha sector. The second closest branch to Lark's home in Dillois. A lady named Pree runs the bookstore leading to the branch hideout. This bookstore is a little, ordinary-looking rectangular prism, but its walls are pure white. Yet, pure white buildings are not unusual on Drell.

When you go through a hidden door, you see a lilac and crimson place. There are gel-plastic objects (oloe tubes) on the floor, like in the backroom of Haus's chemistry shop. There are also emotographs on the walls, showing a myriad of different emotions, but with predominantly cheerful and optimistic colors. When Lark first came here, there were some people sitting at panels doing things. This was where he saw Raoul with his mirror shards fondal structure.

Then you go on a levitating panel to go up to a veiled door. Go through it into a blue and metallic grey room, with green machines called teeleopes. In this room, there is also a human-sized hole full of brown matter that looks like soil. These are the freet minerals for feeding laminae.

Next, ask the computer to teleport you to the Ramisen enclosure. This is a vast meadow with a lot of urlassens. You ride on an urlassen to a purple and black building. Inside this building, you see cyber, metallic, and light blue floors and walls. There are various machines all around. One of these machines is pink and purple with a shiny glass cover, and is taller than Lark.

Afterward, you go into this great rectangular hole and are sucked up via the suction soarer. You then alight in a purplish-pink room. Open a white door, and immediately white smoke rushes out and engulfs you. This is cleaning gas. Then you get into a lab.

The Larence ("lair-rens") Branch

In the Oftonoss sector. The activity of Aira dance was highest here, and Arach activity was present in this area too.

Miha ("mee-ha") Branch

In the Darra sector. The first branch to arrive at the Larence branch for the Aira dancing event.

THE CENTER

In Vénus.

Lark and Raoul went past acaija trees in Vénus, walked on yellow sand, and across many places until they reached the path to the building. This path was bordered by dark purple gravel-like material, and the building is black and jagged. But these dark colors might only be so because it was at night. The path curves until you get there.

When you go through the entrance to the Center, you see a hallway with a red floor (dull red, not violent red), and very light blue and grey walls. The first room you come into has an orangey-yellow faded floor, and white walls. The next few rooms Raoul and Lark walked into have the same color scheme. There were interesting things in these rooms, mostly machines; but there were also some emotographs, paintings, sculptures, and decorations.

The next room Raoul and Lark went into was a copper salt blue (aquarium or bright blue). There was a strong sense of laminae in here but Lark couldn't see any. This was where they saw Liara walking through, looking away from and shuffling past them.

As for other rooms, there is the great room with a stage where the fondal experiment participants stepped onto. There is also a training room with propellers and other machines.

Liara herself, while waiting for the fondal participants to finish their athletic ability testing, was sitting on her stri seat in a green room. Her stri seat is gold, but a darker and more intense gold than her hair, which is airier and lighter. The stri's back is smooth and solid in color, undecorated. But the back is bordered by scary-looking laminae that are jade-colored in some areas but faded red in others.

THE FIVE LEVELS

There are five governing levels in the Rarerus. The higher the level, the more governing authority they have.

Level 1) Liara Grae, 17 years old, is their much revered leader.

Level 2) The Beams—2 people—the children: Amber, 12 years old, and her younger brother Eventii, who is 8.

Level 3) The Spikes—3 people, including Monna, a woman in her fifties.

Level 4) The Scythes—4 people—Marius, Haus, and 2 others.

Level 5) The Drills—5 people.

THE SENIORS

Are the former leaders or wise people who decided to help them.

Jax, a senior, was the previous leader. He is now 30. He started leading the Rarerus when he was 17. He stopped leading because he didn't want to anymore, for some reason.

Bulwark was another senior, an advisor and combatant who died in battle ten years ago. There is an emotograph of him in the Breemil branch.

CHOOSING NEW LEADERS

It doesn't matter what age the candidate is, as long as the former leader thinks they are fit for the job. It is not revealed in the story whether there is a democratic vote for the new leader, or if it is simply decided by the previous leader.

THE LEVEL-LESS (THEY DON'T REALLY HAVE A CATEGORY NAME)

The people who work for everyone but have no governing power. Yet, any of them can lead missions, scientific investigations or the like if they are capable of doing so; plus, they are all still very well respected by the Rarerus. Braiven and Centuri are two examples of the level-less.

FAMILIES

Most people in the Rarerus society are single. As a matter of fact, most members elect to remain single for the rest of their lives, because it's traumatizing to think that the one you love more than your life may one day be gone and replaced by a clone without you knowing it.

The Rarerus tend to avoid recruiting married people or those involved in romantic relationships for the same reason.

However, there are a few exceptions. There are a few married people in the Rarerus. But even these recruits will have to keep the Rarerus a secret from the rest of their family (unless their spouse or another family member is also a recruit), because *knowing* about the Arach will put that knower in more danger. The Rarerus tells all its single members to keep the Arach and the Rarerus a secret from their family too.

HOW THEY HIDE THEIR OPERATIONS FROM CIVILIANS

Now when the Rarerus enter a house, it would be considered burglary if they don't use their detector to confirm that there is Arach activity inside first. And in case they bump into anyone in the house, they have forged Order identity pads they can call up on their computer.

The Order issued these ID pads to the Rarerus because they agreed that the Rarerus should operate unknown to as many people as possible. Order members are also told not to tell their friends or family about the Arach or the Rarerus, lest this knowledge should harm them.

Also, as neighbors and passerby will hear the commotion whenever the Rarerus members fight against the Arach, the Order and the government made up this cover story: the Rarerus members are Order agents cracking down on criminals or criminal organizations and their overlords. This is actually believable as everyone on Drell knows that organized crime and formidable evildoers exist, and the Order and the government military have to protect Drellian citizens from these villains. Children involved in the Rarerus missions are easily explained, because some undercover operations require the assistance of such young recruits.

Of course, there will always be people within the civilian population who doubt the veracity of this cover story. But that can't be helped. There are conspiracy theorists in the world who are sometimes right too.

The reason why the Order and the Drellian government don't directly battle the Arach, is because the Rarerus alone have the forces, power, resources, and knowledge to deal with these unpredictable and unknown viruses.

PERIODIC DNA CHECKS

In the Rarerus, from time to time (e.g. every two deca-weeks), they get all members to take out a sample of their DNA—to shake off some flakes of skin, for instance, and they tell them to do so in the full sight of other Rarerus members so they can't hide; the computers automatically analyze the DNA on the spot. So any Arach clones will show up as having bluamine and zanyliline DNA bases.

NOT KEEPING MANY CHEMICALS AT HOME

Neither Raoul nor many other Rarerus scientists keep many chemicals at home aside from some bare essentials, in case of accidents, or thieves with exceptional hacking skills causing trouble with them.

APPRENTICESHIP JOURNEYS

Journeys to learn or master something. For example, a chemist could follow some other Rarerus chemists on a journey (whether long or short) to significantly increase their expertise in science.

RARERUS TECHNOLOGY AND ITEMS

Epics

Long blades with golden, orange, or yellow glowing edges. When you press a button, the blade becomes a series of short golden flashes that slash the enemy at a distance.

Hand Beams

These are attached to the wrists by being locked into the skin, and are transparent and invisible to the naked eye. Hand beams are the same as guns, except that you only need to *will* them to fire, so they are more efficient than guns. The sensor in this hand beam device will detect your brain cell (neurons and glia) signals, so when you very clearly and unambiguously desire to fire, it will fire.

Arach activity detectors

When an Arach virus lays a web egg on a person, and the egg starts spreading its web, the egg emits a kind of radiation. Each Rarerus branch, as well as the Vénus Center, has a detector to sense these radiations and help find victims. But there's only at least one branch per sector, and each detector has a limited radius in such a huge sector (though the Rarerus Center in Vénus has a stronger detector than the branches' with a larger radius). That's why Liara predicts that they can only detect 10% of the Arach victims.

You also need a good amount of radiation generated first before it can be detected: the egg needs to have spread a good bit of web already before you can detect the Arach's activity.

Oloe Tubes ("oh-loe")

Gel-plastic curly objects strewn all over the floor in the Breemil branch and in the backroom of Haus's chemistry shop. Oloe tubes are there to comfort and massage your feet, and to provide nourishment for your feet to become stronger and healthier. If you stand in the midst of oloe tubes for long enough, your feet and legs will become cleaner as well.

Gas screens

Used if you want to go into a smoked place. But the oxygen supply runs out after some time.

Soft Bomb

Recent invention. Small yellow ball. Raoul activated it and threw it over the heads of the Arach clones, Lark, and Karrin. The soft bomb releases tracking dust, and can track any life forms the dust touched. The dust is invisible.

The Glass

Liara's vehicle. The fastest vehicle in the Rarerus: at maximum speed, the Glass is two times faster than an inter-super-sector Coaster. It can change to whatever color the user prefers (it was purple on Lark's first mission). It's also very shiny, with a highly aesthetic and strong appearance.

The Silver

Newly made and still in the process of improvement by Vénus scientists in the Rarerus Center. The Silver is small enough to fit through doors, and one person can ride in it. This is the vehicle Liara suggested Centuri ride in, to be the first tester of the Silver.

Streeto ("street-toe")

The large Rarerus vehicle: sleek and pale green. Streamlined for speed but can fit a lot of people, e.g. 30 something people from the Breemil branch.

At maximum speed, the Streeto is 1.5 times faster than the inter-supersector Coaster. But the Rarerus members usually only take the Streeto for important speed trips, because they would have to keep it invisible to avoid questions from curious passerby, so they'll have to use a lot of invisibility spray. This spray is expensive, so they don't want to use it on this big machine too often. It's better to just use invisibility spray on people.

Gel armor

Protects against some physical blows—or at least absorbs much of the shock.

Ray Reflectors

Bounces the energy beam rays back at the Arach.

Teeleopes

Dark green machines. Some soar around, while some are stationary in the air. As for shapes, some are triangular or angular, whilst others are smooth and round but not circular or spherical.

There are some teeleopes in the Breemil branch. They record and process the information on the products, projects, and other things the researchers are working on, and integrate all this data to form a big picture of what the Rarerus are doing to combat the Arach. These green machines are different from the average computer because no average computer can process that much information at that speed—faster than thought and almost instantaneous.

Teleeopes have other functions that the average computer can't do either, but these are not revealed in the story.

Energy Dispensers

Generate liquids to restore energy. These liquids will taste like your favorite food.

Freet Minerals

Nutrients used to feed most laminae.

Suction Soarers

After getting into a black, rectangular hole (not the "black hole" in outer space, but literally a hole that looks black), this sucks you up and you glide rapidly up to the level you want to go to.

Cleaning Gas

You open a door, and a lot of white smoke engulfs you. It cleans away the microbes from your skin, but leaves the benign microbes alone.

Electricity Absorbers

Removes electricity by absorbing it.

Healers

These items are filled with healing chemicals. Wounds need to be widened slightly for the healing chemicals to flow in and treat it. This is why you can't use healers during a fight. It would be too dangerous to widen the wounds during combat because it would make those wounds more vulnerable.

Lock picking using lasers

Instead of picking a lock with a piece of wire like on Earth, some Rarerus specialists can use their hand beam lasers to open a lock.

RARERUS-RELATED CHEMICALS

For the chemicals below, see relevant sections under "Chemicals."

- Octamethyst
- Brachiorsor
- Trichloroes
- Par-the-air
- Amosti
- Green substance (Chrystacience)
- Brachiorsor Barrier

FONDAL ENHANCEMENTS

The Physical, Athletic Boost:

Increased speed, stamina, strength, and suppleness. Even Lark became better than an average five-year-old at all four of these.

The extra enhancement:

The ability to shapeshift certain body parts according to your situational needs. But it seems like you can only shapeshift if that feature occurs in nature. I.e. No invisibility, no x-ray vision, no eye lasers. But this shapeshifting ability will not enhance your current athletic capacities. The initial boost by the fondal's first physical enhancement has been done already.

WHAT WORKED SO FAR FOR THE SHAPESHIFTING:

So far, this function only works for aged 5 (and presumably even younger) children. Yet, by the end of the novel, when Lark is 18, it works for children up to the age of 15. But the maximum age limit keeps increasing every year as science advances in the Karerus.

Also, both the physical and extra (shapeshifting) fondal enhancements seem to be permanent. At the age of 18, Lark and Karrin still have their elevated athletic abilities and their shapeshifting powers.

Wings and Bones Hollowed

When they grow wings, their bones get hollowed too so they'll be light enough to fly.

Claws

For digging.

APPARATUS FOR BREATHING UNDERGROUND SO THEY DON'T SUFFOCATE

Spikes

For climbing.

Semi-transparent lids

Protect against overly strong sun rays.

Whitening of Skin and Clothes

This reflects off excess sunlight and heat.

Camouflage

Changes their body color to fit into their surroundings, like a chameleon.